FROM LAURIE BELL:

IN *THE STONES OF POWER* SERIES:
THE BUTTERFLY STONE
THE TIGER'S EYE

MORE FROM WYVERN'S PEAK PUBLISHING

THE RECALCITRANT PROJECT
BY LAUREN LYNNE

CHARLIE SULLIVAN AND THE MONSTER HUNTERS
BY D.C. MCGANNON & C. MICHAEL MCGANNON

THE TIGER'S EYE

THE TIGER'S EYE

WYVERN'S PEAK PUBLISHING
An imprint of The McGannon Group, Ltd. Co.

The Tiger's Eye

The Stones of Power, Book 2

Written by Laurie Bell – www.solothefirst.wordpress.com

Copyright © 2020 Laurie Bell

Published by Wyvern's Peak Publishing. 2020
An imprint of The McGannon Group, Ltd. Co.

Cover design by www.FlirtationDesigns.com

The Tiger's Eye / by Laurie Bell – 1st Ed.

Summary: Tracey Masters and her friends face conflict from all sides, and from within, as they try to prepare not only for their enemy's next inevitable attack, but also for the new threats that loom over their futures.

1 2 3 4 5 6 7 8 9

ISBN-13: 978-0-9990212-3-1

All rights reserved. No part of this publication may be reproduced, distributed, or transmitted in any form or by any means, including photocopying, recording, or other electronic or mechanical methods, without the prior written permission of the publisher, except in the case of brief quotations embodied in critical reviews and certain other noncommercial uses permitted by copyright law.

This book is a work of fiction. Names, characters, places, and incidents are either the product of the authors' imagination or are used fictitiously, and any resemblance to actual persons, living or dead, business establishments, events, or locales is entirely coincidental.

Except in the United States of America, this book is sold subject to the condition that it shall not, by way of trade or otherwise, be lent, re-sold, hired out, or otherwise circulated without the publisher's prior consent in any form of binding or cover other than that in which it is published and without a similar condition including this condition being imposed on the subsequent purchaser.

www.WyvernsPeak.com

The Tiger's Eye is dedicated to my mum and dad. You keep reading no matter how many times I send it to you. You are my biggest supporters! Thank you for everything. I love you heaps.

To Taylah, Skye, Mark, Bree and Amy, Mia, Chloe and Bryce, Elsa, Emily and Hannah, Cody and Corey, Luneah, Lisa, Jen and Kathy — here it is at last. Thanks for waiting.

And to every child who opens a book and gets lost in another world. You are why I do this. Be brave, be strong. Always help where you can and read to whoever will listen (and to those who don't, read to them anyway). Magic is inside you if you believe it is. Be awesome.

-Laurie Bell

Tales
by
The Lost

Following <u>219</u>, Followed by <u>0</u>
click **<broken link>** to follow <u>The Lost</u>!

Day 1

Today is my birthday!

I'm eleven today

<u>0</u> *likes,* <u>0</u> *comments,* <u>0</u> *reshares*
click **<broken link>** to like this post!:D

T.B.T.L.

1

Tracey's shield sprang out as an invisible bubble around her body and blocked the incoming baseball-sized blob of swirling orange magic. She only just stayed on her feet. Sweat rolled down her nose. It dripped beneath her collar and soaked through the back of her shirt. She hardened the bubble in front of her face and caught the next hit, drawing in her shield to absorb the magic into her body. *Ha! Bet they didn't see that coming.* She heard a snort but couldn't pinpoint its location.

"Over here!"

Tracey twisted hard, her ponytail flicking side to side until she could see the grinning face of her sister, Sarah. The younger girl tap-danced and waved her hands around. Tracey focused inward and pictured her core — the magical node of muscle beside her heart — and imagined it full of glowing golden energy. She pictured strands of magic snaking from her core down to her fingertips. The bubble around her body worked to protect her from attack. It also protected her attackers from Tracey.

When she first discovered her natural way of using her magic was to pull it from the Mage-kind around her she had been horrified. It had caused her to question everything she'd ever been taught. The battle with the Shadowman and his boss, Timothy, showed her how dangerous her abilities truly were. Luckily, she had saved her sister and her friends, but she'd also hurt them. It showed her the cost of magic could be too high.

Her muscles twitched, exhausted from keeping her bubble in place. The Butterfly Stone pulsed against her chest tempting her to clutch it with her fingers. The necklace was a terrible curse and she wished with all her might she had never put it on. A stone the size of her palm with a painting of a butterfly on it should not be so powerful. But it was, and Tracey couldn't take it off. She had tried and failed. Now it was her burden to carry.

"No shield. Come on, Trace. Free shot! Try to get me," Sarah shouted.

"Put your shield up," Tracey snapped back. To launch an attack, Tracey would have to drop her bubble. She couldn't fire through it. Her sister knew that and was taking advantage.

Sarah whooped and jiggled. "Come on, Trace. You can't get me."

Tracey released a slow hiss from between her teeth and allowed her shield to flicker, throwing a ball of magic up into the air. The ball exploded in a shower of glowing pink sparks, lighting the entire area with her magic. In her mind she could see the clearing they were standing in surrounded by giant trees, and as her magic floated down it settled over several human shapes, exposing them to her magically enhanced vision with an orange hue. Two Mage-kind hid in the trees bordering the clearing. Another crouched several feet behind Sarah, hiding in her magic shadow. Couldn't hide from Tracey's Sight, though. She saw him clear as day.

Blistering sunlight poured down over them — too hot for early autumn — burning Tracey's skin. Her nose practically glowed. If only her bubble could block out the sun along with magic. If it did, it would block the air too, and that would kill her.

"Cheating!" Dave shouted from the tree line. Tracey spun in his direction and strengthened her shield, blocking the blast he fired toward her. The once bully, now reluctant friend, radiated joy. He sure loved battle practice.

"I'll allow it," said the man standing at the edge of the clearing. Agent Malden's stern face was carved with lines of deep thought as he watched the battle. Their mentor, the M-force agent, was determined they would be prepared for Timothy's next attack. Tracey just wished he wasn't so sure there would be one.

A chorus of complaints filled the air. The momentary lull in the battle slowed Tracey's reaction time as three blasts, all from different directions zoomed in at her simultaneously. She dove and the energy balls collided above her head, erupting in sparks of energy that shot out in all directions like fireworks. A buzz criss-crossed her skin sending her into a fit of giggles.

"Seriously team? Okay, that's enough for today." Agent Malden strode toward them, his hands outstretched in the order to stand down. Tracey brushed dirt from her jeans and camp t-shirt, still chuckling as she walked toward the gathering group. Tony knocked his shoulder against her arm. His camp t-shirt, identical to hers, was still pristine. He didn't quite meet her gaze. "Hey."

"Hey," she replied. "I didn't get hit."

"You didn't fire back at all." Tony, one of her best friends, stood an inch taller than Tracey and his light brown hair dangled over his forehead in sweaty clumps. His voice didn't carry the sarcasm she had expected. She searched his face for a hint of what was bothering him. *Maybe he's just tired.*

"I outlasted you all," she said.

He shook his head, denial on his lips. Tracey pretended to scowl as she stopped beside Sarah. No one looked as filthy as Tracey. Even Dave's camp shirt was cleaner than hers. She was always the messy one.

Agent Malden clapped his hands and Tracey focused her attention on the only adult in the group. The M-force agent straightened his camp shirt—the same one they all wore—and went to adjust his tie. Tracey stifled another giggle. He kept forgetting he wasn't wearing a tie. Agent Malden said the first step to acting like a team was to look like one. Tracey didn't think it helped. "It's only day three of your intensive skills training. Don't be disheartened, you're all doing really well."

Dave barked out a laugh. Tracey felt his glare against her face and tried not to squirm. "She's not even trying," Dave accused, pointing a finger in her direction.

Agent Malden's sharp stare locked onto her. "Tracey?"

Dave didn't give her time to come up with an excuse. "When Timothy comes back, he'll slaughter us."

"He doesn't want us. He wants the stones," Sarah said. She pressed against Tracey's side and clutched her sister's hand tightly. Tracey squeezed Sarah's fingers reminding her sister she would always look out for her.

Dave threw up his arms like he knew it was an argument he was never going to win. "We're not a threat to him. We defeated him, but we didn't stop him. He's coming back, and Tracey will be his first target."

Tracey stared at her grubby shoes. It wasn't fair. She had only taken possession of the Butterfly Stone to stop Timothy from getting his hands on it. The magic in the stone, and Tracey's family connection to it, prevented her from taking it off. She could feel the stares of her friends crawling all over her skin and didn't want to look up. Eventually, she *did* force her eyes up to look at them. She had made the decision to wear the necklace. She had to own it.

Tony scrubbed a hand over his face. "Two weeks isn't long enough to learn what we need to stop Timothy from finding the other four stones. We don't even know what they look like. The only one we know about for sure is the one around Tracey's neck. If Timothy needs all five stones to restore his body, he'll have to come for Tracey." Tony turned to face her, his worry and fear fighting a battle in his brown eyes. The anger won. "Dave's right. You weren't trying."

"I know."

"Tracey, these two weeks are for you to work on your magic. It's also to get Dave and Sarah up to speed. A tough ask I agree, but I know you're all determined to succeed." Agent Malden's words burrowed into Tracey's skin. "Tracey, we need to talk about this."

"Later?" Her voice wobbled. Sarah squeezed Tracey's hand tighter. Tracey bit down hard on her bottom lip determined not to cry.

"Okay." Agent Malden scanned the rest of the group. "Dave, how are you feeling with your magic? It's been a little over a month since you discovered your Mage-kind status, hasn't it?"

Dave rubbed his neck and shuffled his feet in the dirt. "I dunno. All right, I guess."

All right? Tracey thought he was doing amazingly. Most Mage-kind magic started seeping into their bodies when they were six years old. At fifteen, Dave had only just discovered his power and he'd had a fiery initiation, thrown straight into a fight with Timothy over the Butterfly Stone.

"All right everyone. Do you have any questions?"

Why aren't we trying to find the other stones? Tracey didn't give voice to her question.

A hand shot up from every student. "Ah, okay." Agent Malden's thin lips quirked at the corner. "Perhaps I should have asked for questions earlier. Let's start with Sarah."

Sarah's face pinked as she fidgeted. No one liked to be picked first. "I know this training is special, and we have to learn how to protect ourselves for when Timothy attacks again, but we only have two weeks here. What happens when we're back at school? You said we have to work together, but I'm at a different campus and all by myself."

Agent Malden's eyes creased when he smiled. "There will be agents placed around both campuses. You will not be alone, Sarah, and your training will continue. These are dangerous times and you are all known to your enemy—"

Tracey stopped listening as she pictured Timothy in her mind. She had seen him wear many faces. From the man in the red mask to Officer Jameson, but the face she saw in her nightmares was the one she'd seen in the memory-dream Grandma showed to her: Piercing brown eyes, a sharp nose and a mouth downturned in a forever frown, belonging to a man the same height as her own dad with clipped, dark hair slicked in place with shiny oil. Tracey's hands clenched around the Butterfly Stone necklace before she could think it through, and her head spun as her senses were instantly overwhelmed. When she could see again, she stood in an endless white room.

The woman who haunted the Butterfly Stone was Tracey's ancestor, Stephanie. She stood before Tracey, her arms crossed, and an unhappy expression on her face. She wore the same white dress Tracey always saw, long and lacey. Her hair was twisted up in an immaculate loop, but what was most jarring was that she looked like Tracey, if not a little older and more jaded. Tracey had never smirked like that, nasty and a bit cruel. It was like staring into a funhouse mirror, only there was nothing fun about it.

"You are afraid."

No duh! Tracey barely stopped from rolling her eyes. "Of course, I am."

"Of Timothy."

"Yes."

"You defeated him before," Stephanie reminded her.

She had, but only because she'd used the Butterfly Stone. The magic necklace had once belonged to Stephanie. It was why she haunted it now. If Tracey hadn't used the magic stored inside the stone, Sarah would have been hurt. And in saving her sister and her friends, Tracey had hurt them herself, ripping their magic from their cores to use against Timothy and Doctor Chan. No, she couldn't use her magic or the stone again to attack. Not until she learned how to use it safely.

"Do not be afraid, Tracey. You must practice with it and become familiar with your new strength. Call on me. Use the stone. Why do you fight it so?"

"I can't use the stone. It's too powerful," Tracey said, shaking her head.

"It is yours to use."

"Agent Malden said I shouldn't."

"Timothy, while defeated, is still out there. You cannot deny who you are."

"I know, but…"

Stephanie released a long sigh.

Tracey hated disappointing her ancestor, but it wasn't going to happen. "I'm sorry. Agent Malden said I have to practice my shielding and fight my tendency to draw on other people's magic."

"Then use the stone." Stephanie walked toward Tracey, her long white skirt flaring around her ankles, exposing small boots that looked both soft and cute. "But that is not what has you afraid today, is it?"

"I—" Of course it was.

Stephanie waited, watching her patiently. Tracey closed her mouth and really thought through the ghost woman's question. She *was* afraid. Of everything. How could they go back to school and act as though nothing had happened—that they hadn't nearly been killed by her ancestor's ex-boyfriend? Tracey was also afraid of herself. The one taste she'd had of the Butterfly Stone's magic was… *not enough*. She craved more. She was also afraid of the Shadowman, Timothy's monster henchman made of shadow and magic. She had destroyed him, hadn't she? Could he come back, too? Really, what wasn't Tracey afraid of?

"I am scared," she said. Admitting that truth lifted a weight pressing down on her shoulders. "What if I can't stop him next time? What if he finds the other stones first?"

"Is that really what you fear?" Stephanie's stare drilled into her. Tracey chewed on her thumbnail.

"I do want to use the Butterfly Stone." The words were a whisper on her breath. Even now, Tracey could sense the necklace begging her to open up and let it in. The hunger gnawed on her bones. She wanted — oh, how she *wanted* — another taste of that pure chaotic magic.

Stephanie smiled, her eyes alight with joy. "Why would that scare you?"

Tracey poured all of her fear and anger into her words. "Because it killed you!"

Her body yanked sideways. Tracey found Tony squatting right in front of her. She was lying on the uneven ground. Broken twigs dug into her back and she could feel leaves and dirt beneath her hands. Tony's eyebrows made a V shape as he shook her shoulders gently. "Tracey?"

Agent Malden shifted Tony aside. "Tracey? Are you dizzy? Is it another blackout?"

She glanced from Agent Malden to Tony and Dave before finding her sister sitting cross-legged beside her head. Her face was scrunched up in worry. Tracey gulped and lifted a hand. She had dirt under her fingernails. "Ah, I—" She squeezed Sarah's hand. "I'm fine. Sorry. Must have spaced for a second."

"It was way longer than a second, Tracey," Sarah told her.

"Whoa." Shock hit Tracey like icy water, and she tried to sit up. Sarah grabbed her arms and helped her upright. "I—uh."

"Let's head back to camp and prepare some lunch. We have a few things to go over and I'll try to answer the rest of your questions while we eat. Come on." Agent Malden waved at the path that led to the campground.

Tracey didn't let go of Sarah's hand. Giant trees towered above the overgrown path casting them all in cool shadows. Tracey imagined the trees were watching her, judging her. Did they know her secret desire to use the Butterfly Stone? This isolated area of Mount Hawthy showed no signs of civilization—a primitive world free from technology and modern conveniences. Much to Tracey's annoyance, there were no WI-FI towers out here. Not that it mattered. Agent Malden had confiscated their cell phones.

The ground was rock hard beneath her feet, bugs attacked her exposed skin and they were at the complete mercy of the elements. Supposedly, this helped their training. *Ha!* It just made Tracey miserable. Lack of sleep from her nightmares about the Shadowman didn't help either.

Tracey's thoughts drifted to her fellow Mage-kind. They walked around her like Prince Henry's bodyguards. Tony was at her back, Sarah was beside her, and Dave was two paces away. It was weird, Tracey was stronger than all of them, but their protective behavior made her feel safe. "How do we pretend everything is normal when we go back to school?" she mused.

Sarah's lips ticked up on one side. "At least you won't be alone."

"I can't do anything about that, Sars. I wish you weren't alone, but it is what it is."

Her sister shot her a snotty look.

Dave waved his arm around like he held a streamer—a funny look for the muscular boy who would have been more at home on a football field than attending magic camp. His nearly shorn head and blue eyes could have been mistaken for a tenpin bowling ball. The new Mage-kind identification student wristband on his left wrist glowed bright emerald. "How do I hide this?" The tremble in his voice was clear under the veneer of anger lacing his tone. Tracey hated her ID bracelet too, now that she understood it as the way the government kept track of Mage-kind. Every bracelet had a green stone or bar that flashed red when Mage-kind used magic. Tracey's band had been altered by her parents when she was little. That probably should have warned her that her magic was different.

Tracey eyed Dave's wristband. The light stayed green. His control was getting better. "It'll be o—"

"Don't, just don't. It will be hell. All my friends…" Dave's frown was etched deep in his face. Tracey's heart went out to him. How hard must it be to grow up thinking you were a Norm only to learn you were not. Norms were not wholly accepting of Mage-kind, even though they looked exactly the same. To make matters worse, Dave had spent his entire school life bullying Mage-kind before finding out he was one himself. He was right to be worried.

"We're your friends," Tony offered, though he didn't look up from his feet when he said it. Tracey hoped he was okay. He had been really quiet over the last few days.

"Dave. We're a team. Well, we're supposed to be," Tracey said. "Besides, we have other problems. Timothy is still out there, and he knows who we are."

The tension in Dave's frame didn't diminish. If anything, it grew tighter. Tony shot Dave a dark look. *Whoa! That escalated quickly.* Tracey expected anger from Dave, but Tony's abrupt mood swing surprised her. She moved between the two boys. "Guys come on. This is not helping." Would she now have to worry about Tony as well? Tracey's stomach twitched as Tony continued to ignore her.

A tired voice greeted them from the middle of their camp site. "You're back early." Tracey's stomach growled at the sight of the picnic table laden with food, sending flames of embarrassment over her whole body. Prince Henry—or Hank as they had come to call him—waved at the campfire.

She still couldn't get her head around their training being conducted by an M-Force agent and a prince. A prince she once had a celebrity crush on. Hank's smile was not as bright as usual, and dark hair hung over a face that was a little too pale. The lines around his chocolate brown eyes were more pronounced too. Camp life didn't suit the actor prince, who seemed far more comfortable around starlets and five-star hotels. Hank's training sessions had taken the sheen off Tracey's affections. That and the fact that even a camping prince smelled of boy sweat and wood smoke. Without his hair perfectly made up and his skin gleaming, he was just like one of Tracey's brothers.

Thinking back on when she had first met Prince Henry, she couldn't believe she'd had no idea he was Mage-kind. How had he hidden his abilities? She thought about Dave and his wristband. Prince Henry didn't wear one, probably because he was Agent Malden's undercover operative.

Tracey rotated her wrist. The heavy weight of the bracelet was a hand cuff encircling her life. What would it be like to be a Norm? Her other best friends—Laura and Jonny—were Norms, as was her brother Simon. She had always thought they were missing out not getting to play with magic. Maybe they were the lucky ones.

Between Hank's acting lessons and Agent Malden's fighting drills, Tracey was exhausted. And it had only been three days. The Butterfly Stone pulsed against her chest. She warned it she was not in the mood and silenced its urging. With her burnt hotdog still smoking, she slumped down on one end of the wooden picnic seat and groaned, happily taking weight off her aching feet. Sarah slid onto the bench seat beside Tracey, adding her own moan to their chorus. "I'm so tired."

"Me too," Tracey shared a grin with her sister. The best part of all this training stuff was the time she got to spend with Sarah. "Wonder what Mom and Dad are doing?"

"Didn't the boys have some football thing this week?" Sarah asked.

"Oh yeah, Mom's probably been bouncing back and forth, taking them from training to school and back again. I can't believe we're missing it."

"Pfft! You hate football."

Busted! Tracey laughed. Sarah joined in, bumping her shoulder into Tracey.

Agent Malden cleared his throat. "As I know from experience you can talk and eat at the same time, so let's continue. Tony, how are you feeling? Any questions?"

Tracey glanced across the table at her friend. Tony's stare burrowed into his plate, his bread roll torn to shreds by worried fingers. When he looked up, Tracey was shocked to see a shimmer in his reddened eyes. "What happens to us now?"

Agent Malden sat at the head of the table in the red director's chair Prince Henry had brought with him. He leaned back, the chair creaking with his weight and studied Tony. "You return to school."

"And then what?" Dave grumbled, waving his lunch around. Ham and bacon poked out of his flattened bread roll. Tracey eyed it with fascination, wondering when it would fall out and hit the dirt.

"You study hard and continue your training."

Tracey frowned. "But what about Timothy? We have to find the other stones before he does."

"Hank and I will continue the search, alone," Agent Malden announced, his voice firm.

Tracey shot a quick look at her friends. Tony's mouth hung open. Sarah tilted her head and Dave gritted his teeth, his eyes narrow and suspicious. What worried Tracey was that Prince Henry wouldn't look at her. "But you said finding the stones was *my* mission," she said.

"I did, Tracey, but right now, your magic is too uncontrolled. Can you honestly tell me you feel comfortable using your abilities at the moment? We will call you when we find him. I promise you that. You all need time to heal."

"How can we act like everything's normal?" Tracey's voice matched her anger. The Butterfly Stone pulsed hot against her chest. The urge to explode something was growing harder and harder to fight.

"Tracey!"

She spun on her sister. "What?"

"You're doing it again," Sarah warned.

Tracey's shield had weakened while she wasn't concentrating on it. The pressure waves of five protective bubbles were raised against her. Her skin tingled from the raw power. With her inner eye she examined her own core, aghast to find tendrils of golden magic, like dental floss, stretching out from her chest to her friends. Not to, from. She was pulling magic from her friends. Tracey's core, like a black hole, was forever hungry. She slammed her mind down on it, and in her heart heard five little pings as she cut off the transfer of magic.

Tony held up a hand. "Breathe, Tracey."

"Nothing has changed," she shouted, leaping to her feet. "Three days of practice in using my magic differently and it's not working. It's too hard keeping a shield up all the time." Her heart pounded. She spun away from Sarah's pained expression and glared at Agent Malden. "You said you'd fix me. I—I can't do this." Tracey ran for the woods. "Pathetic," she snarled at herself.

"Tracey!" Sarah called out, but Tracey ignored her. She ignored all of them.

Picturing her core behind a little door, Tracey locked her magic away inside her chest and blinked back tears. Trees appeared as sentinels, looming over her, casting judgement and finding her guilty. Behind them, shadows waited to consume her. Tracey darted off the stony path and plunged into the unknown, uncaring where she headed, just desperate to disappear.

Tales
by
The Lost

Following 219, Followed by 0
click **<broken link>** to follow The Lost!

Day 1

[cont …]

I find I have a need to write

my journey down, though

I know it will never be read.

0 likes, 0 comments, 0 reshares
click **<broken link>** to like this post! :D

T.B.T.L.

2

Spying a tree with low branches that acted as uneven stairs, Tracey climbed until she found a wide perch. She braced her back against the thick trunk and stared out over the canopy of green around her.

I can't believe I ran away again. Just like a little kid. Her stomach ached with all of the bad feelings that twisted and bit at her insides. With her shield bubble around her, the world seemed cold and frighteningly unreal. The sound of birds, even the wind, was muffled and hard to distinguish from her heavy panting. Colors faded and blurred. Even her sense of smell seemed off. No one was around, who would know? She pressed a hand against her chest and threw open her inner closet door. Her body tingled with warmth as color exploded before her eyes, every shade of brown and green. Golden motes danced in the sunlight. Her skin sparkled. *Glorious!*

For a while she watched the finger-sized leaves shudder in the light breeze. A bug crawled the length of a twig at the height of her eyes, fortunately heading away from her, but she could see its tiny feet grip and release the wood. Birds tweeted to each other and she wished she understood their conversations. Were they laughing at the silly girl hiding in the tree? *Fruit tingles. What am I doing?*

Tracey swiped her tongue over her dry lips. She should have remembered to grab a bottle of water when she ran away. Mottled sunlight painted her arms, bringing shadows of cool air and gooseflesh to her skin. Closing her eyes, she breathed slow and deep, and focused on slowing her racing heartbeat. Angry quivers of heat and fragmented thoughts drained out of her along with her anger and fear.

She became aware of the bark beneath her fingers, flaking off the branch. Speckles of heat kissed her skin as sunlight found her hiding place.

How much time had passed since she had run away? She opened her eyes on a ladybird sitting right in front of her nose, startling back before she stretched forward to follow it, wishing she could shrink herself down to join it on its grand adventure.

Sarah was angry Tracey had left. The strange sixth sense they had shared since Tracey merged their magic to defeat Timothy had not faded. Even at this distance she could feel Sarah's emotions and Tracey hated that she had upset her sister again. Maybe Sarah got a taste of Tracey's emotions too. Could she feel how angry Tracey was? She would have to ask Sarah if she shared this weird connection, hoping it wasn't one-sided. Maybe then Sarah wouldn't feel so alone. She wasn't alone. She had Tracey and Tony, even Dave. There were heaps of Mage-kind for her to hang out with now who would look after her. She just had to see that.

Hank and Agent Malden wanted Tracey to keep her shield bubble raised all the time, but it was harder than she had imagined. She had to be conscious of her core at all times, and couldn't resort to magic to do even the simplest of tasks the way she used to. Her body ached like she stood still holding up bags of groceries. Muscles she didn't know she had hurt. Even her teeth hurt, which was the strangest feeling ever. She touched the Butterfly Stone and thought of Stephanie. Knowing she shouldn't, Tracey called on it. Power filled her mind instantly, flooding her veins with magic. She swelled with it, her skin fighting to contain the stone's raw energy. Suddenly, it was easy to hold her shield. The ache in her tired muscles disappeared and she felt buzzed like she had drunk a whole energy drink without taking a breath. Why shouldn't she use the stone's magic if it helped her feel better? What was wrong with that?

She felt alert, wide awake, like she could take on Meena, Carla, and Dave One all by herself. The school bullies would be unable to stand against her. She could take on Timothy and defeat the Shadowman, and no one could stop her. Laughing a little at her wild imagination, she patted her pockets. *No cell phone, remember?* A crinkle in her back pocket reminded her of the poem she had shoved there last night before changing into her pajamas.

It was the story of the stones Tony printed for her a few weeks ago.

The one he had found on the M-net. *The Five Stones of Power.* She had been unable to stop reading it, pondering its message, sure it was a clue to the rest of the stones. She removed the creased paper and spread it out over her jeans, straightening the folds until she could read it.

Five spirited mages,
Five stones of power.
Spelled to hold, will and wish,
Binding soul to life, forever.

To contain or conceal,
Enslave or ensnare?
Bewitch or betray,
Deceive or repay?

Dealers of death,
Absorbing magic through dreams.
Strength growing, unknown proportions.
Their end will reveal,
The mistakes they've made.

The one who leads,
Who dreamed of more,
Lost her mind in the fire,
Her charge now her curse.

Another in love,
Betrayed by fear.
Trapped, bitter and frozen;
Vision lost.

One full of passion,
For learning and love.
Left bereft and empty,

Wind burnt and cross.
One filled with hope,
A fire for the world.
Destroyed all that he loved,
Heart black, soul scorched.

The last held desire,
For power and purpose.
His soul, but shadow,
Alone in his curse.

Together, bound to the flame,
Five stones to carry their name.
But as with magic,
Truth begets truth.
Death, loss, and madness marked,
Their lives now accursed.

There was no author named. She sighed and crumpled the page in her hands. Without her cell phone she couldn't research it further.

One of the five passages had to be about Stephanie, but which one? From the memories Grandma shared with her, Tracey suspected her ancestor was one of the masterminds of the group. Stephanie's ghost told Tracey her Butterfly Stone had once been known as the Ice Stone. *Fruit tingles. Why does everything have so many names?* It was all so confusing.

The fifth passage spoke of being frozen and lost. Stephanie did speak to her from inside the so-called Ice Stone. Perhaps that part was about her. Was Stephanie stuck inside the Butterfly Stone as Timothy was trapped inside the missing stone Officer Jameson had held?

Chewing on her thumbnail, Tracey tasted blood. The eighth verse had to be about Timothy. "His soul, but a shadow," she mumbled.

All Tracey knew of Stephanie was from the memory-dreams Stephanie had passed down through the generations until Tracey's nana—her mom's mother—gave them to Tracey's grandma—her dad's mom—for safe keeping, to protect them from her rapidly attacking dementia. Grandma showed them to Tracey, but even then Stephanie kept her secrets. The memories were locked, to be shown to Tracey only at the right time. And who determined that? *Stephanie*.

In the memory-dream Grandma showed Tracey, Stephanie had called the rest of the Sect of Five her friends. If only Tracey had kept a copy of the image she had seen, the photograph Doctor Chan had of the four people with her ancestor–three men and a woman. She had seen the woman, Millicent, in the memory-dream and the other man named Charles. She remembered his long-drawn face and tiny eyes. There had been another name too. Stephanie had said it—Matthew, her future husband.

All Tracey really had was a heap of clues and no real information. If Agent Malden and Hank were not going to let Tracey help find the stones, then she would have to find them on her own. If she didn't, Timothy would come for her again. And she feared this time he wouldn't just threaten Tracey. He would kill her.

Tales
by
The Lost

Following 219, Followed by 0
click **<broken link>** to follow The Lost!

Day 1

[cont …]

The simple act of putting words

onto the screen and sending it out

into the world gives me hope.

0 likes, 0 comments, 0 reshares
click **<broken link>** to like this post!:D

T.B.T.L.

3

She stayed away until dark, slinking back into camp as the group was cleaning up after dinner.

"I kept you a plate," Sarah said, hunching her shoulders as if expecting Tracey to shout at her. Tracey took the plate with the burger and chips from the picnic table and carried it over to the campfire with a soft word of thanks to her sister and plonked down beside Tony. No one spoke to her. Actually, they completely ignored her, and she was thankful for it. Their disinterest helped keep the peace.

She picked at her cold dinner in silence. Dropping the paper plate onto the grass at her, feet she stretched her hands toward the flames to warm them. The campfire crackled, hungrily consuming the wood. Popping sap sounded a counter-beat to distant animal cries. The wind shifted, swirling the sharp scent of smoke and burning paper. Tony coughed, waving a hand in front of his face. His movement acted as a siren announcing the silence was over.

"Hey," she mumbled, checking her shield was in place. The strain of keeping it in position bunched her neck muscles. Before coming back she had closed off her link to the Butterfly Stone, knowing Agent Malden would be pissed she had used it. "Awful habit."

"What is?" Tony glanced at her from the corner of his eye, his gaze fixed on the campfire.

"Me running off."

"Yeah, you should stop doing that." He shifted on the tree stump he was using as a seat. "Are you okay now?"

"I just needed some alone time, you know?"

"It's been a crazy few days," he said.

He had to mean since the attack. The afternoon alone had given her plenty of time to reflect on what had happened since the events that had changed her life. After the battle at the film studio, Agent Malden had swept them all off to a "safe" room—what he called it—and within hours had spoken to all of their parents, dropped Laura and Jonny off at home and then hiked Tracey, Tony, Dave and Sarah out here, the middle of nowhere, for magic training. If they had wanted to talk about what they'd been through, there had been little opportunity. Agent Malden and Prince Henry often disappeared to "plan" leaving Tracey and her friends alone, and Dave, well, he was not a talker. Tony wanted to be by himself and Tracey had been so worried about Sarah's trauma, she had let her sister prattle on about whatever she wanted. Tracey hadn't mentioned her fears or her ongoing nightmares of the Shadowman. She worried her friends were scared of her and if she was honest, she sort of was too. She wanted to call Mom.

Sitting next to Tony, Tracey realized she was worried about him too. Her friend had been acting weird since their arrival and whenever they were alone, he closed in on himself. She bit at her little fingernail. *Is he afraid of me?* She didn't want to ask in case he said yes.

In a camp full of people, Tracey had never felt so alone. Today in the woods she'd had an epiphany. She was suffering from trauma too and she needed to talk to someone—*had to*—or she would go mad. *You are not alone*, Stephanie whispered. Tracey ignored her. Stephanie was *not* the one she wanted to talk to. She needed her mom.

"Hey? You in there?" Tony nudged Tracey's shoulder.

Her gaze snapped to his. "Ugh yeah, what did I miss?"

"Agent Malden."

She tilted her head. Agent Malden sat across the campfire examining her through narrow eyes. "Tracey?"

"What was the question?" Her face burned. If she covered her cheeks with her palms it would only make her embarrassment obvious.

"You seem distracted."

"I'm tired." It was all she felt comfortable revealing.

His expression softened. "Go on."

Why did he have to push this? "It's exhausting holding up my shield all the time. It's worse when I fight. You're making me split my brain in two directions. I can't focus on what's happening because I'm too busy making sure I don't do anything bad. There must be an easier way."

"It will take practice, Tracey. You are starting to learn your strengths—"

"Not all of them," Dave muttered, scowling in Tracey's direction. She snarled at him. He knew why she couldn't use her powers.

Tony touched her arm. Sighing, Tracey focused on her shield, unsurprised to find a crack in it. A thin stream of fiery orange magic whispered through her cracked bubble. "Sorry." She tightened her grip on her shield and sealed the split. *Use the Butterfly Stone,* Stephanie whispered. Tracey shook the ghostly voice away.

Tony waited a moment longer and then removed his hand. Nausea swirled in her belly. She rubbed her stomach, hoping the burger she had just eaten would stay down, and breathed slowly through her nose. The campfire smoke smelled funky—like one of the pieces of wood was rotten.

"Let's speak more tomorrow," Malden suggested. "Head on to bed."

Sobbing woke Tracey from her unsettled sleep. All was darkness. A hiccup and a soft sniffle from her sister's sleeping bag brought her upright. "Sarah?" Snoring from the tents outside would block her voice from waking anyone else.

"What?" Sarah's voice was phlegmy.

"Are you okay?"

"Yeah, I had a bad dream."

Tracey scooted closer, still inside her sleeping bag, and pressed against Sarah's side. She stretched out a hand to rub Sarah's shoulder, feeling the minute jerking as her sister tried to hide how upset she was. "Do you want to talk about it?"

"Not really."

Fair enough. Tracey was pretty sure she knew what Sarah relived in her sleep. If it wasn't Sarah waking Tracey with a nightmare, it was Tracey waking Sarah. Tracey leaned her head against her sister's shoulder, hoping that just being near would provide comfort.

"Your hair smells funny."

"Needs a wash," Tracey murmured. "Yours too."

"Yeah." Sarah cleared her throat. "Where did you go today?"

"Climbed a tree."

"Really?" There was a tiny laugh inside Sarah's voice.

"Yeah. There's this really cool old tree about, I don't know, fifteen minutes away toward the river. Giant branches look like a ladder. There was a fat branch to sit on."

"You climbed a tree?"

"It was nice up there. All I could see was green. There was a cool breeze, but it was hot too."

"Sounds nice. Maybe you can show me tomorrow?"

"If Agent Malden gives us time off."

"I wanna stay with you, Tracey. I don't like it when you leave me alone."

"You weren't alone." She took a deep breath. "I'm sorry I left you with the boys. I was, uh, grumpy."

"You're always grumpy, Trace. I just don't wanna get left behind again."

She breathed silently and listened to her sister's sniffles. "Hey, since uh"—she hated to bring it up—"that night we merged magic, have you had any strange senses. Like—"

"Your emotions? Yeah, they're pretty clear to me now. Do you think it will always be like that?"

"Dunno, I get your feelings too. I know you're sadder than you tell me."

"And you're madder."

A faint light made one side of the tent slightly brighter than the other side. Someone had a light on. Tony's tent was on that side.

"Why does Timothy want the stones so badly?" Sarah asked suddenly.

"To come back? To make a new body? I don't even know how he

can do what he does."

"Why is he so angry?"

"I don't know. He... I think he was in love with Stephanie, but she didn't love him back."

Sarah sat up. "How do you know that?"

"Nana's memories."

"Nana has dementia, Tracey. She doesn't—"

"Grandma's holding onto her memories, special ones that Stephanie passed down. Grandma showed me."

"So that's where you two kept sneaking off to? Why couldn't I come with you?"

"Sorry, Sarah."

"He's horrible. Why try to hurt Stephanie if he loved her?"

"I don't know." Tracey remembered the memory-dream Grandma showed her. Timothy had wrapped Stephanie up in his magic "I think he wanted her to be in love with him. I think he wanted to control her."

"That's not love." Sarah sniffed.

"Yeah."

"How did he lose his body?"

"I don't know. There were five Mage-kind, friends of Stephanie's. Somehow, they put their magic into the stones and now they're all lost. Timothy thinks if he has them all, he can come back." Tracey had the crawly sensation that Sarah was staring at her in the dark.

"Can he really do that?"

"He thinks he can."

"What's it like? The Butterfly Stone. What is the magic like?" Sarah's voice sounded softer, like a whisper against Tracey's skin.

Fruit tingles. It took Tracey a while to speak. "It's different."

"How different?"

"I dunno. Different."

Sarah was quiet for a moment, then hummed. "Before that night, you used to be like you, but softer, more yellowy. Your magic I mean. Then we—together—we like, mind-melded and now you feel sharper, more like the edge of a blade. It's hard to explain."

Tracey stared at the lighter side of the tent. "Weird."

"I feel your edges more. Like I always know where you are."

"I get it. I know when you're close by too."

"Weird, yeah?" Sarah's voice was growing soft, sleepy.

"It's a good weird, Sars," Tracey whispered. She listened to her sister's breathing deepen and become regular. *Do I feel different to anyone else?* Mom would know. Again Tracey wished she had her cell phone. She scooched away from her sister and wriggled back to her spot in the tent. A bird cried out making her jump inside her sleeping bag. It didn't seem to wake any of the other campers. Tracey brushed her fingers over the Butterfly Stone and stared up at the dark canvas of the tent. Her mind whirred.

A little while later she crouched outside Tony's tent. "Tony, are you awake?"

"Yeah." His voice sounded croaky, as if he had been sleeping, which was silly because she knew he hadn't been asleep. She had listened to him toss and turn for ages. A flashlight clicked on.

"Can I come in?"

"Tracey, it's late." His shuffling increased. She jumped her sleeping bag backward as his shadow grew to fill the wall of the tent. The zipper sounded way too loud even beneath Prince Henry's snores and Dave's heavy breathing.

She had no idea how Sarah and Agent Malden managed to sleep through it all.

Tony peered around suspiciously but Tracey was the only one moving. He shuffled backward — still in his sleeping bag — and beckoned her inside. She wrapped her own sleeping bag tighter, poked her feet into the corners, and shuffle-walked inside, nearly falling on her face twice. Rocking unsteadily, she flopped onto his blown-up mattress, bouncing back up as Tony sat down. The up and down motion slowly settled and then all she could hear were snores broken by the occasional snort.

Tony's tent smelled of boy sweat and socks. It also smelled of sugar. Her eyes sprang wide. "Have you got sweets hidden in here?"

Lit by only his flashlight, Tony's face darkened. "Is that all you came in for?"

She gulped. "No. I wanted to ask if you're feeling okay." She kept her voice low, aware the other tents were pretty close. She didn't want to wake everyone up.

"I'm really tired."

Well, so was she. That didn't explain why he was giving everyone the silent treatment. She wriggled on his air mattress and stared at the tent wall. "I wanted to talk to you."

"You think it's my fault." He hissed the words as though wanting to stay quiet but shout at the same time.

She snapped around to face him. "What? No. What … what's your fault?"

"You ran off because of me, right?"

She thought about grabbing his arm but clenched her fists inside her sleeping bag instead. "No! Of course not. Why would you think that? My magic is out of control. *My magic.* Why would you think I blamed you? What would I even blame you for?" She told herself all this whispering was hurting her throat and that it wasn't sore because she was trying not to cry.

He hunched his shoulders and turned away. "What did you want to talk about then?"

Sorrow burrowed into her heart. It hurt to breathe. "I — do you want me to leave? I just wanted to … well, I've been …" How could she ask for his help when he was scared of her? "The stones," she blurted, needing a way to start.

"They want to keep us out of it," he said. So, he had picked up on that too? Agent Malden *was* being shifty. The way he had spoken to her, as if he was already distancing her from the investigation? "I think we —"

"— should look for it ourselves. Yeah, me too. Actually, I've already started." Tony pulled his cell phone from beneath his pillow. Blue light refracted off the cracks in the glass, creating crazy shadows along the walls of the tent.

"What? How have you got signal…? Wait. Hang on. How did you get your phone back? We had to give them to Agent Malden."

He didn't answer. She didn't press.

"So, what did you do?"

"Redirected Doctor Chan's mail."

"Why would…?" Her head snapped up as realization dawned. "The journal?" When they had first met Doctor Chan, he was working at the university and investigating the history of the stones. The man had shown Tracey the photograph of her ancestor, shocking her when she realized she and Stephanie looked almost the same. Doctor Chan had told them he was waiting for a book, a journal he thought had been written by one of the Sect of Five.

"Yeah. He said it was coming from a collector's estate and, well, when Doctor Chan disappeared from the University, I wondered if he was real or not."

"I wondered that too." They had discovered Doctor Chan was a bad guy when he'd fallen for the trap Tracey and her friends set at the film studio. He had betrayed them all in his desperation to get the Butterfly Stone.

"Mail is real, and to get mail you have to have an address. So, I sort of got into the mail records."

"That's super illegal, Tony."

"Trace!"

"I know, I know, just… we are in so much trouble already and, no… sorry, go on. Did you get the journal?"

He held up his phone. "Please."

She shouldn't be surprised.

"They're holding it for me at the post office. We just have to collect it."

Finally, things were going their way. "Tony, that's great." In the past, she would have hugged him or at least grabbed his hand. She clasped her fingers together and bounced up and down on the air mattress. "That's just great, Tony." There was no way Agent Malden and Hank could keep Tracey and her friends from searching for the stones. With Tony being his genius self, they now had their first real clue. They just had to suffer through the rest of this training camp and get back home so they could get that journal. She grinned at Tony. "Awesome."

Tales
by
The Lost

Following <u>219</u>, Followed by <u>0</u>
click **<broken link>** to follow <u>The Lost</u>!

Day 1

[cont...]

Perhaps one day my

story will be known?

I cannot imagine it.

<u>0</u> likes, <u>0</u> comments, <u>0</u> reshares
click **<broken link>** to like this post!:D

T.B.T.L.

4

"Good morning, campers!" Hank's voice exploded across the campground like one of Jonny's stink bombs. Tracey moaned and pressed her fingers into her skull. If Mom was here, she would have let them all sleep in.

"I have a new activity for you if you've all finished eating," Hank bellowed. He bounded into the middle of the camp. After five days, the prince was looking and acting more chipper. Tracey stifled a moan. *Ugh. Why is he such a morning person?* Grumbles followed the happy announcement. There was a cool breeze, and it brought the scents of the camp wafting over them — grass, the dying campfire smoke, boy sweat. *Ew gross!*

Tracey shifted on her uncomfortable log and squinted up at the smiling prince. "It's not even 7 a.m." Her breakfast bar lay unopened in her lap.

"Trust is a feeling that must be earned," Hank said loudly, ignoring her complaint. *Trust games? This is going to go well.* As though he could hear her doubts, Hank's gaze locked on to Tracey. "Without trust, a team is not a team. Trust builds confidence and confidence builds trust. Lack of trust can break a team apart and create gaps that can be exploited by the enemy."

Great! Another role-playing game. Tracey left her breakfast bar on the log and trailed after her team as they followed Hank out of camp.

"We'd work better if Tracey would use her magic," Dave grumbled from the back of the group. Tracey scowled over her shoulder at him. Dave used a finger to show his response to her glare. Tony barely opened his eyes as he walked along and Tracey kept expecting him to trip or stumble, but he somehow stayed upright. Sarah's fear leaked through their mental connection. Tracey sent back positive feelings while trying to disguise her own concerns. Could she use her magic today like Dave wanted? Her palms were damp with nervous sweat. She scrubbed them against her jeans.

Hank's face was stern as he glanced over his shoulder. "To truly be a team you need to rely on each other in the face of the unexpected."

Tracey peered around the overgrown path. No Agent Malden. He must be off preparing the test.

Hank held up a bent branch weighed down with thick green leaves for them to pass under. They stepped into another clearing, different from yesterday's arena. This one was square-ish, almost the exact length of an actual football ground. The boundary line was an impenetrable wall of foliage. In the middle of the grassy area was a small mound with a pole that held a little white flag fluttering in the breeze.

"Let's discuss today's activity." Hank's smile stretched across his face, reminding Tracey of the Joker. It was off-putting. For an actor, he sure wasn't good at hiding how uncomfortable he was. Maybe he didn't enjoy mornings any more than she did and was just faking it for the rest of them. "Huddle up."

Tracey scrunched between Dave and Sarah. Tony didn't meet her eye. "Your goal is to protect the flag." Hank stared at them expectantly. When the silence stretched into eternity, Tracey asked, "Is that it?"

"Yep. If you last thirty minutes with your flag untouched, you get the rest of the day off." He walked away with a smirk on his face.

"Come on, we can do this," Dave said pumping his fists.

"This is not a game," Tony snapped.

Tracey sighed. They were off to a great start. She missed Laura's level headedness and Jonny's awful jokes. *I wonder if they miss us? School must be awfully boring without us there to entertain them.* Nibbling at her pointer fingernail she glanced over at Sarah. "What do you think?"

Sarah shrugged. "Aren't you the boss?"

"No. I... Am *I* the boss?"

"You're the strongest," Dave said.

Tracey waited for Tony to chime in, but the boy remained silent. "But I can't use... being powerful doesn't make me or anyone else the boss. Tony's the smartest. He should decide."

Tony shook his head. "Not me."

Sarah peered up at Tracey and smiled. Feeling encouraged, Tracey glanced at the white flag. *Ha! Poor symbolism.* Such an open area should be easy to defend. They would be sure to see any attackers coming and have plenty of time to set up a response. She examined her team.

"We should—"

"—I'll take that end. They'll come at us from the woods." Dave took off before Tracey could call him back. Of course the attack would come from the woods, they were surrounded by woods. She scowled. Dave hadn't listened to the instructions at all. This was a trust exercise, they were expected to work together... right? With four of them they could each take a side. With three, things would be more difficult. Well if Dave was at one end, she, Tony, and Sarah could still take the other sides.

"Sarah, what about you go over to that spot over there?"

"I don't want to go by myself." Sarah's magic sparked an orange halo around her head.

"I could stay with her," Tony offered.

Ugh. That split them unevenly. She glared at her sister. "No, Tony. Take that end down there." She pointed to the side opposite Dave's current location.

"Are you sure we should split up? Aren't we meant to work together?" Tony asked.

"You didn't want to be the boss, remember?" She stared at him. "*Do* you want to be the boss?"

"No."

"I want to stay with you, Tracey," Sarah's voice drilled into Tracey's right ear.

Urgh! She stepped toward Tony. "What do you want to do?"

He shrugged.

"Then go down there please." Tracey smiled at him brightly. The look on Tony's face said he doubted her decision. She threw up her hands. "Fine, do whatever you want." She stomped away not bothering to look back.

Dave, in his haste, had headed north, so Tracey moved in the opposite direction. If Sarah followed or stayed with the flag it didn't matter because Tracey and Tony could form a long triangle with Dave at the end. Hank said this activity was about trust. Tracey would have to trust her team to hold their corners while she did the same. It was hard not to want to protect the flag herself. She glanced at the mound. Sarah stood beside it. She caught Tracey looking and her shoulders slumped. Tracey turned away, Tony's doubtful expression staying in her mind. It was so obvious he thought she had made the wrong decision. He kept saying he didn't want to be the leader. Then who should it be? She couldn't be the boss. None of them listened to her anyway.

A shout snapped her head up. That was Dave.

Tracey took two running steps before she skidded to a stop. This was a trust exercise. She had to trust that Dave could take care of himself, unless... was she supposed to help him? Could this exercise be about Dave trusting Tracey to save him? *Fruit tingles. What am I supposed to do?*

A roar lifted her head in time to see a fireball burn across the sky. She could feel its heat bloom against her skin and when it reached a spot above her head, it burst apart. Smoke poured out quickly obscuring the clearing. She coughed, her eyes streaming tears at the metallic taste in the back of her throat, and the hairs on Tracey's arms rose as something landed nearby. The ground trembled. Tracey strengthened her magic bubble around her body and reminded herself not to use her magic to attack, only defend. "Sarah? Tony?"

No reply came at her shout. "Dave?" They should have heard her. Tracey's heart gave an almighty thump. *What do I do now?* She had to help her friends. The purpose of the exercise sprang into her mind. Make sure no one touches the flag. *Ugh.* She held her position and used their weird connection to reach out for Sarah. Sarah's magic reached back. Good. Okay. Sarah was okay.

I need to see. Agent Malden and Hank would radiate strong magic. They should be easy to find if she searched for their Mage-kind presence. Closing her eyes, Tracey sneakily drew a bit of the Butterfly Stone's magic out. It pulsed like a beast anxious to be let off the leash. She wrapped her mind around it, determined to keep control and drew a fist-sized glomp of power down into her hand. She dropped her shield and threw it up into the air.

Exploding the sense ball, she followed the golden, glittery magic as it settled back down around her. Nothing stirred. *Where are they?* She could see her sister glowing off to her right, and in the distance she found Tony and Dave's magical presence. There was no sign of Agent Malden or Prince Henry.

Stephanie whispered into Tracey's ear. *Use your anger. Don't hide from your power. Open yourself up to the chaos. Hold the flag. Attack anyone who reaches for it.*

Tracey flicked the voice away with a snarl. She didn't want to use her magic to attack, only to defend. Stephanie's presence buzzed with displeasure. The grey smoke enclosing her crept closer. With an audible pop, Sarah's magic presence disappeared.

"Sarah?" Tracey shouted.

A male voice called out in response. "Tony?" Tracey spun in a circle. *Which way?* What could she do if she couldn't see? She dropped her shield. All she could hear was her own heartbeat thudding in her ears. She focused on the sound and closed her eyes. Breathing deeply, she drew another fist full of magic from the Butterfly Stone. She tugged it up to her ear and Listened, letting her magic thicken inside her body. Through the oppressive smoke, she made out a hiss. And beneath that—or through it, she couldn't tell—was the rustle of a bird's wing. She turned. Whistling wind caressed the nearby trees. She turned again and found Sarah's rapid breathing. She latched onto the sound and started running. Smoke was fading. Tracey ran until the mound with the flagpole reared up like a ghost rising from the murky mist in front of her. Sarah knelt beside the flag, her hands clasped tightly around the pole.

"Sarah!"

Her sister's eyes sprang open. "Where were you? I was shouting. You disappeared." Her voice was broken, as if she had screamed so loud her voice had fled from the force of it.

"You've got the flag," Tracey praised. Sarah looked up in surprise, or perhaps she had forgotten. A roar right next to Tracey rattled her ear drums and made the ground tremble. Sarah screamed. Tracey spun, thickening her shield bubble as a blast of magic hit her full force. She rocked back from the strength of it, ears ringing. Her shield held. She had sensed nothing. Where had that blast come from?

Sarah's scream changed pitch. Tracey turned as Sarah flew past, propelled by an impossible force. "Sarah!"

Another blast hit Tracey's shield and exploded. Smoke swirled and coalesced into the shape of a man. *The Shadowman!* Tracey's mind went blank. The Shadowman's throaty laugh grew manic. Her tongue flared with hot pain and Tracey tasted blood. Her shield flickered. She willed her shield to hold.

Fear won and her magic fizzled out. The man-shaped smoke monster floated toward her. His head twisted side to side, searching for her. Arms outstretched, his terrible tentacle-like fingers extended in her direction. A scream bubbled in Tracey's throat. She couldn't breathe around it. The Shadowman reached for her sister.

"Sarah!" The scream tore out of Tracey's mouth and she jumped in front of Sarah. *Not this time.* Tracey wrapped her hand around the Butterfly Stone and opened herself fully to power beyond her wildest dreams. The world became clear. The thrumming of her blood faded to a whisper as Tracey filled her palms with white hot power and threw everything she had at the Shadowman. The figure shattered into wisps of iridescent magic. Tracey reveled in her magic. It filled every part of her body. Her fingers prickled with pins and needles, her lips tingled. Her whole sense of being was alive with sound and taste and smell. *Sarah!* Tracey spun, searching for her sister and saw the flagpole was bare.

"No!"

She ran to the mound, hoping she was hallucinating, but she wasn't. The flag was gone.

Dave ran up, puffing hard, his hand brushed over the dirt stuck to his shirt. Tracey eyed the long tear down one leg and wondered what he had been attacked by. *He could have just fallen over?* Sarah clambered to her feet, her skin pale and shiny. She wrapped her arms around her waist and trembled. Tony appeared, trudging with his head bent, staring at the ground. There were drops of blood on his shirt. When he glanced up, his skin was stained red under his nose.

"What the flipping heck was that?" Dave demanded. Tracey was sure he would have sworn, but Hank and Agent Malden were already hurrying toward them. Hank shook his head. Tracey knew what he was going to say before the words left his mouth. Still, when they came out, they cut like a thousand knives.

"You failed."

Tales
by
The Lost

Following 219, Followed by 0
click **<broken link>** to follow The Lost!

Day 1

[cont …]

To have a friend, a true

Mage-kind friend, is

something I desperately

want, and I know it is

something I will never have.

0 likes, 0 comments, 0 reshares
click **<broken link>** to like this post!:D

T.B.T.L.

5

"I thought I'd find you here." Agent Malden lowered himself to the cracked tree stump beside Tracey. She didn't shuffle over or even look up. In her hands, she fiddled with a stone she had picked up from the river's edge. She stared out across the moving water and focused on a hummingbird that dipped in front of her. It darted up and zoomed off on some fabulous adventure, leaving Tracey behind, alone. Well, not quite alone. Not anymore.

"What do you want?" She shouldn't snap, but her stomach bubbled with fury and her chest felt so tight it hurt to breathe.

"Do you want to talk about it?"

The Butterfly Stone was a hot coal against her chest. She gritted her teeth and suffered through the pain. Various answers sprang into her head. None of them were appropriate given Agent Malden's self-appointed role as her mentor. Instead, she focused on steadying her breathing. It was an effort to unclench her fists. "I failed."

"Your team failed, Tracey. All of you."

She knew what she had to admit. She had been thinking about it a lot over the last half hour. Still it was hard to say. "We're not a team."

"No."

Peeking at him from the corner of her eye she saw that he was staring at the river. "It's not working, is it? What you brought us here to learn."

The drain on her strength from holding her shield in place was unnerving. Even now she was tired, like marathon-running tired. A weariness weighed heavy on her bones making it difficult to raise her arms.

"Not yet, Tracey, but we have time. It's going to take a lot of practice and hard work from each of you. Communication, teamwork, trust. Even adults struggle with these issues."

Tracey snarled and threw the stone she was playing with into the river. "You said time was running out. That's why we came here. Two weeks of intense training. In case he... Timothy... comes back."

"Tracey."

"It's been a week and we're hopeless. It's all just... crap."

His silence rubbed on her skin, making her itchy. She rocked her butt to inch further away from him, but still, when he inhaled to speak, she flinched.

"Is this about your magic?"

No duh! "It's broken. I'm broken." She couldn't look at him.

"You seem to be doing quite well. You overcame your fear and used your magic against the image of the Shadowman and you didn't take magic from your sister to do it. I'd say you are improving."

"I can't keep my shield up all the time. It's exhausting. When I fight, I have to drop it and that's when I need it the most. That's when I'm likely to hurt someone."

He shuffled on the log and stretched out one leg. She heard his knee click. "You didn't hurt anyone today. This is trial and error, Tracey. We have to find something that works for you. It's not like we can refer to a manual."

"It's too risky," she mumbled staring at the dirt between her feet.

The agent made a few sounds like he was trying to figure out what to say. His head tilted in her direction. She didn't look up. "I've asked some questions and reached out to some friends. I know your grandmother is looking into it too. We'll find something. In the meantime..."

"Shield all the time," she sighed. "Who are you asking for help? M-Force?"

He shuffled again. "No, this has gone up the chain. I have to be circumspect to keep this out of the council's hands."

"The council?"

He froze. "Forget I said that."

"Agent Malden?" He didn't respond. When she examined his face, it was clear he wasn't going to say any more on the subject. *Who are the council? Why do you need to keep my problem a secret?* "Who are the council?" she demanded.

The rumpled man stared at the river. There was more grey in his hair than she remembered and when he moved his head, his flappy neck skin looked like a chicken gullet. The lines around his mouth cut deeper. He rubbed at the skin between his eyes. "Tracey."

She glanced back down the path. "School," she blurted. "We have to go back soon. How am I going to keep my shield up all the time?" She picked up another stone and tossed it between her hands. The edges were round and smooth like glass. Like the Butterfly Stone.

Agent Malden said nothing. Tracey threw the stone and picked up a pebble, running her fingertips over the gritty surface. It was cracked and there was a hole in it. The sharp edges dug into her skin when she formed a fist around it.

"I'm concerned."

She snorted. *Join the club.*

"Right now, you want to lash out at me. Burn me to a crisp, blow me into the woods and blast me with your magic, don't you?"

She did. But how did he know that? She didn't confirm his comment. By the river's edge the grass quivered. The same cold breeze ruffled the hairs on her arms. A bird burst from the tree above her head, squawking like it was scared. She watched it race away, her heart beating fast.

"We both know the Butterfly Stone is tempting you, wearing you down, weakening your self-control. You want to embrace it, am I right? It would be so easy to use its power."

This time it was Tracey who said nothing. Her face burned hot. Was this what a bug felt when it was examined under a magnifying glass? She feared Agent Malden would squish her or trap her in a glass jar to study later.

"What should I do?"

"You should take it off."

Her hand sprang to her chest. "I can't."

"Tracey, it may give you the space and time you need to work on your control—"

"No, I can't," she snapped. "I've tried to take it off. Every night, I—" She threw the pebble and listened to it *plonk* into the water. She picked up another stone and rolled it between her fingers. "I get sick. I start shaking and get dizzy. I—" The words stuck in her throat. She coughed but couldn't continue.

The older man hummed.

Tracey bounced between wanting to run, or shout at him to leave her alone. Surprisingly, it felt good to finally say, "I'm scared."

"Of the stone? Or of your magic?"

"Of me." She finally gazed at him. His gaunt face made the lines around his eyes more obvious and his pale skin held a waxy sheen. If she hadn't heard him snoring each night she would wonder if he was getting any sleep. None of them had truly recovered from their battle with Timothy and the Shadowman. Poor Agent Malden. He had to be still mourning his partner, Agent Striker. Tracey hadn't even asked if he missed her. As his gaze focused on her face, she wondered if he was feeling as helpless as she did.

"I think we went about this all wrong."

The words cut into her chest, slicing her into little pieces. Her vision wobbled as tears filled her eyes. *I want Mom.* She looked away, blinking quickly but couldn't stop their fall. Agent Malden didn't comment as Tracey pulled a used tissue from her pocket and scrubbed under her nose with it. She sniffed and poked her fingers into the corners of her eyes to stop more tears from forming. "Mistake?" At least she knew the truth now. He thought she was hopeless. Or dangerous. Probably both.

"I ... usually I have ... Brig would do all the planning. I'm not good at making these kinds of decisions."

Brig must be Agent Striker's name. The words *"I'm sorry"* stuck in Tracey's throat.

"I should never have asked for your help to find the stones. You are all children. Dave has no experience, Sarah is too young. Tony, perhaps, is ready, but your magic is—"

"Out of control?" The words whispered out of her. Her stomach churned.

"I was going to say volatile. You need to learn to trust in your abilities. You all do. But Tracey, you must pay particular attention to your strengths and weaknesses. Throwing you into group work was a hasty decision on my part."

Tears filled her eyes. "But Timothy…"

"Is gone for the moment. It will take some time for him to amass enough power to possess someone else. I've rushed your training, Tracey, and I apologize."

She clenched her fingers into fists and ground her teeth. "So, we just go home?"

"Yes. I'll speak to your mom and grandmother when we get you home about creating individual lesson plans for each of you. We'll give you some new exercises to try and Hank and I will continue to work with you—"

Tracey exploded, jumping to her feet. "But the investigation? The other stones? Who is going to find them?"

"We—"

"You can't train us and track down the other stones at the same time."

Agent Malden stood up, his gaze searching the tree line. Tracey's tummy swirled as realization dawned. He didn't know what to do. The thought of an adult without a plan was scary. Adults were supposed to have these things figured out. *What does that mean for me?* Tracey stared at her feet. *I'll figure something out.* She couldn't leave the hunt for the stones up to these adults. Only Tracey held the Butterfly Stone, and only she knew how truly dangerous it was. Without her help they would never track down the other stones. *I'll do it myself.* With her hands on the log, she pushed to her feet. "We should get back to the others." She would keep her and Tony's plan a secret for now. Malden and Hank couldn't know what she was up to or they would stop her. "You're right. I should just concentrate on school. Maybe Hank can help us get into the school production this year or something. What do you think?"

He raised an eyebrow and let out a soft laugh. It was a weak sound, but at least he was trying. Pity it didn't make her feel any better.

"Tracey, we'll work this out."

Yeah. Sure we will. "Why did we fail the test?" she asked. At least she could get an answer to that.

He shook his head. "You need to figure that out for yourself."

Tales
by
The Lost

Following <u>219</u>, Followed by <u>0</u>
click **<broken link>** to follow <u>The Lost</u>!

Day 954

I almost did it today.

I was in a Mage-kind store,

watched by the Mage-kind

storekeeper and I almost

put the lipstick in my bag.

<u>0</u> likes, <u>0</u> comments, <u>0</u> reshares
click **<broken link>** to like this post!:D

T.B.T.L.

6

Only Tracey's dad was awake to greet them when she and Sarah came home. Agent Malden stood in the doorway as they headed inside. "Bathroom!" Sarah shouted and raced past their dad up the stairs. Tracey gratefully lowered her stinking camp bag to the carpet and launched into her dad's arms. He mumbled something she didn't catch. She was content to stay wrapped in his embrace forever. Eventually, he pulled back. Concerned brown eyes stared into hers. She shook her head, halting any questions he might have had. "Where's Mom?"

Dad held a finger to his lips. His greying hairs were staring to outnumber the brown strands and looked like he had been running his fingers through it. "Mom's in bed with a migraine. Just tell me you're okay. The rest can wait until tomorrow."

Unable to answer, Tracey hugged him again and buried her face into his shoulder. The hand patting her back felt big and warm, his body solid and safe beneath her cheek. "Tracey, let me talk to your father for a moment," Agent Malden said. Tracey pulled away and crept up the stairs leaving the two men alone in the living room.

She didn't remember cleaning up but, somehow, she ended up in her pajamas and in bed. She couldn't sleep. She stared at her bedside clock as the hours ticked by. Her brain wanted to go over every detail of the last few weeks but her body wanted to switch off. Huffing, Tracey rolled to her back and stared up at the ceiling. Beneath her pajama top the Butterfly Stone vibrated as though it heard her anxious thoughts and wanted to help. No one could help. In less than a minute her alarm would start to blare and she would be forced to get out of bed and face her nightmare head on.

School.

THE TIGER'S EYE

I don't want to go.

5:59 a.m.

A huge sigh surged from her mouth. Her breath was awful, and her teeth furry because she hadn't brushed them before going to bed.

Bleep! Bleep! Bleep! Bleep!

Tracey smacked her hand against the alarm cutting the noise off mid-bleep. Rolling over, she stared at the opposite wall and listened to feet thunder past her bedroom door.

Her insides were frozen like she was a human-shaped shell around a core of ice. Tugging her dressing gown on, she decided to face the inevitable interrogation downstairs and ensuring her shield was finally in place, thumped into the kitchen.

Dad, Simon, and Peter sat at the table eating toast. Tracey felt the buzz of her dad's magic and the slightly faster vibration of Peter's presence brush against her shield. There was a void of emptiness around her brother Simon that itched at Tracey's skin. No one knew why some people were born with the Mage-kind node and some weren't. Tracey worried her brother Simon — a Norm — was missing out because he was unable to sense magic. He never said anything to indicate he was bothered by it, but how could he not be? Magic was awesome — when it wasn't awful.

"We're out of cereal," Simon rumbled. His hair stuck up in the air like he had stuck a finger into an electrical socket. His pimples were growing pimples and his face was splotchy, the little white bumps looking nasty and swollen. Sarah stumbled down the stairs behind Tracey.

"Hey girls." Dad stood up. "Toast?"

Like they had a choice. Tracey collapsed at the table beside her sister, and pulled the butter close, nudging raspberry jelly toward her sister.

The younger girl dragged her sleep-tangled, dark brown hair out of her face and mumbled what was probably a thank you.

Tracey waited for the first question to be asked. Simon's stare darted from Tracey to Sarah and back again.

"Go on," she sighed.

"What did you learn? Did you get to use a lot of magic? What's Prince Henry like? Did Agent Malden—"

"Where's Mom?" Sarah mumbled.

"Still in bed. Bad migraine," Dad said pointing to his temple.

Ouch. Poor Mom. She got them fairly regularly and said they were hormone related. Both Sarah and Tracey hoped they wouldn't get them. Given all her problems with her magic, having hormone related issues just didn't seem fair. "So, you're dropping us at school today?" Tracey asked.

"Yep, so talk while you eat," he urged waving his toast around. Tracey sighed. They always got toast when Dad was on drop-off duty. And it was always burnt.

"Careful," Tracey warned, as jelly dripped close to his white business shirt.

The toaster popped. Sarah scored the first piece, Tracey got the second. "Lots of magic drills and practicing basic shielding. Heaps of study, too. It was like school and camp combined into one evil dream," Sarah told Simon.

"Yeah," Tracey agreed. "Sarah was pretty awesome though."

"Really?" Dad looked at Sarah with pride. "Great to hear that, honey. Mom will be happy."

Tracey didn't mention the test they failed. She hoped Sarah wouldn't say anything about it either. When her sister remained silent, Tracey glanced her way. Sarah's face was flushed. Hopefully she wasn't sunburnt. Tracey was sure she had reminded her sister to put on sunscreen. Typical. Sarah never listened.

"Trace, what about your magic? I don't sense your, ah, wobble. Did you get some help with your shields?" Peter asked. His hair was wilder than Simon's this morning. Brown curls twisted in all directions like they were trying to escape his head.

She sighed. "I have to shield all the time. Agent Malden raised the threshold on my bracelet again. Can't you feel it?"

"That's what that is?" Peter mumbled.

"Sounds dumb. How does that help?" Simon said.

Tracey shrugged.

Sarah leaned over and poked Tracey's arm. "It's not a real shield. It's a shadow one. To stop her power from leaking out."

"That sounds gross." Simon grinned.

"Shut up," Tracey said.

"Tracey." Dad's voice held a familiar warning.

"Sorry, Dad. Agent Malden is still trying to figure out what I can do and what I can't do. I just have to keep shielding for now."

"Do what he says."

"Yes, Dad," she grumbled.

"Just pretend you're a spaceship," Peter offered, running a hand through his wild curls. Crumbs from his toast latched onto his hair. "Even the smallest speck of dust damages the hull, so they use shields all the time in space."

"Great, I'm a spacewoman. I just need a suit and helmet."

"You can borrow my bike helmet." Simon smirked. Tracey threw her toast crust at him.

"Go on—get upstairs and get ready for school," Dad ordered, passing Tracey and Sarah another piece of toast. With slightly more energy than before, Tracey followed her siblings upstairs.

When Simon and Peter were out of earshot Tracey slowed and whispered to Sarah. "Did you get any sleep?" They stopped at the top of the landing. Pictures of her family covered the wall. Tracey stared at a photo of the two of them climbing all over their mom.

"Not much. You?" Sarah rubbed her eyes and let out an enormous yawn.

"Barely at all. Be careful at school, yeah? If anything happens, anything at all, text me."

Sarah's eyes narrowed. "You think he'll attack at school?"

Tracey wished she knew for sure. She yawned. "Just be careful."

"I will. I wish you came to my school, Trace. It's just... I'm so alone there."

"Not alone. What did I tell you?"

"Yeah, great. Such a help." Sarah waved a hand around and stomped away. Tracey sighed.

Beating Peter into the bathroom, Tracey showered and dressed in her most comfortable jeans and favorite green superhero T-shirt. After a week in her stinky camp clothes, it felt great to be back in comfortable, boring, old school clothes. At the impatient toot of the car horn, she grabbed her bag and cell phone and raced downstairs to pile into the car next to her brothers. Simon squashed her into the door. She shoved him back. He poked her in the leg. She elbowed him in the side.

Ah, it was good to be home where people didn't tiptoe around her. Sarah peered over her shoulder from the front seat and grinned, probably sensing the direction of Tracey's thoughts. She could feel nervousness hiding beneath Sarah's wide smile.

Tracey understood it. It was strange pretending everything was back to normal. She and Sarah had not told their parents everything that happened at the movie lot that night a few weeks ago, though she was sure Mom suspected they had faced more danger than they'd let on. She always knew stuff like that. It was like Mom had a sixth sense about all her children. Agent Malden had explained what happened, but Tracey hadn't mentioned the soul crushing horror of that moment when she had known they were going to die.

Tracey was the first one out of the car when Dad parked outside the school. Waving to Sarah and the boys, she made her way toward her usual spot for meeting her friends — the side gate off Elm — and sat on the stone fence.

Laura arrived first. Tracey checked her watch and then the clock on her cell phone. "Am I late?"

"Very funny," Laura moaned, and then gave Tracey a brief hug. "It's way too early to be awake. How are you?" Lowering her voice, she added, "How was camp?"

"Awful," Tracey told her eyeing Laura's red blazer, white lacey shirt and what looked like new jeans. Laura's dark hair hung loose around her gorgeous face. Not a pimple to be seen. "How was school?" Tracey scratched at the blemish on her nose. "Any nightmares?"

"Ugh, all the time, yeah," Laura said. "What do you mean awful?"

Tracey opened her mouth but closed it again at the sound of Jonny's bike motor. He coasted to a stop and pulled off his helmet revealing he had shorn his hair even closer to his scalp. "Hello there, lovely ladies. You both look well rested." He pressed his glasses higher up on his nose and blinked at them through the smudged glass.

Tracey smacked him on the arm as Laura moaned at him. The black boy wore an emerald green tie around his bare neck. It matched the color of his trousers. "Where's the last member of our Scooby Gang?"

"I don't know," Tracey said. A sick feeling wormed its way through her stomach as the first bell rang.

Laura squinted and peered around holding her hand up to shield her eyes against the early morning sun glare. "It's not like Tony to miss school."

"Maybe he slept in?" Tony *had* been super weird at camp, really withdrawn. Maybe he was sick and his parents had kept him at home. Tracey chewed on her middle fingernail.

"Gross. When did you start biting your nails?" Laura asked.

"Oh, I dunno. At camp I s'pose." She hid her hands behind her back, eying Laura's chip-free pink painted nails.

Laura waved her hand around. "Use nail polish, it stops you pretty quick. Tastes gross."

"Yeah okay, I'll try that." Tracey peered around searching for any sign of Tony. The bad feeling in her tummy was growing.

"Hey, what's going on in your head?" Laura nudged harder than she had to. "You're writing some big story in your head about why Tony's not here. Did something happen at camp?"

Tracey rubbed at the bruise blooming on her arm. "No, nothing like that. Just basic camp stuff. Except, well... There was this test we... we kept failing. I really wish I knew why, but Agent Malden said we had to figure it out for ourselves."

"What about the next stone?" Jonny asked.

Tracey sighed. "No internet access. Tony worked his magic though — not literally — so we might have a place to start."

Laura's eyes lit up as Jonny leaned in. Tracey smelled chocolate milk on his breath. "Come on, we'd better get to class. Are you going to Donny's later?" he asked.

"Yeah, I have to check in and see how much paperwork he's left me." Knowing her uncle and his not very busy detective agency, there wouldn't be too much paperwork waiting for her. Her friends knew it too.

"Great, we'll come over tonight," Laura said.

Jonny nodded. "Yep, gotta start planning."

"There you go with the planning again, Jonny. Are you feeling okay?" Tracey asked, grinning wildly.

He laughed. "I have an affinity."

Though distracted and laughing with her friends, Tracey's thoughts drifted back to Tony. She would text him that they were meeting at Uncle Donny's later that afternoon. Hopefully he would meet them there and she could find out what was wrong.

Laura nudged her again. "So, I heard something." Her perfectly sloped eyebrows wobbled up and down.

Tracey's mind went straight to Damian, the cute Norm boy at school — the cute Norm boy she *totally* had a crush on. She pictured his dreamy brown eyes, muscular football body and tousled hair. "Don't keep me waiting."

"Damian broke up with Meena."

Tracey's jaw dropped. She stopped walking and stared at Laura. "What? Really?" Her mind darted through a number of what-ifs. Eventually, she shook her head and started walking again. "It doesn't matter."

"What do you mean it doesn't matter?" Laura grabbed Tracey's sleeve. Tracey stopped.

Jonny looked back. "What's the hold up?" he called.

"What do you mean *doesn't matter*?" Laura repeated. "I thought you liked him."

"He was weird to me. I-I just, he's weird okay. Come on, any guy who likes Meena and wants to spend time with her must be touched in the head, right?" Tracey's laugh sounded forced. Her heart pounded at the news. *They broke up?*

"Uh, yeah, right, I suppose. But he's not with her anymore." Laura's eyes narrowed. "Hey, does that mean I can talk to him if you don't want him?"

Tracey's stomach fell out of her body. She imagined it hitting the ground with a wet smack. She actually looked down to check the pavement.

THE TIGER'S EYE

Nope, just her imagination. "You like Damian?"

"Well, he's cute. What's not to like?" Laura winked and tugged on Tracey's arm to get her walking again. *Laura likes Damian?* Tracey's brain melted. It shouldn't surprise her that Laura would want to date Damian. They would make a really cute couple. Why hadn't Laura said she was interested before? Tracey's hands trembled. She shoved them deep into her pockets and plodded after Laura toward Hall B. Beneath her shirt, the Butterfly Stone pulsed.

When Damian sat down beside Tracey, she recalled with a bang that Mr. Michaels had assigned them to work together before she left for the emergency training camp. Meena had been furious about it. Tracey smiled at the cute boy nervously. He looked yummy in his leather jacket and she had to tear her gaze from his beautiful face before she made an even bigger fool of herself by drooling or sighing.

"Hi Tracey." His lips curled up. Light shone from his eyes. *Oh, fruit tingles.*

"Hey," she muttered and flipped through her notebook. Damian's presence seared into her soul. She tried to convince her brain that leather was a cliché and that it wasn't the eighties, but his tight muscles rounded out the edges of the jacket and the scent of wood and sugar drifted to her nose. She sniffed, searching for the source. It came from Damian. Her face heated. She pulled a tissue from her bag and blew her nose. "Allergies," she said, hoping her face would not combust. Laura's voice in her ears kept saying he and Meena had broken up.

Mr. Michaels bent over to tie his shoelaces. His bald spot looked particularly shiny today. Tracey forced her mind to focus as he started talking about persuasive texts like the articles you read online, click bait, and the power of the media.

"What power—fake news!" Dave One shouted. Everyone in the room groaned. Mr. Michaels glared, his face beet-red, until they all fell silent. He stood up and paced the front of the room, his slacks making a swish sound between each squeak of his right shoe.

"We know there is bias inherent in every persuasive article you read. A writer writes with purpose to sell a story. You can learn to read what is behind the author's intent if you study the text of the article properly. Words such as... anyone?"

"Emotional words?" Meena suggested.

"Like?" Mr. Michaels urged.

"Like in the old diaries you're making us read, when they describe girls as *weak* or *delicate*. Total rubbish if you ask me."

"Yeah," Carla piped up from Meena's side. "The women have to be stronger to put up with those attitudes!"

The class snorted and giggled. "Focus, class," Mr. Michaels warned. "Today, to help you with your team assignment—which I am sure you are diligently working on—"

What assignment?

"—we will look at a few first-hand accounts. Read the two letters on pages eighty-seven and eighty-eight. Highlight all instances of the persuasive words used to sway the reader. What is the writer trying to convince us to believe?"

Tracey raised her hand. "Sir, I don't—"

Mr. Michaels' thunderous expression caused her to hunch her shoulders. "Get to work, Miss Masters."

Damian leaned over and whispered in her ear. She shivered as his warm breath caressed her skin. "He gave us the assignment last week. We have to write about the Week of Terror from the perspective of a townsperson. He wouldn't assign me a new work partner, so I started without you. Are you feeling better?"

She nodded, unable to meet his gaze. He leaned back and she stared at the two letters on her tablet. The description bubbles said they were written during the Mage-kind Rebellion. *Ugh*, it was bad enough they had to study the 1820 Mage-kind Rebellion in her History Studies class with Mrs. Arctalie, but did they have to do it in Mr. Michaels' English class too? It pained her to read the very one-sided accounts. The first was written by the Mayor of Chirnside to his mother, dated the day before the uprising.

My Dearest Mother,

The weather is most unusual for this time of year. Torrential rains, frost, and hail continue to plague us. I am afraid your prized roses did not survive the unseasonal change, though I am pleased you are away at this time. Strange happenings have occurred in town of late and I know little what to make of it. Many have taken to locking their doors at night and I fear our once trusting townsfolk are becoming hard and cold toward one another. Something is coming. You will perhaps call me foolish. I look forward to assuring you all is well upon your return a month hence.

Your loving son,
Bertrum Jeffers.

The next letter was also written by the mayor, dated a week after the Week of Terror.

My Dearest Mother,

The worst of news, I'm afraid. A terrible reckoning has occurred. Many of the good townspeople you have fond memories of have lost their lives in a revolt of horrific science. What you and I long feared has now come to pass. There is wickedness inherent in many a good soul. Dark aspirations I dread to name lest they strike me down as well. Witches are among us. Too many in the populous are infected. The demons have gone rogue, striking down the innocent without impunity. Last night, a council—or so they claim—came upon my door insisting they be heard. Sworn, they have, that they can end the bloodshed but for some concessions. I fear for my children, your beloved grandchildren, for I am positive I saw their young cousin in town during the battles. I do not know what to do and wish that I had your wise counsel. Time runs short. I must have an answer for them within the hour.

Think well of me, mother.
Your loving son,
Bertrum Jeffers.

"Well? Who has a comment?" Mr. Michaels sat at his desk in the front corner of the room. Tracey could see his right shoe had a hole in the sole. The laces were different shades of brown.

Her hand snapped up. "Sir, the Mayor is a Norm. What about Mage-kind accounts? Are there any letters from them during the same time period?"

The class sniggered. Mr. Michaels rolled his eyes. "No, Miss Masters, we don't have letters from the murderers."

That was not what she meant.

"He was scared, Sir," Meena said. Tracey twisted to glare at the leading half of the bully girls known as the Evil Queens. Meena sneered at Tracey. Her perfect eyebrows slanted, her caramel skin gleaming. Tracey felt she was staring down a snake, one who was very hungry.

"What makes you say that, Miss Gulpta?"

Tracey tuned out, not wanting to hear what gross thing Meena would say next. She turned the page in her tablet. "Hey, I'm sorry about before," Damian whispered, leaning in close. His arm brushed her skin as his lips came close to her ear.

Goosepimples rose up over her skin at the feel of his warm breath. "What?"

"The Meena thing. Look, I was weird. I'm sorry."

"Oh yeah, okay," she mumbled. Tracey stared at her tablet not really seeing it, not wanting to look up. *Why is he telling me this?*

"Would you like to meet my sister?" he whispered. She snapped her gaze to his face and caught him checking to see if Mr. Michaels had noticed them whispering. "You remember I told you she's Mage-kind."

Tracey examined his face. He stared at her so intently she hoped she didn't have toast stuck in her teeth, or butter smeared across her forehead, or... "Um."

"She's scared of school. Scared and angry. Enough to make herself sick. She hasn't come to school at all since we moved. Mom and Dad don't know, but they'll find out soon. I'm sure it would help to talk to someone like you."

Tracey couldn't say no to those gorgeous deep-set brown eyes. His hand touched hers when he pressed a piece of paper into her hand. She agreed to text him later. *Damian just gave me his phone number!* She felt faint, but she also felt giddy. Her heart pounded. Taking the paper, she assumed she said something like, "Sure, happy to help." Her racing heart slowed as realization dawned. *Oh, he's probably only being nice to you because of his sister.* She let out a soft sigh and turned her head to hide her disappointment. Her gaze returned to the letters. *Why can't we study the ... Oh!*

Tracey had long suspected Stephanie was directly involved in the Mage-kind rebellion. If there were any first-hand accounts of that time maybe she could use this assignment as an excuse to research her family further. There might even be clues to the stones somewhere in these first-hand accounts. *I've got to tell Tony.* She surreptitiously glanced at her cell phone. No messages.

Where could Tony be?

Tales
by
The Lost

Following 219, Followed by 0
click **<broken link>** to follow The Lost!

Day 954

[cont …]

I wouldn't have been caught.

As soon as I left the store

the storekeeper would have

forgotten me. I almost did it.

0 likes, 0 comments, 0 reshares
click **<broken link>** to like this post!:D

T.B.T.L.

1

Lunch time came quickly and the gossip around the hall was centered on Dave Two and his Mage-kind bracelet. The buzz against Tracey's skin was electric. The table favored by the Evil Queens and the Double Ds was minus one of the Ds and the lack was made up for by Meena and Carla growing louder. Two more beef-heads from the football team and two vapid girls with more hair than brains made up the rest of the table. Tracey swore she could smell their hairspray from where she sat at her usual table against the back wall. She wasn't sure why she thought Dave Two would sit at her table now. She supposed it was because she thought he was part of her team. The scowl on Dave One's face as he glared across the room at his once best friend was scary.

Dave Two sat alone at a table in the far corner, opposite Tracey's group and at a diagonal to the cool kids' perch. Meena and Carla preferred to sit either side of the double entrance doors where they could preside over the lunch room and cast judgment over students as they entered. Other kids gave Dave Two's table a wide berth.

"Dave One looks cut-up. It's like he thinks Dave Two decided to become Mage-kind just to peeve him," Jonny whispered. It wasn't that Jonny was genuinely trying to keep quiet. It was more like one of those fake whispers you get in a stage play that still needed to be loud enough to be heard by the audience.

Laura picked cheese out of her salad. "Can't say he doesn't deserve a little payback though, right Tracey?"

"I guess." Tracey yawned and spun her apple around with one hand, watching it rotate unevenly before catching it.

Laura raised her eyebrows. "Seriously? You don't think he deserves it?"

"I would have once, but any flack he gets as Mage-kind trickles down onto me and Tony. And Sarah."

"How is she?" Laura asked, flicking glossy dark tresses over her shoulder.

"Having a lot of nightmares." Tracey moved her gaze from the lone boy back and to her friends. The empty seat beside her was a black hole sucking her attention toward it. *Where is Tony?*

Jonny waved a hand in Tracey's face. "So how did camp go?"

She deflated, dropping her head to the table with a clunk. "We totally suck at everything." When there was only silence in reply she dragged her head up.

"But your magic..." Jonny's eyes widened behind his gold-framed glasses. "I've seen you. You're amazing."

She shot him a smile. It quickly fell off her face. "No, Jonny, we totally suck. We failed every teamwork task. Every single one."

"Yeah but, Dave—"

"—not just him. Me and Tony, too." *Mostly me.* "I can't figure out how Agent Malden and Hank beat us every time. It's driving me crazy. We never saw them coming."

"Hank?" Laura asked, her eyes twinkling.

"Yeah, we got used to calling him that." Tracey's gaze drifted to the empty chair again. To change the subject, she poked Laura's arm. "So, what's been happening here? Anything going on last week I should know about?"

"Meena and Carla got in a fight. They must have worked it out though, because yesterday they were back to normal," Laura said nibbling at a large lettuce leaf.

"Aw, I missed that?" Tracey's attention flicked to the girl in question. Meena's straight black hair had a strand of beads dangling in front of her right eye. She said something that sent Carla into peals of laughter.

"I'm in love," Jonny announced.

"What?" Tracey screeched, her head snapping back to Jonny. "With who, what?"

"It's only in his head, Tracey. Jilly doesn't even know who he is,"

Laura said shaking her head at the boy.

The name didn't ring any bells. "Jilly? Is she new?" Tracey asked. The Butterfly Stone beneath her shirt warmed slightly. She pressed her hand against it to quiet it.

Jonny tilted his head, his nose scrunching. "Nooo, not new exactly. She started this year."

"I don't think I know her," Tracey said.

"She has lunch classes, violin, or something. She's like super isolationist. Really pretty though," Laura said, giving Tracey a long look. "I'm sure we've talked about her before."

Tracey wriggled her eyebrows at Jonny. "So, she's really pretty, huh?"

"She is," Jonny confirmed. He closed his eyes and hummed as if he was picturing her. Tracey laughed.

Laura's face still looked weird, all creased. "I get a weird vibe from her."

"That's because you're threatened by her gorgeousness. You're both like magnets. Your beauty repels each other." Jonny dropped his chair to all four legs.

"Shut it, Jonny," Laura rolled her eyes.

Intrigued, Tracey leaned in. Lowering her head and her voice she asked, "Who is she?"

Laura leaned in too. "I can't believe you don't remember her." Laura sighed when Tracey continued to stare blankly. "Her name is Jilly Cho. Long black hair—"

"Skin that glows. Dreamy, deep, soulful eyes and a body that just—"

"Jonny!" Laura and Tracey snapped in unison.

The boy subsided with a grin.

"Is she nice?" Tracey asked, curious. She couldn't put a face to the name. The last few weeks must have wiped all non-consequential things from her brain to make room for the Butterfly Stone and the Shadowman. She rubbed a hand over her neck and massaged her tight muscles. Maintaining her shield, especially at school, drained her down to her bones. She pushed a little more power into it and slumped further down in her chair.

"Can I sit with you?"

Tracey's head nearly twisted clear off her neck as she sat upright. Her gaze snapped to the boy standing behind Tony's chair.

Damian's gorgeous brown eyes locked onto her face. The question was clearly meant for her. No words formed. She gaped.

"Sure, man," Jonny said when Tracey kept silent. Laura grabbed her phone and tapped into it with fast moving fingers. Any moment now Tracey's phone was going to vibrate, and she knew what it was going to say. Her palms grew damp.

"So, um hey," Damian said sitting in Tony's chair.

Tracey nodded. "Hey." Did spontaneous combustion still happen or was it just a myth? Because she was seriously close to finding out. The table's occupants fell into a really awkward silence. The cafeteria noise rose to fill the gaps. Still, Tracey heard her phone's soft buzz. She slapped her hand over it while trying to avoid Laura's all-knowing eyes.

"So yeah, um… I thought we could discuss the assignment for Mr. Michaels?" Damian said.

Jonny leaned his chair back up to rest against the wall, his gaze glued to Tracey's face, his lips quirking. Laura's ankle boot connected with Tracey's shin. She would have yelped but Damian was watching so she bit her lip and glared at her friends. The scent of sugar filled Tracey's nose. She shoved her apple into her mouth to hide her groan.

Laura put her fork down and turned her full attention on Damian. "What do you have to do for the assignment? I haven't got mine yet." Laura was in the advanced English class. She was in a lot of advanced classes.

"Mage-kind rebellion letters." Tracey told her. The face Laura pulled in response was dead right. *It was gross.*

"At least you don't have to work with Dave Two," Jonny moaned. "He barely said two words to me. Just glared at Dave One the whole time."

Tracey tried to keep her voice steady as she replied to Damian. *Be cool.* "The assignment? Sure, what did you want to go over?"

"Could we meet in the library after school to talk about which question we're going to answer?" There were three to choose from and she hated each one. All Norm-positive, they made the Mage-kind rebels sound evil.

"I work at my uncle's after school." She debated inviting him to come there. *Too soon, too soon,* her mind screeched like a fire alarm. "How about Friday? I could meet you in the library before school?"

"Okay, sure." Damian peered at the river of students splitting the lunch room in half. "Hey, Dave Two is sitting on his own. What's that about?"

Tracey glanced down at Laura's text message as Jonny answered Damian's question with an elaborate theory. She sucked in a sharp breath and choked on it, coughing loudly and waving off concern. She avoided looking at Damian as she typed a reply into her phone.

`We have to work together. Mr. Michaels teamed us up, that's all.`

Damian started talking again. Tracey wasn't really listening to what was being said. His voice was a deep, hypnotic drone as she read Laura's reply.

`Thought you weren't into him?`

`Maybe I am,` she replied, her ears burning. She looked up at Damian. His face was animated, his lips moving fast as his tongue darted out to wet them. She felt herself falling. *He's so dreamy.* What it would be like if she *did* invite him to Uncle Donny's? It would be just her and Damian, staring into each other's eyes, pretending to work on the assignment, but getting distracted, leaning in to kiss, his hand warm over her fingers and …

"Ouch." Tracey jerked upright, her shin smarting at another of Laura's well-placed kicks.

"Earth to Tracey." Jonny grinned.

"What?" Her gaze flew to Jonny, catching Damian's smile out of the corner of her eyes.

"I asked you about the hack you used on level 18—you kinda spaced."

She scowled. Why were her friends embarrassing her in front of Damian? "What?"

"Oh hey, Tony's here," Laura said, pointing toward the double entrance doors. Tracey twisted, searching for her friend. Tony headed toward them, T-shirt wrinkled like he had slept in it. He didn't look sick, though there were those dark bags under his eyes. Or maybe it was just that his face was so pale it made them look darker.

"Hey," he said drawing near.

"Are you okay?" Tracey tried to convey all of her questions into one look.

He nodded and mouthed, "Later," as he noticed Damian sitting in his spot. "Hey."

"Hey," Damian offered. The awkward silence from earlier returned with a vengeance.

Normally Tracey would have commented on the genius quality of their conversation, but she didn't want Damian to think she was weird or rude. After another, longer silence, she turned to Jonny. "So, level 18?"

Tony's reply to her earlier text message came as she stepped into Uncle Donny's Mage-kind detective agency. Blowing the fringe off her face, she noted the window hadn't been cleaned. *Weird.* She was the one who had arranged the regular cleaning. The sign *Donald Master's Mage-kind Detective* had a big black smudge over the word *Mage*. She frowned and pushed the door open with her butt as her hands were full of junk mail. Why hadn't her uncle checked the box? She had only been gone a week.

Uncle Donny wasn't a very good detective, so business was slow at the best of times. When it was busy, like when he had taken Miss Tearning's missing necklace case, then it could be full on, but it looked like her uncle had hit another dry spell. Dust lined the inside window sill, the bookshelf, and even her desk. She sighed at the sight of dirty cups in the little kitchen sink along the wall. Old coffee pods filled the overflowing bin. She eyed the red two-seater sofa that acted as the waiting room. One cushion sagged from the weight of a stack of books.

"Uncle Donny?" If he had a client, he would be annoyed she had called out. "Not professional. Whoops." She dumped the junk pamphlets, magazines, and past due utilities notice onto her desk and swiped away the dust. *A week! How is it so dusty?* Thumbing on her computer, she pulled her cell phone from her pocket. Uncle Donny's door remained closed. Since he hadn't replied or stuck his head out, she assumed he wasn't there. She plonked down in her chair and opened Tony's text.

Was late to school because of an appointment. I can't come to Donny's tonight.

What appointment? Are you sick? she typed back, and while she waited for his reply, deleted the spam emails in her inbox.

Psychiatrist. Mage-kind one.

What for? She hit send and willed Tony's reply to come quickly.

Mom and Dad thought I needed to go. It's dumb. Don't worry about it. Hey, meet me tomorrow before school. I have to show you something.

The journal, you got it?

Yep.

Tracey sat back happily and stared at her phone. *Finally.* The journal might contain a hint about the other stones. Maybe more than a hint, it might actually tell her where the stones were. That had to be why Doctor Chan was so anxious to get his hands on it. She swiveled excitedly in her chair, raising a pile of dust and sneezed. Muffling the noise with her hand, she raced to the little kitchen for a tissue. The box was empty. Sneezing again, she grabbed the last paper towel off the roll and used that.

Balling it up, she went to throw it in the bin and found it already overflowing. Pulling the bag out of the bin, she tied the edges and jammed her snotty paper towel inside. She dumped the trash in the stinky alley through the side door and returned to wash her hands. The soap dispenser was empty. Curious now, she opened the fridge. Uncle Donny always kept bottles of water on hand for clients. It was empty. He hadn't been to the market.

A shiver crept down Tracey's back. She took a closer look around the office. Scuff marks and lint balls marred the worn carpet. Books on the sofa would stop a client sitting on it and of course there had been the overflowing trash. What on earth had Uncle Donny been doing while she was away?

Thank goodness she hadn't invited Damian here tonight. *I go away for a few days and the place becomes a pigsty.* She spent a frantic few minutes dusting. By hand she picked up the obvious lint balls and grass clippings off the carpet and shot a worried glance at the closed door. If Uncle Donny *was* in and talking to a client, he wouldn't want her to use the vacuum. She restacked the books on his bookshelf and to pass the time flicked through the book on lock picking. When she looked up again it was nearly 4:30 p.m. A noise from Uncle Donny's private office drew her attention to it as the door popped open. *Fruit tingles. I should have been quieter.* An unfamiliar man froze in the doorway when he spotted Tracey sitting at the desk. His mouth made an "oh" shape. Tracey's heart jumped into her throat until she spied the messy hair of her uncle behind the man. Oh, he was a client. Her attention returned to the man. He hadn't moved, still staring at her with squinty eyes. He wore a neat, skinny brown suit and clean, polished black shoes. Short greying hair and small spectacles made his head look weirdly skinny and his eyes tiny. He looked like a colored-in Slenderman. *Creepy.* She dropped her shield to scan him and snapped it back up at the vibration on her skin. Mage-kind.

She didn't say anything. The man walked out without a word. Tracey waited for the front door to shut properly before she leapt from her desk. "Uncle Donny?"

Her uncle scrubbed a hand through his unruly curls and gave her a tired smile. There were dark smudges under his eyes that reminded Tracey of Tony. "Kiddo, hey. Welcome back." She gritted her teeth at the sight of his wrinkled shirt and the blue ink stain on his sleeve.

"I cleaned up a bit. Do you want me to vacuum now or do you have another client coming?"

He shook his head. "I need to pop out for a bit. Will you be okay here? Just flip the closed sign and lock the door."

"Sure. I've got a school assignment I can do. Was that an actual client? What's the case he—"

Uncle Donny shut his door on her question. A second later he popped his head back out. "Great to have you back. We'll talk when I return, okay?"

The feeling that crawled up Tracey's spine grew legs and scuttled across her back.

He bustled out of his office, now wearing his jacket and carrying his emergency magic bag. Before she could ask what he was doing, he raced out of the building. The bell above the door rattled madly and then the office fell eerily silent. Tracey huffed out a breath that was part annoyance and part worry. It took next to no time to do her usual clean—well, a little longer because everything was really dusty. Now she knew why she had been sneezing earlier. Sitting at her desk, she tapped her fingers against her keyboard. No query emails. No messages to follow up and no files to type. She sighed and shifted the lock picking book to the side to grab her school bag. Not to pull out her assignment, but for the creased poem page and her highlighter pens. With a different color she marked each stanza of the poem and put a question mark next to it.

The Five Stones of Power. The middle stanzas had to be a clue about the stones' owners. Nothing that sounded like a butterfly though. She jumped online but her search engine questions came up blank. *I need Tony.* She typed *butterfly* and spent some time reading about the different species and colors. Dave Two had once listed a bunch of different flies—she tried that but quickly lost interest. Flies were the most boring insect ever. She leaned back in her chair. What else could she search?

Her phone buzzed. She expected it to be Tony, but it was a message from Damian.

`Hey, so what we were talking about earlier? Do you have time to come to my house tomorrow morning to meet my sister?`

Her face heated. Damian messaged!

`Sure, happy to help,` she replied. Then cursed her quick response. She had promised to meet Tony before school. She typed an additional text, `Uh, it might be pretty early.`

Damian's reply came quickly. `No problem. My folks both work so it'll just be me and Kylie.`

`Sure. See you then.`

Un-freakin-believable. She was going to Damian's house. Nibbling on her lips, she bounced in her chair. This had to be the best week of her life. She couldn't stop grinning.

Tales by The Lost

Following 219, Followed by 0
click **<broken link>** to follow The Lost!

Day 954

[cont …]

But I couldn't.

That's not who I am.

0 likes, 0 comments, 0 reshares
click **<broken link>** to like this post!:D

T.B.T.L.

8

Tracey bolted upright, breathing the kind of fast, wheezy breaths Uncle Donny made when he had to run any kind of distance. The nightmare that woke her was the weirdest one yet — talking birds and butterflies. There was a tiger with glowing eyes who told her in a high-pitched growl to keep running. The dream faded and in moments she couldn't remember what the dream had been about at all. Her alarm clock read 2 a.m. She flopped back onto her pillow and groaned. She was not going back to sleep now. *Damian's house!* Her bedroom was super quiet so the soft knock on her door sent her heart rate into orbit. It was Sarah. The odd connection between them was a vibration that wobbled her brain. *Let's test this.* Dropping her shield, she said, *Come in.*

The door creaked open. "Hey."

"You heard me?" The thought sent a shiver of excitement through Tracey's body.

"What?"

"I spoke to you in my mind. I told you to come in."

"Oh, I didn't hear that. I just felt like you were awake."

Disappointment stabbed through Tracey's excitement like a deflating balloon. She raised her shield and the drain on her magic renewed the ache in her muscles.

"Well, I felt like I could come in. So maybe I did hear you, but, like, with no words."

"Yeah." Tracey's head hung low while her fingers ran through her disheveled hair. That just wasn't as exciting as mind reading. "What do you want?"

"Can't sleep." Sarah slunk into the room. "Can I sleep in here?"

Tracey wriggled over on her bed. Sarah slid under the covers next to her. Her cold skin shocked Tracey. She pulled away, squealing softly.

"Sorry," Sarah mumbled.

"What's wrong? Why can't you sleep?"

"I don't want to go to school tomorrow." Her sister's toes were freezing.

"I don't either. It'll be fine. We'll all be fine."

"My neck hurts."

Tracey bit her lip, immediately picturing the hand shaped bruise Timothy had left on her sister's neck. "I'm so sorry, Sarah."

"I wish I was at your school. I hate being so alone."

"You will be. Soon."

"Two years is a lifetime."

Tracey wanted to apologize again. She mashed her lips together. "Try to sleep."

Sarah burrowed her head into Tracey's side. "I feel safer when I'm with you," she said, wriggling her head into Tracey's pillow. The smaller girl closed her eyes and seemed to fall instantly asleep. Tracey stared at her sister for a long time.

Eventually, she closed her eyes. Her own sleep was a long time coming.

Five hours later, Tracey stood outside Damian Carter's front door. Exhaustion from a lack of sleep and constantly holding her magical bubble in place around her body dragged at her shoulders. She slumped, feeling as though she had aged a lifetime since returning from camp.

Her stomach moaned because she had forgotten breakfast. Mom was still unwell, so Peter had dropped her off at the neat little townhouse. She pressed the front door buzzer with a sweaty finger and watched as the door opened wide.

"Thanks for coming," Damian said, his warm voice wrapping around her like a hug. He wore jeans and a plain grey sweatshirt, his dark hair damp and tousled.

Should I hug him? Ugh, no. Don't be weird. "Hi—um, I'm not too early, am I?"

"Not at all. Come on in. My sister's in her room. She's kinda grumpy today. Do you want to talk to her out here, or go on up?"

Tracey would have preferred to be alone with Damian, but there was a purpose for her visit. "It might be more comfortable to meet her out here first."

He seated Tracey at the kitchen table and disappeared upstairs.

Tracey peered around, curious to get an insight into the cute boy. The kitchen was spacious and clean, unlike her kitchen at home which always seemed to have someone standing in it eating over the sink. Every pot sparkled and hung according to size above the bench island. Tracey couldn't spot a single crumb anywhere. There was a photo stuck to the fridge. She jumped up to have a look. Four smiling faces grinned at the camera. Damian was pictured horsing around with a blonde-haired girl who had to be his sister. The man in the military uniform had his arms wrapped around a pretty blonde lady. His uniform was a tan color so that was... um... Army? She smiled at the photo finding the grins infectious. Hearing footsteps, she dove back to her seat not wanting to get caught snooping.

"Tracey, this is my sister Kylie," Damian said, walking into the room. All Tracey could see of the figure behind him was flowing blonde hair and a pretty red dress with a high neck. Damian tugged the reluctant girl from behind his back, revealing a scowling freckled face with lovely, sky blue eyes and long lashes.

"Hello," Tracey said, waving.

"Hi." Kylie kept her head low, her eyebrows drawn tightly down toward her nose. She whispered something to her brother, and he mumbled something back. Tracey risked thinning her shield bubble and stretched out with a little power immediately encountering the buzz of Kylie's magic. It seemed to vibrate quicker than her family's magic, or Tony's. No wonder Kylie was moody. It would be hard to control a power that energetic.

"Damian, can you get Kylie a drink?" Tracey suggested.

He crinkled his eyebrows before he rose from his chair. As soon as he stepped away Tracey pressed her hand to the table top and flipped her palm up. "Damian told me your family is all Norms? You're the only Mage-kind? Have they taught you anything about basic scanning at summer camp?"

Kylie's eyes didn't meet Tracey's as she grumbled, "Yes."

"Do you want to scan me?" It might put Kylie at ease if she could feel Tracey's magic and realize she was not that different. Tracey flicked her eyes to where Damian stood near the kitchen bench. He had poured his sister's juice and now leaned back against the counter waiting patiently.

The younger girl stretched out a shaking hand and touched Tracey's wrist. Tracey thinned her shield bubble to let Kylie get closer to her magic. "I can't feel anything." Tracey hadn't wanted to drop her shield completely in case she hurt the girl. She focused on her core and pressed down tightly on her magic. Finally, she lowered her shield. Kylie's power flowed over Tracey's hand like an invisible bug with hundreds of legs. It traveled up her arm. Closing her eyes, Tracey imagined good feelings and candy bars, keeping her own power locked away. After a moment Kylie pulled back. Tracey restored her shield bubble and opened her eyes. A very slight upturn of Kylie's lips gave Tracey hope.

"Cool," Kylie said. Though her brows were still drawn together, anger now simmered rather than boiled beneath her skin.

Tracey smiled as Damian put Kylie's drink down on the table. He sat next to her. "I wish I could do that," he said, knocking his shoulder into Kylie. She snorted and pushed him back.

"No, you don't," she grabbed Tracey's hand and yanked her to her feet. "Want to see my room?"

Tracey shot a quick look at Damian to check it was okay. He shrugged. "Sure," she told Kylie. The younger girl pulled Tracey down a hallway toward a bunch of closed doors.

"Don't be long," Damian shouted after them.

Kylie shot a sly smile over her shoulder. "I'm not going to school today."

"Are your parents at work?" Tracey asked. Damian had already told her, but she wanted to get Kylie talking. Even with her shield up she could feel Kylie's magic bouncing around, more so as they approached her room. Tracey guessed Kylie wouldn't need her shields at home since her family wouldn't be able to feel her magic anyway. It was a sad thought.

A lopsided pink cardboard name plate hung on a little nail over the door Kylie opened. "Mom's a nurse. Dad works at the Army base."

Kylie's room was the same size as Tracey's. All her furniture was made from white painted wood — a single bed, a desk and along one wall a great big bookshelf packed to overflowing with books. Tracey gasped. She ran her fingers over the spines, finding many she wanted to read. A book lay open on Kylie's chest of drawers. "Oh, I love that one. Isn't Lizzy brilliant?"

"Yup." Kylie plopped down onto her perfectly made bed, mussing up the covers. "That's lame nail polish."

Tracey held up her hands. The pink color was more orange than she liked. "I'm trying to stop chewing my nails," she admitted.

Tracey hoped Kylie would open up and tell her why she was so scared of school, but the younger girl fell silent. A slight air of aggression surrounded her. Kylie seemed more angry than scared. Tracey sat down on the end of Kylie's bed. "It's hard starting a new school, especially when you don't know anyone."

Kylie picked at the tassel on one of her many pillows. Her movements sharp, stabbing at it with her fingers. "I've been to a lot of schools."

"That sounds rough." Tracey thought of Camp Mindflower, the Mage-kind summer camp where she had first met Tony. "New summer camps too, huh?"

"Yeah."

"But you must have picked up a lot of different magic techniques, different skills?" Tracey sat still, waiting. She had been dragged in here after all. What did the girl want to tell her?

"Not really. Different camps just make things more confused. Too many people teaching the same thing in different ways. It's like school."

"Maybe you'll end up at my camp next summer?"

Kylie shrugged. Her mouth became a twisted line. "If we're still here."

That sounded like a sore point. Did Damian feel the same resentment from moving all the time? He hadn't said anything, so maybe not. "My sister always complains about the brain wobble switching between school and camp causes. She's the same age as you."

Kylie stilled. She pursed her lips. "Is she Mage-kind?"

"Yep, all of my family is. Well, except for my brother Simon. He's a Norm, like your brother."

Kylie wriggled down the mattress to sit next to Tracey. "I'm the only one in my family who's Mage-kind. It sucks." She tore at the hole in the pillow making it wider, her lips pressed tight together.

"That must be hard." She would have to ask Simon if he felt left out and alone because he didn't feel what they did. She had never really thought about it.

"Yeah," Kylie mumbled.

Tracey worried that if she said the wrong thing, she would upset Kylie further. She really wanted the girl to like her. Maybe if she did, Damian would want to hang out more after school. Her stomach gave a little jolt at the thought. She jumped up to stare at the bookshelf and ran her fingers along the book spines. "My sister freaked out about her first day of junior high," she added. *Come on Kylie. Give me something.*

"I don't want to go."

Tracey turned around. "Why?"

Kylie shrugged, but didn't raise her head, too focused on pulling at a thread in her pillow. "I don't know anyone. People will pick on me," she said.

"Have you ever been to a mixed school?"

"No. I usually get sent to a different school than Damian. But at least they are all Mage-kind. I don't ever really know anyone, and I get weird looks but it's not the same." Kylie threw the pillow down on the bed and mashed her fist into it.

"My sister will be at your campus. What if I introduce you before school tomorrow? Then you'll know someone and she's Mage-kind too."

"Yeah, maybe."

"Sarah would like to be your friend," Tracey said. *She'd better.*

Kylie turned her head and skewered Tracey with a sharp look. "What if she doesn't like me?"

"I'm sure Sarah will think you're great. Seriously, I'll bring her around tomorrow, so you can chat."

"Um."

Tracey examined another family portrait in a pink fluro frame on Kylie's desk. Her dad was in uniform, his shaved head almost completely bald, his nose and facial shape the same as Damian. Kylie's mom was in her nurse's uniform. Her smile was bright and wide. Kylie stood a little out of frame. Her gaze locked on the distance, shoulders slumped, eyes hidden by sunglasses. *What's she looking at?* "I think it will be cool having another Mage-kind at school. You seem to have really good control over your magic — much better than I did when I was your age."

"I don't, not really. I, ah... get angry a lot." Kylie's scowl darkened. "I set fire to the toaster this morning."

Tracey burst out laughing. Kylie looked away, red splotches blossoming in her cheeks. Power jumped, like live electrical wires, sending sparks into Tracey's shield bubble. Whoa! Kylie *did* get angry fast.

"I'm sorry. I'm not laughing at you. I promise." Tracey sat beside Kylie on the bed and patted her hand. "I've done that. My brothers did, too. Mom had to buy three toasters in the space of six months."

Kylie shot Tracey a side-eyed look with a hint of a dare in them. "Show me something magic?"

Tracey spied a pretty ballerina jewelry box on Kylie's desk. She dropped her shield bubble and sent a burst of power toward it. The finger-sized ballerina started to turn.

Kylie jumped to her feet, demanding, "How did you do that? You didn't say anything. Show me?"

"Okay," Tracey said with a smile.

Damian interrupted them a few minutes later, catching them in the act of dancing with a green dressing gown. Tracey spun around, her face on fire. "Hi Damian." Without her attention focused on the fleece, the dressing gown slumped to the ground.

"You ruined it," Kylie groaned. Damian smiled at his sister's over-the-top behavior.

"Tomorrow, yeah?" Tracey reminded.

Kylie's face was flushed from dancing, but her instant scowl took over her whole face. "Show me how you did that," she ordered instead.

A shiver crept down Tracey's spine. "Ah, sure. If you *promise* to meet Sarah tomorrow."

Kylie squinted. "I'll think about it."

Tracey checked her watch. "Oh, fruit tingles, I gotta go." Tony would be waiting for her at school. Damian walked her to the front door.

"I'd come with you, but…" He gestured back to Kylie's room. Tracey nodded. "Thanks so much for this," Damian said and reached for Tracey's hand. She thrust out her hand to shake, not sure what he was doing. He pulled back awkwardly and patted Tracey's fingers.

OMG, embarrassing! Her whole body was on fire. "Okay, bye." As soon as Damian shut the door Tracey hit her forehead with a palm. "Fruit tingles."

Somehow, she still managed to get to school well before most students started to arrive. Her stomach swirled with excitement — it warred with the headache caused from keeping her shield in place. She had to tell Tony about Damian, his house, and his sister. Breathing slowly to calm down she started with the most important question first. "Do you have it?" He sat on the stone fence outside of school in a navy-blue shirt with a picture of Einstein on it and torn jeans. The dark smudges beneath his eyes were not as bad today, but they were still there. A crease marred the skin between his eyes.

"Hello to you, too."

"Sorry. It's been a long morning already," she excused. "Remind me to tell you some stuff later."

"What about?"

"Later. Come on, do you have the book?"

He shot her a tired smile and jumped off the fence. Kneeling, he opened his backpack. Tracey moved closer to peer inside, catching a whiff of his spicy deodorant and suppressed a cough. Strong stuff. There was nothing on the cover of the brown leather-bound book to tell her who it belonged to. A strange buzzing, like a phone vibrating came from the paper. Hairs on her arms and neck quivered as the Butterfly Stone warmed her skin. "Whoa."

"Yeah. I felt it too, as soon as I opened the box it came in."

"Wrapped?"

"Silk, yeah. I... I haven't opened it."

Silk contained magic like a pot lid over bubbling water. "Why not?" He wouldn't answer. "Was there anything else in the package?" Tracey's fingers hovered over the journal, but she didn't take it from his bag. She was a little afraid. What would the information inside teach her about her family? Would it help Tracey find the stones or be another dead end?

"Just a cover letter. About the owner of the estate. The man who died. It's pretty dull."

Tony thrust the book in her direction. "Well go on, take it."

With a gentle hand she took it from him and started flicking pages. A passage caught her attention. Transfixed, she started reading.

> *I'm not sure what to make of her, the woman who has insisted she and her companions join me. I know what they are, though nothing has been said, as they know what I am. Mama tells us every morn not to let others see. My brothers are good, honest men. For their silence, they have found work at neighboring farms. My eldest sister is a housemaid at the Lindaly Estate, and I am yet to look for work. But I admit, my heart is unsettled by our silence. I feel an ache deep inside that yearns for something greater.*
>
> *She — the woman — Millicent — speaks blasphemy. Of becoming more. I can barely write the words. Of using our curse. She calls it a gift. Never have I heard it called thus. She and her companions say the darkness is not evil. I — I don't know what to do. All I do know is that I am intrigued by her. I want to know more.*
>
> *I have agreed to meet with her tonight.*

Rapid footsteps pounded the pavement behind them. Tony stumbled and fell against Tracey letting out a yelp as a blur rushed past. Tracey fumbled the journal as her elbow was jolted. "Hey, watch it," she snapped.

The Butterfly Stone beneath her shirt started pulsing like a heartbeat. She slapped her hand against it.

"She pushed me," Tony said spinning around.

"Why are you just standing there getting in people's way?" A briskly moving Asian girl clad in black stopped a few paces beyond them. Her glare tried to melt Tracey's face. The Butterfly Stone gave off more heat against Tracey's skin. The girl flipped straight black hair out of her face and raised her hand, her Mage-kind bracelet flaring red.

"Hey, whoa!" Tony jumped between them, raising his hands. "I'm sure it was an accident."

Tracey didn't back down. Neither did the unknown girl. There was a tense silence as they faced off. "Don't get in my way again!" the girl snapped. Magic crackled around her, electrical sparks dancing along her skin.

"Maybe look where you're going next time. You would have seen us with plenty of time to go around." Tracey spied a cell phone in the girl's hand. "Oh, let me guess, staring at an app? Trying different filters for your selfies?"

The girl's glare ramped higher. The sparks around her hands grew brighter. Tracey pictured her own face as a mirror. Magic buzzed through her body sending a static charge into her hair. Reluctantly, Tracey suppressed the urge to blast the girl into tomorrow and drew her magic back inside, strengthening her shield bubble. She caught Tony staring and fought to slam the imaginary closet door shut to keep her magic trapped behind it. *Come on, Tracey. Be the bigger person.* Tracey dropped her hand as her magic petered out.

The girl held her defensive pose a moment longer before she spun on a heel and stormed off.

"What's her problem?" Tracey asked, shoving the journal into her backpack. She yanked the zipper closed, the Butterfly Stone hot against her chest.

Tony stared after the girl. "No idea." More kids appeared on the path behind them. "Come on, let's head to the library. Hey, what did you want to tell me about this morning?"

A shiver wracked Tracey's body in a completely different way to the flood of her earlier fury. She bounced on her feet. "I was at Damian's house."

"What?" Tony's voice would have shattered glass if there had been some nearby. Tracey giggled as they walked toward Hall B, all dark thoughts about the angry girl disappearing completely from her mind.

Tales by The Lost

Following <u>219</u>, Followed by <u>0</u>
click **<broken link>** to follow <u>The Lost</u>!

Day 954

[cont ...]

Just because you can do something

doesn't mean you should...

The storekeeper might not have

remembered me, but I would

have remembered what I'd done.

<u>0</u> likes, <u>0</u> comments, <u>0</u> reshares
click **<broken link>** to like this post!:D

T.B.T.L.

9

Tracey put her tray down and scanned the lunch hall but couldn't spot Damian or Dave Two. The smell of burnt toast lingered in the air, along with scrambled eggs, ketchup, and the scent of sweaty kids jammed inside one room for too long. Chatter and laughter filled the air, trays clattered, and chair legs scraped loudly.

"That's Jilly Cho." Jonny's face lit up as he craned his neck to peer at the Asian girl in the black jacket and long black hair sitting on her own near the window. Tracey sensed a buzz of Mage-kind energy against her shield. Her eyes narrowed as she examined the girl. Jonny's eyes glazed over, and he sighed loudly.

"Super-hot scary," Laura commented as she sat down with her lunch. "Isn't that what you said after she totally blanked you?" Laura flipped her hair over her shoulder. Her emerald green satin shirt made her eyes glow. Tracey brushed a finger over the faded superhero shirt she wore. It was so comfy, and she loved the blue color—like the sky. "Trace, before your boyfriend gets here, tell us about training with Agent Malden."

Flames burst across Tracey's cheeks. "Laura!" Her friend ignored her glare, twisting open her OJ bottle with a grin.

Tony slumped down at the table beside Tracey. "Hey."

"Hey." Tracey examined his face with concern. "You look terrible." Bloodshot eyes stood out on his extra-pale face. "What happened? You were fine this morning."

"I've got a headache," he complained, rubbing his temples.

"You should talk to the school nurse," Laura suggested.

"I know, but I don't think she likes me."

"What? Not possible. Everyone likes you, Tony." Tracey pointed with her fork for emphasis.

"Yeah I'll go and see her later." He scrubbed his hands over his face. "Did you find anything in the book about the stones?"

The journal! "I can't believe I forgot," Tracey said, bending over to unzip her bag.

Tony grabbed her arm, hissing, "Not here."

Tracey sat up, searching for the Evil Queens. Meena held court at her usual table by the door, casting judgement over the hungry students forced to enter and slink past her table.

"Where's Dave Two?" Tony asked.

Jonny sneered. "Embarrassed to be seen with us."

Tracey worried at her tray of — what even was it? Grey white mush that could have been mashed potatoes or pureed cauliflower. Maybe it was liquid cheese. The burger was more burnt bread than meat patty. She pushed it away in disgust and glanced around. No Dave Two in sight. He shouldn't isolate himself. "If you see him, tell him I'm looking for him." The table fell silent and gazes lifted over her head. Tracey turned to see Damian standing behind her.

"I can — uh — still sit here?" he asked.

"Of course!" The words exploded out of Tracey, sending a rippling grin over her friends like a wave at a soccer match. *Ugh, so embarrassing.*

"Did you tell them?" Damian asked, his sugary scent dancing up Tracey's nostrils.

"Tell us what?" Laura batted her eyes. Tracey jerked upright realizing she had been leaning toward Damian following the intoxicating scent. She focused on the dreamy boy then darted her gaze to Laura who was staring at Damian like he was made of chocolate. Tracey dug her nails into her palms.

"About helping me with my sister. Which is very cool."

What? She had missed something. Tony stared at Tracey with wide eyes. "Yeah, cool," she said hoping it made sense.

A ruckus drew their heads toward the door. The Mage-kind girl stood before Meena's table glaring at the Evil Queens. Tracey could feel the Asian girl's magic from all the way over here at the edge of the lunch room. The girl's Mage-kind identity bracelet flashed orange on her left wrist. Meena's mouth moved but Tracey couldn't hear her words. Carla, as usual, laughed her head off in a high-pitched cackle that grated on Tracey's nerves. That sound never boded well for anyone. Tracey sighed and focused on her food tray, but the contents didn't look any more appetizing than before. The Butterfly Stone warmed against Tracey's skin. She pressed a hand to it as Jonny jumped to his feet.

"Where are you going?" Tracey called.

Jonny turned begging eyes on Tracey. "No one deserves the Evil Queens, ever, and you know that."

She held up her hands. "New girl should be able to take care of herself."

Jonny gave her a strange look. "New girl?"

Tracey hardened her heart and shrugged.

"Out of everyone here you should support Jilly against Meena," he said.

Low blow. But Jonny was right. Well, he would have been right—usually. Tracey thought her argument perfectly reasonable for not getting involved. Meena was never nice to Tracey. Most of the time, Norms here just put up with Mage-kind. This school was one of only a handful of mixed schools on this side of the country. The general behavior was that if Norms left you alone, you left them alone. Meena never left Tracey alone. And the rules were clear. No magic at school. If Meena shifted her target to the new girl then Tracey might be left alone for once.

"Trace!" Jonny's voice climbed high enough to comfortably sing Beyoncé. Tracey glanced at Laura hoping for support. Laura sucked on her lips. *Ugh, come on, you too?* Jonny didn't relent. It was what cute girls did to him. "Tony?"

The Mage-kind boy shrugged. She turned to Damian. "You were friends with Meena. Can you—?"

"—oh hell no." He smiled, taking the heat out of his next words. "She'll just go harder on Jilly if I get involved." The heated argument was growing louder and now everyone in the hall was watching, like the crowds at an airshow hoping to see a crash. Jilly stood toe-to-toe with Meena. Carla stood near Dave One, her body leaning forward so she didn't miss any details. There was no sign of Dave Two.

Any minute now a teacher would intervene, Tracey shouldn't get involved. The sharp tug to her core drew Tracey to her feet. That settled that. Magic gathered over the two girls in a growing storm of emotion. Tony sighed and climbed to his feet as well. Now they *had* to get involved, if only to stop the school calling the Mage-force police when Jilly used her magic. The news would ripple through school and the blowback would affect Tracey and Tony—probably Sarah and Damian's little sister too. Jilly had to be stopped.

Tracey sprinted to where Meena stood oblivious to the building explosion. Jilly turned sharp eyes on Tracey. Unseen by the students in the room, Tracey expanded her shield bubble to test Jilly's defenses. Beside Tracey, Tony did the same, hiding his wrist and the Mage-kind student bracelet flashing red beneath his long sleeve. The Butterfly Stone pulsed, hot and angry against Tracey's neck. She hushed it with a hand pressed over it.

"Hey Meena, what's up?" Tracey asked. The silence in the room grew total. Tracey could even hear a cell phone notification beep in someone's pocket.

The bully speared Tracey with a death glare. "I don't recall inviting you to join us. This is none of your business."

It really wasn't. So why *was* she getting involved? Jilly had to feel Tracey's magic but didn't respond to her poking. She also didn't back down. Tracey let her shield flicker and sent a push of energy at the angry girl. There was no way she could ignore Tracey now.

Jilly rocked back, her shocked gaze springing to Tracey's face. Tracey's thoughts jumped back to last night and her test in trying to speak to Sarah with her mind. If only she could do it here, talk to Jilly using telepathy, she could tell the girl to back down. "It sure looks like a fascinating conversation. Is it about the new superhero movie? Cause yeah, Tony and I nearly came to blows about that one." Tracey spoke loudly making sure everyone could hear her.

She poked Tony in the side when he didn't respond. He was

concentrating on keeping a magical wall between Jilly and Meena so the bully wouldn't get hit if Jilly lashed out. Tracey poked his side again. "What? Uh, yeah. I didn't think it was that great."

"Scandalous!" Tracey said.

"Stay out of this," Meena tapped her fingers against the table. *Rat-a-tat-tat.*

God, what's her problem?

"Stay out of it," Jilly added.

Tracey was seriously tempted to just throw up her hands and leave them all to it. She jerked a finger at Tony. "Don't tell me you think it too? The movie was great. You're all clearly delusional. I understand your confusion, but come on, it's not enough to actually come to blows over. I thought it was a terrific movie. That part when Jackson stood up to the train full of bad guys and didn't let them taunt him into exposing his identity was brilliant. Tony thought it was lame."

Meena's eyes narrowed. Her mouth tightened. "I wouldn't watch that show — it's for kids."

Tracey faked a loud gasp. "Rude!" She stared at Jilly. *Come on, come on.* Tracey's provided distraction would only work if Jilly took it willingly.

A long moment stretched into eternity. It was finally broken when the electricity that buzzed around Jilly in an invisible cloud wavered and then withdrew. *Finally.*

Once, Meena's sour, scrunched up face would have been terrifying, but Tracey had faced death recently and Meena didn't inspire that kind of fear anymore. Today, she held Meena's stare, taunting her to say something else. The girl's dark eyes flickered and her face twitched.

Good enough. Tracey gestured for Jilly to approach. "Come on then. We can compare movie reviews. I'm sure I can change your mind." They turned away.

"So, where were you last week?" Meena sneered, probably desperate to restore the upper hand. Tracey didn't answer. "How was rehab — did it work?"

What? Tracey spun around. Eager listening students' heads popped up like meercats on one of those animal shows. "I wasn't at —"

"I don't think it worked. You still look kinda strung out, Tracey." Meena lowered her voice to a false whisper. Naturally, it was still loud enough for everyone to hear, "Do you need a time out?" Laughter spread around the room. Tracey's skin boiled.

Tony's fingers dug into her arm. Tracey gritted her teeth and pictured the mean girl imploding.

Meena scratched at her arms and scowled, disappointed by Tracey's lack of response.

Tracey turned to Jilly, "Coming?" For a minute she didn't think Jilly would take the hint. Well, she had done all she could. Laura and Tony stayed with her as Tracey stomped back to her table.

"Whatever!" Meena snapped and flung her hair over her shoulder as she flounced out of the lunch room. Nervous laughter rose up signaling the drama was over, for now.

Laura whistled softly and sat down. "Intense."

Tony huffed, "I loved that movie and you know it." He picked up his orange. "You did good."

Damian sat down beside Tracey. "Meena really doesn't like you, does she?"

Tracey held out her hand, palm above the table. Her hand was shaking. "I shouldn't have got up. It was a mistake. She hates me." Her shield bubble felt suffocating. She pressed her hand to her chest and covered the Butterfly Stone willing it to return to sleep. She didn't turn around or peer over her shoulder. "Where's Jonny?"

"Waiting for Jilly," Laura told her.

"Who? Oh, the cause of all this. Does it look like she's going to go off on Meena?" Tracey couldn't feel the girl's angry magic anymore, but that didn't mean Jilly wouldn't lash out physically.

"I can't te... Wait. They're coming over. Jonny *and* Jilly."

Jonny flopped into his seat but didn't kick his chair up against the wall. Tracey expected him to start blasting Meena, but he stayed quiet. In fact, the whole cafeteria was quiet. Tracey followed Jonny's gaze to the girl standing behind Tracey's chair. She thought about asking Jilly to sit down but really didn't want the girl to join them. Before she could say anything, Jilly leaned down so her silky hair brushed Tracey's shoulder. "I don't need your help." Her sharp stare dropped from Tracey's face to the open bag beside her seat.

The journal! Tracey kicked her bag further under her chair.

Jilly stomped away with a swish of hair, leaving only her floral perfume behind. Jonny breathed deeply and sighed.

"That was heavy," Damian said. His raised eyebrows begged Tracey to explain.

All she could do was shrug. She pointed at Jonny. "How can you like her?"

"She's a goddess!" Jonny said, his gaze locked on the door Jilly just stormed through.

Laura pointed at Tracey's bag. "Did you see—?"

"Yeah," Tracey murmured.

Tony scrunched lower in his seat. "It was like she recognized it."

"Recognized what? Tracey, what is going on? I've missed something, haven't I?" Damian asked. No one answered him. What could she tell him without having to explain everything about the Butterfly Stone? It was too much. Her gaze traveled to the door. *I really don't like Jilly.* The noise level in the cafeteria increased as students returned to their conversations, forgetting all about the odd encounter. Tracey caught Tony's eye. He shrugged.

"You should hide the book," Laura suggested.

Tracey waved a hand at Damian. "It's just a journal. I dunno why Jilly was weird about it." She speared Laura with a look and wiggled her eyebrows, glancing at Damian.

Laura nodded. "Yeah, maybe she has one like it. Whatever. Weird, hey?"

The bell blared angrily ordering them to class.

Tracey grabbed her bag and clutched it to her chest as if it contained precious jewels. She followed her friends out of the cafeteria wondering what else the day would contain.

THE TIGER'S EYE

All was strangely quiet in Mr. Michaels' English class that afternoon. Tracey crossed out the last paragraph she had written and groaned. Damian smiled at her. "Yeah, I struggled with that too," he whispered. "Maybe we should just skip the opening and go straight to the body of the essay. Pick out some words and leave the intro for the end?" Tracey leaned her head closer to Damian. He had little freckles on his nose. *Adorable.* Her gaze dropped to his lips. He was so close. She could just press closer and ...

His eyes scrunched. "Yeah that would make sense." He tapped his pen against his perfect teeth and flipped over his class notes. "I don't think you missed a lot last week."

She moaned. "I hate this speech. Why do we have to write about it? Why can't we just pick our own text?"

"Quietly. I said work quietly." Mr. Michaels' red face appeared behind Damian. Tracey reared back, startled. *Fruit tingles!*

"Yes sir," they obediently said and shot each other a wide-eyed look while their fellow students snickered around the room. Tracey peered over her shoulder. Dave Two and Jonny were working together, whispering and pointing at their tablets. Neither caught her glance. Meena and Dave One worked silently. Dave One kept shooting Dave Two dirty looks. Tracey turned back to her work.

The document was a transcript of the police chief's speech, dated the day after the Week of Terror.

Good people of Ellisborough Commons. I am pleased to announce an end to the bloodshed we have suffered these last seven days. An agreement has been reached and I can confirm the insurgents have been captured and duly punished by their own kind. Good people, please, please calm yourselves. How can I inform you of what has occurred if you cannot hear me? My friends, the murderous behavior of the demons is over. We shall create a record of all townspeople who suffer from this terrible affliction. Sir, yes, they have hidden themselves from us. They have lied, you are correct, sir but*

*Speech ends here as the townspeople abruptly end the public hearing.

Tracey's heart beat faster than normal. *How awful.* Words kept jumping out at her. *Insurgents. Murderers. Demons.* Her stomach swirled dangerously. Over and over she was forced to read letters from the Norm point of view describing Mage-kind in revolting ways. It made her rage inside. She felt sweaty and cold at the same time. The journal in her bag was a Mage-kind account. She longed to yank it out and read it instead of the Norm accounts. There had to be information inside the journal about other Mage-kind. Perhaps even Tracey's own ancestor.

Woop woop woop!

The familiar alarm had Tracey groaning along with the rest of the class. *Stupid drills.*

"Again?" Mr. Michaels gestured to the door. "Leave your bags. Let's go, kids, single file." Tracey's hand fell to her bag. No way was she leaving it behind. Not now she finally had her hands on the journal. She pressed close to Damian and hoped his height would hide her as she headed for the door. Chatter increased as complaints were drowned out under half-hearted cheers.

"How lucky are we?" Damian uttered under his breath. Dave One kept his distance from Dave Two, acting as though he had cooties. Dave Two's breathing hitched.

"Hang on," Tracey told Damian. She slipped through the crowd of students around the door and tapped Dave Two's shoulder. "Hey Dave." He ignored her. "Dave?"

"Miss Masters, your bag." Mr. Michaels held out a hand to stop her from exiting the room.

"But sir..."

The teacher peered down his nose at her. "Leave it, Masters."

"It's just a drill sir," she complained. "I—I have to take it with me."

Everyone stopped to stare at her. Even Damian gave her an odd look. *Ugh, he's going to think I'm weird.* Mr. Michaels blocked the doorway. "Come on, Masters. In an emergency, it would already be too late to evacuate. You are putting other students at risk. Move. Now."

Her hands started sweating. "But I need—"

"MOVE!"

Tracey lowered the bag to the floor beside her desk and followed the line of students out through the door. Mr. Michaels' eyes narrowed as Tracey passed him. What did he think she was going to do, sneak back in to get her bag?

"That was odd," Tony commented as she joined him in the long line of students cramming the hall. Damian peered back at the line. His gaze locked onto Tracey and he smiled. She waved.

"Tracey." Tony pulled her attention back. "That's odd, right?"

"What is?"

"Another drill. And Michaels making you leave your bag."

"I don't like it," she said, yawning loudly. Her jaw cracked. *Stupid magic bubble draining my strength.*

"Hey, what's wrong?" Damian asked, appearing at her side.

She shook her head at him, sneaking out of line. "It's nothing."

He glanced back at the classroom. "Yeah, okay. So about tomorrow morning… Hopefully I can convince Kylie to come with me to meet you and your sister."

"No pressure," Tracey said, giving him a wide smile.

His lips twitched. A hot flush traveled the length of her body. She tore her gaze away and examined paint chips in the wall. The line moved at last and they made their way out to the evacuation point. Damian's hand brushed her arm. *OMG!* Tracey couldn't stop a smile from blooming across her face.

Dave Two stood alone at the edge of their waiting place. Finally, she had a chance to talk to him. "Sorry, Damian. I'll be back," she said and raced over to the sullen boy. "Hey."

Dave Two didn't look at her. It wasn't going to deter her. "Hey," she tried again. "Dave?"

"I can't talk to you," he mumbled, turning away when she moved into his line of sight.

She stumbled. "What?"

"I can't be seen talking to you. Leave me alone."

"Dave, what's wrong?"

He walked away leaving her confused. She spied a big yellow bruise under his shirt sleeve. "Dave, I—"

"Come on kids, back to class." Mr. Michaels shouted, helicoptering his hands around. Tracey hesitated. The swirling in her belly told her to insist Dave Two talk to her. Reluctantly, she let herself get dragged back to class. Finding Jonny on her walk back, she told him what happened. "You have to talk to Dave. You're assignment partners. He *has* to talk to you."

Jonny sucked on his lips. "Only about the assignment and that's barely a grunt. I do most of the talking."

"Then, we need to find him after school. I'll message him to come over to Uncle Donny's." Urgency colored her voice. Something was seriously wrong, and she had just forgotten about him. Dave was her friend whether he liked it or not. She should have insisted he tell her what was wrong. *I'm a horrible person.* She knew why she hadn't followed up on her concerns. Too much was going on and their friendship was still new and fragile. He didn't pop up in her thoughts as often as he should. Perhaps their past history still infected her mind. *I'm as bad as he is... was.*

"If he's avoiding us, he won't come," Jonny said.

"I'll ask Mom, she'll know what to do," Tracey answered him. She looked into the classroom and froze in the doorway.

Damian and Tony came up to her side. "You two walk fast. What were you talking about that was so—?"

She raced into the classroom. "Tony?"

"Over there," he said, pointing to the window. Goosepimples rose all over her skin. She hadn't left her bag there.

"Tracey? What's wrong?" Damian followed her inside.

"I—Damian, sorry. I must seem so—" The bag's zipper gaped open. Tracey grabbed the thick material with sweating hands and rummaged through the insides. Her heart stopped beating. "The journal's gone!"

Tales
by
The Lost

Following <u>219</u>, Followed by <u>0</u>
click **<broken link>** to follow <u>The Lost</u>!

Day 954

[cont …]

One of my uncles does the wrong thing.

Mother does not know that I know,

but I heard them talking one night.

My mother and father, voices

raised, shouting across the room.

<u>0</u> likes, <u>0</u> comments, <u>0</u> reshares
click **<broken link>** to like this post!:D

T.B.T.L.

10

"Who do *you* think took it?" Tracey repeated for the sixth time. Laura groaned at her—loudly.

"What? You know it's her. It's so obvious."

It wasn't a long walk from school to Uncle Donny's office because they took the side streets, walking through the new estate to see the houses being built. The hot afternoon sun pressed heat against Tracey's back, and the smell of cut grass made her think of late summer not early autumn. She pushed her sleeves up to her elbows.

"You don't know that for sure," Laura jabbed.

Tracey didn't understand why Laura was being so contrary. "I thought you hated her too."

Laura stopped walking. "I don't hate her."

It took Tracey four steps before she realized Laura wasn't beside her. She peered back. "What?"

"I don't really know her, and yeah, she hasn't exactly been very nice to you, but I don't hate her." The breeze was kicking up, blowing both Laura and Tracey's hair around.

"Don't know her? Meena? You do know her—she's the worst."

Laura pulled hair out of her eyes. "Meena? No, Jilly."

"Who?"

Laura's eyebrows rose. "Jilly. The Mage-kind girl at school. The one that almost had that meltdown at lunchtime."

"Mage-kind?" The Butterfly Stone throbbed against Tracey's chest. She covered it with her hand. Why was it behaving so weirdly? She willed it to settle as she thought back to lunch. Something had happened, hadn't it? She couldn't quite put her finger on it. "What are you talking about?"

Laura's eyebrows were dancing wildly as she stared at Tracey. "She ran into you this morning. You told me. And then she was arguing with Meena at lunch today. Don't you remember?"

Tracey tapped her forehead trying to get her muddy thoughts to clear up. Nothing came to mind. She couldn't even picture Jilly. "Another Mage-kind at school? Do you think she took the journal?"

"Well, maybe she's just... you know... Mage-kind stuff."

Tracey stared. "What? Mage-kind... I can't believe you."

Laura threw her head back and growled at the sky. "Really? Look Tracey, not every person, not every Mage-kind, is like you."

"What are you saying? I was barely away for a week. When did the whole world flip upside down? That's never... You've never said it bothered you before." Every muscle in Tracey's body tensed.

Laura's voice was sharp, her words snapping out like a whip. "It doesn't—don't do that. I didn't say that. Tracey, you used to be more empathetic."

Tracey's mouth dropped open. "Used to be?" She pressed a hand to her sternum. Her chest ached something terrible.

Laura let out a slow breath. "I don't want to fight."

"Neither do I. So why is this Jilly girl getting the nice treatment and not me? You know what I've been through lately."

"I know." Laura stared at the pavement beneath her feet. "But because of that, don't you think you could be a little kinder?"

"Maybe *she* should be kinder. Why are you defending her?"

"I'm not defending her," Laura shouted. She grabbed her wind-whipped hair in one hand and held it out of her eyes.

"You are!" Tracey's own hair whipped across her face. *This stupid wind! So annoying.* With the hair tie around her wrist she tied her hair into a ponytail. "Let's not talk about Jilly anymore."

"Yeah." Laura spun on a heel and continued walking.

Tracey didn't immediately try to catch up. Her blood thrummed in her ears. Why was her friend acting so weird? And when had she become so chummy with the new girl? Her eyes sprang wide. Laura said Jilly was

Mage-kind. Jilly must have put a whammy on Laura! She spelled Laura to like her.

Dropping her shield, Tracey drew a little bit of magic from her core and flung it up into her sense ball to fan out in its large blanket-like shape, invisible to Laura's eyes and senses. It settled over Laura searching for the spell that had hijacked her mind.

"What are you doing?" Laura stumbled backward. Her hand rose up against Tracey as if to fend her off.

"What do you mean?" Tracey asked as innocently as she could while tugging her magic blanket around Laura's body. It should jiggle or buzz if it found traces of a spell. There was no reaction at all. *Where is it?*

"I can feel that. What are you doing?" Laura's voice was louder than ever.

"Nothing." Unable to find any magic residue, Tracey released her magic blanket and it faded away. Tracey raised her shield bubble again. There was nothing, but Jilly must have put a spell on Laura. Why else would she be acting so strangely?

"You did something. The hairs on my arms are up. What. Did. You. Do?" The accusation popped out like the pellets from Simon and Charlie's paintball guns — sharp, hard, and loud.

"Nothing. I just... I had to check if Jilly did something to you." Laura shouldn't have been able to tell what Tracey had done. *Fruit tingles.*

"What?" Laura's eyes bulged and she backed away further. "You used magic on me?"

Tracey followed. "Only to check—"

"—Tracey!"

"Laura, I had to see..." Tracey stepped forward, but Laura stumbled away, her hands raised to stop Tracey from coming closer. Tracey froze. Laura's face had paled like she'd seen a ghost. Her eyes were wide, and she was breathing heavy. So was Tracey.

"Don't ever! Tracey..." Laura spat the words like she was really mad. *Oh no!* "I'm sorry. I—"

"Just don't."

They stood in silence on opposite sides of the pavement, staring at each other. *She's afraid of me.* Tracey gnawed on her bottom lip and twisted in the direction of Uncle Donny's office. They were only a block away. It felt like miles. "Um, we should—"

"—I'm gonna go home," Laura said, her voice suddenly soft. She blinked a lot and turned her head away, staring down the street at the cars slowly moving past.

Tracey wanted to race to her friend's side. She forced her feet to stay still. "Laura no, please."

"Tracey. I need..." Laura backed up again and turned toward the street. When she glanced back, she wouldn't look Tracey in the eyes. "I'm sorry. I just can't. Not right now."

Tracey swallowed the plea in her throat. Blinking back hot tears, she watched her friend go. Laura didn't look back. *What did I just do?*

Tracey stepped into Uncle Donny's office in a daze, her body numb and tingly. That was the worst fight she and Laura had ever had. She glanced at the phone in her hand. *Should I call her? Text her?* Fingers twitching, Tracey replayed every word shouted between them. Laura wanted Tracey to play nice and not pick on... whatever her name was. It was *her* fault Laura and Tracey had that big fight. If that new girl hadn't been around, the fight would never have happened.

"Hey, Tracey?"

She focused on the black boy in front of her, "What?"

"Whoa! Chill." Jonny held up his palms. "You didn't answer. What's wrong?"

Tracey placed her phone on her desk with deliberate care. "Nothing." She didn't want Jonny to know what she had done. Swallowing hard, her mouth bone dry, she grabbed a bottle of water from the fridge and gulped. The cold liquid rushed down her throat and swirled in her stomach. She put the bottle down, suddenly queasy. Jonny watched her with a confused twist to his mouth. Would he leave if she told him what she had done? She swallowed a few times to make sure the water she had just drunk stayed down.

"Where's Laura and Tony?"

"Tony? I don't know. Laura said she had to ... ah ... go home."

Jonny fell onto the sofa. "Sooooo, Damian?"

Luckily for her, Jonny didn't ask for further details. The bell above the door chimed as Tony pushed it open. He gave them a short wave. "Hey."

"Hey," Tracey and Jonny echoed.

Tony itched his neck and speared her with a sharp gaze. "How's your shielding going?"

She shrugged. It was horrible but she was growing used to the ever-present exhaustion weighing her down, making her body ache. The momentary lift when she used her magic acted as a release valve, taking the pressure off for a short period of time. She waited for Tony to ask about Laura. He seemed to sense something was up and shot her a squinty look, raising both his eyebrows. She shook her head and turned her vision inward, picturing her inner closet and behind it her magical core safely locked away. Scrubbing sweaty hands against her jeans, she said, "So, uh, missing journal. How do we find it?"

Tony glanced at Uncle Donny's closed office door. "What about your uncle?"

Turning on her computer, she typed a quick message and sent it to his computer. If he had a client, he wouldn't respond. She snuck over to the door and Listened. *It's spelled you idiot.* She shrugged at Tony. "No idea." Tracey waved the boys back to the sofa. Squeezing in at the end she sneezed as Tony's cinnamon body spray tickled her nose.

"No, I mean can he help?"

She shrugged again and looked at the closed door. "Tony, do you know—"

Uncle Donny poked his head out of his office. He caught sight of Tony and Jonny and coughed, choking on what he was going to say. Finally, he managed to get out, "Tracey, can you come in here for a moment?"

"Ah, sure. Hang on guys," she left them on the sofa and stepped into her uncle's office.

"Hey guys." Uncle Donny shot the boys a weird one-handed finger wiggle and followed her inside. He shut the door. "Sit down." He sounded weirdly formal, like she was a client and not his niece.

The chair was cold beneath her butt. "What's up?" The silence was creeping her out. "Uncle Donny?"

"How often were you helping me? With my magic?"

Pent up air exploded out of her. "Oh, that."

Leaning his elbows onto his desk he rested his chin in his hands. Tracey squirmed. She didn't want to hurt him, but she also didn't want to lie. "Just, uh, sometimes with really complicated spells... I, um, sent little bursts to... make... to help." She sunk into her seat and peered through the window. "Not much. Really, Uncle Donny, I just sort of..."

"Stabilized me?"

She winced. "Yeah."

He sighed and leaned back, scrubbing his fingers through his hair. "I never even noticed. I should have." A little smirk twisted his lips. "You're very good, kiddo, and I'm not a very good detective."

"Do—uh, Uncle Donny, do you want me to stop?"

His eyes popped wide. "What? No. I'm just trying to figure out how to convince your mom to let you help me more."

"What?" She sat up straighter.

"Leave it to me, honey. I'll figure something out. Now, how did your training go with Agent Malden? Did he and Hank help you? Any word on the other stones?"

Tracey burst out laughing. "If it was that easy to find we'd have the other ones already. I've found nada. Have you got anything?"

"Keep on it. I've got a few contacts I'm talking to. It's like finding a needle in a world-sized haystack." Uncle Donny furrowed his eyebrows then laughed with quizzical eyes. "How's your shield bubble?"

"Meh, it's fine."

"I want to help you find the stones, but given my... ah, lower level magic, I... ah... I realize I may not be the best person to help you."

"Don't be silly, a low level doesn't mean you—"

"It's okay. I get it. It's always been a strain. My spells often don't work the way I plan. Luckily, I don't think you're going to take after me.

You're more like your grandma." Grandma rated as a Significant. Out of the three levels Tracey now wished she rated more like her uncle, or even mid-range like her parents. Being too strong just made everything harder. He leaned forward. "You should know I've been, well, looking into things from a detective standpoint."

Tracey sat up straight, wondering if he would be upset if she brought her friends in to listen. "What did you find?"

"Something odd is... I'm not sure what to make of it." His voice drifted away as he stared at the door. "That man you saw in here the other day—"

"The guy that looked like a bald eagle, with the hooked nose and beady eyes? Yeah, I remember."

"He collects Mage-kind memorabilia."

"We're not sports heroes. Why would he... oh, you mean like a war buff?"

Uncle Donny's eyes drifted to the window again. "Something like that, yes."

Tracey thought about the missing journal. What a strange coincidence. *Or was it?* "What was he looking for? That's what he came here to ask, right? For you to find something for him? What was it?"

"He didn't say." Uncle Donny tipped the back of his chair until he lay almost horizontal. He put his hands behind his head and stared up at the ceiling.

"Why was he here then?" Tracey glanced up. The paint had round water stains near the lone lightbulb. She could smell curry from the takeout place on the corner. Ducking her head, she spied the empty container in her uncle's waste-paper bin.

"Checking me out, or so he said. Once he confirms my credentials he'll be back to explain the case."

Weird. "Did you check him out?"

"Of course. He's British, from a large estate in the southern part of the UK. I'm waiting on a contact to get back to me with further details." Uncle Donny sat up, his chair springing upright with a clang.

"So, he didn't actually tell you anything about the case?"

"He said it had to do with a missing book."

The journal! "Oh?" She tried to sound bored. Her voice ended up squeaking. She cleared her throat. "What about it?"

"He was tracking it. And guess what, kiddo? It was sent here to Miltern Falls."

Fruit tingles. "Who was it going to?"

"That's the thing. It was being delivered to Doctor Chan. But the package was redirected and it's disappeared."

"Really?" Her voice was way too high. Uncle Donny was going to get suspicious. She coughed.

"I'm looking into it from here, but the redirect happened online. I've left a message with Agent Malden because I need his resources for the computer stuff."

Tracey's brain was going a hundred miles a second. "Aha, sure ... ah ... do you —" *Don't do it.* "— want to ask Tony? He's pretty good with computer stuff."

"Tracey, I'm not getting your friends involved in this. I'm just giving you the heads up. Doctor Chan might be here in town. I want you to be careful. He's come after you once. I'm afraid you might still be his target."

Fruit tingles. "Thanks for warning me."

"Hang in there, kiddo. We'll get him. I know Malden has men dedicated to finding Doctor Chan."

Tracey stood up. "Do you want me to leave the door open?"

"Close it. I'll call Agent Malden now and get an update."

She paused in front of his closed door. "Did you tell him about the book?"

"No. Why? Do you think it's important?"

Tracey's next move made a rock-like lump in the bottom of her stomach. "Nah, it's probably nothing."

She opened the door to find the boys crouched in front of her. "Hey," she said.

"Hey," they both replied, their faces red.

Tracey stepped out of Uncle Donny's office and made sure the door was shut tight behind her. She dropped her voice to a whisper. "Tony, we have to find that book."

"Well, yeah. I know." His gaze darted to the closed office door.

"No! Uncle Donny's new client is looking for it, too."

"Fudge!" Jonny hissed. He glanced at Tony, mouth open. Both boys turned as one to stare at Tracey.

"Worse. Uncle Donny wants Agent Malden to get one of M-Force's tech guys on it and trace the delivery."

Tony paled. "What do we do?" He stumbled to the sofa and sank down, dropping his head into his hands.

"Do you know a spell to track who stole the journal from my bag?" She really wanted to ask him if he knew a spell that could convince a person to like someone better than their best friend. Laura had to be under a spell. There was no way she would prefer the new girl over Tracey. Right?

Tony shook his head. "I was looking for one while on my way over." He swallowed and scrubbed both hands over his face. "I'm going to get in trouble, aren't I?"

"Only if they work out it was you."

Jonny leaned close and whispered. "Then we're good, right? Tony's the best." Tracey could smell orange soda on his breath. It made her tummy growl.

"M-Force," Tony reminded him. "Maybe we should tell them."

"No, Tony, we can't. They'll take the book. They might not even give it back to us." Maybe they should fess up. But then she would have to admit she lost it. She clenched her fists tighter.

"—Whoa!"

Tracey's head snapped up at Tony's hushed exclamation. He was staring at his cracked cell phone screen.

Jonny pushed his glasses up his nose and poked Tony in the side when he stayed silent. "What?"

Tracey leaned over. "Tone?" She couldn't make sense of what she saw. Lines of gibberish scrolled across the screen, pages and pages of it.

Tony locked eyes with them, his face flushed. "Our trap just went off."

"What trap?" Tracey lowered her voice to match Tony's barely audible whisper. Jonny leaned his head in until they were all touching.

"You remember how we thought we could catch the Shadowman by setting up that trap in Sachorn Forest, at the movie lot?"

"The thumb drive you put the virus on? The one that went missing after Timothy's attack? The one with the fake data about the Butterfly Stone? The one Doctor Chan stole back?" Jonny said without taking a breath.

"It just activated."

Tracey blinked at Tony feeling a little stupid. "Which means what?"

"It means I know where Doctor Chan is. Or I will."

Jonny grabbed Tony's arm and let out an excited yelp. Both Tracey and Tony shushed him quickly and glanced up to check Uncle Donny's door was still closed. Tony jumped to his feet.

"We should tell your uncle," Jonny said.

Should they? Of course they should.

"Uh, Trace?" Tony's lips mashed together in a way that worried her.

She *should* tell Uncle Donny, but if she did, she would have to tell him about *how* they knew where Doctor Chan was. And that would put Tony under the spotlight with his illegal hacking and computer virus stuff. Tracey nibbled at her bottom lip and held up a hand. "We don't actually know where he is yet, right?"

Tony nodded as his expression lightened. "Right. I still have to track him down. It shouldn't be too hard if I get back to my computer before Doctor Chan discovers the virus."

"Right," Tracey said. "So, we shouldn't tell Uncle Donny yet. Not until we know exactly where Doctor Chan is."

Jonny's tilted head dripped with skepticism. "Ye-ah, okay."

"Okay," Tony gushed. "I gotta go."

"Call me!" Tracey ordered. He waved and ran out through the door sending the little bell jingling loudly.

"Well," Jonny said in the sudden silence left behind by Tony's exit.

"Yeah." Tracey laughed. Jonny joined in. It felt great to just enjoy the moment. All too quickly reality set back in. Laura wasn't there to enjoy it with them. And that was Tracey's fault.

Uncle Donny's office door sprang open, and he scowled over at them.

"What is going on out here? I'm on a call. Keep it down."

"Sorry, Uncle Donny," Tracey said as her giggles tapered off. Uncle Donny scrubbed a hand over his face and scratched at his beard shadow. "Head home, Tracey. There's not much left for you to do today."

There wasn't much to do most days. She jumped to her feet and pulled Jonny up after her. "Okay." Waving goodbye to her uncle, she dragged her friend outside.

"Man, I feel like stuff is happening, but to everyone else. I don't want to go home yet," Jonny moaned.

Tracey wrapped her hand around his arm. She didn't want to go home either. She would only stress about Laura, Tony and Dave Two. "Let's go get ice-cream."

Tales
by
The Lost

Following 219, Followed by 0
click <broken link> to follow The Lost!

Day 954

[cont …]

I mean I could hardly

have not heard them.

My uncle.

The criminal.

The Betrayer.

0 likes, 0 comments, 0 reshares
click <broken link> to like this post!:D

T.B.T.L.

11

Nana's small bedroom at Tavel House was full of shadows. Light snuck in through the closed blinds. It cast an eerie glow into the room and sent weird shapes up onto the walls. A feeling of de-ja-vu washed over Tracey's body. She was in another one of her horrible nightmares.

Nana sat up in bed. The gloom illuminated enough of the room to see her Nana's tiger covered flannel pajamas. Funny, Tracey didn't remember her mom buying Nana tiger pajamas. Tracey avoided her nana's vacant gaze for as long as possible, staring instead at her tight grey curls and glasses reflecting her worried expression, but eventually she was drawn to Nana's lax skin and thin lips. Her glasses were glowing. No, it wasn't her glasses, but her eyes behind the glass. Orange orbs flared brighter, stealing Tracey's sight. Shrinking what she could see until only Nana's glowing eyes remained. "It's coming," Nana said, sounding cold and dead. "You need to remember."

"Remember what?"

"Remember," Nana repeated. "You will be blinded to the truth."

"I don't understand." Tracey reached out but found Nana's body frozen, like a giant popsicle.

Nana's eyes weren't eyes anymore. They grew wider at the edges, the pupils elongated through the middle. Like a cat. The eyes blinked. "Remember."

Tracey bolted upright in bed, her heart pounding.

Remember what?

Tales
by
The Lost

Following 219, Followed by 0
click **<broken link>** to follow The Lost!

Day 954

[cont …]

He is looking for it.

The cursed stone.

The Tiger's Eye.

0 likes, 0 comments, 0 reshares
click **<broken link>** to like this post! :D

T.B.T.L.

12

Tracey couldn't get back to sleep. The next morning, she was grumpy and tired and her sister wasn't making it easy to remain civil.

"I already have friends," Sarah grumbled, shooting Tracey a dark look.

"Come on, Sarah. Kylie Carter is new and Mage-kind. You could be nice and just meet her. She might end up at Camp Mindflower next summer you know. Having a new friend might make that more fun, don't you think?" If Sarah was difficult, Tracey was afraid their meeting with Damian's sister would go badly. The two girls stood near the school gate waiting for the Carters to appear.

"Doesn't look like she's coming," Sarah said as she picked at one of her fingernails. She didn't look up at Tracey, her body screaming *I don't want to be here*. This was one of those times being able to sense Sarah's emotions was not that great. Well, Sarah would have to suck it up.

It did look like Kylie and Damian weren't coming though. "We'll give them a little more time. I told you, Kylie's scared." *Angry, actually.* Tracey checked her cell phone. She was going to be late meeting up with Tony and Jonny. *Will Laura come?* Thinking of their fight made Tracey's stomach twitch.

"Great," Sarah muttered.

"What's your problem?"

"I didn't sleep well last night."

"You too?" Tracey noticed dark smudges peeking through the makeup under her eyes. It was a cooler morning and both girls were wrapped in thicker coats. Tracey's breath puffed out of her mouth in little white clouds. "I'm sorry, but please try and be nice to Kylie."

"What's your interest, Tracey? Is this connected to another one of Uncle Donny's cases?"

"Look, she seems like a nice girl. Didn't you say you don't like being alone at your campus? She's Mage-kind, Sarah."

"She's not you," Sarah snapped back, scuffing her school shoes on the pavement. Mom would be mad when she saw the state of them.

"I can't come to school with you, Sarah. This is the best I can do. So be nice, please." They were silent for a few minutes. "Hey, Mom's migraine seems to be hanging around, do you think—"

"Is that her?" Sarah asked, pointing across the road.

Damian and Kylie stood at the corner, waiting for the lights to change. Damian wore his leather jacket and his hair was spiked up in all directions like he had been running his fingers through it. Kylie's grey coat hung open over a pretty grey dress, and pink tights. Her hair was tied up in a high ponytail. "That's her."

Sarah eyed Tracey curiously. "Her brother's cute."

"Is he?" He was chatting to Kylie and hadn't looked up yet. That wasn't the reason Tracey wanted Sarah to meet Kylie. Well, maybe initially. But after meeting Kylie, Tracey just wanted to help the poor girl. When the light changed Damian looked up and caught Tracey looking. He shot her a wide smile. The cold coating her bones disappeared in an instant. The look Sarah gave her said she knew what was really going on. Tracey screwed up her nose at her and turned to watch the Carters cross the road.

"Hey Kylie." Tracey pushed upbeat energy into her voice.

Kylie grunted.

Tracey smiled at Damian, impressed he had managed to get his sister this far. "Hi." Tearing her gaze from his dreamy face she glanced again at Kylie. "This is my sister Sarah."

Sarah growled quietly but perked up as she stepped forward, smiling brightly. "Hi. That's a pretty necklace."

Tracey was so proud of her in that moment. Sarah was trying. Tracey edged closer to Damian to give the girls some space. "Hi Damian," she said again. *Ugh, way to be a doofus. You said that already.*

"Morning." He watched his sister from the corner of his eye.

"I like your bracelets," Kylie said to Sarah, though she had barely even glanced at Sarah's wrists.

Sarah shook the chunky bracelets around. They almost hid her Mage-kind ID bracelet. She led Kylie down the path toward the junior school campus, talking about her teachers the entire way. She didn't look back at Tracey at all. Tracey narrowed her eyes after her sister, picking up a sense of grudging acceptance. A thank you would have been nice.

Damian watched them leave. "Thank you so much for this. It looks like it's working."

"Yeah, Sarah can be good sometimes. Just don't tell her I said that."

He laughed as they turned toward the main campus. "I'm sorry about the other day," she blurted.

His nose crinkled, "What do you mean?"

She waved her hand around. "All that stuff about my bag and the journal. I know I was acting—"

"It seemed important. Did you find it?"

"No."

Jonny stood waiting outside the door to Hall B.

"Is Jonny your boyfriend?" Damian asked. "You guys hang out together a lot."

Boyfriend? Why ask that? Oh, is he going to ask me to be his girlfriend? She squealed internally. "Jonny? No. He's my friend." Her voice was strained as she worked to hide her excitement.

"But he's not Mage-kind."

Tracey stopped and eyed the tall boy at her side, hopes dropping into her feet. "Does that matter?" He met her gaze without flinching. He seemed so nice and she had hoped... well... they had been getting along so well. She didn't like to think he was weird about Mage-kind and Norms. His sister was Mage-kind after all.

His skin pinked. "Oh. No, of course not. I just wondered..." He glanced back at Jonny. "Never mind."

Tracey pondered Damian's question as they approached the door. So, *was* he interested in her as a girlfriend, or not? Now she was totally confused. *Why ask about Jonny?*

Jonny bounced on his toes. "What are you thinking about? Your face is all scrunched up."

Tracey just shrugged and let out a giant yawn. *Why did boys have to be so confusing?* "Nothing."

Laura didn't join them before school and there was no sign of her in the lunch room either. Tracey was stewing. Tony sat beside her and mumbled, "Hey." She turned toward him happy for the distraction, dying to ask what he had found out about Doctor Chan. Did he know where the nasty man was hiding yet? Damian stood just behind him. Tracey's shoulders dropped. Now she couldn't ask Tony anything. Tony scowled as he realized they couldn't talk. She shrugged, a minute movement her friend would pick up on. She couldn't ask Damian to leave. They would just have to make time to talk privately later. Damian caught the tail end of her weird look and his smile fell away. "Can I —?"

"Of course, sit down," she blurted. Her skin tingled as he put his tray down at Laura's spot. Tracey didn't correct him and Jonny's eyebrows rose under his baseball cap. Tony's hands unclenched around his tray and he twitched his shoulders. Maybe she should tell Damian about the Butterfly Stone? Then they could tell him everything and she wouldn't have to keep secrets anymore. But what about that weird thing earlier about Jonny? He might freak out if she told him about Timothy and the stones. Especially now that she had introduced Kylie to Sarah. It might be best to keep him out of it.

Everything felt so wrong, lopsided, and off-balance. Laura's absence dug into her chest like a spoon had scooped out parts of her body leaving her full of holes. She jerked when Jonny's chair crashed back down on all fours. He leaned forward and glared at Damian.

"What's going on?" Tracey blurted, wondering what she had missed.

"You didn't hear that?" Jonny demanded. Tony's breathing was heavy, his fist clenching around his phone. Okay, she had clearly missed something major.

"What did you say, Damian?" she asked. *Does he have a problem with Mage-kind?*

"What? The thing about Dave One and Dave Two?"

Oh, not a Mage-kind thing. "What about them?"

"They were fighting at the morning break. Me, Jack, and Lin had to pull them apart. Dave One isn't happy."

"About what?"

"The bracelet. Dave Two's bracelet."

Tracey had wondered when this was going to come to a head. Dave One and Dave Two's friendship was on the line now that Dave Two's Mage-kind status had come out. As Dave Two feared, Dave One—the bully who hated Mage-kind—had turned on him. She had always wanted Dave Two to understand what it was like to be bullied, but now that it was happening, she felt awful about it. His friendship wasn't going to survive this.

"He's pretty angry about how he found out Dave Two is Mage-kind." Damian rubbed his neck. "Oh, I guess you probably know all about—"

"Hey, cut that out! Back off!" Every head snapped toward the shouting. Dave Two stood facing off against Dave One. Both boys held trays piled high with food, probably the only thing stopping them from coming to blows if Dave Two's expression was anything to go by. Peels of high-pitched laughter erupted from the table behind Dave One. Meena's predatory lean forward turned Tracey's stomach into a hard stone. Carla's laughter grew louder as Dave One rumbled something Tracey couldn't hear. He bared his teeth in a feral grin.

"Oh no," she muttered at the sight of the confrontation. Why couldn't Dave One just leave Dave Two alone?

A sudden swell of power around Dave Two forced Tracey to her feet. "Dave!" she shouted across the cafeteria, succeeding in getting everyone's attention. Both boys turned, not knowing which one she addressed. She let them wonder, stalking forward until she stood between them. Inwardly, she couldn't believe she was getting involved. Her life used to be so much simpler.

Jonny and Damian followed in her wake. She could have done with

Tony's help, but he hovered behind Jonny and wouldn't meet her gaze.

"What do you want?" Dave Two's voice scratched like an old DVD skipping in the player. A deep purple bruise poked from beneath his Mage-kind bracelet.

Tracey made her shield bubble thicker, knowing Dave Two would feel it and understand what it meant. She turned toward Dave One. The boy's blue eyes narrowed at her, daring her to get in the way. She pretended not to be intimidated by his larger body or clenched fists. *Come on Tracey, you faced down Timothy. You can stand up to Dave One.* "What's up, guys?" She pulsed her shield at Dave Two reminding him she could still feel his magic simmering beneath his skin.

"Go away," Dave Two snarled.

Tracey ignored him and stared directly at Dave One trying—and obviously, failing—to scare him. *If only he knew.*

"Protecting your own kind?" Meena called. Her sharp voice cut through the cafeteria silence. Tracey heard a text message ding out across the hall. She also heard shoes squeak on the linoleum and a chair leg creak. *Why do I keep getting involved?*

"I guess so. Even the dumb ones," Tracey said. She received scowls from everyone. Carla's braying laughter frayed Tracey's nerves. Doing her best to ignore it she held Dave One's stare. "I thought you guys were friends, what's going on?"

"Seriously? Friends with *that?*"

Whoa! She fought back her own reaction as Dave Two dropped his tray and shoved her aside. "You're a d—"

"Hey," Tracey shouted to be heard over the feuding boys and Carla's incessant cackling. She pushed the brawling boys apart with her hands and an assist from her magic. The boys sprang apart.

"You hanging out with *her* now?" Dave One gasped.

Tracey paused, actually curious to know what Dave Two would answer. Beneath the verbal sparring there was another battle going on. Tracey pushed her magic bubble at Dave Two. He pushed back. She wouldn't let him attack his ex-friend in front of all of these kids. *Where the heck are all the teachers?* Shooting a glance toward the food counter, she spied a cell phone in the head server's hand. *Not far away.* This had to end now. Without looking at either Dave Two or at Tony, she dropped her shield and let Dave's magic hit her full force, drawing it inside her core by turning her whole body into a black hole. She staggered on unsteady legs. Dave's magic whipped at her skin, but she gritted her teeth and stood her ground. Her exhaustion fell away as his magic soaked into her body.

He didn't have the strength or experience to stop her. Tony's shield bubble sprang up like a wall between her and Dave Two, cutting off the power flow. She glared at Tony, but he stared back, undaunted.

Tracey straightened her shoulders. It didn't matter, the danger had passed for now. It would take Dave a while to rebuild his magic. He was still so new to all of this he hadn't known how to stop her. It was a basic parental protection, mostly used on kids under ten years old. Tracey had basically left Dave Two defenseless. Tony stared at his feet, shaking his head and she had the weird feeling she had disappointed him. *I stopped the fight, why are you upset with me?* She checked on Dave Two. His shirt was damp under his armpits, his face shiny and minute trembles traveled the length of his body. That wasn't what caught her attention, however. It was the utter fury radiating from his aura.

If she hadn't just depleted his core she would have imploded from the strength of his glare. Tracey felt—peaceful. Her skin tingled. She could hear birds singing and overhead, a plane flew past. A mix of perfumes and aftershave surrounded her, yet she could distinguish each scent as a separate smell. The sweaty socks were not as pleasant. Wondering if she could, Tracey separated the negative scent from the rest and switched off her ability to smell it. Cool. That was new.

Dave's magic swirled inside her chest, thumping along her veins. She felt invincible. "Listen, Dave," she said, turning to Dave One. "You know as well as I do what Dave Two thinks of me and my friends. Stop being such a douchebag. No one can help being what they are. Otherwise, you'd be smarter, right? You want to trigger a Mage-kind outburst? Well try me."

The bully's eyes fixed on her, but other than that he didn't move a muscle. Tracey wished she knew what he was thinking.

"It's always about you, isn't it, magic girl?" Meena's voice was nothing more than white noise in the background. Tracey easily ignored her, didn't even look her way.

"What about the game on the weekend, Dave? You'd rather lose to Harrietville than play beside your best friend? Training, pregame, postgame, all of that gone? School, class everything? What kind of friend are you?"

"He lied," Dave One growled.

"He didn't know," Tracey snapped back.

"What's going on here — break it up you three." Mr. Rachette's appearance threw cold water over all of them, sending them scurrying back to their tables before he could give them lunch time detention. The bell rang as Tracey and her friends gathered their belongings. Dave Two disappeared.

"Tracey, how could you do that?" Tony hissed.

She was stunned at the venom in his voice. His eyebrows drew down from the weight of his disappointment. "What? Stop the fight? Come on, Tony. He had—"

"You took Dave's magic."

Tracey's eyes narrowed. "I had to — you felt how close to the edge he was." If Dave Two had lost control, they *all* would have faced trouble.

"He has to learn to control it," Tony told her. "You shouldn't have taken his choice away."

"What are you talking about?" Now a fire was burning inside her chest — or maybe it was from the hot stone hanging from her neck. "People would have gotten hurt, Tony." *Why is he so angry with me?* She had stopped the fight and saved Dave whether Tony saw it that way or not. "He was going to explode."

Tony walked away.

Tracey stared after him. "Tony?" Her friend didn't look back. Damian and Jonny's shocked expressions swung from Tracey to Tony and back again.

"What in the …" Jonny ran to catch up with the furious boy. He would find out what was wrong with Tony and tell her. Tracey gritted her teeth. Why were all her friends acting so strange? Her thoughts flittered to the day before — Laura's anger, now Tony's questioning. Dave was always angry, but still, this was way worse than usual. It was like watching a reality TV show with only melodrama shown. *Wait.* Something danced at the very edge of her memory. She couldn't quite grasp it. It felt as though her friends were turning against her one by one, which was crazy unless… Tracey dropped her shield and threw up a sense ball. It exploded in an invisible shockwave over the students still seated in the cafeteria. They peered around wondering at the sudden gust of wind that blew over them when all the doors and windows were closed. A very faint taste of residual magic flared in her Sight. Dave or Tony? She couldn't pinpoint who it belonged to.

"That was amazing," Damian said. "You stood up for D2. I knew you were brave, Tracey but whoa. Meena and D1 just don't get it. My sister says magic is hard to control, but you seem really good at it. I'm glad I introduced you to her."

Tracey spun around to face him, her body filling with warmth at his gushing. "Ah, thanks."

They made their way toward class and Tracey tried to push the questions about her friends away. Hopefully they would return to normal soon. Damian's fingers brushed her hand and Tracey's heart skipped a beat. *Fruit tingles.* She didn't look up but let her fingers touch him back. A shiver raced over her skin and she broke into a big smile. She glanced up and around to check if anyone had seen them, and spied a black SUV idling on the street beyond the yard. When Tracey's gaze moved over the darkly tinted passenger side window a wave of cold air flowed over her, chilling her body and sending a different kind of shiver down her back. She froze. It was the same feeling she used to get right before the Shadowman appeared.

"Tracey?" Damian stopped beside her.

Her gaze was fixed to the SUV. The passenger window wound down and a silver cylinder appeared. There was a flash of light, then it disappeared from view. The window wound back up and the car inched away from the curb, moving well under the speed limit as it drove away. She stared after it. The Butterfly Stone beat a warning against her chest and she rubbed a hand over her sternum to ease the ache. The cold feeling didn't leave her until the SUV was well out of sight.

"Tracey? Are you okay?"

Her friends' suddenly odd behavior and now this weird SUV...

Timothy! He's found a new body to possess. He *must have put a whammy on my friends!*

She shook her head to clear the paranoid thoughts and forced a smile. "Sorry, bit distracted." *I have to tell Agent Malden.* Damian smiled back and took her hand again. *Fruit tingles.* Her grin felt bright enough to be a sun all on its own. She caught sight of Laura up ahead, walking next to someone. The person flipped long straight black hair from side to side and laughed brightly. She peered over her shoulder and caught Tracey staring, scowled and took Laura's arm to hurry her along. "Hey, did you see—"

"Jilly and Laura?" Damian shrugged. "I thought Laura was your friend?"

"So did I," Tracey said watching her friend disappear. *What is going on?*

Tales
by
The Lost

Following <u>219</u>, Followed by <u>0</u>
click **<broken link>** to follow <u>The Lost</u>!

Day 954

[cont …]

How I wish I'd never heard of it.

How I wish my family

had not been cursed by it…

<u>0</u> likes, <u>0</u> comments, <u>0</u> reshares
click **<broken link>** to like this post!:D

T.B.T.L.

13

Tracey was unable to concentrate in her English class that afternoon. She kept coming back to *why?* Why was Laura hanging out with *that* girl? She was clearly still angry at Tracey. Did Laura have any idea how Tracey's stomach ached to have *that* girl chosen over her? Tracey's notebook remained blank. She sagged in her seat, her pen rotating between her fingers as her confusion mounted. When her phone vibrated, she hoped it was Laura, quickly swiping the screen to read her friend's apology.

The message was not from Laura. She sagged in her chair and thumbed over the message from Uncle Donny.

`Need you at the office exactly at 4 p.m.`

Rather than question him, she typed `Sure` and returned to staring at her notebook. Why hadn't Laura texted? "Hey!" Damian's elbow against her own drove her head up. Mr. Michaels stood in front of her desk. Damian shifted back quickly and pretended he was working.

"Miss Masters?"

"Sir?"

"Your page is blank."

"I'm — uh — thinking about what to write." Her hands were sweating. She gripped her pen tighter.

"Are you playing with your phone?"

"No sir." *Liar.*

"Then get writing."

"Yes, sir."

Mr. Michaels stormed away, and Tracey released the breath she held. She leaned forward and rested her chin in her hands. "Thanks for the save. What are we writing about?"

Damian shook his head and mumbled. "The next letter, page eighty-nine."

Tracey suppressed a moan and turned to the correct page on her tablet.

It is said, with hand on heart, that they are not evil. But what lies fall from cursed tongue, for they are wicked through and through. Seven days of terror and blood, seven days of horror most foul. Their very existence an affront to God. Demons cursed to walk in the light and destroy good men's hearts. Children, whose innocence is led astray. It is a temptation that cannot be overcome. They are bewitched and stained with evil evermore. The demons must carry a mark so that our souls cannot be seduced by their wickedness. For their goal is to destroy us and blacken our hearts for their evil purposes.

Tracey covered her mouth and swallowed back bile, her stomach swirling. This author was talking about Mage-kind. Her family wasn't evil, Tracey wasn't a demon. How could people think this way? Her skin crawled and she thumbed her tablet off, not wanting to read any further. No wonder Mom warned her to be careful around Norms. Tracey fingered the identification bracelet around her wrist. Tagged—like animals. She examined her fellow students. In her mind she heard them whispering and felt their eyes on her skin. If the Norms in the room didn't think this way already, would reading these kinds of letters encourage them down a path of hatred? Tracey stood, her chair screeching against the floor and excused herself. Not waiting for Mr. Michaels reply, she scampered into the hallway.

Mr. Michaels yelled out, "Where are you going?" and she heard, "Mr. Carter freeze."

She hit the bathroom door hard. It sprang back, bouncing off the wall as she vomited into the first cubical toilet. She had known this was how some people felt about Mage-kind, but she'd never truly understood it.

Had Stephanie listened to this kind of thing every day? Being called evil and a monster? Tracey scrubbed her mouth and collapsed on the floor. A moment later she realized how gross it was to sit on the toilet floor and jumped to her feet. She scrubbed her hands with a heap of soap and spat again into the sink. Rinsing her mouth, she washed her hands again.

Somehow, she had to write about the rebellion and the abuse of Mage-kind at the hands of the clearly terrified Norms. And Mr. Michaels was going to expect her to say it was right that Mage-kind had been shunned and tagged like animals. She understood now what Peter had meant all those weeks ago. Her face was a pale reflection as she stared into the mirror. She raised her hand until she could see her green glowing bracelet. Dave Two was right. It *was* a form of punishment, designed to remind her that she had been made wrong. She clenched her fist and punched the wall beside the mirror leaving a hand-sized dent behind.

A tentative knock sounded on the outer door. "Tracey?"

Damian followed me? She checked her face was clean in the mirror, cupped her hand beneath the tap to wet her mouth and spat into the sink. It took a second splash to her face and take a sip of water before she felt ready to face him. She tugged open the door. "Oh hey. You ah… didn't need to follow me."

"Are you okay?"

She couldn't keep staring into his kind eyes and looked at her feet instead. "Sure. Sorry, that was a bit hard to read."

He moved closer and ducked his head so he could see her eyes. "Mr. Michaels is a creep."

He took her hands in both of his. Her heart tried to squeal with excitement, but she was still too torn open. "Damian, do you… you don't think like that do you? You don't think Mage-kind are evil?"

His eyes popped wide. He stepped back but didn't release her hands. "Of course not."

She desperately wanted to believe him and didn't mean to keep pushing, but the words burst out of her anyway. "It's just, all the weird looks you give me, and you hung out with Meena and Dave One and I just… I don't understand why you were being so weird before. But then you act like my friend now and—" Footsteps sounded in the hallway. Damian pushed her gently into the bathroom. He dropped her hands and sighed, running his fingers through his hair.

"I know I did. I'm really sorry. When you go to new schools all the time it's hard to make friends and you sort of latch onto the first people who treat you nice. I picked wrong and by the time I realized how horrible Meena was, I...well...it was too late. She said all these horrible things about you, and I didn't know what to believe."

"You could have just asked me," she whispered.

"You're right. I should have. But Tracey, I'm trying to make it right. I just wish, well, that you'd talk to me. I promise you can trust me." He looked so earnest and she really did want to trust him.

She sighed. "I've been going through some things. Look, I—I want to tell you about it all, but you have to see why I didn't—" *Can I trust him?* Everyone else was acting so squirrelly. She desperately wanted to tell someone what was bothering her. The bell rang and their time ran out. They looked at each other and smiled. Tracey took his hand and squeezed it. "We'd better get back. Can I call you after school tonight?"

"I'd love that," he replied, he ran his hands over his hair and straightened his shirt.

"We'd better get you out of the girl's bathroom before anyone catches you," she told him.

He laughed. She joined in. "Come on," he said and let her lead the way into the hall.

We need to talk. Away from other people. Tracey's text to Tony gave no inkling to her inner turmoil.

Come over tonight.

I can't. Uncle Donny needs me.

This is important.

I know. Come to Uncle Donny's.

I can't. I'm...not allowed.

What? Why? Tracey tapped her phone case as she waited for Tony's answer. Why wouldn't he be allowed to hang out with her? His parents wouldn't do that to him, would they? There had to be another reason.

She gasped. Tony was lying so he wouldn't have to come over. He must still be mad about what she'd done to Dave.

Mom says it's too dangerous.

Her mouth dropped open. At Uncle Donny's?

Yeah.

That's ridiculous. The office is not dangerous. Tony couldn't be giving her the real reason. It had to be because he was still angry with her. Fine. I'll try to get away early tonight and come over before dinner.

She was still waiting for Tony's reply when she walked into her next class. Her science teacher Mrs. Burke called Tracey toward her desk. "Phones." She pointed to the tray filled with colorful devices. *Fruit tingles — a pop quiz.* Though reluctant to part with her phone she had to hand it over. "Make sure it's off please."

Tracey grumbled but did as asked. The next forty minutes were hell on Earth. Tracey preferred facing off with the Shadowman over this. She answered maybe a third of the questions correctly. Several she just took a wild stab at. Too many answer boxes were left blank. *Mom's going to murder me when the results come out.* Turning her phone back on, Tracey jumped as it began vibrating madly. She nearly dropped it.

One message was from Sarah. I need to talk to you.

From Hank. Good and potentially bad news. Text me when you get out of school.

And then there was one from Damian. I have an idea for the assignment.

Nothing from Laura. Tracey's heart ached. Tony wasn't at their waiting spot after school and neither was Jonny. She thought about texting Damian, but she was calling him later tonight, and besides, she needed time to think about what she was going to say. Should she tell him about the Butterfly Stone? Doubts sprang into her mind. If she told Damian everything, he might think she was too dangerous to hang around with, but she couldn't *not* tell him. *Urgh, what to do?*

Her shoulders slumped. As she walked alone toward the bus stop, she typed out a quick reply to Hank. Her skin tingled. An SUV passed too slowly for the street's speed limit drawing her attention from her phone. She searched the road ahead wondering what had slowed it down but there was no traffic in front of the dark-colored vehicle.

Tracey squinted. *Why does it look familiar? Oh!* The same make and model she had seen that morning while she was with Damian. *I really need to learn more about cars.* It passed her and then sped away. Tracey stared after it. *Creepy.*

Tales
by
The Lost

Following 219, Followed by 0
click <broken link> to follow The Lost!

Day 1105

I've been tasked with finding him.

This was not what I had wanted

my destiny to be. My training has

focused on attack. I should have

realized they had plans for me.

0 likes, 0 comments, 0 reshares
click <broken link> to like this post!:D

T.B.T.L.

14

Memories of the creepy vehicle stayed in her mind as she entered Uncle Donny's office. The door was open, but her uncle was absent. Grabbing a pen, she jotted down the registration plate number and figured she would use Uncle Donny's computer access to the DMV to find the owner. She popped open the button on her jacket. Uncle Donny must have forgotten to slide his window open again. Her cell phone rang as she wrestled with the stuck window frame. She left it partially open and grabbed the phone. "Hey, Sarah," she said recognizing the name on the display. "What do you want?"

"I don't really want to ask this, but it's all your fault I'm in this mess in the first place, so you have to help me fix it," Sarah grumped, clearly unhappy.

"What are you babbling about?"

"Kylie."

Tracey straightened. "What happened? Is she okay?" Tracey's brain jumped to Damian. Sarah better not have ignored Kylie after Tracey went to all that work to introduce them.

"You know that guy—Dumb-dumb Dave, the one that annoys you all the time?"

"Yeah."

"Dave's brother Michael is in our class. He's a pain, but he's not normally too bad, you know?"

"What did he do?"

"He keeps bugging Kylie about her powers, trying to get her to show him stuff. Kylie gets super upset about it. I was able to calm her down today, but she gets angry fast. Like, really fast. I thought she might hit him with a mind blast or something. Trace, she's the only Mage-kind in her whole family. She doesn't have anyone to practice with or to answer her questions. I'm not even sure she's ever been to summer camp."

"She must have. It's mandatory."

"Well if she has, she didn't say." Sarah's voice was snappy again.

Poor Kylie. It must be hard to be on your own. Tracey and her sister had practiced on their brothers since they were little. By practicing, she really meant using her brothers for target practice and avoiding becoming a target in return. No one was more annoying than her brothers. It must be so hard not to have anyone who understood what that buzz against your skin was trying to tell you, or what it felt like to lose control—to feel magic bursting out of your pores. "Maybe we could practice with her?" Tracey suggested. "We haven't done a group practice since camp. We could start the afterschool club up again." *Though where I'll find the time will be the hard part.* Why don't you ask Mom if you can invite Kylie over tomorrow night?"

Sarah sounded a lot happier when she said goodbye.

Tracey could also find some games to give Damian for Kylie. It wasn't right that the younger girl could get into trouble in only her first week of school. If Dave Two's brother kept pushing, there was no way to know what would happen.

She shoved her phone into her pocket. *What else can go wrong today?* A red Turbo Jetfire roared up to the curb outside and parked illegally. Tracey jumped up to grab the door for Prince Henry as he hurried inside. "What are you doing here?"

"Your uncle called me in," he said. The actor prince wore a blue suit with a white shirt that didn't fit very well. It was an awfully strange look for him. Tracey had known him a few weeks now, but she still found it strange that he even talked to her. She had seen every one of his movies. That he was also Mage-kind was a very well-kept secret. When he came to her rescue in Sachorn Forest and helped her save her friends from Timothy she had learned another side of him. It made him so much cooler. Of course, she couldn't tell anyone about it.

"Huh. He called me here, too," she said.

"Don't you work here?" he asked, giving her a quizzical raise of one eyebrow.

"He specifically told me to get here at four o'clock, but he's not here." She pointed to the open office door.

"Weird." Both of his eyebrows danced up and down.

What's he doing? She shrugged and leaned back in her chair. "Not really. You sort of have to know my uncle."

Hank's eyes narrowed. "What does that mean?"

Another shrug and a sigh was her answer to that. "So, you messaged me earlier. What did you want to tell me?"

"I did?"

"Yeah. Don't you remember?"

"Uh, about that."

"Yes?"

His face screwed up and a sneeze exploded out of him. His eyebrows wobbled and he moaned, bending over and clutching his stomach. "Crap, not now."

Recognizing the signs of a disguise spell breaking down — after all she had gone through it herself not that long ago — Tracey jumped out of her chair and raised her magic bubble against the rippling man. His face puffed up and expanded like a balloon. He would be helpless under the onslaught of the collapsing spell, so Tracey dialed Agent Malden's cell phone number, while keeping her gaze glued to the …

"Uncle Donny?" Tracey disconnected the call as soon as she recognized the exhausted figure. She dropped her shield bubble and sucked her magic back inside her core. Uncle Donny sagged onto the sofa, his eyes wet and face pale. His hands trembled. Tracey squatted in front of him.

"Hey kiddo."

"You scared me." Her heart pounded hard enough to break right out of her chest.

"Sorry, I didn't expect the spell to break down quite so soon."

"What were you doing?" She gestured to the car parked haphazardly outside. "And how did you get Hank's … I mean, Prince Henry's car?"

"It was a test."

"Of what?" Her breathing was too fast and she was getting dizzy. Grabbing a handful of tissues from the dispenser on her desk she thrust them into his hands and sank down onto the sofa beside him. *Test?* "Why? What on Earth were you doing?" she asked.

Uncle Donny wiped his eyes and sniffed hard. "It wasn't supposed to break down so quickly," he repeated.

His spells never did what they were supposed to. It was why she was called upon to help him out so often. Tracey's hands were fists in her lap, nails digging into her palms. "Were you trying to trick me?" The stone on her chest pulsed.

"No, no. I just had to see if it was going to work. You know him—"

"What if Hank found out? He'd be so mad."

"Not to worry. I already know," Hank announced, appearing from Uncle Donny's office. He wore a sports jacket and black jeans—perfectly fitted.

Tracey squeaked and nearly fell off the sofa. "Wha…? Where did you even come from?"

"It didn't work," Uncle Donny said, his face red. His suit fit him better now, but it was damp with sweat.

"Actually, it did work," Hank told him. "It just didn't last long enough. You thought he was me, didn't you Tracey?"

"Yes, but why? What were you doing?"

"I have a mission and I need to leave the country immediately. To provide a cover story, your uncle has agreed to impersonate me. I want you to keep an eye on him, Tracey."

She sighed and then what he said registered. "You're leaving? Where are you going? How long will you be gone?"

"England. I don't know for how long."

Uncle Donny's weird English client? Tracey leaned forward. "Is it to do with the stones? Do you know where one is?"

Hank didn't respond. *Ha! Guessed right, but wait…* "Shouldn't I come with you then?"

"Relax. We need to find the stone first." Tracey squinted at him, but his face didn't break out of its serious expression. "I need you to work with your Uncle."

"What does he have to do... oh, he doesn't have to act, does he?" She almost burst into laughter and schooled her face when she caught sight of Uncle Donny's frown.

Hank did laugh. "Good God, no, nothing like that. I just have some publicity interviews I need to do for *Saving Time*."

Tracey smacked her forehead. Prince Henry had been filming *Saving Time* when she had first met him. It was why he had found them so quickly at the Sachorn Forest film lot. "But it's only just finished filming. Won't it have heaps of post-production? Why are they interviewing you about it now?"

Hank laughed. "You sure know your stuff. Right on all counts. This is just early hype. A bit of a teaser."

"I hope you've left him a script. Uncle Donny doesn't watch a lot of movies."

Her uncle straightened his back, poking his chin forward to peer down his nose at her. "I've been catching up on Prince Henry's films."

Tracey groaned even louder, much to Hank's amusement.

"I know you've seen them all, Tracey. That's why I want you to tag along to the interviews if you can get away from school. Help Donny with the curlier questions. Besides, he'll need you there to assist with the disguise spell."

"This has disaster written all over it, you know that, right?" Tracey said, talking into her hands.

"Hey!" Uncle Donny could have been Sarah his voice was so high and whiny.

Hank chuckled. "I've given him a list of standard questions and answers. These things are usually pretty repetitive and straightforward. It'll be fine."

No way would it be fine. What a nightmare! "Magic scanners?" she asked.

"I've brought a few of my tricks with me. I want to show you how they work," Hank said. Tracey relaxed as she remembered when she had first met him in his hotel room. She'd had no idea he was Mage-kind.

"Okay, but if he blows your cover or ruins your reputation it is totally not my fault," she warned.

Hank nodded. "Fair enough." He stood up and handed Tracey a large suitcase. "Let's go over the PR questions."

They sat in Uncle Donny's office and spent what felt like hours going over Hank's schedule. Tracey finally asked the question that was bothering her. "You're going to England? Can we call you if we need to, like if it's an emergency?" There would be an emergency. With her uncle, there was bound to be an emergency.

"Actually, we're sort of swapping jobs," Uncle Donny said. He looked a lot better now that the spell had worn off properly. He sipped from a bottle of water and leaned back in his office chair. The chair overbalanced and he wobbled awkwardly before he snapped upright.

Tracey ignored him through long practice. "What do you mean swapping jobs?"

"My new case—"

"The mystery man in the brown coat? The British one—oh, that makes sense." The leather-bound journal popped into her mind. The *missing* leather-bound journal. *Should I tell him that it's missing?* She thought of Doctor Chan and Tony's illegal hack of the mail system. *Urgh.* She should really tell her uncle they had found Doctor Chan. But she hadn't had a chance to talk to Tony yet. She was going to his house straight after here. Not telling Uncle Donny or Hank gave her a squinchy feeling, but it would be better to wait until she knew what Tony had found before she explained everything.

"You certainly are a detective, Tracey. How did you connect the client with my trip?" Hank asked leaning back in his chair.

She grinned at the compliment. "It was obvious my dear prince," she said, affecting her own version of a British accent. It was terrible and it made him laugh. "Uncle Donny said his client was from England and you're going to England. Doctor Chan wanted the book because he thought it was linked to the stones. So, who is the mystery man?"

"Funny you ask. At first, I thought you already knew him. The tip came from you," Uncle Donny said.

"Me?"

"A few weeks ago. We had a phone enquiry on the machine. You took the message and emailed it to me. I found it after the — uh — incident."

The incident was what Uncle Donny called it now. Tracey didn't like thinking about her uncle's kidnapping. Seeing him at the mercy of the Shadowman was not something she ever wanted to relive. The Shadowman had only taken her uncle to force Tracey to give up the Butterfly Stone. She had given up a different necklace instead and saved her uncle's life.

"His name is Frank Transcenni."

"How did he know about you?" she asked.

Uncle Donny shrugged. "My reputation clearly transcends borders."

Yeah, no. Not likely. So why had this Mr. Transcenni contacted him? Did he know about Tracey? Uncle Donny stared through the window at a bird tapping on the sill. She squinted. He wasn't supposed to put bird seed out there.

"Transcenni insisted the book he was searching for had been sent here by accident. He wants it back."

Did Hank know Tony had redirected the mail? Tracey couldn't tell them. If they didn't know yet, she would get Tony into trouble. Besides, the book *was* missing. "So, the book is important?"

"We know Doctor Chan wanted it badly. There must be a connection to the stones and with Doctor Chan in hiding, perhaps the book will give us some answers."

Blah, I should tell him. "Why are you going to England then, isn't the book here?"

Hank leaned forward, resting his elbows on his knees. "Donny will keep looking here and I'll investigate at the other end."

Tony was already mad at Tracey. If she told on him, he might never speak to her again. She decided not to mention it. If she and Tony could find Doctor Chan and the book, then she could give it to her uncle and not have to mention Tony's part in it. She changed the subject. "Something weird happened at school today."

"Oh?" Uncle Donny leaned forward, brow furrowed, scenting a mystery.

"Uncle Donny, can I use your tracking program to find a license plate number?"

"Sure—what for?"

She told them about the strange SUV. "It was so weird, but…"

"I don't like it," Hank said, standing. His expression darkened. "No driver should behave that way around a school."

"There was a Mage-kind in the SUV."

"What's the number?" Uncle Donny asked, spinning his chair back to his computer. He spun too far and had to tug himself back into place.

While he was focused on the search, Tracey pointed at Hank, whispering, "What do you know about all of this? Is there a stone in England?"

Hank lowered his voice. "Don't know for sure. Malden's checking into Transcenni's background. Don't worry, I'll be back soon." He shot her a big grin exposing his shiny white teeth.

"Aha! Found it—hmm."

Tracey jumped up and moved around Uncle Donny's desk to see his computer. "It says it belongs to a red Hyundai," she read aloud. "That's wrong. This one was a black SUV."

"Stolen number plates?" Hank straightened.

A cold chill pressed against Tracey's spine. "He was watching me."

Hank sucked on his teeth. "I don't like it. I'll call Malden. He needs to get back here so you have extra protection while I'm gone."

"You think it's Timothy? Is he back?"

"I don't know," Hank rubbed the side of his nose and peered at Uncle Donny. "Maybe I shouldn't go."

Tracey spun around. "No, don't be silly. You should go."

"That's right. She has me," Uncle Donny said.

Tracey shared a look with Hank. "And Agent Malden."

"Right, of course. And Agent Malden, when he gets here. In the meantime, I'll keep Tracey safe," Uncle Donny said.

Tracey shared another look with Hank.

"Right, well Tracey will be with you at the press junket where you can keep a close eye on her," Hank said.

Where she could watch her uncle make a fool of himself. This was going to be such a disaster. "Maybe, you should stay," she said to the prince. He laughed.

Tracey's cell phone beeped. She checked the display. "Oh fruit tingles. I'm supposed to go to Tony's tonight. Uncle Donny, do you need anything else?"

"Nah, go on kiddo. I'll finish up with Prince Henry."

Hank held out a hand to stop her from leaving. "The disguise spell, do you know what to do?"

"Yep. I've done one with Uncle Donny before. Piece of cake." Especially because this time it wouldn't be her inside the spell.

Hank was an actor. He could school his face into any expression. Right now, it was blank, but Tracey knew he wasn't reassured from the slight twitch of his nose. He knew Uncle Donny pretty well by now. He was right to be concerned. *Whose great idea was this anyway?*

"Before you go, I want to show you these." Hank lifted the suitcase onto Uncle Donny's desk. Raising the lid, he pointed to one of several small boxes. It was as large as his hand and had two straps dangling from either side. It looked a bit like her dad's old CD carrier that he kept in the car until they taught him to use the Bluetooth and his phone. "This blocks magic. Not to Donny. He'll still have access to his core. It's more like a... a giant silk sheet only a millimeter from his skin. All of his magic will be locked inside, invisible to anyone on the outside. Malden will remove his Mage-kind ID as well. We strap this to your uncle's waist and once it's on, he'll feel like a Norm to any outside Mage-kind. He won't be able to monitor the disguise spell though, so you'll have to make sure he's not leaking any magic."

"So that's how you did it," she said, and took the box from his hand. It was lighter than she had expected and only a little thicker than her pinky finger. Explosions went off in her brain. "You used this at camp, didn't you? That's why we failed the test. We... I was looking for magic. Not a Norm." *Urgh, I should have known. That's why Timothy picked Officer Jameson to possess in the first place. Who would suspect a Norm?* "How will the disguise spell work?"

"It's complicated. They can't suspect your uncle is Mage-kind." Hank removed the watch from his wrist. "This will be spelled. As an Object of Power, it will anchor the disguise spell. Rather than your uncle spelling himself with the disguise, I'll spell him with my likeness. The watch will hold the spell, but because your uncle's magic will be suppressed he won't sense it if the spell starts to weaken."

It sounded impossible. "Then how…"

He pointed to the last box. Inside it were two plastic rings that looked like plain gold bands. Dad's wedding ring looked exactly the same. "Tracey, you will wear these. They may fall off so wear them on your thumbs. They'll vibrate against your skin if the person you're speaking to is lying. Use them sparingly, because you'll need to cloak your own power too."

This was getting way too complicated. "It's not going to work," she said, shaking her head.

"It will, Tracey. Have a little faith."

"What excuse do I have for being at the press junket?"

"You'll be a fan who won a competition to spend the day with me. Lucky you!"

"Yeah, lucky." Tracey glanced at her phone again. "I've got to go or I'll miss the bus." She waved goodbye and raced out the door, making it to the bus stop with seconds to spare. Bounding up the steps, still puffing, she checked her phone again. No message. She clutched it to her chest and stared through the bus's grimy window. Three days. She and Laura had never gone three days without talking before. Her phone vibrated, tickling her fingers. It was Damian.

Hey, can't talk tonight. Family stuff. Can we catch up tomorrow?

Tracey sighed. Maybe he had changed his mind about liking her. She swiped away the tear welling in her eye. Everything was just so messed up. Hopefully Tony would know where Doctor Chan was and then everything could go back to normal.

Tales
by
The Lost

Following 219, Followed by 0
click **<broken link>** to follow The Lost!

Day 1105

[cont …]

I just thought, well, that I was gifted with my staff. My movements like a dance, smooth like water, gentle like a stream.

Mother has told me it is a spear, not a staff.

0 likes, 0 comments, 0 reshares
click **<broken link>** to like this post!:D

T.B.T.L.

15

When Tony opened his front door to let her in, a mouth-watering smell of roast chicken swept out to greet her. *Oh no, dinner time.* "Sorry I'm so late, Tony. Is it okay that I'm here?"

"Uh, yeah. Come in." He tugged her inside. "Dad, Tracey's here to talk about a school assignment," he called. Tracey peered around curiously, anxious to get a glimpse into Tony's home life. Maybe she could use this visit to show his parents she was not as scary as they thought she was.

Mr. O'Shae poked his head through the kitchen doorway. Thin blond hair was peppered with grey and stuck to his head in sweaty strands. "You've got twenty minutes." He focused on Tracey, staring at her for a long time without blinking. His thin lips seemed to disappear as his expression darkened. She checked her shield bubble to make sure it was holding. *Look innocent.* She forced a smile onto her face, faking energy she didn't have. Mr. O'Shae's expression didn't change. "Hello, Tracey. A bit late isn't it?"

"I was at Uncle Donny's," she excused. It didn't appease him. She had been wishing she could stay for dinner, but Mr. O'Shae's expression gave her a weird feeling in her tummy so she wasn't going to ask. He was probably still angry about Tony being questioned by Agent Malden. No one wanted their kids involved with the Mage-kind police. Her mom and dad used to tell Tracey and her siblings that if they didn't stop messing around and go to bed, they would call M-force! M-force locked up dangerous Mage-kind. And now Tracey knew M-force kept lists on underage Mage-kind who used magic outside the safe zones of home and camp. She knew because Agent Malden told her she was on it! And then there was the whole Timothy thing. Was that why Tony had to see a counselor? She rubbed her cold hands together and shot Mr. O'Shae an even bigger smile. "I won't be long. I promise."

"Okay then," he said. Spinning on a heel he returned to the kitchen.

Tony's front hall was really clean, if a little dark. Tracey realized with a start that this was the first time she had ever been inside Tony's new house. A little orange lamp on the side table provided enough light to see the ceiling was painted white and the cornices deep maroon. Along with the red wood slates over the small window, the hall felt smaller than it actually was. As Tracey followed Tony to his room, she noticed the red color went right through the house. Deep red curtains covered the windows and as she peered into the living room, she figured Mrs. O'Shae must really love lamps. Some were ornate, some were plastic, and some were really garish, but there were lamps everywhere.

Tony led Tracey to his room and shut the door. It was so quiet. Tracey's house echoed with the noise of too many people. Here, it was like a library. She expected Tony's mom to appear suddenly and shush them if they talked too loudly. She glanced around. No lamps in here. "Did you find Doctor Chan?"

He plonked onto his bed and gave her a tired grin. His bed was a double with a comic book covered comforter. "Oh, you have the new version!" she exclaimed, pointing to the game station on his desk. "I want dual screens too."

"Yeah, I got it last Christmas." Tony turned one of the screens around so she could see it. "I've tracked the virus to an IP address in Miltern Falls West. On Acacia Street."

"So, Doctor Chan is hiding in town? There are hotels on Acacia Street. Do you know which one he's in?"

"Working on it. He must have turned his computer off. I have to wait until it's on again before I can ping it."

"Never mind. This is great news. We can tell Agent Malden and get Doctor Chan arrested." That would be one less problem to deal with! She slumped onto Tony's mattress, suddenly wobbly.

Tony scratched his arms. He jumped off the bed and paced the floor.

"Trace, before you call Agent Malden..."

A shiver danced along Tracey's skin at his tone. "Tony? What is it? What have you done?"

He shook his head. "I didn't, uh, well I haven't done anything yet. Sort of."

She sighed. "Tell me."

"What if Doctor Chan has a stone?"

"What makes you think...? Tony, how do you...?" Her thoughts raced. Tony seemed to understand her question anyway.

"I've been watching him. Electronically. He never leaves Acacia Street. There's high security all over the place. Cameras and such. The stone Officer Jameson was carrying that night, the one that let Timothy possess his body, disappeared when Doctor Chan did. So, I wondered, what if he took it?"

"Agent Malden said they couldn't find it, so yeah, Doctor Chan might have it. That's why Agent Malden wants to catch Doctor Chan. But what if he lets Timothy possess him?"

"He wouldn't, would he?"

"Doctor Chan could literally be hiding Timothy." She shook her head. "Okay, yeah, you're right that *is* crazy. We'd better tell Agent Malden. Let them handle—"

Tony's lips quivered. He spun around and stared at the wall. "Tony?"

"It's Agent Malden."

"What about hm? Tony, what is it?"

"He's M-force. He has more resources than me, Trace. How did I find Doctor Chan first? And... my... ah, therapist, has been working on my nightmares. She's Mage-kind, Trace. She suggested meditations and readings, and I keep... stuff keeps coming up, all to do with Agent Malden. I know you like him, but what if... What if he's hiding something?"

Stunned silent, Tracey gaped like a fish searching for water only to find air. "You think Agent Malden is... what... a bad guy now? He saved us, Tony. He helped us defeat Timothy and save Sarah." The stone against Tracey's chest began to heat. "He did."

"Did he?"

She jumped to her feet. Tony stepped back, putting space between them. "Yes. You were there." *I don't believe this.* How could Tony suggest Agent Malden was... what? Lying to them?

"You weren't there. Not the whole time, Trace."

"What are you saying?"

"When you were hiding from Timothy in the woods, we were left fighting the Shadowman. Agent Striker had the Shadowman trapped. And then..."

"Then what?" Tracey whispered. She remembered the horrific sight of Agent Striker's mummified body laying where she had fallen protecting Tracey's friends. No wonder Tony was seeing a therapist.

"I don't... I don't remember. That's the thing, Tracey. I don't know what happened next," he fell onto his bed and buried his head in his hands.

So, this was what he had been stressing about? Why hadn't he told her? *Agent Malden?* No, the M-Force agent couldn't be the bad guy. "I don't understand what you're saying."

"I don't think Agent Malden is everything he says he is. Those tests at camp? He was supposed to be teaching us how to protect ourselves, wasn't he? And teaching you how to use your magic safely? What did you learn, Trace? Because I don't think I learned anything." His gaze locked onto his computer screens. "We need a real teacher."

"Like my grandma?"

He glanced at her and blinked. "What?"

"Grandma's a Significant, remember? She was teaching me and Sarah before you all came over for training." With Hank leaving town, Tracey would feel better if a strong Mage-kind was nearby. Especially since her mom was in the middle of a cluster migraine. "Maybe we should—" Sarah's voice popped into her head reminding her that Kylie Carter needed help. She paced to the wall and back to the bed. "Yeah, yeah we should do that."

"Do what? Speak English, Tracey."

She spun around. "I'm going to ask Grandma if she can come back and continue teaching me and Sarah, I'll add in Dave and Kylie. So if you want, you can come too."

Tony sat up. "Do you think she would? What if she has things to do and can't come?"

"I'm sure she'll come back if I ask. She's supposed to be looking for ways to help me with my shielding anyway. She can help everybody." Tracey's gaze darted to the closed bedroom door. "Do you think your parents will let you join us?"

Tony slumped back on his bed. "I dunno."

She sat down beside him. He flinched. Biting her lip to stop from snapping at him, she checked her magic and found it locked safety behind her shield. "Ask them if you can come over." She glanced at the door. "I'd better go. Your dinner is probably ready."

He followed her to the front door. Clanging pots and the sound of cutlery and china hurried their steps. "I'll ask," Tony promised. "In the meantime, I'll narrow down Doctor Chan's exact location."

"Say goodbye to your dad for me," she whispered at the door. Tony glanced over his shoulder and scrunched his face.

"Yeah." He closed the door.

Tracey turned around and stared out into the front yard. *Agent Malden is a bad guy? It's not possible.* Night had set in while she had been inside, bringing with it a chill that cooled her breath and raised goosebumps on her skin. Tony's suburban street was lit in yellow streetlight patches. The shadows in between seemed to move, creeping closer as she stared at them. She should call her dad to come pick her up. Tony's dad would be okay with her staying a little longer, probably.

Remembering the older man's stern expression and sharp stare, she decided against going back inside to ask. *I've got this.*

A breeze picked up, tugging on her jacket and making trees dance. Two bright orange lights appeared at the end of the street. She could hear the rumble of a car's engine, though the lights didn't move. Tracey squinted but couldn't make out the color of the car. Her pulse sped up. Thinking about the creepy black SUV Tracey spun around and ran up the porch steps. She froze in front of Tony's front door, hand raised, ready to knock. Tony's dad wouldn't be happy if she interrupted dinner. That look on his face freaked her out. He had never looked at her like that before — like she was bad. Tony had been weird inside the house too. He didn't... did he think she was bad? She could just stay up here on the porch until the car drove past and then go home. She turned to watch the car. It didn't move. *Who is in there?* Her palms grew damp the longer she waited.

Engine revving, it rumbled a challenge. Headlights, like piercing eyes, stared her down. The Butterfly Stone pulsed against her chest and fear bubbled up inside her body. She spun around to knock on the door and get help and then spun back to face the car. Tony was already traumatized, Tony's dad was mad at her. Everyone seemed upset with her and it wasn't fair. She had done nothing wrong. This vehicle was trying to scare her, or the driver was, but Tracey was tired of being scared. Tired of running all the time. Of being bullied for who and what she was. Well, she *was* Mage-kind and she *was* powerful. *Right pal, you just picked the wrong person to intimidate. You should be scared of me!* Tracey returned to the footpath, all of her attention focused on the headlights. She held her ground, thinned her shield bubble and drew enough power into her hands to make them glow. "Bring it on, pal."

Use the stone, Tracey. Stephanie whispered into her ear. *No, I can't.* She couldn't let Stephanie convince her. Agent Malden said not to use it, Mom and Dad too, but this could be life and death. Cars don't usually rev and drive straight at people. *Do it.* Her heart rate shot up as the vehicle revved loudly. A quick glance around confirmed she was alone, so there was no one she could suck magic from and hurt. She dropped her shield bubble. Energy sprang into her body as her exhaustion disappeared. The glow in her hands grew bright. The streetlight above her head popped and went dark.

The standoff held. Part of Tracey wanted the confrontation to hurry up, reveling in the power now spreading through her body. People were afraid of her—Laura, Tony, Dave Two.

Well they should be.

She didn't need help. She didn't need anyone. "Come on," she urged, stepping forward. Cold air tickled her nose. Weird, how a person could actually smell rain.

Sparing a little of her concentration, she threw her sensory ball up into the air and let it spread out over the front yard and down the street. The Butterfly Stone compensated for the use, pouring more magic into her body. Her blood thrummed with power. The sense net illuminated the car as though she had turned on a spotlight. "Come on!" she urged under her breath. The driver's window wound down with a whir. A dirty brown shadow spewed out and gathered in front of the car like a filthy cloud.

Her heart clenched. *The Shadowman!* But it was unlike the Shadowman. The creature appeared to be living sand, spinning rapidly upward into a mini tornado. Sand swirled and the sky turned dark. It was thick too, like a really bad fog. She couldn't see through it or past it. The scent of dirt and dry dead things filled her senses, getting up her nose and into the back of her throat. The air filled with its monstrous form. Even her ears itched. *OMG I'm going to suffocate.* "Help!"

Her cry was answered by the Butterfly Stone. Magic poured into Tracey and out into the sky pushing the dust away. It swirled away from her reach and coalesced into a wavering dervish. She felt it was watching her, waiting. Tracey's magic kept the area lit like a reflection off a mirror, but it couldn't last. The dirty tornado came straight for her moving like that cartoon devil on TV.

Tracey widened her stance and raised her hands feeling her magic pulse inside her. She chose a point of no return — the end of the O'Shae's driveway. And as if it guessed her thoughts, just before it reached that point, the Dust Devil stopped.

"Tracey!"

Twisting to keep most of her attention on the twirling sand, she glanced at Tony's front door. Tony and his dad stood on the porch, their raised hands alight with power. "Tracey, come inside," Mr. O'Shae yelled.

Disappointment flared inside her chest, sending heat into her face. *No, I want this.*

The Dust Devil retreated, spinning back to the car and poured inside the open window. With a squeal of tires the vehicle spun a tight circle, burning rubber onto the asphalt and fled into the night. Two red brake lights were all that could be seen of it until they faded too. Tracey's galloping pulse and short gasps kept her alert. She didn't lower her hands.

Her stomach twisted with disappointment. The Dust Devil had to be Timothy. He had come back.

"Tracey. Inside, now!" Mr. O'Shae ordered. Letting her arms fall, Tracey walked backward until she reached the porch steps. Heaving a reluctant sigh, she turned her back on the street and raised her shield bubble, her body sagging with the sudden muting of her energy.

"I should go home," she said, not moving any closer to the door.

Mr. O'Shae shook his head. "Come inside, Tracey. I'm calling your parents and Agent Malden."

Tony wouldn't meet her stare. "Sorry Tony," she whispered.

"You're okay," he said.

She wasn't sure that she was. Had Tony heard her urge the Dust Devil to attack? What would he think of her if he knew she had wanted it to happen, that she'd wanted a fight? She followed them inside where they all stood in the front hall. Not a word was spoken. *Awkward.* Now she had to stay where she wasn't wanted, with people who were afraid of her power. *Just great.*

Though they were expecting it, the knock on the door startled them all. Mr. O'Shae appeared as relieved as Tracey. "Thank you for your help tonight, Mr. O'Shae. Tony, I'll see you tomorrow."

"Yep," Tony said, a sad smile dusting his lips.

When Mr. O'Shae opened the door Tracey's eyes popped wide. "Grandma?"

As she turned to say goodbye to Tony, the front door was shut in her face. Tracey bit back a nasty comment and threw her arms around the old lady standing on the porch. Almost the same height as Tracey, Grandma was a little heavier and a lot stronger. She nearly squeezed all of the air out of Tracey's lungs with her hug. Over Grandma's shoulder Tracey searched the empty street for evil cars and dangerous dust clouds. "What are you doing here?" she asked. Her heart thumped. "Do you have another memory for me?"

Grandma shook her head, her pink curls frozen in place as she peered through her glasses at Tracey. "Your dad called."

"Why?"

"Your mom's still unwell, honey. I'm going to help out for a bit." She smoothed her wrinkled hands over her hand-knitted hot pink cardigan.

Tracey's voice fell. "Is she really sick? I thought it was just a migraine."

Grandma didn't answer, she simply shooed Tracey toward the car. Tracey swallowed around her suddenly dry mouth. "How long are you staying for?" she asked.

"For as long as you need me," Grandma promised.

Tales
by
The Lost

Following 219, Followed by 0
click **\<broken link\>** to follow The Lost!

Day 1105

[cont …]

I have discovered they have been training me to fight. To track. To kill.

Why? I am still a child. I should be focused on my schooling, on my future.

But what future could I have had?

0 likes, 0 comments, 0 reshares
click **\<broken link\>** to like this post!:D

T.B.T.L.

16

Tracey slumped in the passenger seat, playing immediately with the wireless connection on her phone to send a playlist to her grandma's sound system. Grandma flicked it off with a touch to her steering wheel. "Tell me about the monster you saw." She stayed quiet as Tracey spoke, not even humming encouragement, examining the road ahead, eyes flicking occasionally to check her mirrors.

Inhaling the comforting scent of lavender, Tracey spoke about the Dust Devil and when Grandma continued to stay quiet, went on to complain about Tony's parents treating her weird and making Tony see a psychiatrist. She blurted out about her fight with Laura, only she didn't admit she started it, twisting her hands in her lap and biting her lips. After a moment of silence, Tracey took note of her surroundings. She didn't recognize anything. "Grandma, where are we?"

The woman's smile could barely be seen inside the dark car. "You needed to talk."

Tracey rubbed the palm of her slightly warmer left hand with the fingers of her right. "Did you find a way to help my magic?"

"Honey, I've only been gone a week."

"Grandma?"

"Possibly. I have a new exercise for you to try. It encourages a different focus and—"

"It's gotta be better than Agent Malden's idea."

"Your shield?"

"All the time. I'm so tired. And I can't keep it up at night so I'm not even doing it all the time anyway. Can't you put a spell on me or—"

"The problem is with how your magic works, Tracey. We need to figure that out first."

"What's the council?" Tracey blurted. She pulled her sleeves down over her wrists.

"What? Who said anything …? What council?"

With that answer, Tracey knew her grandma wouldn't be telling her the truth. "Agent Malden said… well, he let it slip but then he wouldn't tell me anything about it. He seemed, I don't know… scared. Who would an M-Force agent be scared of?"

"Honey, let's not talk about that."

"But Grandma—"

"Tracey."

"What about my magic?" Tracey stretched the material of her shirt further, twisting it around her hands.

"The shield is a good start. But it's not a long-term solution. We'll try the exercise I found and go from there."

"Could you teach all of us? Tony, Dave, and Sarah too, like before?" Tracey paused. "There's another girl, um, a new friend of Sarah's. Her name is Kylie. She's uh, a bit like Dave."

"Anger or fear?"

"Anger." Tracey huffed out a breath. "Ugh, it might be good for me too," she admitted.

"What about your work for Donald?"

"I'll figure something out, oh um, except Hank—Prince Henry—gave me and Uncle Donny a mission, so I'll have to help him with that first. I'll fit it all in somehow."

"Anything else?"

Tracey giggled. She couldn't help it. "How long have you got?"

"As long as you need."

"We failed the tests Agent Malden gave us at camp." Her chest grew tight as she told her grandma how awful it had been. Failure gave her aches in her belly and her in chest. It made her hands sweat and her head pound. She didn't mention her suspicions about Agent Malden. She only had them because Tony put them into her head in the first place. He had to be wrong. Agent Malden wasn't a bad guy.

"Honey, failure is the way life teaches us to improve. It's how we deal with failure that makes us strong or weak. When your sister was a baby, did she give up walking when she fell over?"

"No. She got back up."

"Right. If babies gave up when they failed they'd never learn how to walk. When you first became aware of your magical core and started using magic, did you succeed the first time you tried?"

Tracey snorted.

"Did you give up?"

"No, I kept practicing."

"Right. Failure is how we learn. Practice is how we get better."

Looking at it that way her problems didn't seem all that bad. "So, I keep trying?"

"Yes."

Her thoughts, once settled, rapidly changed direction again. "Grandma, I've been looking into the story of the stones."

The ticking of the car blinker signaled Grandma pulling over. She stopped the car and let out a long breath. Warm wrinkled hands wrapped around Tracey's clammy fingers. "Didn't Agent Malden and Prince Henry say they were going to look into that?"

"I feel like I'm being left out of things. Things I'm supposed to be involved in. Stephanie is inside the Butterfly Stone. She's in my head. I should be looking for the stones. I'm—itchy. I need to do something and I'm not doing anything."

Grandma *tsked* softly. "You're still young."

Tracey snatched her hands back. "I had to fight Timothy, Grandma. I'm the one wearing Stephanie's stone. Timothy wanted *me* to unlock it. I'm involved in all of this and I don't think it matters how old I am. It didn't stop him before did it?" She gritted her teeth, her heart pounding. *Doesn't Grandma understand how screwed up everything is?*

"You're right, honey. I'm so sorry. You're young and it hurts my heart that you are going through this. I fear it is only going to get more dangerous, not less."

"A Vision?"

"Perhaps."

Tracey wished she knew what Grandma could see in her face or her aura or whatever it was her elder was trying to read. "Is there another memory-dream of Stephanie's you can show me?"

Grandma shook her head. "Only when the time is right."

"Oh, come on," Tracey moaned.

"I wish I could. I want to show the dreams to you, but whatever Stephanie did when she passed the memories to your nana stayed with them."

"How do you know when the time is right?"

"I just know." Grandma took the car out of park and pulled onto the road, not saying anything for the rest of the drive home. As they drove into the driveway Grandma spoke, her voice filling the car with soft tones and love. "You have a lot on your mind, honey. I think you need to slow down a little. Take one problem at a time. Start by being honest with your friends and with yourself. Miscommunication is the seed to many a war. I'm sure your fears can be laid to rest by talking to your friends. Be honest with how you feel."

"Thanks, Grandma." Tracey's skin tingled when they stepped inside the front door, the silence grated against her already sensitive nerve endings. "Where is everybody?"

"In their rooms I suppose," Grandma said pulling off her shoes and stepping into her slippers.

Since when? Home was a madhouse — a deafening one. At the moment, it was as still as a graveyard and reminded Tracey of Tavel House. Memories of Nana intruded into Tracey's thoughts. Mom's headaches. Nana's dementia. There was no need to panic, right? Mom's perfectly fine.

Isn't she?

The Butterfly Stone vibrated like a text message alert on her cell phone. "I'm pretty tired. I think I'll go to bed. Are you going to tell Mom and Dad about the Dust Devil?"

Grandma hummed. "Right now, your mom is in a lot of pain and your dad is worried about her. He's also looking after all of you kids. We will tell them, but perhaps not right now. It will only worry them. I'll call

Agent Malden tonight."

Ha! So much for always telling the truth. Tracey kissed Grandma's soft papery cheek and trudged to her room. She plugged in her phone to charge overnight outside her room—Dad's new rule—and plonked down onto her bed. She pulled the stone from beneath her shirt and stared at the butterfly painted on it. "Stephanie?"

In an instant she stood in that familiar all white room. The two weird shapes, a square and a diamond, undulated in front of Tracey in flashes of red and blue.

"Why are we playing this game? I know it's you, Stephanie," Tracey said.

"Are you so sure?" A voice said out of the nothingness.

Tracey pondered that. While the voice was that of a British woman, it didn't sound like Stephanie. Tracey's eyes sprang wide. If it wasn't Stephanie talking to her, then who was it?

The voice answered her unasked question. "While an impression of Stephanie is contained within the stone you hold, I—we—are so much more."

It was the clearest answer Tracey had ever gotten from the stone and yet she was more confused than ever. "What do you want?" she asked.

"What do *you* want?"

Seriously? "Are we really doing this again? I want to talk to Stephanie."

"Why?"

"I want to know about Timothy and the stones. I want to know why I can't see all of the memory-dreams she left behind and ask her why she left them for me?"

"Why do you think she did?"

Ugh! Impossible. "Send me back so I can go to bed." Tracey's sigh disappeared into the silence. Everywhere she looked was white, her voice continued to echo around her and the only objects she could see were those strange red and blue shapes. Tracey bounced from foot to foot determined to out silence the silence, but the urge to make noise was growing inside her. A soft tune like the sound of a lone piano played just out of the periphery of her hearing. A song once known, now unremembered.

Tracey focused on it and tried to bring the music into being. She couldn't grasp the melody.

"I don't understand," she said at last.

The shapes laughed.

Fury swelled inside her chest. "Stop laughing at me!"

"You are filled with questions."

"No kidding." Tracey glanced at her feet and debated sitting down. There was no floor, only white stretching away beneath her. She stood on something, she just couldn't see what it was. In the end she remained standing.

"What are you afraid of?"

Why did everyone keep asking her that question? "Nothing. Everything. I don't know." She imagined stamping her feet or puffing magic out of her chest to push the shapes away. In a blink she found herself back inside her bedroom. The silent house burrowed into Tracey's mind. A thick, heavy sound as if she wore noise-cancelling headphones. Humming to check she hadn't gone deaf, she lay back on her bed. What was it Grandma said? Be honest with herself? The shapes kept asking what she wanted and what she was afraid of. She shrugged. "I don't know."

"Tracey?"

That was Mom's voice. Tracey bolted out of her bedroom running straight to her mom and dad's room. "Mom?" she whispered cracking the bedroom door open. She heard a mumble and poked her head inside. It was pitch-dark. "Mom?"

Mom said migraines made noises twice as loud and twisted into the side of her skull like a sharp knife. Tracey tiptoed into the bedroom, being careful to close the door softly but securely behind her. Mom and Dad's bed was against the back wall. It was only a few steps forward, but if Tracey went too far to her right, she would hit the bedside table. She shuffled to the bed and found Mom's hand. It was icy cold. "Hey, Mom. Feeling any better?"

"Not really, honey. Is everything okay? I... I feel like something is upsetting you."

"It's fine, Mom."

"Don't lie to me, Tracey, I can feel—"

"Mom, don't worry. Just concentrate on getting better."

"What about Sarah and the boys?"

"Grandma's here to look after Dad and the boys. I'll keep an eye on Sars. Just rest." Wiping a hand over her damp eyes, Tracey smiled, though she doubted her mom could see it. The room was clean and cold, like Dad had turned the air-conditioner up. There was a faint flowery smell that made her nose twitch in a sneeze that wouldn't come out. She also made out the scent of cut apples. It was a good sign if Mom had tried to eat something.

Her mom's magic pulsed low and heavy, practically filling the room. She must be in a lot of pain to lose her control of her magic like that.

"Want some help?"

"Could you, hun?"

The pleading tone broke Tracey's heart. She laced her fingers in her mom's hands and knelt beside the bed. Mom's sour breath caressed her face in little puffs. Tracey shut her eyes on the dark room and pushed her worries out of her mind. Focusing on her mom's breathing, Tracey tapped into her own core to draw out a little magic. It flowed down her arms and into her mom's skin, warming her body with little pulses. Tracey pushed out with her senses until she could feel the entire room. She didn't know how else to help. "Stephanie?"

Tracey?

"Can you help my mom?"

A little. There is something… I …

"Stephanie?"

She is in a great deal of pain. Sleep is an important healer. Allow me.

Tracey relaxed and let Stephanie take control. Tracey was pushed to the back of her own mind and watched through her eyes she was unable to control as a glow of white energy filled her hands where she held her mom's fingers. Tracey's mouth moved as Stephanie's presence filled her body. Mom's breathing grew deeper, heavier, as tension left her muscles. In Tracey's mind she imagined the room had become a giant pillow, thick and soft and comfortable. Suddenly she could move again as Stephanie released control. The Butterfly Stone was cold and lifeless against her chest once more.

"Thank you," Tracey whispered.

It is not a cure.

"Mom always gets migraines," Tracey told her ancestor. "But thanks for helping." After a moment spent watching her mom sleep, Tracey crept out of the room.

"Mom's sleeping," she whispered, spying Dad and Grandma waiting for her in the hall. They headed downstairs. The smell of burnt toast grew with each step closer to the kitchen.

"We felt the magic," Dad said when they reached the ground floor. "What happened? Where did you learn how to do that?"

"Internet," Tracey answered. Grandma's sharp gaze burrowed into Tracey's shields. She pushed back making Grandma scowl. Dad handed Tracey a plate with some toast on it. "I ate at Tony's," she said, but she took the plate anyway. "Thanks."

Dad pointed, staring hard at Tracey. "Did you use the stone?"

"Just to help her sleep. Why are the migraines so bad this time?"

"Tracey, I don't want you using that stone," he said.

"Mom's hurting. I just wanted to help."

"I'm taking her to the doctor in the morning," Dad told Grandma over Tracey's head.

Grandma sucked on her false teeth. "I'll be here, Tommy. The kids will be fine. I promised to help Tracey with her magic, though I'm not sure I'm truly needed. She seems to be managing quite well on her own." As she said it, Grandma shot Tracey a squinted side-eyed glance that Tracey pretended not to see.

"Dad, can I invite Tony, Dave, and Sarah's new friend Kylie over to practice with me and Grandma tomorrow night?"

Dad's frown took up half of his face. "I don't want that many people in the house while your mom is unwell."

"Tommy, I'll ensure they stay outside. We do need to work on Tracey's shielding and you know that's always easier in a group."

"I don't think Beth will be comfortable," he said. Tracey didn't like the worried expression on her dad's face. He shouldn't look like that. Ever.

"Please Dad, Sarah will be with us. The boys have footy training tomorrow night and Peter will be out driving." *Probably.*

"All right. But promise me you won't make too much noise."

"You bet," Tracey said. She wrapped her arms around him and buried her nose in his pullover. He returned the hug and rocked a little. Held tightly in Dad's arms, Tracey felt safe at last and let her mind go blank. When she opened her eyes, Grandma was sitting on the sofa watching them, her lips upturned in a little smile. The elderly woman looked smaller, frailer than Tracey had ever seen her. Worry did that to people — turned them into shadows of themselves. Dad hadn't even asked Tracey what had happened at Tony's house. She realized Grandma was right about not telling Dad. He had too much to worry about already. She wouldn't say anything. It was their secret to keep. She tightened her grip on her dad's waist and rested her head on his shoulder.

Tales
by
The Lost

Following 219, Followed by 0
click **<broken link>** to follow The Lost!

Day 1105

[cont …]

I could not work in a Mage-kind career,

a Mage-kind boss would never remember

they had hired me. And I could never

work for a Norm. A Mage-kind forced to

only associate with Norms? Untenable.

0 likes, 0 comments, 0 reshares
click **<broken link>** to like this post!:D

T.B.T.L.

17

Branches like fingers reached for the stars from the tree that stretched high above Tracey's head. She tightened her legs around the trunk and clutched the scratchy bark tighter. Sharp pieces dug into her hands. Blood pounded beneath her skin and her chest was so tight, it was as though she couldn't expand her lungs properly. Spots bounced in her vision. Swiping a hand over her eyes she blinked and resumed searching the ground below. *Where is it?*

A growl answered her question. Movement drew her frightened gaze to the beast prowling at the base of the tree. It clawed, tearing great chunks of bark from the tree—the only thing keeping her out of its reach. It let out an almighty roar and leaped, digging its claws into the tree and slid back down stripping her safety away. She felt every tremor and shudder through the trunk and bit back a scream. The monster's next leap sent her scrambling further up into the branches, slipping a little as her sweaty hands desperately clutched the wood tight. Two glowing orange eyes sent her heart into her throat. She could just make out a muscular feline body in the shadows. A tiger. The creature opened its mouth wide, exposing wicked, sharp teeth.

"It's coming."

Tracey bolted upright. Darkness surrounded her, but she knew without turning on the light that she was safe in her bed. Heart pounding, she scrunched her eyes, clamping down on the tears welling beneath her eyelids. The tiger growled in her mind.

"It's coming."

Tales
by
The Lost

Following 219, Followed by 0
click <broken link> to follow The Lost!

Day 1105

[cont …]

So, what would I do? Work alone?

Live alone? It is as though

I would be an outcast.

Unknown, unremembered.

0 likes, 0 comments, 0 reshares
click <broken link> to like this post!:D

T.B.T.L.

18

Unable to sleep, Tracey grabbed her tablet. She played around on social media for a while and then tapped into her favorite search engine — the M-Net, the Mage-kind portal on the internet. She closed her eyes and opened her heart to the Butterfly Stone, asking for information on the stones of power as she typed in her search. *What had Grandma said? Be honest.*

Tracey's desire was to find the stones. Closing her eyes again, she focused on that wish and tapped on a random page. Her gaze was drawn to the third hyperlink. Another tap brought up a blog. The last post was dated several years ago. Disappointed, Tracey was about to close out of the page when her eyes focused on another link embedded in the text.

```
            Tales
             by
          The_Lost
```

An anonymous blog? Her skin tingled as she tapped on the link. The Butterfly Stone pulsed hot against her skin. She pressed her hand against it. "Shhh."

```
    The Tiger's Eye is what they call it. Orange
in appearance, the dark shadow in the stone gives
the appearance of an eye. Imbued with power, the
stone is cursed, and with good reason. It is said
to bring bad luck to those who possess it. You
```

```
might wonder how I know this? The Tiger's Eye
belongs to my family and it has brought us noth-
ing but heartache and pain. When it was lost to
us...Well, anyway, I am searching for it because
even without the stone the curse continues to
haunt us. Any information I find vanishes without
a trace. As soon as I post this, it will be lost,
deleted, or the link broken, never to be seen
again. That is my family's curse. To be forgot-
ten. Invisible. Unremembered.
    I will keep trying. I must keep trying. The
Tiger's Eye can restore my family name and allow
us, at last, to be remembered. If I do not
hope—then all hope is lost. For I am lost and
that is how you shall know me.
```

Tiger's Eye? Her dream! Tracey jumped to her feet and nearly shouted in glee, only remembering it was the middle of the night at the last second. The Tiger's Eye had to be one of the stones of power. If the curse keeping the stone hidden worked like the spell on the Butterfly Stone, now that she knew what to search for, she should be able to find more references to it. *Right?*

Her gaze drifted to the name at the end of the post. *The_Lost.* Who was The_Lost? If the curse was as powerful as The_Lost said it was, then would Tracey forget what she had just read? She copied the story onto the notepad near her wrist, then popped open her bedroom door to unplug her phone from the charger and copied the website link into an email that she then sent herself. With her purple pen she scribbled the link on her hand. What else could she do? She dialed Tony's number, but he didn't answer. *Tiger's Eye, Tiger's Eye.* How long would it take to forget? Magic was magic, and magic was powerful, so who knew?

She dialed Grandma's cell phone.

"Tracey? Why are you calling me in the middle of the night? I'm in bed."

"Grandma, help. I found information on the next stone, but there's a curse on it—a forgetting curse. I need to remember."

"Remember what, dear?"

"I..." *Fruit tingles, what was it?* "The stone."

"What is it called?"

"Ah..." Tracey's gaze dropped to the tablet. The screen was blank. "Honey?"

She stared at her hand. There were two words written on her skin, but her mouth froze, unable to voice them. "Ugh."

"Tracey?"

"I just read about it, I just—"

"Tracey listen to me. Drop your shield and open up to your magic. The memory spell I used with your nana, do you remember it?"

"I... ah..." The words were right there. Why couldn't she make sense of them? Animal? Face? Ugh, what was it? Purple ink smeared across her palm. Grandma's voice faded. Tracey dropped the cell phone, her hand clutching at the Butterfly Stone and called to Stephanie.

The white room appeared. "Help me."

"With what?" Stephanie stood before her in a long white dress with puffy sleeves. She waited patiently while Tracey searched her memory.

"I... ugh." *Nothing.* "I... I..."

"Tracey?" Stephanie's brow furrowed.

"Something I was supposed to remember." Tracey scrubbed at the purple stain on her hand.

"Tracey?"

"It's gone. I... never mind."

Tracey blinked herself out of the white room and stared at her phone. Who had she been talking to?

Tales

by

The Lost

Following 219, Followed by 0
click <broken link> to follow The Lost!

Day 1105

[cont …]

So instead, I am to be a hunter.

That is what they are. My family.

Hunters.

I never knew…

0 likes, 0 comments, 0 reshares
click <broken link> to like this post!:D

T.B.T.L.

19

Dragging her eyes open, the green glow of her LED clock burned into her sleep-fogged mind. 6:52 a.m. Eight minutes until her alarm went off. Tracey smooshed her face into her pillow and tugged her blankets tighter around her body. *I don't want to get up.* If only she could freeze time and make Friday cease to exist. *How can I pretend everything is normal?* She rolled onto her back and stared up at the ceiling. She was sick of being confused. All she had were questions and no answers. She was tired of being angry all of the time, and most of all she was completely over worrying about everything. *I'm just a kid! This is grown up stuff and I don't wanna be grown up yet.*

So, what *did* she want?

Tracey glanced back at her alarm clock and waited for another minute to tick over. "I don't want to be angry or worried or confused anymore." She sat up and let her bedsheets fall to her lap.

Enough feeling sorry for herself. Nobody has any answers. Last night, she had seen how helpless Dad was and how Grandma didn't know what to do. It was time for Tracey to find her own answers, starting with her friends and why they were acting so squirrely around her.

She reached the bathroom first, a minor miracle, and took it as a sign her day was off to a great start. Texting Laura, she made her way downstairs. We need to talk, meet me at our spot. Something firm stopped her progress. Peter grinned, his arm held out in front of her.

"What do you want?" she grumbled, eying the giant pimple on the side of his nose. *Yowza!* She blinked, unable to tear her gaze away. What had she asked? The sight of that volcano of white ready to erupt scattered her thoughts.

"Grandma will lose her mind if she sees you texting and walking, especially on the stairs."

Tracey rolled her eyes, though she knew Peter was right. It was bad enough that they had to charge their phones overnight outside their rooms—Dad's idea—but she could lose her phone privileges entirely if she was caught texting and walking. "Did you see Mom?"

"Yeah, she looked better. Said she slept well last night."

Tracey's shoulders straightened. A grin bubbled at her lips. "How's everyone else?"

"No one wants to go to school," he said, shifting to the side to continue up the stairs.

"What else is new?" she called after him. Tracey poked her head around the kitchen doorway to examine the lay of the land. Charlie ate from his bowl like a robot, his eyes barely cracked open. Simon sat beside him, a reversed mirror, hair sticking up in all directions. Sarah was …

"What are you wearing?" The question popped out before Tracey could slam her mouth shut. *Fruit tingles!*

Sarah glared at her from under straight bangs. Her long-sleeved, button-down shirt was fully buttoned, even at her wrists, and her jeans looked … ironed? Tracey scrubbed her eyes and blinked—nope, nothing changed. "Grandma said I look nice." Sarah's frown was epic, oozing displeasure.

Tracey glanced at her own wrinkled, three-day-old jeans and superhero shirt. *Grandma won't try to dress me, will she?* Sarah read Tracey's mind and her glare turned into a grin. Tracey sighed. "Grandma's going to work with us after school. We're starting the training group again. Do you want to invite Kylie to join us?"

Sarah shoved a spoonful of white mush into her mouth and talked around it. "Yeah, I'll ask her."

Tracey's phone danced a jig in her pocket. She covered it as Grandma walked around the bench island and put a bowl down in front of her. Milky oats. She bit back a groan. "Porridge?"

"It's good for you, dear. Spoonful of honey, Sarah." Grandma smiled and gestured for them to eat. "Oh, and Tracey, I have your school clothes hanging in the living room." Tracey moaned. Sarah cackled madly and shoveled another spoonful of porridge into her mouth.

Tugging on her shirt collar didn't stop the itch. If anything, it made it worse. Tracey couldn't figure out what Grandma had done to her clothes. Her usually soft emerald shirt was hard and scratchy, and her skin felt raw where she kept scratching her neck. Her cell phone lay in her lap. She had received a text message from Agent Malden but nothing from Laura. Her day had started off so well, but after Grandma's interference it had gone downhill and was still rolling.

Hear you had some trouble last night, call me.

Tracey kicked her feet against the stone fence and shifted uncomfortably, a pebble poking into her butt. Suppressing a yawn, she stared down the path hunting for her friend. Any minute now the bell was going to ring. Laura wasn't coming.

She pressed a finger to her phone to wake it up and checked the time. Approaching footsteps snapped her head up, a smile on her lips to greet her friend. Her body deflated. She could almost hear the blart of air, like blowing a raspberry or letting air out of a balloon. It wasn't Laura. She cracked a smile. Damian Carter. It wasn't totally bad. "Hi," she said.

"Hi. Can I sit?"

She hesitated too long. "Ah…"

"Sorry I—uh, never mind." Damian turned away.

Tracey jumped off the stone fence. "Don't go, Damian, I'm waiting for my friend Laura."

His face scrunched. "Does she know you're waiting for her?"

"Yes."

"Oh," he tilted his head and bit down on his bottom lip.

"What?" Her heart sank a little as she stared into his handsome face. He wouldn't meet her eyes.

"I just saw Laura with Jilly Cho. They were headed into the library with your friend Jonny."

Tracey clamped her eyes shut. *Traitors!* All she said out loud was "Oh." So much for having a great day. All her positive energy vanished in a snap. "You can sit down I guess."

"I'm sorry. Do you want to be alone?"

"Nah, its fine." He sat down beside her and the smells of sugar and cinnamon wafted off his shirt. "Any further ideas about—"

"—the introduction? Nope. But that's not why I came over," he said.

Her heart lurched. "Oh?"

"Kylie texted me about Sarah's invite. I wanted to thank you."

Her whole body flamed. *Oh, don't let my face turn hot rod red.* He stared at her like she was a superhero who had saved his life. "I…"

His eyes sparkled like stars. Was it her imagination? No, they were actually sparkling. "Well, I just… ah…" *What am I doing?* Grabbing her bag, she yanked out several pages covered in drawings.

"What's this?" he asked, looking adorably confused.

"Some magic games. For Kylie. You could, uh, play them with her. They're pretty easy. You don't have to be Mage-kind to help her play."

As he took the papers from her hand, his fingers brushed hers sending a tingle up her spine.

Peering up at him, she offered, "If you need any help with them let me know."

"Of course." His smile was like staring directly into the sun. He swayed toward her and she breathed in his sweet scent. Her eyes fluttered closed. After a moment of silence, she popped her eyes open. He had straightened and was staring down the path.

Her tongue glued to the inside of her suddenly dry mouth as a wave of embarrassment flowed over her body. At the same time, she felt a shiver of cold pass over her skin. She peered around, expecting to find that creepy SUV circling the school.

"Tracey?" Damian's voice sounded far away, even though he was sitting right next to her.

She heard him, but couldn't shake the feeling something was coming. Something bad. Touching the Butterfly Stone nestled under her shirt she thinned her shield bubble and expanded her senses.

"Tracey?"

"Shhhh." The air felt dry, silent… "Something's wrong."

"Wh—"

She silenced him with a look.

Her hair flopped across her face. She whipped it back and sniffed. She could smell dirt. Springing to her feet, Tracey tugged back her hair with one hand and searched the school ground. The bell to signal the start of the school day blared, startling her and she almost dropped her phone. "I—uh…"

"Tracey?" Now Damian sounded annoyed.

The feeling was gone. She spun in a circle, but nothing caught her attention. *Weird.*

"We'd better get going," Damian said, giving her side-eye.

"Yeah. I… I just have to make a call."

"I'll wait."

"No, no. It's fine. You go. I'll be there in a minute." He walked away. Her skin prickled when she caught him glance back twice.

Agent Malden answered on the first ring. "Tell me about last night."

"Grandma called you." Of course she did. "What did she say?"

"I'd rather hear it from you," he said.

Tracey detailed as much as she could remember of last night's confrontation with the Dust Devil. He asked her for details. It reminded her of her interrogation about the Shadowman. "Smells like dirt and it moves like a tornado. Not a man shape, um, unnatural temperature. Gritty, creepy feel—like darkness—and thinking… um… intent."

"Malevolent?"

"Yeah, that's the word. Is it Timothy?" she asked.

"I don't know. From what you're describing this creature is of a different nature to the Shadow."

"It didn't feel like the Shadowman," she told him.

"Go on."

She pictured the Dust Devil. "It smelled weird, all wrong. Not like the Shadowman at all."

"Like what?"

"Steam off an iron, like when my mom does the laundry." She stood up and made her way toward the school buildings. "If it's not Timothy, then who is it?" She continued talking, more to herself than the man on the other end of her cell phone. "If it *is* someone else, how do they know about me? If Timothy isn't controlling the Dust Devil, then who is?"

Agent Malden couldn't give her any answers. "I'll look into it."

Tracey ended the call and raced into class. *Who is after me now?*

She was still thinking about the question on her walk home from school. Dave Two was waiting in her front yard, his bike tossed on the ground. "So, your grandma is teaching us now? Why can't you do it?"

His teeth were bared in a snarl. Angry pulses of energy cycled around his body. He looked the same as always, decked out in his team jersey and torn jeans. She examined his arms and neck for bruises. There was nothing obvious. His scowl deepened as he realized what she was doing. Tony appeared at the gate. His gaze swung from them to the front door where Grandma stood watching them. She was in her favorite walking clothes — grey slacks and blue cardigan.

Tracey led the way through the house and into the back yard. Sarah sat on the back porch. She jumped to her feet and gestured to the blond Mage-kind girl hovering in her shadow. "This is Kylie."

Kylie mashed her fingers together and grumbled what might have been hello. Her brows were drawn together, her mouth pressed into an unhappy line.

The group mumbled hello. Grandma strode past them and into the middle of the yard. "Sit in a circle please." They all plonked down on the grass. "I'm going to talk to you about anger," Grandma said.

Before Tracey could blink, Kylie's face became thunderous. "Way to be obvious."

She glared at Sarah, who wilted under the harsh look.

"I didn't say anything."

Dave tilted his head and pointed to his own chest. "Not everything is about you, kid."

"Kid?" Kylie snapped.

"Hey," Tracey inserted herself into the argument before it could escalate. "Let Grandma speak."

"Thank you, Tracey." The elderly woman remained standing, forcing them all to look up. Tracey scratched her inside elbow. Kylie and Dave were not the only ones with anger issues. Well, probably not Tony. Grandma had to be talking about Tracey. "What does your body do when you feel angry?" Grandma asked.

No one spoke. If they felt anything like Tracey, then they didn't want to draw attention to their own weakness. Guess she would have to be the bigger student. "I lose my magic," she said. Kylie's eyebrows rose. *Yup even me.*

"Right, but why? What is your body doing?" Grandma encouraged.

Stephanie whispered into Tracey's ear. *Anger is sweet. It is adrenaline. It strengthens you, makes you fearless. Anger can be focused into a scalpel to cut into the heart of any matter.*

Tracey shook the voice away muttering, "Not now." Grandma was still talking and Tracey realized she had missed another question.

"—blood pumping in your chest and your ears, exactly right, Sarah."

"What about breathing?" Kylie offered, her voice noticeably softer.

"Yes, certainly. What happens to your breathing?" Grandma asked, smiling at the girl.

"My chest gets tight, like I can't get any air. I feel faint, but not. Like I'm really focused, but I can't see anything."

"I get really hot," Sarah added, sharing a look with Kylie. Both girls were sitting scrunched up like balls, their arms wrapped around their knees. Dave snorted.

Grandma eyed him with an intensity that made him shift on his butt cheeks. "Everyone has a right to their opinion. Tell us about your anger?"

He seemed to realize he had annoyed Grandma and tore his gaze away to stare down at the back fence. Silence fell over the group as they waited for him to speak. When he didn't, Sarah snorted in retaliation.

"So, what do we do about it?" Tracey asked.

Tony opened his mouth, but no sound emerged.

"What do you think you can do?" Grandma asked.

"I don't know, that's why I'm asking," Tracey tore a piece of grass from beneath her leg. She twisted it between her fingers.

Grandma didn't answer. Tracey figured she wanted them to come up with the answer on their own. It was infuriating.

Clearly Dave felt the same. "How do I know? That's ..." he huffed out a breath and flopped onto his back.

Tracey leaned forward, elbows on her knees. She thought about Stephanie. "Grandma, why does anger affect our magic?" Grandma speared her with a sharp look, like she was trying to dig around inside Tracey's brain. "And don't ask me what I think."

Everyone laughed, even Tony. Tracey shot a glance at Kylie. Yup, a tiny smile. Grandma gestured for them to stand up. As Tracey did, a pressure pushed against her skin. "Whoa!" She strengthened her shield bubble against the strange pressure, unsure where it was coming from. Tony, Dave, and Sarah raised their shields. Kylie's appeared a second later. The downward pressure became heavier, harder. Tracey's concentration faltered when a piercingly loud squeal erupted inside her head. She slammed her hands over her ears to block out the sound. Her shield bubble popped. The noise grew louder.

Stop it! Tracey's confusion gave way to fury. Pinpricks stabbed at her skin, a never-ending explosion of pain as the remnants of her concentration were torn to shreds. She couldn't focus on any one irritant. They all merged into one giant nightmare of sensation. She wailed, hearing the sound echoed by her friends. One scream dug into her heart. *Sarah!* Tracey's fury mounted and her eyes sprang open. *Sarah!* Tracey fought to raise her shield bubble again, searching for her sister. Her vision was smeared like a finger painting in the rain. The screeching continued, growing louder. The prickles grew sharper. *Sarah?* And just like that, the pressure and the noise stopped.

Tracey blinked. She lay on her back staring up at the blue sky. A cloud shaped like a bird swept over them. Tracey's gasps were loud, her heart even louder. Once her breathing settled she forced her body to sit up and searched the shocked faces around her for answers.

Grandma's expression hadn't changed. She smiled at them sweetly. "That is what high emotion—any high emotion—does to magic," she said. "It shuts down your senses and makes it difficult to concentrate. Anger does not help you, it hinders you. You cannot give in to anger. Your entire being loses when you give in to anger."

Tracey moaned, a headache pounding behind her eyes. She perched her elbows on her knees and dropped her head into her hands. "How do we control it?" she whispered. Even her whisper was too loud. The drums behind her eyes beat louder.

"That is what each of you must figure out. You all feel anger differently, so each of you will have a different way to manage it. And that is your lesson for today."

Tales
by
The Lost

Following <u>219</u>, Followed by <u>0</u>
click **<broken link>** to follow <u>The Lost</u>!

Day 1176

...my grandmother Dreams. It is spoken of in hushed circles amongst my family. She has Seen that I will find my uncle. We are moving to a town called Miltern Falls.

<u>0</u> likes, <u>0</u> comments, <u>0</u> reshares
click **<broken link>** to like this post!:D

T.B.T.L.

20

The next day passed without incident. A nice pause. Tracey ate Grandma's breakfast, dressed in her chosen outfit, got through school without a Mage-kind battle and worked at Uncle Donny's office in the afternoon. *Spreadsheets. Yuck!* She went home, worried about Mom with her siblings, and went to bed.

Wednesday was not quiet at all. Dad slept in, which meant they were late to school. Running through the school yard, with her backpack bouncing against her back with every step, Tracey moaned at the chirp from her cell phone. Now she would be even later. She stopped to answer the call. "Hi, Agent Malden, the bell just rang, and I have—"

"I'm arriving in five minutes to pull you from class."

Her eyes popped wide. "Why?"

"Your uncle needs help."

The interviews! She had completely forgotten. "Today?"

"Now."

Tracey changed direction and ran for the school office. Within five minutes she was escorted to Agent Malden's car. He wore what looked like a new navy-blue suit with a white shirt. Weirdly, he didn't wear a tie. It was the first time she had seen him without one and his neck looked odd—skinny and naked—without it. She hesitated before climbing into the car. Tony couldn't be right. Agent Malden wasn't hiding anything, was he?

For as long as she had known the man, he hadn't done anything strange or unexpected. Not that she really knew what was normal for an M-Force agent. Tony had to be imagining things. He was scared, he wasn't sleeping, and his parents had him visiting that shrink. He had to be wrong. But if he was wrong about Agent Malden—what else was he wrong about? He had said he didn't know where Doctor Chan was hiding. Would Tony lie to her? Tracey glanced at Agent Malden's profile. There was a small scar under his ear—a straight white line, and a closed hole in his ear lobe. *An earring?* He soooo did not seem the type.

"Come along, Tracey. Get in, we have to go."

She nodded and slid into the back seat. The scenery through the window quickly changed as they approached the city center. More grey concrete, less greenery. They would reach the Grand Central Hotel before she knew it. It was such a strange sensation to be driving around on a school day. Traffic was light and there were more people in suits striding the streets, eyes glued to their cell phones, ignoring the sunny day around them.

Darkness fell as the car turned into the underground carpark. "Tracey, keep your magic closed down until we reach the interview room. I have Hank's suitcase in the trunk."

"What do I say when they ask why I'm here?"

"You're a fan who won a competition. Just stay quiet and look excited. Subtly scan everyone who comes into the interview room."

"Is the disguise spell already working?"

"We activated it last night. The booster strapped to your uncle should keep it active until tomorrow. It wouldn't hurt to monitor that as well."

"Sure."

"Tracey, just keep your uncle calm." Agent Malden parked the car in a spot reserved for hotel staff. Tracey jumped out. Pretending to be excited wouldn't be too hard. Her blood thrummed like she'd had some of her mom's coffee. For the first time in a while she didn't feel tired. Maybe her excitement hid it. Agent Malden opened the trunk and popped the lid on Prince Henry's suitcase. The magic suppression box was gone. Agent Malden handed Tracey the small case with the truth rings. She pulled them out and slipped them on over her thumbs. The gold was cold against her skin. She handed the case back and followed the agent through the dim concrete carpark and into a tiny elevator. He swiped a black card across a sensor.

"Penthouse?" she queried.

"The interviews are being held there."

Cool! Some days she just didn't believe her life. The door *dinged* and *shooshed* open.

"Ready?"

"Yup." She stepped into a short grey corridor filled with people. A man stood playing with a camera the size of his arm. Dressed all in black, a big bag hung from his shoulder. He glanced up. "You the prize winner?"

"Yes, sir," she said, bouncing on her heels.

The balding cameraman rolled his eyes. "Third door. He's already here." A tense woman in a white suit and two men in grey stood in a line outside the door. They glared at Tracey as Agent Malden hustled her past. Tracey recognized the lady from the television news her parents watched.

Hank—no, Prince Henry—who was actually Uncle Donny in disguise, paced before a wall-length window. He spun around at their entrance and his eyes lit up in a way she had never seen them do before. He raced over and whispered, "Well?"

"It's good," she confirmed.

"Can you feel the…," he peered around, "magic?"

Tracey tilted her head. She lowered her shield bubble. Nothing leaked out that her senses could pick up. "Wow."

"Right? Amazing stuff."

"Tracey, take a seat over there." Agent Malden gestured to a faded blue sofa against the wall. "Whatever you do, don't be obvious. I'll be right outside."

Uncle Donny, in his Prince Henry disguise, ran a hand over his shirt and sat down in a chair positioned in the center of the room. The director's assistant appeared and placed a chair down opposite him. Behind Uncle Donny was a tripod stand that held large metallic panel reflectors. The lighting guy, who appeared out of nowhere, put two giant lights behind the empty chair. They flared on a moment later putting Tracey's disguised uncle under a literal spotlight. Tracey plonked down on the surprisingly comfortable sofa and scrubbed sweaty hands against her trousers.

"Ready?" someone asked. Uncle Donny nodded, though his

eyes—Prince Henry's eyes—looked wider than they should be. His nostrils flared.

"Let's get started, shall we?" A rotund man in a white suit entered and clapped his hands. "Tell the first interviewer to come in."

Tales
by
The Lost

Following 219, Followed by 0
click <broken link> to follow The Lost!

Day 1176

[cont …]

I am angry with my mother.

Angry that she kept this secret

from me. Angry that my destiny

has been decided without my input.

0 likes, 0 comments, 0 reshares
click <broken link> to like this post!:D

T.B.T.L.

21

Five lives in search of power and fortune,
  Five hearts in a tangled mess.
  Five stones their magic pours into,
  A choice that love cannot suppress.

Ice, fire, sun, air and earth,
Purest minds,
Blackest hearts,
Driven by fear,
Forgotten by time.

Tracey's phone flashed a red low battery warning. She turned off the poem she was reading and sighed. The thud of her feet against the leather sofa base earned her a displeased glare from the cameraman. Spying a power point on the rear wall she tugged her charge cable from her back pocket and crept over to plug her phone in to charge. Her movement drew another glare from the cameraman. It also distracted Uncle Donny.

"Uh, catering tent?" he answered. Tracey was pretty sure the question had been about CGI.

"Sorry," she mumbled and snuck back to the sofa. While her phone charged she couldn't use it, the cable didn't reach the sofa. She slumped back against the cushions. *Ugh! Soooo bored.* Watching Uncle Donny play acting as Prince Henry doing the same interview over and over again was as dull as school. The research she had done before her phone battery died had mostly been about butterflies. She found several fluffy romantic stories of transformation or lightness of being. Transformation was sort of right, wasn't it? Tracey couldn't use her magic the way she had been taught and now she was forced to use it in a different way. She clicked on various meanings but kept coming back to the one about becoming who you were meant to be. That would mean change was normal, which was a comfort. There were several images of the cycle of birth and rebirth. Rebirth would mean you would have to die first, wouldn't it?

Nana had drawn The Devil card a few week ago when she had done Tracey's tarot reading. Maybe death wasn't scary if it meant being reborn? In between one interview and the next, Tracey had clicked on a link about freedom and self-expression. Maybe her magic wasn't really broken. If change was normal, shouldn't she embrace it? Stephanie kept saying she had to let go, but Grandma and Agent Malden—as well as Mom and Dad—told her she shouldn't. Who should she listen to?

Concentrate Tracey. Heaving a long silent sigh, she slumped further down on the sofa and stared at Uncle Donny.

He sat rigid in his high-backed chair, sweating under the spotlight. The current interviewer sat opposite Tracey's uncle, leaving Tracey to stare at the woman's sharp nose and chin. Maybe it was just the way she seemed to sit taller than Uncle Donny in his Prince Henry disguise, but the woman appeared to stare down her nose at him. Her super sharp pumps and crossed legs added to the impression of a predator staring down at its prey.

Tracey lost track of how many reporters came through the door. It felt like hundreds. Uncle Donny must have upended the bottle of Prince Henry's aftershave, because the thick woodsy scent was giving her a headache. It did nothing to mask the stink of Madam Raptor's cheap smelling sea water perfume. It was probably called something fancy like *Ocean Heat* or *Flame of the Sea*. Tracey hid a yawn behind her hand, wishing she could lay back on the sofa and take a nap.

Uncle Donny's laugh sounded fake to Tracey's ears. "Oh yes. My co-stars are fabulous, just wonderful to work with."

He had given the same answer maybe eleven times so far and it still sounded scripted.

Prince Henry's notes had been brief, and little wonder why. The interviewers all asked the same dumb questions. The only action Tracey saw was in the first minute of their entrance. Tracey would let her magic seep into her hands and gather in the truth rings she wore. For a split second she would lower her shield bubble as they were introduced to Prince Henry. So far, she had been met with a void, even from her uncle. The truth rings did nothing. No vibration, color or sound. She wasn't even sure they were working.

Sunlight pouring in through the window faded, turning the room shadowed and gloomy. "Oh … for crying out loud." The cameraman lowered his camera. "I need more light. Get another lamp in here."

"We're done with this one anyway." The studio's agent was the round man in the white suit. His pants were hemmed too high, showing his socks. One was decorated with grey and black diamonds, the other with brown and black diamonds.

The current interviewer, whose hair looked wet even though it was over a hundred degrees, stood and stretched her hand for Uncle Donny to shake. Tracey jumped to her feet and interrupted her. "Excuse me, Prince Henry. Can I get a picture now?" Uncle Donny snapped his hand back, before he could touch the woman's skin.

"Oh, yes of course. Let's take a break," he said. In moments the room emptied and they were left alone. Tracey grabbed her phone from the wall for show in case someone came back in and sat down on the sofa.

Uncle Donny flopped down beside her. *Whoa!* His body odor was eye-watering this close. He had to be sweating profusely. He didn't look it, which impressed her anew. Pity the disguise spell didn't work on smell.

"You can't let them touch you," she reminded him.

"I forgot. Covering for Prince Henry is exhausting. I hope he'll be back soon."

Tracey felt the same way about her shield bubble. Jumping to her feet she stomped toward the window. "Uncle Donny, you need to …" The strange darkness outside appeared to be a swiftly approaching storm. It looked like no storm Tracey had ever seen. Her breath caught as she stared at the dirty brown clouds swirling and rolling in angry waves straight toward them.

"What is it?" he asked.

"A storm, I think." The whole sky was covered, and it was moving fast. Uncle Donny appeared at her side and peered through the glass. "Dust storm?"

Tracey shook her head. "I don't know." Fear stirred in her stomach. *Dust?* It raced toward them like a giant wall of sand.

He didn't hear her. "It's huge! That cloud must cover half the city."

"It's searching," Tracey whispered, feeling the pull against her shield.

Uncle Donny tore his gaze from the view outside to stare at her, "For what?"

"Us? The stones? I don't know." *Me.* She rested her hands on the window sill. The fine hairs on her arms quivered.

Before their eyes, a few strands broke away from the main dust wave. Holes appeared, as the strands stretched and grew. Through the dust gaps she could see blue sky.

"Not to worry. Look, it's breaking up."

He was right. The dust cloud was disintegrating, the wave falling to the ground the way a sand castle fell apart when hit by an ocean wave. The fear in Tracey's belly still danced, making her squirm.

The door to the penthouse burst open. The cameraman's assistant lugged in another light, knocking it against the doorframe with a loud bang. He was followed by the studio's director.

"Shall we get back to it, Your Highness?"

Uncle Donny cleared his throat. Tracey could see by his slumped shoulders and dead-eyed gaze that he just wanted the day to be over. With the slow steps of a man walking to his own hanging, he returned to his seat. A new journalist entered. "Prince Henry, my name is Hayley Evans, I'm from Starshine Magazine."

Tracey felt an immediate surge of power slam into her shield bubble. The rings on her thumbs buzzed with a violence that shocked her. She raced forward to stand between her disguised uncle and the suited woman. "Oh, um — Prince Henry, we forgot to take a selfie. You did promise."

Uncle Donny startled back a step, his eyes widening at Tracey's interruption. "Excuse me a moment," he said to Hayley Evans.

Tracey stood close to her uncle and held up her phone to take a picture. They both smiled. Tracey muttered, "She's Mage-kind and she's lying."

"Right-o."

"Thanks, Prince Henry," she said and skipped back to her seat, determined to remain alert. Hayley Evans's red hair cascaded around her shoulders, brushing the collar of her ashy grey power suit. Uncle Donny *um'ed* and *ur'ed* his way through her first question, stirring in his seat as if he was sitting on rocks. Maybe Tracey shouldn't have warned him, he was distracted, and it affected his performance. She allowed magic to seep into her hands and flickered her bubble to check on the spell keeping her uncle's disguise in place. She jerked forward, as if pulled by an invisible string. The journalist didn't move, not even flinching at Tracey's probe. So, what had Tracey latched onto? Her gaze snapped to the wall. Someone or something stood behind it. The tug on her mind didn't feel malevolent. It felt... *curious*.

Tracey leaped off the sofa. Uncle Donny stared at her with confusion, the cameraman looked annoyed, and the director's anger peaked. "Um, I'll be back," Tracey said and raced out through the door.

There was no one in the hallway.

She spun in a slow circle, her hands held out in front of her, and let her shield bubble drop completely. Nothing. Her chest fluttered with confusion. She raced back into the interview room to find the journalist on her feet.

"I know who you are. *What* you are!" The woman accused, her voice setting Tracey's teeth on edge.

Uncle Donny sat back in his chair, eyes wide and mouth open.

"What's going on?" Tracey asked.

"Faker!" the woman screeched.

Tracey jumped between Hayley Evans and Uncle Donny. "You're bonkers, lady."

"Security!" Uncle Donny called toward the door.

"This man is not Prince Henry." The woman froze. Her mouth hung open as her eyes turned sickly green. Dust poured out of her mouth in a vomitus stream.

"What the hell?" The director and the cameraman dove for the door. It slammed loudly behind them. Tracey dropped all pretense of being a fangirl and flung out her hands, calling on her magic. Two streams of power raced toward Tracey, sucked from her Uncle Donny in a thin stream, and a wider stream from the journalist. The dirty cloud rose up into a swirl and let out a high-pitched wail. Tracey shoved an invisible wall between Uncle Donny and the journalist, trapping the woman with her dusty interloper. Twisting her hands and pushing out with her magic, Tracey turned it into a blanket and flung it over Hayley Evans and the monster. The whirling dirty wind stretched its blob-like body sideways and Tracey's throw missed. Hayley Evans collapsed.

Tracey refocused her attention on the monster. "Uncle Donny, we have to get out of here." She snapped her magic back into its bubble shape and solidified it. Tentacles of dirt lashed at her like a cat with a toy, slapping at her shield bubble, first one way and then another, sending showers of dust around the room with each movement. The dust disappeared before it hit the ground. Tracey didn't think the monster would stay amused for long. She glanced at the solid door blocking the room from the hallway outside. "Security will be here any minute."

Uncle Donny crouched beside Tracey. "We can't leave her behind."

"The journalist? She's the bad guy—"

"—victim, Tracey. Whatever that thing is, it's out of her now. We have to help her."

Of course they did. Tracey didn't have time to scold herself, she was too busy keeping her shield in place to hold the monster off. "So, what do we do?"

"I don't know."

His admission sent a coil of fear around her body like a snake, squishing the air right out of her chest. She pinched her arm, hard. *Stay focused. Stay in control.*

Her magic would falter if she gave in to fear. Timothy had used that against her once and she refused to let it happen again. Forcing more power into her shield, she expanded it over the fallen journalist. The Dust Devil let out a roar that rattled the windows. Tracey expanded her shield further, pushing it back. Dust and grit swirled, hissing angrily above them, the smell penetrated her barrier filling her nose with dry, desiccated death.

A plan. She needed a plan! Tracey slapped her hand over the Butterfly Stone and cried out for Stephanie.

Let me in. The whisper sent a shiver down Tracey's spine. With conscious effort Tracey let go and released control of her body to the ghostly memory.

Magic filled her mind and sent her blood racing. Her thoughts, fears, and desires disappeared. Stephanie took full control quicker this time and Tracey's mouth spoke words that were not hers. A euphoric feeling swelled around Tracey and washed her away. She drifted. There was no worry, no hunger, no fear. Nothing was of consequence. After a moment — how long of a moment she couldn't say — a thought surfaced. It was not an urgent thought, but something about it caught her attention. She was supposed to be doing something. What was it?

Where am I?

Tracey tried to blink but couldn't. All was darkness.

I can't see.

Fear exploded inside her. Somehow, she forced her consciousness forward. In that brief second, she was able to see through her physical eyes. Uncle Donny — behind Prince Henry's face — stared at her, mouth open wide, skin shiny with sweat. She could taste his fear.

He was afraid of her.

Tracey couldn't feel her chest move as she breathed. Her body was neither hot nor cold. She couldn't touch the warmth of her magic or her core, or her love. In the room, the tornado raged. The wind blew harder, spinning the dust madly. The monster let out a screech and exploded, sending glittering dust particles all over the room. They disappeared as quickly as they appeared.

Stephanie still controlled Tracey's body. Tracey felt like a passenger on the back seat of a bike, allowed to watch but unable to reach the handlebars. Stephanie didn't let go. Tracey felt her mouth stretch into a smile, one she didn't share. She could feel Stephanie's joy, her pleasure in simply breathing. Stephanie turned her hands over, made a fist and then spread her fingers wide.

Stephanie? Tracey called. There was no response.

Tracey tried again. *Stephanie — let me back in.*

For a moment Tracey didn't think Stephanie was going to let go. *Of course. My apologies.* The wall stopping Tracey from feeling her body disappeared and Stephanie's voice was back inside Tracey's head. Tracey blinked, staring stupidly around the empty room, overjoyed to feel her chest expand as she breathed. She trembled at the chill in her skin and flexed her hands. Her wrist was on fire. Beneath her student bracelet, her skin was swollen, with mottled grey and purple bruises.

Uncle Donny climbed to his feet, his gaze focused on the unconscious woman sprawled on the floor. Tracey raised her shield bubble again. This time not to attack, but to protect him — from her.

"Are you okay?" she asked.

He didn't answer. He knelt beside Hayley Evans, his trembling fingers finding her neck. "Is she okay?" Tracey asked. It took him a moment to answer. He squeezed the journalist's hands and shook her gently, calling her name.

"She's not responding. Her heart rate is too fast. We should call for help." He wouldn't look at Tracey. The longer he refused to look up, the more Tracey's skin crawled with little ants of fear. "Don't just stand there. Get help!"

Chastised, she tugged open the door and found the director, the cameraman, his assistant and several security officers milling about outside. "What's happening in there? Is Prince Henry okay? We've been trying to get in. Why didn't you open the door?"

Tracey glanced over her shoulder to check on her uncle's disguise. She was sure she had just seen him with her uncle's face, but now he looked exactly like Prince Henry. "Get help, please. The — ah — journalist collapsed," she told the worried man.

"We heard screaming," the director said.

"Did you?" Tracey hoped the tremors wracking her body didn't affect her voice. The director's assistant jumped on his phone.

Prince Henry came to the door. "I think we should end the sessions for today. This young lady should be checked over for shock."

"I'm fine," Tracey blurted.

Prince Henry's face was set in stone.

"Are you okay?" she asked her uncle beneath his Prince Henry disguise.

"The security team will escort me back to the hotel," was his only answer.

She endured the long wait for the paramedics with the director, afraid Uncle Donny hated her now. *Why won't he look at me?* "I really am fine," she told the director.

"I insist. We must take care of our competition winner, right?" His gaze barely stayed on Tracey's face. *Yeah, like he cares.* The paramedic, a ginger-haired man with bright blue eyes and a toothy smile gave her a cursory examination. She spied his Mage-kind bracelet and exposed her own. He gave her a wink. "Agent Malden called us." The paramedic's black-haired partner examined the journalist. Tracey feared what Hayley Evans — if that was even her real name — would remember when she woke up. Would she continue to insist Prince Henry was an imposter? The paramedic examining Hayley Evans called for the man with Tracey. "Memory loss is in evidence, must have hit her head. We should get her to the hospital." The ginger paramedic tapped Tracey's knee and moved to help his partner. The director's assistant ran up, brandishing a ream of paper.

That was when the director became all charm. He smiled broadly, exposing all of his yellow teeth. "Miss, if you would just sign these, I believe we can get you on your way home."

"What is it?" Tracey questioned.

"A confidentiality agreement. Of course, I know you would never dream of telling anyone of what happened here today. This is just to make our lawyers happy. You won't tell anyone, will you?"

Like he even knew what had happened. Tracey wasn't entirely sure what happened herself. They had whisked her uncle off so fast she hadn't had a chance to talk to him. She pressed a hand to the Butterfly Stone. *What was the Dust Devil after? More importantly, why hadn't Stephanie let Tracey's body go when she first asked?*

Tales
by
The Lost

Following <u>219</u>, Followed by <u>0</u>
click **<broken link>** to follow <u>The Lost</u>!

Day 1176

[cont …]

I do not want this.

I just wish that I was normal…

<u>0</u> likes, <u>0</u> comments, <u>0</u> reshares
click **<broken link>** to like this post!:D

T.B.T.L.

22

In hindsight, the email Tracey sent Hank on her way home was long-winded. She only meant to ask him if he thought anyone might have discovered his Mage-kind secret, because somebody had sent that possessed journalist to expose Prince Henry. Was that why he asked Uncle Donny to stand in for him? She ended up rambling about her uncle's odd behavior after the attack and asked if Agent Malden's paramedics would cover for them if the journalist regained her memory. When Tracey got home, she found another lesson in store. A magic lesson.

Sarah, dressed in black jeans and a sequined heart top, sat with Kylie on the grass in the middle of the yard. Kylie's wavy blond hair was loose and blew all over her face. She had to keep grabbing it with her hands to get it out of her eyes. Her pink crop top showed skin which had to be driving Grandma crazy. Kylie whispered in Sarah's ear and the two girls broke into soft laughter. Sarah glanced at Tracey and laughed louder.

"Pay attention," Tracey hissed at them. Her sister rolled her eyes and poked Kylie in the side, then straightened and shot a dark look straight at Tracey.

Gee, gratitude much? Kylie was only here because Tracey had thought to invite her. Shaking her head, Tracey let it go and focused on Grandma. After the day's events, tiredness was settling into her limbs and the longer she sat there the heavier her eyes grew. *I need to stand and get my blood pumping. Come on, Grandma. Enough talk.* The elderly woman stood at the bottom of the garden, her pink crocheted cardigan buttoned all the way up against the wind. "Pair up. Today you will focus on shield-sharing." Tracey jumped to her feet and stood next to Tony. Sarah and Kylie moved to the bottom of the garden putting distance between them all.

"No Dave?" Tony commented softly, his head tilted toward Tracey.

"I'm going to have to talk to him, aren't I?" she said.

"Do you want me to?"

She examined his downturned lips. "Are you sure?"

"Yeah, you have a lot going on. Besides you look pretty tired."

That was sad coming from him, his eyes were still really red, his hair wild. Tracey thinned her shield at Grandma's order and raised a second one over it. Holding two shields in place was even more exhausting than holding one.

"Do you want me to do this?" Tony asked. "I can shield us."

"She'll swap us over anyway," Tracey told him. Keeping her shadow shield in place so she didn't pull at Tony's magic, she strengthened the larger shield and stretched it wide, making sure Tony was fully covered and waited for Sarah's strike.

Tony's eyes narrowed. "Ready?"

"Yep."

He prepared a pinprick-sized magic ball. "Straight after her shot," Tracey told him.

"Okay."

She staggered as a punch of magic hit her shield. "Whoa!"

"Now."

Tracey barely adjusted her outer shield before Tony launched his magic. Another strike from Sarah exploded right in front of Tracey's face, rebounding off her restored shield. "Hey, cheating!" Tracey shouted. Sarah and Kylie laughed like cartoon bad guys at the bottom of the yard. "Come on, I'm serious. Grandma?" Tracey whined.

"Focus, Tracey," Grandma ordered.

"They're using too much power and they're not waiting," Tracey called back.

"Can't wait in a battle, Trace!" Sarah shouted.

Tony shook his head. "What's going on with her?"

"I dunno. Hit them harder," Tracey ordered.

"Trace, I don't—"

"—do it." She dropped her shield. Tony wasn't ready. Tracey jumped in front of him and launched her own magic ball. "Ha!" she shouted.

A splatter of orange and pink electrical sparks exploded in front of her eyes, reflecting off the invisible shield Tony threw up. "Fruit tingles!" That had nearly gotten her. It would have hurt too. "What the heck?" In the distance, two high-pitched screams told her Tracey's shot had penetrated their defenses.

"Grandma!" Tracey and Sarah shouted at the same time.

"Enough!" The experienced Mage-kind's sharp tone shut them all down. "If you are not taking this seriously, we are stopping now." Her glare was as epic as the stormy swell of her magic.

Great. They had upset Grandma. Tracey had been hoping for another private lesson on her magic use. "Thanks for the save, Tony," she said as they walked toward the house.

"What's up with your sister and her friend?" Tony asked. "No worries by the way. You could have waited before dropping the shield in the first place. I was nearly ready."

"Sorry." She shot a dark look over her shoulder. Sarah and Kylie stayed at the bottom of the garden. Sarah's face was full of anger, her dark hair blowing wildly around her in the wind. Standing beside Tracey's sister, Kylie was doubled over laughing. A nasty smile twisted her face into shadows.

Anchored to each stone, animal souls mirror hope and creation,
A dreamer's desire,
A lover's mad fire.
Broken promises,
Instant damnation.

One breath binds all together, unending and lost,
Invisible to fate,
Unremembered by life,
Shadows twist in heartbreak.
Pain is the true cost.

Mom was still unwell, so Dad dropped Tracey and her siblings at school early the next morning. Sitting in the school library Tracey was using her phone to do more research into the stones. She had looked into butterfly meanings and symbols yesterday, but what about other animals? A simple search brought up hundreds of different animals and almost every one had associated traits and connections. Nothing reminded her of that poem.

She yawned loud enough to echo in the silent library and pressed her chin into her palm. *I love it in here.* The quiet usually soothed her frayed nerves, but not today. Today she couldn't find peace. The giant, high ceiling room was flooded with a heap of natural light. Windows at the top of every wall acted as sky lights, sending early morning sunlight straight into the study area. Tracey sat at the last table in a row of six. Bookshelves filled two thirds of the library, creating a labyrinth of walkways that was fun to get lost in. A second level housed even more books. A wide staircase joined the two floors and though the librarian's desk was shoved beneath the staircase, it didn't stop her seeing and hearing everything that went on in the library. It was weird sitting in here alone. Usually Tracey would have Laura and Jonny to whisper with and share notes. She could have looked up animal books on the library's computers, but her cell phone was closer. There were zodiac animals and the Chinese procession. Native American totem and spirit animals. Hindu, Japanese, Aboriginal, Magekind. So many to look up and she had no idea where to start.

Tracey tapped her pen against the side of her phone. She had been dreaming of tigers. With one finger she typed *Tiger*. Lots of information came up. One website referenced the tigers that appeared in dreams. Fighting tigers could mean fighting with friends in real life. *Fruit tingles.* She had been fighting with Laura and Dave fought with everyone. Tigers could represent strength and courage, but also aggression and fear. Unpredictable emotions. *Ha!* That could be anyone in Tracey's life, including Tracey herself.

Her head pounded. In one ear she heard Grandma talking about controlling her anger and in the other Stephanie argued against it, making her swing her head from side to side like that Gollum scene in *Lord of the Rings*. Perhaps, it was more like listening to a good angel and a bad angel on her shoulders. She only wished she knew which one was which.

Damian sat down and brandished a hardcover book.

Tracey sucked in a sharp breath, her tiredness fading in his presence. His blue polo shirt reflected in his shiny gaze. "What's that?" she asked.

"What you're looking for. Well, uh, I think."

She took the book from his hands. *An Untold Story*. The library stamp was from Daleford North, a few towns over from Miltern Falls. Opening the cover Tracey discovered crude drawings and a heap of profanity. "Someone didn't like it, huh?" A lot of someones if the different writing styles and pen colors were any indication. "You went all the way to Daleford North for this?"

His face pinked. He licked his lips. "It seemed really important to you."

The smile she gave him covered her whole face. He looked down at the book and scratched his neck. "Well, you've helped me with Kylie."

"How is she?"

"Still angry, but she's been a bit better. She likes Sarah. It's good for her to have a friend."

Tracey wasn't so sure. Sarah's behavior had grown worse since the two girls became friends. She started flicking pages. The book was packed with tiny text. A name caught her eye. *Stephanie*. Tracey slammed the book closed and clutched it tight to her chest. "Can I... do you mind if I borrow this for a few days?"

"Of course. Just get it back to me before the date on the return slip. Do you want to pick a topic from this?"

"You're okay with writing from a Mage-kind point of view? What if Mr. Michaels marks us down."

"If we have cited sources he can't fail us, right?"

Tracey snorted. Mr. Michaels so could.

"You hangin' out here now?" The bitter familiar tone set Tracey's teeth grinding. "Freak," Meena hissed as she approached Tracey's table.

"I didn't know you knew what a library was," Tracey sniped back.

"Tracey," Damian sighed. He drew circles on the table top with his fingers and avoided Meena's nasty stare.

"Where's your protection detail?" Meena asked.

"Where's yours?"

Meena didn't rise to the bait. She peered down her nose and stopped right beside Damian. The boy's shoulders hunched as if he expected an attack.

Tracey would never let that happen. "What do you want?" she asked, prepared to stand up and confront the bully.

"You skipped school," Meena accused.

"No, I didn't, I had a pass." How had Meena found out about Tracey's mission to help her uncle?

"Please," Meena sneered.

"Looking for a book or just browsing?" Tracey asked

Meena flicked her long hair over her shoulder, her eyes narrowed. "None of your business."

"I doubt you'll find any of your friends in here," Tracey said. *Why won't she just leave?*

Tapping a sharp nail against the table top, Meena's stare shifted to Damian. "Really? The freak?"

"Leave now, Meena, before I get angry," Damian said. Tracey spied his hand clench into a fist beneath the table.

"I thought you were cool, Damian. Don't stay with her."

"I am cool," Damian replied. "So is Tracey."

That validation made Tracey grin up at the mean girl. Meena huffed and spun on a heel. Damian shook his head at her dramatic exit. "I'd better get going. I have practice," he said. The press of his hand on Tracey's arm sent a different kind of shiver through Tracey's body. "Text me later. We still need to confirm a topic."

"Sure."

In moments Tracey was alone again. She rubbed her hands against her jeans. Damian had protected her from Meena. Her eyes fell on the book and her smile returned. He had even gone all the way to Daleford North just to get a book for her. Tracey wished her friends were here so she could tell them. Letting out a sigh she flipped back to the page she had found earlier.

... Her name was Stephanie Walters. I wish I'd never met her...

Whoa! Tracey turned back to the start of the chapter, her hands trembling.

It was an unseasonably warm day the day I met her. A day suited to iced lemonade and resting in the shade. I recall the music of birds singing romance to one another and the honk of swans doing the same. A shadow fell over me, bringing sweet relief from the oppressive heat. I peered up into the sweetest face I'd ever seen. She smiled so prettily, her lips cherry red, her eyes breathtakingly bright and full of humor. Long dark tresses surrounded her face. She held out a delicate umbrella offering to share it with me. Standing in her presence, I felt immediately cooler and somehow more at peace, as though her mere smile acted as a comforting embrace.

Her name was Stephanie Walters. I wish I'd never met her, though at the time I was besotted, as many in her company were. I, unlike my friends, was granted a singular gift. I was to be her friend and companion. In time I was also to learn her secrets. Oh, how those evil lips bewitched me, trapping me in a life I could barely have imagined. For beneath her honeyed words, deceits of such magnitude as I can scarcely comprehend even now lay in wait. Her lies were spoken as freely as her truths. All I know now is that on that fateful summer day my life did surely change.

I am a fool, for I miss her even now.

The book was snatched from her hands with such speed Tracey couldn't keep hold of it. Dave One towered over her, his shorn head blocking the library's lights and cast her in shadow. "Homework? Nerd. Meena sent me to fetch her book. You shouldn't take what doesn't belong to you mangy-mage."

"It's not Meena's book," Tracey said. Dave One *tutted* at her, patted her hand and walked away. Tracey fumed, fire igniting in her chest. Her page of notes burst into flames. "Shhhhhoot!" She dove on her bottle of water and extinguished the fire, cursing and patting at the remains with a handful of tissues. When she looked up, Dave One was gone, along with the book Damian had given her. *Oh, it's on.*

Tales
by
The Lost

Following 219, Followed by 0
click <broken link> to follow The Lost!

Day 1283

Sometimes I think I could

take advantage of this curse.

If I were not a better person.

Like some.

0 likes, 0 comments, 0 reshares
click <broken link> to like this post!:D

T.B.T.L.

23

"Where are Sarah and Kylie?" Tracey asked, peering around the empty backyard. She was still furious over Dave One and Meena stealing the book Damian had given her and was plotting how to get it back. Two books stolen in only a week. It was a bad precedent. How was she going to tell Damian? She would get the books back and Dave One and Meena wouldn't know what hit them.

Dad hadn't mowed the yard in a while and the grass was long enough to scratch her ankles as she and Tony walked to the back fence. It added to her irritation. Grandma stood waiting for them. Tracey glanced at Tony. "At least you made it."

"Yeah. So, no Dave Two either?" he asked.

"Did you talk to him?"

"I tried. He just walked off."

Tracey stopped in front of Grandma. "If the others don't come, can we work on that exercise you mentioned. The one for how to use my magic?"

Grandma's gaze sprang to the house and came back to Tracey. "If you like. Tony are you happy to stay and assist?"

His brow creased. "Will it confuse me? The way I use my magic, I mean?"

"I do not believe so," Grandma said with a shake of her head. The pink tinted curls didn't dare move out of place.

"I'd love your help, Tony," Tracey said. It was scary to think of resetting her skills. Would it be like restoring a cell phone to factory settings? Would she lose everything before she could learn it all from scratch again?

They sat on the grass and crossed their legs. Grandma waved at the house and Dad's garden chair floated off the porch toward them. When Grandma sat down, she closed her eyes. "Tony dear, raise a shield. Tracey, I want you to focus on your core."

"And do what?"

"Just focus on it."

Tracey shrugged, "Okay." She closed her eyes. Through her shadow shield, she could make out Tony's magical presence. His shield snapped on and she lost him completely. For a moment she floundered in the darkness behind her eyelids.

"Focus," Grandma ordered.

"Right." Tracey thought about the little muscle inside her chest, the node barely the size of a peach pit just beside her heart. In her imagination it glowed orangey-white hot and pulsed with a beat that echoed her heart. All outside noise faded until she no longer heard Tony breathing or Grandma tapping the arm of her chair. She could not feel sunlight on her skin or the itchy grass beneath her butt. The orange-white light grew brighter. Eventually, Tracey could see a white center surrounded by waves of orange magic.

"This is about finding your natural magic," Grandma said, Tracey stopped hearing Grandma's voice and thought of the butterfly stories she had read about, the natural life cycle of living beings. Babies didn't learn to breathe or poop or feed. They did it naturally. Tracey touched the moving life inside her and a streamer of orange untangled from her core. It swept down her arm toward her hand and tickled her palm. She held it, enjoying its excited dance. It disappeared with a pop. "Tracey, call for your magic again, but not like that. Imagine it appearing in your hand like it has always been there."

Tracey released her breath and in the silent emptiness before she drew her next breath, pictured her core again, only this time in the palm of her hand. Light swirled inside her chest. It crawled down her arm toward her hand and popped out of existence.

"Try again."

Guh! This is impossible. Tracey stared at her palm and the faint lines bisecting her skin, forming branches and stars. She stared and stared, imagining her magic filling the center of her hand. A flicker of light preceded a pea-sized orange ball zapping into being. It popped away like a balloon. Tracey rubbed at the ache between her eyes.

"Again," Grandma said.

Tracey waved as Tony walked away and stared out at the street, overcome with sadness. Her skin didn't fit right. It felt too tight over her bones. She pressed a hand to the ache in her chest and touched the Butterfly Stone, shooting a glance over her shoulder for her grandma's presence. She must have gone inside. Holding the stone, Tracey called for Stephanie. In a blink she found herself in the white room, staring at a dancing red diamond and blue square. She searched for Stephanie, but the woman in white wasn't there. Tracey stared at the shapes wondering if she could find a pattern in the undulation. "Something is wrong," she announced. Her words echoed around her body, growing louder before fading away.

"Is it?"

She should have expected a question for an answer. The shapes only ever asked questions. Realization hit her like a lightning bolt. "Oh," Tracey gasped. "You ask endless questions, because I already know the answer. You're making me think about the question in a different way. Something *is* wrong."

Another blink found her standing on her front porch. The streetlight outside her house had grown brighter as night fell.

Her feet moved without conscious thought toward Tavel House, the home for mentally unstable Mage-kind. Trusting her instincts, Tracey headed to her nana's room. Nana's dementia meant she couldn't control her magic. The doctors said it made her dangerous to be around. Tracey didn't believe that. She had never seen proof Nana was dangerous, but the government had rules and you had to abide by them. Nana pulled open the door and a giant smile spread across her lips. Her grey curls were a little messy, her dull brown eyes not quite focusing on Tracey's face.

"Tracey, what are you doing here at this time of night?"

Nana's coherent question brought a smile to Tracey's lips. It meant her nana was not in the middle of one of her increasingly frequent vague episodes. "Hi, Nana." She launched herself into the familiar embrace, trying not to squeeze too hard. Lavender and roses filled her nose. Super soft skin pressed against Tracey's cheek. Tracey pulled away slowly and sank into the chair at the little table beside Nana's bed. She glanced around the small room. There was not a crease to be seen in the floral bedspread, but the mug on the table had a brown tea ring on the bottom and two other mugs were in similar condition, pushed close to the stacked tarot card deck.

"Tracey, dear, what's wrong?" Nana sat in the chair opposite Tracey, pulling her pale blue dressing gown tighter around her body.

"I feel like there's something I should remember but I... I'm not sure what. Is that what you feel all the time?"

"Honey, I... yes and no. Most of the time, when I don't know how to do something, I don't remember ever doing it and sometimes, yes, I have a... word, name and I should... Why do you ask?"

Could that be what was troubling Tracey? Had she lost something she didn't even know that she knew? Could she be affected by the dementia that affected Nana? No. She was too young, right? Her hand brushed the Butterfly Stone. Something *was* wrong, she just didn't know what it was.

"Nana, how old were you when you started forgetting things?"

The face that looked so much like her mother, only older and more experienced, frowned and brushed the front of her dressing gown. "I don't know, honey. You reach a certain age and it's easy to forget little things. It adds up, but you don't notice. Why are you asking? Is your mom okay?"

Urgh, now Nana was worried. "She's fine. It's just a migraine. Well, a few of them. But you know how it is."

"Oh yes. I still get those. Horrible things."

"Hey Nana, weird question... Do you wear pajamas with tigers on them?"

"No, Tracey, I wear nighties. Your mom buys them for me." Nana popped the first two buttons on her dressing gown to expose a pink flannel nightie with flowers."

"No tigers?"

"Well, I... maybe? No, I don't..." She pointed to a drawer. "Have a look, honey."

Tracey couldn't find anything even remotely like a tiger. She closed the drawer with a sigh and sat back down at the table.

"Why did you ask?"

"Oh, it's a silly dream I had."

"About tigers? Have you been fighting with your friends?" Nana asked.

"How did you know that?"

"Tigers are quite symbolic, Tracey. You should look into it."

Tracey smiled. It was like an ordinary conversation, reminding her of the old days when she was little. You would never guess Nana was sick. "Nana, can I ask you about Stephanie?" Dropping her shield, Tracey reached for Nana's magic. As always, she found only distracted wisps.

"Stephanie?"

"Your ancestor." She reached across the table and took Nana's chilled fingers in her own, warming them up with a press of magic.

Nana's face became troubled. "Should I remember?"

Tracey wet her dry lips with a sweep of her tongue "You were keeping her memories."

"Was I?" Nana's gaze darted around the room as if searching for answers she couldn't remember. Her breathing increased, little short gasps speeding up.

"Grandma has them now, Nana." Tracey smiled, trying to calm her. She rubbed Nana's wrinkled knotty hands.

Something told Tracey there was a reason she had come here tonight. She had something to learn, but how could she get anything from a woman who couldn't remember?

"Beth, you're very sick. You must go to hospital," Nana said suddenly. She turned her head and stared at the wall, or perhaps she was looking beyond it.

"Nana?" Tracey prompted.

"It's coming."

The familiar words sent a chill down Tracey's spine. "Nana, please focus, I need—"

"Beth, don't go home."

"I'm Tracey, your granddaughter. Beth is my mom and she's at home. She's safe."

"Tracey?" Nana turned away from the wall, looking right through Tracey.

"Nana?"

"What are you doing here, Stephanie?"

Tracey's breath caught. She leaned forward. "Do you remember me?"

"Of course, I remember. You wouldn't go away."

The sharp tone set Tracey back in her chair. "What do you—"

"I gave you to Adele. You shouldn't be here anymore. Go away."

"I know, Nana." *This is a waste of time.* Tracey had felt such a strange urge to come here. She hadn't fought it. She wanted to see her nana and needed answers. Maybe she had only come here because she had felt so alone. Once upon a time Tracey and her nana had so much fun together, driving to the library, stopping at coffee shops, sneaking out for ice-cream. Sometimes with Sarah, but mostly just the two of them. Tracey had wanted to feel that joy again. She didn't have her friends to hang out with anymore. Well, she had Tony when he wasn't being weird. And Damian too. Maybe she wasn't really alone. She just missed Laura.

Nana leaned her head closer to Tracey. "Sarah's new friend ... watch out for her."

Tracey blinked, and then she blinked again. "What?"

"Beth, you need to rest."

"Nana, I'm Tracey."

"Oh Tracey, dear. You should stop looking for the stones. It will only bring you trouble."

That cold shiver was back, dancing down her spine. "Stop looking for what, Nana?"

Her nana straightened her glasses and held up a tarot card. She placed it face up on the table. It was a picture of a girl sitting up in bed, her face cradled in her hands. Above her was a heap of sharp swords.

The little hairs on the back of Tracey's neck quivered. With a trembling hand she picked up the deck of cards and fanned them out, face down across the table. She slid one toward Nana, bit her bottom lip and waited. Wrinkled hands trembled as Nana turned the card over. The familiar red eyes of The Devil stared up at her. Nana waved a hand. "Two more."

Tracey took her time, sliding the requested cards forward. Nana flipped them over. One was of a man holding two stones as if they were scales and he was weighing them. The other was of a woman with her eyes covered.

"Choose carefully." Nana blinked and leaned forward to pat Tracey's hand. She gathered the cards into a pile. "Beth, honey you need some sleep. You look tired."

Without bothering to correct her, Tracey gave her nana a hug and headed home, her head filled with questions.

Sarah met Tracey at the front door already wearing her pajamas. "Where have you been?"

"I went to see Nana." Tracey closed the door. "Where's Dad and Grandma?"

"Grandma's in the kitchen." Sarah squinted at her. "Nana? What did she say?"

"Not a lot. Hey, how's Mom feeling?" Tracey headed for the stairs. She could hear the TV playing an advert in the living room, the music super loud. The house smelled of lasagna.

Sarah's silence brought Tracey to a quick stop. She peered back down at her sister. Sarah twisted her hair, twirling it around her fingers. "Mom's at the hospital. They kept her in for observation."

Tracey's heart froze. "Where's Dad?" Her hands were as cold as the chill that settled in her chest.

"He stayed with her. Grandma made dinner. She kept you a plate."

"Is she angry I snuck out?"

"No. She probably knew where you were going."

Tracey sat down on the third step. "Is Mom okay?"

"Dad says it's precautionary."

Nana's voice sprang into Tracey's mind. Sarah stared up with big eyes, making Tracey bite back what she was going to say. She didn't want to worry her little sister. *What about me? Who worries about me?* "Well the hospital would know, right? Maybe Mom just needs new tablets." Tracey forced herself to turn around and continue up the stairs. Sarah followed. "Oh hey, how's Kylie doing? Is Dave's brother still upsetting her?" Tracey asked.

"She's okay. I mean, she's... you know, Kylie. Grumpy and sarcastic."

"Be careful around her?" Tracey blurted. The family picture hanging on the wall right in front of her was of Mom and her five sisters. Nana sat in a big garden chair, laughing at the girls' dance poses. Mom's little sister, Tracey's Aunt Gemma, was on the ground as if she had fallen over just as the photo was taken.

Sarah waved her hand around. "You were the one who wanted me to be friends with her in the first place."

"Yeah, I know. But..."

"I'm fine, Trace. Stop worrying."

What a crazy thing to say. Tracey would always worry about her little sister. She touched the photo. "Are you coming to practice tomorrow?"

"You're not Mom, you can't make me."

"Sarah, Grandma said—"

"Kylie doesn't want to come anymore. She says it's dumb and it doesn't help anyways."

"Yeah, but Sarah—"

"I know, I know. Grandma gave me the lecture already. I don't need you to yell at me too."

Tracey sighed. "I'm not yelling. Sarah. Timothy is still out there and I just... I want you to be able to protect yourself."

Sarah stomped up the stairs. She looked older than Tracey remembered. There were tiny lines around her mouth and her eyes looked sad.

Sarah rubbed the back of her neck and Tracey caught a glimpse of the hand-shaped bruise beneath her hair. "Does it still hurt?"

Sarah's hand dropped away from her neck. "Sometimes."

Tracey hugged her sister, squeezing hard. Sarah didn't stop her, but her hands didn't come up to wrap around Tracey like she wished they would. They hung limp at her sides. "I love you," Tracey whispered.

"You too." They pulled apart. "Are you okay, Trace?" Sarah tilted her head, squinting as if trying to see inside Tracey's mind.

Tracey forced her gaze away and looked at the picture of her own family beside the one of Mom and her sisters. Tracey must have been eight, Sarah six. They had their arms wrapped around each other, dressed in swimming suits, with wet hair and skin, grinning like loons at the camera. Tracey wished she could share her worries with Sarah, but her sister didn't need to be stressed out too. "I'm fine," she promised.

That night Tracey's dreams were filled with battling tigers. One tried to bite her hand, and in another dream a tiger appeared sitting on the bleachers at school watching her run endless circles around the track. The Shadowman hovered above the tiger. Meena and Kylie sat to either side. The Shadowman's smoky darkness reached long tendrils around Meena and Kylie, keeping them close. Both girls' eyes were black, and they cackled like evil witches — rough hacking sounds that made Tracey's hair stand up on her arms. Tracey bolted upright in bed. She gripped her knees and scrunched into the tightest ball she could manage, covered head to toe in a sweat that chilled her to the core. Though it was already fading, she fought to recall the nightmare that woke her.

Nana.

The last dream was always Nana. Dream-Tracey had entered a cold, shadowy room and tried to get her nana's attention, but Nana didn't look away from the wall. Her skin hung slack around her mouth, a creepy grey color making her look more like a zombie than a live person. Her head turned, creaking like an old wooden door and her empty stare fell on Tracey. "It's coming."

Tracey scrubbed cold fingers into the corners of her eyes and wiped away sleep grit. Her heart pounded. *What's coming?*

By the time morning made an appearance, Tracey had decided on a plan of attack. She was going to break into Meena's locker and find the book Dave One had stolen.

Untangling herself from her bedsheets, she smacked her hand against her tablet. She must have fallen asleep while reading. *What had Nana said?* She had a choice to make? Snapping her duvet into place on her bed, Tracey wished the tarot cards would just tell her what she needed to know instead of being all mysterious and cryptic.

Sitting at the kitchen table, Dad was quiet. Too quiet. He didn't even say hello when Tracey entered. She was afraid to ask about Mom, fearing the answer would be something she didn't want to hear. She eyed Charlie and waggled her eyebrows. He shrugged. Simon wouldn't look at her. "Where's Peter?"

"Work," Dad told her.

"When did he get a job?" she asked, startled.

"While you were at camp," Dad said, blowing on his coffee. One gulp made it disappear.

"Dad, how's Mom?" The table fell quiet as each sibling held their breath. Dad jumped to his feet. "Chop, chop, kids. Let's go. Don't want you to be late for school."

"Dad!" Tracey stood up, her voice rising. "Please?"

He stopped his frantic cleaning. "They're running tests, Tracey. We just don't know yet. Get a wiggle on."

Tracey followed her brothers upstairs. *What's wrong with Mom?*

"She'll be fine, Trace," Simon said.

"Yeah, of course," Tracey answered, rubbing her fingers together. She hurried to her room. In a blink she was back downstairs and following Sarah to the car.

"Grandma will pick you up from school," Dad announced as he drove. "I'm going back to the hospital to stay with your mom."

Simon and Charlie protested loudly. "Football training," they both said.

Car tires crunched over stones as Dad raced into the school parking lot and skidded to a stop. *How'd we get here already?* Tracey climbed from the car, stepping on the painted parking lines. *Weird.* Dad never parked across the lines.

"Right, right. Just you and Sars then, Tracey," Dad called. Tracey peered through the window at him as Sarah leaned down to speak through the open door. "Dad, I'm going to Kylie's after school."

Their dad huffed out a breath. "Right."

"Just me then," Tracey mumbled.

As they scattered toward school, Dad reversed the car and with a squeal of tires drove away. Tracey shared a wide-eyed look with her siblings. His odd behavior was freaking them all out. "Hey, Sarah, remember what I said last night."

"I will, I will." She didn't look Tracey's way.

"Try to convince Kylie to come to training." Tracey's tone was weak. She knew Sarah wasn't going to try very hard.

"I can't make her if she doesn't want to come. You can't make me either."

"Sarah, I'm not trying to make anyone do anything. It's just…"

"Yeah, yeah. I'll try."

Her sister stormed off toward her campus. Tracey worried. Hanging out with Kylie Carter seemed to be changing Sarah. Her sister had never lied to Tracey before. Surprised, she realized she couldn't sense Sarah's emotions anymore. Somehow her sister had found a way to block her. It sent prickles of concern over her skin. Tracey had introduced Sarah to Kylie. Perhaps that had been a mistake. *Remember what Nana said.* What if, instead of Sarah helping Kylie manage her anger, Kylie was negatively influencing Sarah's emotions? Great, now she had to keep an eye on Sarah, too. Another stress to add to her overloaded mind.

Tracey made her way to the lockers and stopped in front of the one belonging to Meena. If she got caught, she would be suspended. Using magic at school was a big no-no, but she had to find that book. And what if it had been Meena who had stolen the journal from Tracey's bag? Tracey could get both books back!

Her hands shook as she pressed her palm to the locker door. Shooting nervous looks over her shoulder to check for witnesses, Tracey closed her eyes.

Uncle Donny had a book on picking locks. She had read it when she had nothing to do while manning the phone—the one that very rarely rang. Tracey pictured the inside of a basic combination lock as she sent a spurt of magic into her ear to increase her hearing. As she turned the dial she Listened for the echo of empty space as the wheel fell into place. Right turn click, left turn click, right turn. On the final click the door popped open. Peering suspiciously over her shoulder again she made sure the hallway was clear by using her magic-infused hearing to Listen for approaching footsteps. Nothing. She examined Meena's locker. *Jackpot.* The library book was tucked away under Meena's science diorama, but no journal. Tracey checked three times. "Darn."

"What are you doing?"

Tracey screeched and spun around, slamming Meena's locker door shut and rubbed her ear. Her hearing still spelled, Tony's voice had rattled her eardrums. She killed the spell and grabbed his arm, dragging him away from Meena's locker.

"What were you doing?"

In response she held up the book.

"Mage-kind Rebellion? Tracey, are you doing homework?"

"Sort of," she checked over her shoulder again. "This is the book Damian gave me."

"What book?"

"Damian found it. It's a book with a Mage-kind point of view."

Tony's mouth dropped open. After a moment he asked, "Where'd he find that?"

"He went to Daleford North," she said, bouncing on her heels.

He raised an eyebrow. "Really?"

"I was just getting it back."

Tony pulled free of her grip, giving her a sharp look. "Did you use ma—"

"—ahhhhh Tony. Meena stole it first."

"Tracey, if you get caught—"

"I won't, okay? Come to the library with me." They moved quickly, not quite running because that wasn't allowed at school either.

"Did you check for—"

"It wasn't there. She didn't have the journal."

They hit the library doors hard, both sides popping open to admit them. They slowed to a walk through the scanner and headed straight to the open center where all the study tables were located. Tracey glanced up at the second level. No students in sight. Tony pulled her to the rear table. She couldn't hold his gaze. "I'm looking into the rebellion because I'm pretty sure Stephanie was involved. I was hoping to find a clue about the stones, but information is hard to find. Actually, it's really annoying." Shooting another glance up at the second-floor stacks she checked for students. No one should be here this early other than a few nerds like her and Tony. Still, she kept her voice low.

"Why didn't you ask me to help? I love books," he said.

Tracey eyed the bags under his eyes and his pale, drawn face. "I didn't want to bother you." She dumped her bag on the table and pulled out the library book.

"Yeah, but come on. You know I'd help."

"How's your—uh—visits with the doctor going?"

He shrugged.

"Am I not supposed to ask?"

He shrank back as if he could no longer sit straight. "It's fine."

The only sound came from Tracey flicking the book's pages. A dusty, old person smell wafted up from the paper.

Tony shook himself off and sat up, leaning over to look at the book. "Have you tried the city library? And what about the university? They'd have books on the... rebellion. Ugh! I hate calling it that. Probably better books there than in a high school."

"Do you think I should see a shrink?" Tracey blurted. Stunned by the words that spewed from her mouth, she clapped a hand over her lips. "I didn't mean to say that," she mumbled between her fingers.

His eyes widened. "What? Why?"

"I—um..." What could she say that wouldn't make her sound like a freak? That the voices in her head argued all the time? That she was forgetting things and was afraid she was going to end up like her crazy nana? That Mom being sick left her feeling helpless? That she was fighting with Laura? "Weird dreams."

"About Timothy, the Shadowman?"

Nightmares about turning into my nana. "You?"

"Yeah."

She wanted to ask him if he was scared. Instead, she changed the subject. "What did you think of the training with Grandma?"

"It was interesting."

"Did you try it? Using your magic differently?"

He shot her a side-eyed squinty stare. "Why?"

"You did, didn't you?"

"It's hard," he admitted.

"Yep, but once I got it... it was, I dunno, easier."

"Yeah. It was."

"Ha! You did do it."

He responded to her grin with a small tilt of his lips.

She flicked through more of the book. Tony took it from her hand and checked the back pages. "What are you doing?" she asked him.

"Looking at the index."

"Oh." *Why didn't I think of that?* She leaned over to see Tony looking for Stephanie's name. Her thoughts drifted back to the training with Grandma. "Have you talked to Dave Two?"

"Not yet. I think he's avoiding me. Have you?"

"I keep feeling like I need to check up on him, but then stuff happens and I forget."

Tony put the book down, keeping his fingers in the pages and stared at her. "Tracey, you have a lot going on."

"Yeah, but..."

"If he wants to talk to us, he will." Tony's face pinked. He looked down at the book. "Besides, the assignment is what we really should be doing."

"Tony, I had the journal. It could have told us everything and both the journal and this book were stolen from me. It's like I'm not supposed to learn anything."

"Tracey, maybe you're not supposed to know?"

"Where's Doctor Chan hiding?" she asked abruptly, scratching at a smudged purple ink stain on her hand. Annoyed when it didn't rub away, she licked her finger and scrubbed at it. *How did I get this?* For a second her brain stuttered over the question. Another thing she had forgotten. She was going to have to tell Grandma. Sweat broke out on her neck and lower back. Surreptitiously, she tugged her shirt away from her skin. *Gross.*

Tony tugged his cell phone from his pocket and swiped the screen to read from it. "I've narrowed it down to Miltern Falls Motel Seven. I'm not sure what room he's in yet though. Why? You aren't going after him, are you?"

"Yes! We should go after school. Call Jonny. He can come with us. He's always up for a crazy mission."

Tony thrust out a hand. "What about your uncle? Shouldn't you tell him? What if Doctor Chan is behind the Dust Devil that's been chasing you? He might have Timothy's stone."

"How could he have it?"

"Maybe he picked it up after Officer Jameson dropped it? Or pick-pocketed it from Officer Jameson. We never found it at the movie lot. Officer Jameson must have had it at some point for Timothy to possess him. Agent Malden's team searched for ages and found nothing," Tony said.

Unless Agent Malden *did* find it. Would he have told her if he did? *Gah*, why would Agent Malden keep it a secret when he was the one who had given her the mission to find the stones in the first place. "This is our chance, Tony. We can capture Doctor Chan and get the next stone." In the silence after her outburst they heard familiar voices coming from the double glass door entrance. Laura, Jonny, and a dark-haired girl entered, laughing and hushing each other to be quieter. Spotting Tracey and Tony, they stumbled to a stop.

"Oh, Tracey, hey," Laura said. Tracey's chest constricted as all three faces became somber.

She wanted to ask why Laura was ignoring her text messages. Glaring at the girl next to Laura, Tracey figured she knew the reason. The Butterfly Stone pulsed hot against her skin. *Yeah, me too buddy.* "What are you doing?" Tracey didn't try very hard to keep her anger from infecting her voice.

"Whoa! Settle down, Tracey. Don't get angry. Come on, Jilly. We should go," Jonny said tightening his grip on the girl's hand.

If flames could burst from Tracey's mouth they would have incinerated him where he stood. The girl dropped Jonny's hand and held her ground, glaring back at Tracey.

"Who is that with Jonny?" Tony asked. Tracey checked her memory but came up blank. Another missing memory. Her heart clenched at the realization that something was seriously wrong. The Butterfly Stone pulsed again. Tony didn't know who she was either. It didn't matter. This Jilly had taken Tracey's friends away and that made her the enemy.

Laura tugged on Jilly's jacket.

Fighting the urge to set fire to something, Tracey pointedly turned her back on her ex-friends. Her fingers clenched into fists so tight her hands ached. Jilly's Mage-kind aura pressed hard on Tracey's shield bubble. *She's Mage-kind?* Tracey's head snapped up and she spun around. Jilly must have put a spell on Laura and Jonny! It was the only explanation. Tracey's hand crept to her chest. A power boost would uncover the spell.

Ignoring the fear that Stephanie would take over her body the way she had last time and not let go, Tracey opened her core and called on the Butterfly Stone's magic. Power flooded through her—glorious, musical magic. Her hands relaxed as it seeped into her very bones. She focused on Jilly. The enemy.

"Tracey. Tracey, no!" Tony's voice was sharp in her ear. She waved him away, her whole being focused on Jilly, searching for the telltale buzz of a spell. Nothing. She needed more magic. Music played in her mind, soft and melodic. The tinkle of piano keys. Above it she heard a feminine laugh. Tracey's magic emerged as a golden smoky hand, searching for the magic that had ensnared Laura and Jonny. They wouldn't be able to see the hand, but Tracey and Tony could.

So could Jilly.

Laura stumbled back. Jonny's eyes widened for a split second behind his glasses before he planted his feet, making sure Laura was behind him. "Tracey!"

Jonny's voice became Tony's in her ear. "Tracey!" Magic burned fire into Tracey's arm. She flinched, snapping her attention to the boy at her side. Tony's hand stretched toward her, his shield blooming out to smother her search, pressing her smoky hand to the floor.

"What are you doing?" she shouted.

"What are *you* doing? Stop this. Stop it now, Tracey!"

She turned her back on him to face the enemy. *Keep searching. It's there, you know it is.* With a flick of her wrist she pushed Tony and his magic away. He stumbled back several steps, emitting a squeak of surprise.

"Tracey, stop it! You can't do this!" Laura turned to Jilly. "We have to go."

"She can't bully me," Jilly hissed.

"Please Jilly, we need to back off," Jonny pleaded.

You stole my friends. Tracey stepped forward, pushing her attack. "You took it, didn't you? The journal from my bag. You're a thief and a liar."

Something hit the side of her body, knocking her to the ground. Tony landed on top of her, squishing her into the floor. A shockwave of pain spread from her hip, along her side.

"Stop it!" Tony shouted in her face.

Tracey was so shocked she lost her grip on her magic. The glow in her hands died. The buzz and the warmth faded, leaving her cold to the core. Trembling, Tracey blinked up at Tony. "What just happened?" Tony rolled off. He wouldn't look her in the eye.

"I ... I ..." Tracey peered around. She and Tony were alone in the library.

"What on earth is going on down here? You students are making far too much noise!" The librarian scowled as her feet pounded the carpet toward them, "Out, both of you."

"Yes, Mrs. Stevens," they said and scampered for the door. Tony kept walking when they got outside. He didn't look back. Tracey stopped and stared down at her hands. The bruises on her wrist beneath the bracelet ached anew.

What just happened?

Tales
by
The Lost

Following <u>219</u>, Followed by <u>0</u>
click **<broken link>** to follow <u>The Lost</u>!

Day 1283

[cont …]

If you are not remembered then

anything you say, anything you do,

has a shelf life.

<u>0</u> likes, <u>0</u> comments, <u>0</u> reshares
click **<broken link>** to like this post!:D

T.B.T.L.

24

Motels, at least this one, were creepy during the day. There was a weird stillness — a holding your breath heaviness where echoes seemed louder and made Tracey think people were creeping up behind her. No one was actually there. Her pulse thudded, her senses hummed. She drew on her magic and stretched out with her thoughts, searching for the illusive Doctor Chan. A thought fluttered through her mind, gone quicker than a camera flash. *I wish Tony was here.* She shook her head. *No, I can do this myself. I don't need anyone.*

You have me, Stephanie whispered. The Butterfly Stone pulsed as if to add, *You have me too.*

After the blow up in the library, Tracey skipped the rest of school. Tony, her former friend and fellow Mage-kind, had betrayed her. He had stopped her from getting justice on that … that girl. He had been holding her back, stopping her from hunting down Doctor Chan like the monster he was. Her thoughts jerked to a stop. Why couldn't she remember the girl's name? She was sure Jonny had shouted it. Tracey shook her head forcing the thought to the back of her mind. The Butterfly Stone was a warm presence against her skin, as if she was already using its magic, but she hadn't called on it yet. *Weird.* Anyway, she'd had enough of listening to everyone else. They were all liars and betrayers. She was going to do this herself.

Tracey straightened her back. *Where is he?* Without a room number she had no idea where to go next. Tracey prowled the corridors, her shield bubble lowered, searching for the taste of familiar magic. He would be shielded but she had the added strength of the Butterfly Stone. And her anger made her invincible. A tug had led her to this floor. Doctor Chan's room was along here somewhere. Stopping dead in the middle of the corridor, realization dawned. She didn't have a plan. What would she do when she found him? Doctor Chan was a powerful mage.

So are you.

At the end of the corridor, a door opened. Tracey sprang back to the bend in the corridor and hid. She almost giggled out loud and clapped a hand over her mouth to stop the sound from popping out. Adrenaline had her blood pumping.

Tracey peeked around the corner. Whoever had come out of their room must have headed straight to the elevators at the end of the hall. No one was there now. Shaking off her nerves she searched for her anger, needing the buzz to drive her forward. As she headed down the corridor, the electricity against her skin grew. Hairs rose up along her arms and her neck tingled. The sensations grew until they covered her body. *Close, so close.*

At the next door—room 407—the buzzing just outside her hearing stopped as if it had been switched off. *Ha! Found you.* Instantly, magic sprang into her hands.

Let me help you, Tracey. Let me in.

"No," Tracey snapped. "I can do it myself. I don't need anyone." She pressed her hands against Doctor Chan's motel room door. Calling upon her lock-picking skills she located the inner locking mechanism. With a bang the door opened, slamming back on its hinges.

Tracey realized her mistake as she came face to face with Doctor Chan. The Chinese man uttered a mix of sounds and Tracey was thrown back through the door and into the corridor wall.

She hadn't even thought to check if Doctor Chan was in the room before she opened the door. Every Mage-kind knew a person's home was strongly defended. By hiding out here for weeks, Doctor Chan's motel room had plenty of time to take on the magic of its occupier. Her arrogance had convinced her she was more powerful than a scared Mage-kind on the run. It was her undoing.

Tracey scrambled to her feet and flung up her shield bubble, reflecting the next blast back at Doctor Chan. She bolted for the end of the corridor.

She made it two steps. Something powerful latched around her ankle and yanked hard. Tracey went flying. A gasp exploded from her as she hit the wall. Something popped in her arm, ripping a scream from her throat.

Her vision shrank until it was a pinpoint shaft of light. Doctor Chan stepped into view, his long face and neatly trimmed moustache exactly as she remembered, as was the smirk dancing at his lips. Tracey couldn't see his eyes behind the colored glasses he wore, but she imagined them tearing into her soul.

His left hand flared with light. She flew sideways and slammed into another wall. Pain seared her side, her arm, her whole body.

She screamed.

Darkness fell, swift and all encompassing.

Tales
by
The Lost

Following 219, Followed by 0
click **<broken link>** to follow The Lost!

Day 1283

[cont …]

Once the memory expires,

you can become a different person.

Nice, mean, sharp, horrid,

evil, sweet, gentle, manic…

0 likes, 0 comments, 0 reshares
click **<broken link>** to like this post!:D

T.B.T.L.

25

Ting.
Ting.
Ting.
Ting.

Tracey pried open her eyes. She saw a blurry off-white painted wall. Blinking, her vision focused on a bench that looked like a mini-kitchen with a little sink. That was where the annoying noise originated. A lone drip of water plopped into the bowl. *Ting.* It became a hammer smacking nails into her brain. Her eyes slipped closed.

Ting.

Ting.

Ugh! Echoes upon echoes, like the noise she encountered inside the white room, thudded in her head. Cold air sent a shiver up her spine. She could smell something metallic... blood?

Dragging her heavy eyelids up again, Tracey squinted under the murky yellow overhead light. Stabbing knives of pain dug into her temples and twisted. "Mom?" Her moan came out as a croak. Her tongue scraped the inside of her mouth like sandpaper. *This isn't my bedroom.* The dripping water came from the kitchen sink. *This isn't Uncle Donny's office. Where am I?*

Her nose itched at the glide of a tear from her right eye. She tried to wipe it away but couldn't raise her hand. Looking down her arm she found a leather strap around her wrist. It tied her arm to the chair.

What happened? Tracey jerked and yanked on her arms but there was no give in the straps. *How did I get here?* Focusing on her core she called for her magic. Nothing happened. There was no warmth, no glow. Nothing.

"Help! Someone help!" Pleas burst from her chest, tearing out of her dry throat at high speed. She could barely hear herself. Breathing like a racehorse after a race, she shouted and yelled and bellowed, but all that came out were muffled grunts, as though she was shouting into a pillow. *Magic.* Something stopped her from making any sound louder than a whisper. *Where am I?* She searched for her core, hunting for the node inside her body to fight the spell, but she couldn't touch it. Her eyes popped wide. *Why can't I touch my magic?*

She remembered the school library. She had flashes of Tony's smile, Jonny's sneer, Laura's high-pitched laugh. Oh, she had skipped class to ... to ... do what?

It poured into her head like liquid from a soda machine, bubbles and all.

The motel.

She had used her magic to get into Doctor Chan's room.

Doctor Chan!

Doctor Chan had captured her.

Her movements turned frantic. She pushed and tugged on the straps holding her to the chair, but there was still no give. Slumping back, she twitched her itchy nose. Hot tears overflowed her eyes, dripping down the side of her face.

Jiggling her upper body, she arched her neck and then folded herself forward from the shoulders. The thud of the Butterfly Stone against her chest was both familiar and weird. It lay against her skin, where it had been for weeks, but she couldn't feel its presence. "Stephanie?"

There was no answer.

The taste of metal woke her to the hole she had chewed in her lip. No one was coming to rescue her. No one knew she was here. She was trapped.

Helpless.

Alone.

Mom! She screamed in her mind. *Dad!*

Nothing.

More tears ran down her cheeks. Dropping her chin to her chest, she sniffed hard. She examined the room that had become her prison cell. A basic hotel layout. Two doors — the way out, and probably a bathroom.

The little kitchenette with a sink was in front of her, so the bed must be behind her. She sat isolated, in the middle of the room. From the corner of her eye she spied a desk. Rocking sideways she tried to move her chair.

The clunk of the door snapped her head up and cramped the muscles in her neck.

"You are awake." Doctor Chan slunk into the room and closed the door carefully behind him. He peered at her through his tinted glasses, moving no closer.

"Let me go," she croaked.

"No." He side-stepped his way around Tracey and headed for the desk near the window. The covers were drawn. She had no idea if it was day or night. How long had she been here? He sat at the desk and sighed as his weight was taken off his feet. His wary gaze did not shift from her face. He had been here a long time, hiding from M-Force. Maybe he hadn't intended to lock her up? She had broken into his motel room and attacked him. He was just protecting himself, right? Perhaps she could convince him to let her go.

"It is time I properly introduced myself," he said. "My name is Steven Cho."

A tingle spread across Tracey's skin. "Why are you telling me—"

"You will give me the Butterfly Stone," he said.

Nope, not innocent.

"I can't." Her heart galloped loud enough to almost muffle his next statement.

"Miss Masters, I assure you that I can make this a most unpleasant experience for you."

"Kidnapping a kid? And now you're threatening me? You still work for Timothy, don't you?"

His flinch answered her question.

"You're hiding from him."

"The stone, please."

She rocked in her chair. "I told you, I can't. Really. I can't take it off."

"I attempted to remove it while you were unconscious." He rubbed at the side of his head, wincing as if in pain.

"It does that," she said.

"I will take it from you."

Good luck with that. Part of her actually hoped he could remove it.

He climbed to his feet and lifted his glasses to rub his eyes, then yanked a drawer from his desk, clean off the rack. He sorted through a handful of items she couldn't see, finally lifting several papers free.

"Do you have Timothy's stone?" she asked. Doctor Chan ignored her. He crouched to drag a piece of chalk around in a circle. Thin black hair stuck to his sweaty head in clumpy strands.

"Where did my magic go? What did you do to me?"

He didn't look at her. "A simple child-lock used on dangerous Mage-kind children," he said. She couldn't see if he had put anything around her wrists as her hands were tied behind her. She thrashed in her chair, fighting the ropes and her increasingly dark situation. "He won't forgive you."

Doctor Chan looked up.

"Timothy hates you," she continued. "You failed him."

The sweating man chuckled and bent back to his circle, continuing the strange shapes and words he was writing. She didn't recognize any of them. "He will open his arms to me."

"You sound crazy. Timothy won't care. It's the stones he wants. You mean nothing to him."

"Once I give him the stones—"

"—he'll kill you." Tracey had no idea if that was true or not, but she remembered the intensity of Timothy's gaze. He didn't want anything except the stones. And he needed her to unlock them. "If you kill me, he'll be furious with you."

"He needs me." The red glow in Doctor Chan's eyes grew brighter. She could see it now around the outside of his glasses. Spittle flew from his mouth. He lit one candle after another and placed them down upon the chalk circle.

"My friends are coming—with Agent Malden."

"No one is coming. No one knows you are here. My room spell will prevent access. You cannot call to them and you cannot touch your magic. No one will find you here." He filled a small bowl with water from a jug and placed it at Tracey's feet.

There was one person who would know something had happened to her, one person who always knew when Tracey was hurt or scared or in pain. "My mom will know." Doctor Chan's laugh froze Tracey's breath inside her throat. The headaches, her mom's illness. "What did you do to my mom?"

"I took care of her first."

No! Tracey screamed. The sound exploded out of her, shattering the window glass, the mirror, even the water jug. "No!" Magic flooded into her as whatever spell Doctor Chan placed on her broke under the onslaught of her raw emotion.

The door burst open. Two pops were heard over Doctor Chan's shout of surprise and smoke filled the room. A smell as familiar as it was rancid. *Jonny?* Tracey's mind caught on the scent and dragged her back into coherence. Magic, in the form of a bolt of light, flew across the room at Doctor Chan. But Doctor Chan was no longer there. The bolt hit the wall and fragmented, climbing the walls in long electrical burns.

A warm hand touched Tracey's arm. She blinked, surprised to find Laura crouched beside her, untying her hands.

"He's gone!" an unfamiliar voice shouted. The smoke cleared quickly, sucked out through the broken windows as Laura pulled Tracey from the chair. Tracey tore the inert red ribbon from her wrist — the simple child lock spell she had broken when her raw emotions took over.

Her friends had come to save her. *Where's Agent Malden?* She searched for the agent but didn't see him. The Butterfly Stone pulsed, heating quickly against her skin, like it was reacting to Tracey's fear. But wait, Doctor Chan was gone. She pressed her hand against it. *It's over now, you can rest.* It pulsed again, hotter this time. *Weird.* A noise drew her gaze to the doorway and her jaw fell at the Mage-kind who had saved her.

"Who are you?"

"Tracey," Laura said with a sigh. "It's Jilly Cho."

"I thought you hated me," Tracey said, her voice laced with confusion. The group walked quickly along Acacia Street heading for Stock Street and away from the motel. Tracey realized suddenly just how thirsty she was. Her mouth was desert dry, and she felt a little spacey too. Like things were not quite real yet.

"I don't hate you," Laura whispered, clutching Tracey's hand so tight it hurt. Tracey could see the truth on Laura's face. "But—"

"Where are we going?" Jonny asked.

"Uncle Donny's." Tracey could get a drink there and it was safe. Uncle Donny had wards up to protect the office. Tracey's hands were still shaking.

"What are you doing?" a voice hissed behind them. Tracey spun around and glared at the dark-haired girl holding Jonny's hand. Tracey's eyes narrowed. The Butterfly Stone throbbed like a heartbeat against her skin.

"That's Jilly Cho." Laura's voice was flat, tired, like she had said it several times before. When Tracey looked at her, Laura's eyes closed and she rubbed her cheeks.

Tracey turned back to Jilly. "What are you talking about?"

"I felt how strong you were in the motel. Now I do not sense... *Oh*, you are shielding your true power. Why do you do that? I can barely sense you."

"Long story."

The Mage-kind girl couldn't sense Tracey's magic? What would happen if she really focused on hiding herself? Would her presence disappear entirely, like Hank's did with his box of tricks?

The thought of hiding her abilities appealed to her in more ways than one. She could use it in public, too, and pretend she wasn't Mage-kind. *One day I'll try it.*

She slowed her steps, the fast walk leaving her breathless. "How did you find me?"

"Jilly," Laura said.

Tracey glanced at Jilly, flinching at the intense look in the other girl's eyes. "Thank you."

Jilly's hard stare softened. She nodded. Tracey pressed hard on the Butterfly Stone. It was hot, almost scalding. *What's wrong with it?*

Tracey led them inside Uncle Donny's office. Luckily her uncle wasn't in, which would give her time to figure out what to tell him. An urgent feeling crawled around her brain. Something important, something she couldn't quite put her finger on. It was right on the tip of her tongue.

"Drink this." Jonny placed a bottle of pop in Tracey's hand. Orange liquid sloshed around the inside of the plastic bottle.

"What do you remember?" Laura asked.

Tracey gulped at the soda until she upended the bottle. "Doctor Chan." Hadn't he called himself something else? She couldn't remember. A shiver ran over her skin. She should have felt safe here in Uncle Donny's office, but she couldn't shake the fear that pressed on her chest. Doctor Chan tried to... to... Her brain couldn't complete the thought. She clasped her trembling hands together. "Um."

"Who rescued you?" Laura asked, her voice deep and slow.

"What are you talking about?" Had Laura hit her head on something? She wasn't making any sense. "You were there."

"Who is in the room with us now?"

Tracey narrowed her gaze. *What is she on?* "You, Jonny..."

"And?" Jonny asked.

"And Jilly Cho. What is going on? Why are you asking such weird questions?" Honestly, Tracey was just glad Laura and Jonny were talking to her again. She wanted to know how they had found her. She pressed her hand to the hot stone under her shirt. *Why is it so hot?*

"You were right, sort of," Laura said.

"I was?"

"There was a spell and Jilly was at the center of it. But, it's not on me and Jonny."

"Who is it on then?" Tracey eyed the strange girl standing next to the door. Jilly's face was scrunched up like she smelled something bad.

Tracey took a subtle sniff to check it wasn't something in the room, but couldn't find anything. The back of her neck tingled when both Laura and Jonny hesitated.

"Do you remember me?" Jilly asked, her muscles tensing as she waited for Tracey's answer.

"Of course I do." Tracey glared at her. "You stole my friends."

Jonny snorted. He pressed his glasses back up his nose. "Tracey, that's the spell talking. Do you remember yesterday with Jilly?"

Yesterday? She remembered the library, Damian, and training with Grandma. There was no Jilly Cho in her memories. Tracey's mind became a rollercoaster, leaping up and down. She knew she had been forgetting things. She had been afraid she had Nana's dementia but, no, it *was* a spell! "I ... I don't remember meeting Jilly yesterday."

"You see. That's the spell. It's a spell that makes you forget that Jilly even exists."

Tales
by
The Lost

Following <u>219</u>, Followed by <u>0</u>
click **<broken link>** to follow <u>The Lost</u>!

Day 1283

[cont …]

It doesn't matter.

I can be anyone I want to be.

<u>0</u> likes, <u>0</u> comments, <u>0</u> reshares
click **<broken link>** to like this post!:D

T.B.T.L.

26

Tracey held up her hands, her mind spiraling. "Hold on, what are you talking about?"

Laura shushed Jonny and leaned forward. She clasped Tracey's hands with her warm fingers. Tracey locked eyes with Jilly over Laura's. Jilly's face was calm, but her hands twisted inside her pockets. She wasn't as relaxed as she was pretending to be. "The spell doesn't affect me or Jonny, and we couldn't figure out what was wrong with you. You never seemed to remember her," Laura said.

"It only affects Mage-kind," Jilly added.

Questions swirled in Tracey's brain, but she was so tired it was hard to make sense of them. "How am I remembering you now? Oh, because you're in the room with me, right? As soon as you leave, I'll forget?"

"Maybe. I'm not sure. It's different for everyone."

"Is that why you keep asking what I remember?" Tracey climbed to her feet and paced the restricted space in front of the sofa. Her neck muscles ached. The Butterfly Stone was super-hot against her chest. *Oh!* The stone knew about the spell. It had known before Tracey did and had been fighting the spell. "Are you cursed?"

"That's a good way to put it," Jilly sighed. She shuffled forward and slumped down on the sofa. Jonny sat and leaned against her legs. Jilly ran her fingers over his shorn scalp. "The curse has affected my family for over two hundred years."

"That's awful."

"Laura confronted me when you couldn't remember me. After I explained what was going on, she said we had to find a way to make you remember."

Tracey looked across at Laura, who stood near Uncle Donny's office door. "You don't hate me?"

"Look, Tracey..." Laura nibbled at her lips, chewing her purple lipstick off. "Come outside with me for a sec. I need you to remember this."

"What do you mean?" Tracey asked. "If I leave, I'll forget Jilly and you'll have to tell me everything again, right?"

"We'll tell you again, but I have to say this and if she's not here then you'll remember it."

Tracey let Laura lead her into the stinky alley. There wasn't a lot of room. The alley was the width of a clown car with the doors open. Tracey scratched the toe of her trainers into the concrete, wishing she could leave scuff marks behind. She was in a scuff mark kind of mood. The smell was slightly better than usual out here. The garbage must have been collected that morning. The smell was only *sort of* gag-inducing rather than *absolutely* gag-inducing. Afraid to hear what Laura was going to say, Tracey knew their friendship couldn't return to what it was without them talking. She bit down on her anxiety and urged, "Go on."

"You made me so cross, Tracey," Laura started.

The burn of embarrassment scorched Tracey's face. She couldn't meet Laura's stare, and glanced up at the brick wall above Laura instead. Her throat was super dry. She swallowed and nodded, unable to say anything.

"We were friends, we *are* friends, but Tracey, you used *magic* on me. How could you even think...?"

Tracey opened her mouth desperate to explain she had only done it to protect Laura, to keep her safe from... from... *ugh*. There was someone she was supposed to remember, wasn't there? She scratched at an almost faded purple stain on her palm. "Laura..."

"Let me finish, Tracey. You went crazy. You didn't trust me. I know the curse made it worse, but you should never, ever use magic on me — us — your friends, ever."

"I..." Laura's glare intensified at Tracey's hesitation. She felt bees buzzing in her stomach.

"You have to promise me, Tracey."

This was it. Their friendship stood on a high wire, an inch too far either way and their friendship would fall. "I promise, Laura. I promise never to use magic on you. You, Jonny, or Tony. Ever. I... Laura, I was trying to—"

Laura's face was a mask. "No, Tracey. No reasons, no excuses. Just don't. Ever again, okay?"

Tracey nodded so quickly she thought her head might come clear off. "I promise."

Laura held out her arms.

Tracey dove into them and hugged her best friend tight. "I don't like fighting."

"Neither do I," Laura whispered against the side of Tracey's cheek.

"I thought I lost you. That you hated me. Please, please don't ignore my text messages again." Tracey finally felt whole. When the two girls separated, tears blurred Tracey's view of her best friend. Laura's eyes were red-rimmed and shiny too. They sniffed at the same time and giggled.

"Why were we even fighting? Why did I use magic on you?" Tracey mused, scratching her nose.

"Oh for crying out loud." Laura dragged Tracey back inside Uncle Donny's office. Tracey stumbled to a halt just inside the door when she caught sight of the dark-haired Asian girl chatting with Jonny. The Butterfly Stone was a hot coal under her shirt. "What are *you* doing here?"

Laura and Jonny exchanged exasperated looks and told her about the curse. It left Tracey even more confused. "So, because I left the room, I forgot everything? It's not just Jilly I forget?"

"This is the second time *today* we've told you."

Tracey heard the word Jonny stressed. "Today?"

"Let's just say we've been getting a lot of practice explaining this story to you. We've got it down to a fine art, now. Short and sweet."

Laura nodded. "It's a crappy spell."

"Jilly is connected to the stones, Trace," Jonny said.

"How?" Her mind jumped to all the weird times lately she had forgotten things, and her nightmares about Nana. The Butterfly Stone was hot all the time. *Because it's fighting the spell!* Tracey's brain ticked over. Her nightmares, were they connected too? "Your ancestor's stone. Does it look like the eye of a tiger?" Tracey asked.

Jilly's mouth dropped open. "How could you possibly know that?"

Tracey waved her hands around. "Nevermind. If Jilly leaves the room, then I'll forget it all again. Jonny or Laura, can you take notes? Jilly, can you describe the stone? Tell me everything you know about it?"

Jilly's eyes were wide, her mouth in the shape of an "oh."

Tracey stared back. *Yes, I'm listening. Yes, I believe you.*

A tiny lift of Jilly's lips betrayed her happiness. "My ancestor's name is Jing Cho. He was a founding member of the Sect of Six. After the murders and when the sect scattered, Jing learned the terrible price of his involvement. A curse had been placed upon his family line. Lost in time. Invisible to memory. Forgotten in history. In Jing's anger he made a terrible mistake. He threw the stone away. But the curse did not lift with the disappearance of the stone. My family has been searching for it ever since. I think the curse can only be broken by the stone itself. Four weeks ago, I began having nightmares. Nightmares with your face, Tracey. When Laura told me about the Butterfly Stone, I knew you were at the center of my quest. But the curse infects me too. How could you possibly help me if you could not remember me? I knew I had to convince your Norm friends first. We've been trying to explain everything to you. I am afraid we did rather poorly."

"I thought you were stealing them away from me," Tracey admitted. Shame filled her body.

Laura snorted. "You can't steal friends, Tracey."

"You dummy," Jonny laughed, tugging on Tracey's sleeve.

Tracey scrubbed at her damp eyes. Her head felt heavier than normal, weighed down by all this new knowledge. She just wanted to close her eyes and sleep for a month. "Wait, go back. You said six. The Sect of Six. That's wrong. There are five stones. It's the Five Stones of Power, not six."

Jilly frowned. "No, it is six. I have researched the curse carefully. There are six stones."

"Then you're wrong, because—"

Jonny started laughing. Tracey stared at him as if he had grown another head. "Jonny? What..."

"Memory spell—forgetting curse. It *is* the Sect of Six. The spell made everyone forget."

Tracey locked eyes with Jilly. "How is that even possible? I've been researching too and all the history books say it was five Mage-kind, not six."

"The curse is powerful, Tracey. Even things that are written down are not safe from it. I keep a blog of my studies called *Tales of The_Lost*, but the posts go missing. Any Mage-kind I talk to forget me. Some days it feels impossible to live."

What a nightmare. To be forever forgotten. Jilly had saved Tracey from Doctor Chan, but doubts swirled. "How did you know Doctor Chan had captured me? He said he'd blocked my power."

"I used a hunter spell," Jilly said.

"A hunter? What's that?" Tracey asked.

"I'm a hunter," Jilly said. Her sharp gaze bugged Tracey, challenging her again.

Tracey fought down her fury. "And what is that?"

"My family business. We're hunters. In my culture, Mage-kind are sacred beings gifted with a touch from the gods. To betray that calling, to betray..." she broke off, breathing heavily.

Being treated as special in a good way sounded like a dream. Tracey couldn't imagine it. Then what Jilly said sunk in. "You're hunting me?"

"No!"

"Then why are you here? Why come to our school?" Jonny asked, leaning forward.

"I am hunting *him*. The Betrayer. You had him." Jilly pointed, making Tracey feel inches tall. "And you let him go."

"Who? I don't—" Tracey's confusion was growing.

"You know him as Doctor Chan."

Tracey and her friends gaped at that pronouncement. Falling down on the sofa, Tracey pressed her fingers into her temples. The ache was becoming a full-on headache. "He ran away when we beat Timothy in Sachorn Forest. He escaped again while you were busy rescuing me." Agent Malden would be furious when he found out.

"Timothy!" spat Jilly. "He got the punishment he deserved."

"But, Jilly, Doctor Chan was going to give the stones to Timothy," Tracey said.

Jilly's eyes widened. "That cannot be."

"That's why we —"

"No, no. The Betrayer would not help that demon. I fear his offer of servitude to Timothy was simply a means to an end. The Betrayer wants the Tiger's Eye. And he will do anything, including betraying Timothy, to get it."

"The Tiger's Eye?" Laura asked.

Jilly shook her head. "That is what we call the stone that belonged to my ancestor."

It all made sense. For a moment Tracey finally felt like she understood. Her dreams, her nightmares. The Tiger's Eye was one of the stones of power.

"Tracey, what if Doctor Chan has the other stone? The one Officer Jameson was holding, Timothy's stone?" Laura asked.

"I don't know — he didn't say." *If he has it why would he stay in town?* Tracey shrugged. "We didn't find it in the forest. Doctor Chan might have taken it when he disappeared."

"If Doctor Chan doesn't want the stones for Timothy, then why does he want them?" Jonny asked.

Jilly stormed to the door and spun around. "He is the Betrayer. It is his nature. Everything that he is — it's all a lie. He wants the Tiger's Eye only for himself."

"But that doesn't make any sense. The curse is on your family. How can — ?" Jonny continued, holding out a hand to the fuming girl.

"He's my uncle," Jilly spat. "Steven Cho!"

Whoa! No one said anything for a moment as that sunk in. Jonny's hand dropped to his side. Tracey leapt off the sofa. "Your uncle? But that would mean he's cursed too. How do I remember him?"

"You don't. He told you his name was Doctor Chan. That is who you remember. You remember Doctor Chan not Steven Cho."

The curse has a loophole? "Why didn't you do that then? Give yourself another name? I would have remembered you and this —"

"I will not deny my name," Jilly snapped. "Tracey, your name is your identity. To deny your name is to deny your family and your ancestors.

But for Mage-kind it is much worse. It severs your link with your family." Her gaze narrowed. "You feel it, don't you? The connection you have to your mother? Your sister?"

Tracey nodded, unable to imagine losing that connection. What a terrible thing to do. A terrible choice. To be remembered but only by losing everything that makes you *you*. "Why would he do that to your family?"

"He does not want to break the curse. He wishes it to continue."

"Why?" Jonny asked.

"Steven Cho is a disgrace to the entire Cho family. Our family is of the upmost importance. We have no one but ourselves. To betray family for criminal gain. Pah." She fumed further, "He only uses his true name to further his crimes. So the authorities cannot capture him.

"So, you're here to stop him," Tracey deduced.

Jilly straightened, in that moment she stood tall, proud. Magnificent. "I am here to take him home. He must face the justice of my family."

Tracey stared at the girl with awe. How hard must it be — to hunt down your own family? "Okay, well *we* need to stop Timothy, which means we need *all* the stones. If we help you find Doctor Chan and he has the Tiger's Eye will you give it to us temporarily?"

Jilly's face was stern. Her lips pressed tightly together and she jerked forward in a nod. "Yes."

"Tracey, if Doctor Chan has Timothy's stone and he's searching for the Tiger's Eye, then that's three stones here in town. We could get three. Timothy can't come back if you have three of the six stones he needs. You'll have beaten him," Jonny said, parking his butt on the sofa.

"So, how do I remember all of this?" Tracey asked and flopped onto the sofa next to Jonny.

Jilly squeezed in between Tracey and Jonny. "I don't know," she admitted. "No one has ever remembered before. I just don't know."

Tracey dropped her head into her hands. The Butterfly Stone hung hot and heavy around her neck.

"We need Tony." Laura said.

Tracey mumbled between her fingers. "Call him."

Tales
by
The Lost

Following 219, Followed by 0
click **<broken link>** to follow The Lost!

Day 1283

[cont ...]

What I truly want to be... is me.

No one knows who I am. Not the real me. Being Mage-kind is hard enough ... add in a curse? I hate it.

I hate my family. They did this.

0 likes, 0 comments, 0 reshares
click **<broken link>** to like this post!:D

T.B.T.L.

27

Tony arrived while Jonny was making hot chocolate for everyone. Tracey examined his disheveled hair and reddened eyes with concern. He looked worse than ever. As he paused in the doorway, his eyebrows climbed into his hairline. "I thought you weren't speaking to each other."

Heat spread across Tracey's cheeks. "I might have been wrong about Jilly."

He followed her gaze to the Asian girl sitting close to Jonny on the sofa. "What did I miss? Who is she?"

Suddenly Tracey had an inkling of the pain Jilly went through daily as they explained everything to Tony. When they finished, Tony's exhausted gaze flipped from Tracey back to Jilly. "I don't know if we can. I mean, your family has been dealing with this for centuries. How can we find something in an afternoon?" Jilly shrugged. Tony's shoulders slumped. "Tracey. I think we need your grandma. She's a level three. If anyone can help it's her."

Tracey nodded. "She knows a lot of magic about memory."

"Your grandmother is a Significant?" Jilly's eyes widened. She clutched Jonny's hand tightly. "Then let's go talk to her."

Tracey locked Uncle Donny's office door securely behind them and glanced around the deserted shopping strip. No cars were parked in the bays and no one walked past. It was eerily quiet. Tracey's hair whipped her face sticking to her lips in the icy breeze. She tugged the strands from her eyes and zipped up her jacket. Jilly, Jonny and Laura stood on the sidewalk, talking softly while waiting for her.

Tony inched to Tracey's side. "Are you okay?"

"Tony, keep an eye on her, yeah? I don't know if we can trust her yet." Bitter wind tugged at Tracey's jacket, trying to find an opening. Cold fingers of air pressed into her skin.

"Are you sure that's not just the memory spell talking?"

She dipped her chin and stared at him. "Doctor Chan is her uncle. She's connected to the stones. Darn right I don't trust her."

"Okay, I believe you. Something is off about this whole thing though."

Tracey heard the wobble in his voice and took a long, serious look at her friend, from the slump of his shoulders to his wind-ruffled wild hair "Are you okay, Tony?" He avoided her gaze. She put a hand on his arm. "Tony?" His shoulder dropped further and he leaned against her. She put her arms around him and hugged him tightly.

He sniffed into her neck. "Not really. I've been fighting with Mom and Dad. I hate talking to the shrink. I'm all tied up in knots and..."

She pulled back to stare him in the eyes. "What?"

"I... I just want to forget everything."

"Tony." Tracey held his gaze. "Look at what's happening to Jilly. It's good to remember things and to talk about them. I don't think forgetting actually helps. We haven't hung out a lot lately. I've been stressed and scared too. Maybe... if you want... after we talk to my grandma we should sit down just the two of us and talk?"

"Yeah, okay. That'd be awesome." The two friends shared a smile. "Besides you have to tell me about Damian."

Tracey pushed at him and they both laughed, turning quickly to join their friends.

Grandma's wide stare swung from Tracey to Jilly, sliding to Tony and Jonny before stopping on Laura. "A memory spell?"

"Please, Grandma Masters. I know you don't sense it, neither does Tracey, but Jonny and I have seen it happen so many times now. Tracey and Tony just forget everything when Jilly leaves the room. Conversations, events, everything. Jilly's family is cursed," Laura insisted. The group stood in the living room of Tracey's home because no one had wanted to sit down.

"Explain it to me again," Grandma said.

Tracey listened as Laura listed school events and activities and searched her memory for a hint of what was described. Nothing. She shook her head every time Grandma looked her way. If Grandma wanted confirmation, she wouldn't get it from Tracey.

"None of it?" Grandma asked, her focus entirely on Tracey.

"Nothing, Grandma." *Oh.* "Wait." She pulled two golden rings from her jeans pocket—the truth rings that belonged to Prince Henry. She slid them on over her thumbs. She stared at Laura, then at Jonny, then Tony, and at last Jilly. "Say it again." The rings didn't twitch. She pulled them off and handed them to Grandma. They wouldn't fit over Grandma's arthritic fingers. Tracey slipped them back on.

Jonny tugged Tracey's sleeve. "Tracey, look at your wrists."

She held up her arms. Purple and red bruises marred the skin. "What? How did I get these?"

Laura sighed.

Jonny slapped his hands against his thighs. "That's what we've been telling you."

Right, memory spell. The stone was a hot force heating her skin. *Oh, the stone was fighting the spell.* Maybe Stephanie knew something about it. Closing her eyes Tracey called, "Stephanie?"

Dizziness hit her. When she felt steady, she opened her eyes on the white room. The colored shapes were gone. "Stephanie?" Echoes built in the non-air around her.

A woman's body formed in front of Tracey. Her flowing white dress billowed in a non-existent breeze. *Is there even air here? What am I breathing?* Stephanie's heart-shaped face was brilliance given form. Dark eyes stared, chocolate cherry lips lifted into a wide smile. "Tracey." Her voice was musical, like an angel.

"Can you sense the other stones?" Tracey demanded, cutting right to the importance of the matter.

Stephanie's eyes widened. "What?"

"Can I use the Butterfly Stone to find the others? I think one stone is close, but there's a curse on it."

"Whose stone do you seek?"

"Jing Cho's Tiger's Eye."

Stephanie's brow furrowed. "Who?"

Oh no. Was the curse so powerful it even affected Stephanie's ghostly remnant? "There's a Hidden One curse on the Tiger's Eye. Jing Cho was a member of the Five... ah... six. He was your friend."

Stephanie's gaze turned inward. A frown etched deep shadows on her skin. "That can't be right."

"It is. I'm with his descendent, Jilly Cho, right now. The curse makes Mage-kind forget everything about her and her family. Timothy is hunting for the stone too. Only his form is different now."

"How different?" Stephanie's gaze snapped to Tracey's face. Her hands twitched as if to grab Tracey by the shoulders and shake her.

"Wind and dirt. A filthy tornado."

Stephanie shook her head. "That is not Timothy. He cannot rebuild his shadowy form until he has taken a host."

"Are you sure?"

"It is not him."

Tracey's heart pounded. "Then who is it?"

"Someone else is hunting the stones. Tracey, you must be careful."

"Can you find the Tiger's Eye?"

Stephanie's expression soured. "If the curse affects me, I cannot help you."

"But..." There had to be something. "A spell?"

The ghostly figure shook her head. "Have you not felt the magic thrumming in the Butterfly Stone?"

"It's been active, warm all the time. Is that what you mean?"

"It is fighting this curse, using much of its magic. Perhaps with the strength of another stone—"

"Timothy's stone. We know it's here. Officer Jameson held it. I need to know more about it so we can search for it. What image is painted on Timothy's stone?"

"I do not know. We kept them hidden from one another. The image upon the stone carries power. It is our soul shape. My Butterfly, your butterfly, is for imagination, transmutation, beauty, strength, fragility and life. Butterflies call to us, Tracey."

"So, what called to Timothy?"

"I do not know."

She blinked and found herself standing in front of Laura. "Whoa!"

"Tracey?"

"I'm okay. Grandma, Stephanie can't help," she said turning to her elder.

"Okay," Grandma said. "Clearly the spell is powerful." Grandma stared at Jilly. If the girl tried anything on Tracey's grandma, Tracey was going to blast her into next week. Grandma's eyes flicked to Tracey and turned black. Tracey, Tony, and Jilly felt the moment Grandma tapped into her core. A buzzing noise rose up from the floor. Pictures rumbled on the table and rattled against the walls.

Whatever Grandma was looking for she didn't find it. "Let's try something different." Standing at the base of the stairs Grandma bellowed for Sarah. Tracey's sister appeared at the top of the stairs. Kylie followed Sarah down. Her lips curled in a snarl as she caught sight of the crowd gathered below.

"Not more training," Sarah complained.

Kylie bared her teeth. "We've got stuff to do," she whispered scratching her chest. She glowered at Tracey. The twins appeared from the back garden, a football clenched tightly in Simon's hands. Grandma waved them into the living room.

"Where's Peter?" Tracey asked.

"He went to the hospital with Dad," Sarah said. "You'd know if you were here."

Ouch. Tracey flinched at the rebuke. She hadn't even asked Grandma how Mom was doing.

"What's going on in here?" Charlie asked shooting his brother a questioning look.

Simon shrugged, "How do I know, I was with you."

"Who's that?" Kylie asked, pointing at Jilly. No one answered her.

An interloper. Tracey scowled at Jilly and then stopped herself, pressing a finger to the damaged skin of her wrist. The sharp pain sent her stomach into somersaults. *Stop that! It's just the curse twisting your thoughts.*

Watching her grandma cast a spell filled Tracey with awe. In moments a circle had been drawn with salt and several bowls placed on the floor. "What are you—"

"—hush, darling," Grandma said, waving her hands. "I'll be ready in a moment."

"What's she doing, Stephanie?" Tracey asked, keeping her voice to a whisper.

The ghostly voice answered immediately. *Your grandmother is a wise woman. She is creating a memory circle, a way to restore your short-term memories.*

"Will it work?"

Perhaps.

"You're not sure?"

It depends on the original spell.

"What else can she do?"

I do not know.

Sooooo, that was super helpful. Not. "It's a spell on Jing Cho's stone."

Who?

"Ugh! Never mind." While Tracey was lost in thought, Grandma finished setting up her spell.

"Gather inside the circle please."

Sarah and Kylie gasped as they stepped over the salt line, careful not to disrupt the loose grains. Their hair floated straight up like they had touched one of those globes in the science lab.

Tracey stepped over the barrier with Jilly and Tony. "Whoa!" Every hair stood on end, electrified with invisible energy. A second later, Jilly's hair flopped down in a messy tangle. Tracey's hand flew to her own head, embarrassed at the knotty tendrils. Her skin tingled. Even Tony looked a bit silly, his hair sticking out everywhere. He looked like one of her pencils with the hairy tops.

"All of you," Grandma ordered. Tracey caught the question in Laura's gaze and nodded. Laura straightened and together with Jonny stepped over the barrier, as did Simon and Charlie. Simon had a massive grin on his face. He didn't get the chance to be involved in magic much, being the twin born without a Mage-kind core.

Power swirled around Grandma. At her silent command, Tracey dropped her shield and let magic gather inside her body. Tracey's skin tingled spreading over her limbs like an ocean wave. She felt Charlie's and Sarah's magic blend in with her own, blurring the edges between them and strengthening the core of the circle. Family magic was a glorious thing. Who would ever want to sever it?

Tracey could feel Sarah's emotions again. Her gaze flew to her sister. So much anger. *Where did that come from?* Sarah wouldn't look at her. Tony's magic pulled her attention away from her sister. She opened herself up to him, but he held her off, not letting her inside. Why was he blocking her?

Kylie's energy was bright and brittle. It clashed with the harmony of the family magic. Tony, and even Jilly, blended with the Masters family song creating a magical harmony. Kylie's magic was like a flat key. It sounded wrong. And someone was missing. Dave's absence was a prickle at Tracey's mind like a missing instrument in an orchestra. She had grown used to his magic's metallic tang. Everyone had a print, as different and individual as a fingerprint. Jilly was a thunderstorm, powerful and angry — a swirling, roiling energy with a bitter eucalyptus bite.

Tracey reached out, wanting to learn more about the mysterious Mage-kind girl. Like with Tony, there was a wall in her way. She knocked politely, hoping Jilly would open up. She was pushed back hard enough to rock on her heels. *Rude.* She glared at Jilly and then recognition dawned. *The curse!* Jilly wasn't fighting Tracey at all. She stared at Tracey — her eyes squinted. Tracey tilted her head. Jilly shrugged. She didn't know what she had done. Tracey's gaze flew to Tony. If Jilly's wall was the result of a curse... *Tony?*

His stare connected with hers. "Did you just speak inside my head?"

She hadn't meant to. *Um, can you hear me?* His eyes widened and he nodded. *Fruit tingles!* This needed to be explored. *Grandma's magic circle?*

"Probably."

There's a wall in your mind. I can't get through it.

"Oh sorry."

I don't think it's you. Jilly has one too.

"The curse?" Tony swore.

Grandma *tsked*, glaring them into silence.

A vibration beneath Tracey's feet caught her attention. She looked down, stumbled and widened her stance. Energy was building in the center of the circle. An invisible hand slammed against Tracey's chest, propelling her backward parallel to the floor. She jerked to a halt inches from the carpet. At least that was how she perceived the motion. Gasping, she stared up at her own frozen body standing still in front of her. *My spirit was thrown out of my body?*

Memories, like a movie on fast rewind, burst into Tracey's head. She remembered talking to her friends in Uncle Donny's office about the curse. Her thoughts wound back further to... Doctor Chan's motel room. Unrecognizable memories rewound too fast for her to follow. *I was in Doctor Chan's motel room?* All of her friends were there, including Jilly Cho. The reality of the moment burned into Tracey's mind. Jilly told the truth.

Tracey assumed the memories would stop and play back at normal speed now that she had remembered them but no, her memories went back further and further until she was alone and... *tied up?* Doctor Chan held her captive and she didn't remember it. Cold filled her body, freezing her heart into a solid mass. What had Doctor Chan done? She couldn't hear what the man was saying. If only the reversing time would stop so she could work out what it was.

Nausea swirled inside her belly, rising up into her throat. The memories came faster and faster. Her head see-sawed, thickening, as if filled with cotton wool. Sharp stabbing pain dug into her temples before a broad pressure wrapped across her forehead. Her nose dripped. Her hand, invisible to her own eyes, wiped beneath but found nothing. The pain crested. Tracey cried out as her thoughts became mush. She was sucked back up and into her body and hit the ground in a collision of limbs, breath bursting from her lungs. "Ouch!"

Scrubbing a hand over her eyes, Tracey wiped beneath her nose again.

Her fingers came away coated with blood. Head aching, she pinched the bridge of her nose and tilted her head back. A white flag waved in front of her eyes. Tracey took the proffered tissue and shoved it up her nostrils. "Tanks," she attempted, her blocked nostrils deadening her gratitude. The Butterfly Stone lay cold and quiet against her chest.

"Everyone hit the ground. I can't get a response from the others. What happened?" Jilly's voice was soft, uncertain, unlike her usually sharp orders. Tracey glanced around the circle. Her friends and Grandma lay unmoving on the carpet.

"Grandma?" Tracey scrambled to her elder and cradled her head gently, shaking her shoulders. "Grandma? Grandma?" There was no response. "Get a pillow or something." Grandma's pale skin was cold. "And blankets!" Moments later Jilly appeared with an armful of soft bedding. Tracey lowered Grandma's head to the pillow and wrapped a blue crochet blanket tight around her shoulders. Fear pricked Tracey's belly. Why wouldn't Grandma wake up?

A quick check of each person showed they were all alive, but unconscious. Jonny had landed on his face, nose pressed into the ground. Laura and Sarah lay crumpled on their sides facing each other. Simon had fallen on Charlie, and Tony and Kylie lay on their backs staring sightlessly at the ceiling. "I don't understand," Tracey said. "Laura, Jonny, and Simon aren't Mage-kind. Why are they affected?"

Jilly shrugged. "The curse is the curse. It's never been broken, Tracey, not in two hundred years. I don't think even your grandma—a Significant—is strong enough to fight it.

"Then why am I awake?"

"I don't know."

Tracey pressed a hand to her chest. "Oh." She tugged the Butterfly Stone from beneath her shirt and examined it. The painted butterfly was cold, but glowed with a silvery light.

"You wear a stone?" Jilly gasped. She fell to her knees. "You're a protector. Why didn't you say anything?"

"What's a protector?"

"God, you don't even know what you are, do you?"

"Jilly, what are you talking about?"

"You wear a stone. The protectors are those connected to the stones. You protect it, act as its guardian. The stone chooses its protector, Tracey. Once you put it on—"

"You can't take it off. Yeah, I worked that out too late."

"Tracey, you can find the Tiger's Eye."

"What?" Tracey climbed to her feet. *I need to call Dad.* Her worried gaze drifted over her friends and family again. "We have to get help."

"No, wait. Tracey, what do you remember?"

"I..." Tracey pressed both hands to her temples as her head swam. She swayed as pain exploded behind her eyes. Restored memories burst forth in bright flashes. "Everything," she gasped.

She remembered Jilly rescuing her from Doctor Chan, and more. She could hear Doctor Chan's voice boasting of his intentions, telling Tracey his true name. *That's why I forgot him.* She also remembered ...

"Mom!" Tracey jumped over the salt circle and bolted upstairs.

"Tracey?" Jilly called after her. Tracey ignored her. Heart pounding, her head feeling as though it would explode, she burst into her mom's empty bedroom.

She's not here.

The last memory to return, the one that sent ribbons of fear through Tracey's body, had been about her mom. Doctor Chan had been taunting her.

"No one is coming. No one knows you are here. My room spell will prevent access. You cannot call to them and you cannot touch your magic. No one will find you here." He filled a small bowl with water from a jug and placed it at Tracey's feet.

There was one person who would know something had happened to her, one person who always knew when Tracey was hurt or scared or in pain. "My mom will know." Doctor Chan's laugh froze Tracey's breath inside her throat. The headaches, her mom's illness. "What did you do to my mom?"

"I took care of her first."

The constant migraines—migraines that were worse than normal... Mom wasn't getting better.

It distracted Dad and Grandma, and even Tracey.

Mom would have known Tracey was in trouble had she been well. It was only because she had been so sick that she didn't realize and couldn't send help.

Doctor Chan said he took care of Mom first.

He did something to Mom!

Tales
by
The Lost

Following 219, Followed by 0
click <broken link> to follow The Lost!

Day 1283

[cont ...]

One act, by one man so long ago, destroyed

the lives of the many to come after him.

My mother and father, my grandmother

and grandfather, my aunts and cousins,

all of us, destined to be forgotten.

0 likes, 0 comments, 0 reshares
click <broken link> to like this post!:D

T.B.T.L.

28

Her heart pounding wildly, Tracey upended the bedside table drawer all over Mom's disheveled bed, hunting through boxes of jewelry, coins, lidless pens and other odds and ends. She tossed mismatched buttons, pins, and hair clips on the floor. *Where is it?* She stretched for the next drawer with her magic and upended it.

"What are you doing?" Jilly asked from the doorway, taking in Tracey's destruction.

"It's not here."

"What isn't here? What are you searching for? Won't your mom be annoyed?"

Turning back to her search, Tracey said, "I remember everything. Your uncle said it's my fault. I should have stopped him. My fault!" *Where? Where is it?* Her gaze shot to the other side table. *Maybe on dad's side?*

"Tracey!"

Cold hands clamped around her shoulders, stilling her frantic movements. She wrenched herself from Jilly's iron grip. "Go away."

"We don't have much time. If you remember what happened, then you know we have to find the stone before we can break the curse."

"Doctor Chan did something to my mom. It has to be here. Whatever he used to curse her or ... or maybe he poisoned her ... it has to be here."

"Then be sensible. Think."

"What do you think I'm doing?" Tracey turned on Jilly. "He's *your* uncle. What would he use to get someone out of the way?"

Jilly shook her head, her gaze glued to Tracey's face. "I don't know. I was only sent to find him, to bring him home."

The urge to tear her hair out and pound her fists against Mom's bed was hard to ignore. Tracey remembered Doctor Chan's office at the university when she first met him, filled to bursting with books, full of dust and coffee smells. He was a teacher. "He's an office guy. Not a fighter, not a scientist. How would he get it to her?" Tracey's gaze fell on the fresh flowers in the vase on Mom's beside table. She leaned in to smell them.

Jilly pulled her back. "Don't get too close."

Tracey sent a burst of magic into her palm and held her hand over the flowers. Forcing her breath to seep from her mouth, she concentrated on the red and yellow blooms and opened herself up to the power of the Butterfly Stone. The scent of dust and coffee filled her nose. The taste of wrongness lingered in the back of her throat when she breathed in. "There. It's the flowers. There is something on them."

Jilly grabbed the vase and ran to the door.

"Wait! Don't destroy them. We might need them."

"So, what—"

"We need to take them to the hospital."

Jilly's gaze narrowed. She snatched a blanket off the bed and threw it over the flowers, wrapping them up tightly. "Tracey, we have to find—"

"—not until I save my mom." The two girls faced off, standing inches from each other.

"What about your family downstairs?"

"We don't know when they'll wake up. I'm not waiting! You said it yourself. We don't know how long we have until my memories disappear again."

"Which is why—"

"My mom!" Spittle flew from Tracey's mouth. Jilly didn't move. Neither did Tracey.

Jilly nodded sharply. "Fine. Let's go."

The bus trip to the hospital took forever. Tracey's mind flashed over moments spent with her mom. Watching her as she inhaled her coffee in the morning. Waving to Tracey from the car as she drove away from school. Standing in the kitchen making dinner, eyes alight with interest, asking how Tracey's day had been. Her face, red and practically breathing fire at Uncle Donny when he told her about the Shadowman. Tracey gripped the blanket-covered flowers tighter in her hand. She needed a distraction. She turned to the Mage-kind fidgeting beside her. "Tell me more about your family?"

"Why?" Jilly's dark eyes were mirrors.

"I need something to focus on. Seriously, there might be a clue somewhere that will help us find the stone. Why would Doctor Chan stay in Miltern Falls? Why didn't he run?"

Jilly traced an invisible shape on the window with her fingertips. "I don't know why he is still here."

"You said he used the curse? What you mean is that he can do anything, and no one will remember if he doesn't want them to. Maybe that's why Timothy chose him."

"I think it's the other way around. I am certain he decided to work for Timothy in order to find the stone."

"Timothy wants—needs—all the stones to restore his human form."

"I don't think he was going to give it to Timothy."

"You think Doctor Chan planned to betray him? Why? What does he want the stone for then?"

Jilly shook her head. "It can't be good. That's why we have to hurry."

Tracey thought about her family and friends lying on the floor—silent, unmoving, waiting. She tapped her arm rest. "How did your family lose the Tiger's Eye?"

"My great-grandfather threw it away after my great-grandmother died. This is the closest I've ever come to finding it. Well, my mother nearly got her hands on it. Once."

"What happened?"

"The package was waylaid."

"Sounds like the stone doesn't want to be found."

"Don't be ridiculous. It is just a stone."

Tracey clenched her hand around the wrapped flowers. Stephanie was a very real presence inside the Butterfly Stone. Timothy was imprisoned inside his. Who was to say the other four stones were not linked with their original owners? "Tell me about your ancestor?"

"Jing was a Hidden."

"I ... I don't know what that means."

"His name was Jing Han Cho and he worked as a house cleaner for a Norm named Matthew Williams."

Tracey jerked in her seat at the familiar name. "Stephanie was promised to marry a man named Matthew. Wait, Matthew was a Norm?"

"You didn't know?"

"I heard her say they were promised, not that he was a Norm."

"I don't understand. How could you hear her, she's been dead for years?"

"My grandmother is holding Nana's ancestral memories, passed down from Stephanie herself. She showed them to me. But I can only see a dream when the time is right."

"Then we must wake your grandmother."

"I know. Right after we save my mom. So, Matthew was a Norm. There are only five stones ... Oh, six stones," Tracey breathed.

"Jing Cho was a Mage-kind hiding in the employ of a Norm. They all did it back then, as you know."

Tracey thought about the photo she had seen in Doctor Chan's office. "I saw a photo of the Five. Jing wasn't in the image. Tell me more about him. Please?" Peering through the grimy bus window Tracey realized they were about to run out of time.

"He was a good man, Tracey. My family didn't deserve this."

"Jilly, he believed in staying hidden from Norms. Don't you see? The curse gave him what he wished. Only instead of being hidden from Norms, he became hidden from Mage-kind."

"Oh my God."

"Sit down back there!" the bus driver ordered.

"Sorry," Tracey called. She sat and whispered to Jilly. "The curse reflects who they were in real life. It's not just your ancestor. I think all six were cursed. I found a poem…" Tracey grabbed her phone and flicked to the email she had sent herself. "Look here — these five passages — Jing's passage must be missing too."

"You think your ancestor is one of these five passages? But which one?"

"That's what I'm trying to figure out," Tracey told her. "I'm sure the last one is about Timothy. It mentions a shadow. Oh, oh!"

"What?"

"Tony discovered the M-Net has hidden fields. They only open after you already know what you're looking for. We need to search for the Tiger's Eye on the M-Net while *thinking* about the stone. I was searching for five stones, not six!" That's why I couldn't find anything.

"It won't work for me," Jilly said, excitement dying in her eyes.

"It will for me."

"You think?"

"I hope."

They jerked forward in their seats as the bus came to an abrupt halt. Conversation forgotten, Tracey bolted from the bus. With Jilly at her heels, she raced into the Miltern Central Hospital waiting room. The last time here she had gone down to the morgue with Uncle Donny investigating Miss Tearning's death. It was where Tracey had experienced her first Vision. "The Mage-kind wing is on level five." The elevator they jumped into had to be the slowest Tracey had ever ridden. She clutched the flowers tighter. Sweat beaded her brow. She swiped it away, but to her annoyance it returned. *Come on.* A soft ding announced their arrival and the doors slid open. Tracey raced to the counter that stretched in a half circle around the room. Corridors branched off at either side. All Tracey could see of the black lady at the desk was black hair scraped into a bun tight enough to stretch the skin on her face. "I need to see Mrs. Beth Masters," Tracey blurted.

The nurse didn't look up. Spying the woman's name tag, Tracey bit back her impatience and tried again. "Nurse Jeffers, excuse me. I'm here to see Mrs. Beth Masters. She's my mother." At Jilly's kick to her shin,

Tracey added, "Please."

At glacial speed Nurse Jeffers peered up through large black-framed glasses. "Yes?"

Tracey sighed. "May I please visit my mother, Mrs. Beth Masters?"

She stared down her nose. "Mrs. Masters is in room 514."

"Thank you." Tracey ran to the designated room, garnering several scowls and voices asking her not to run in the corridors. She burst into Room 514 and stumbled to a stop.

The loud, rhythmic beeping from the machine beside the bed caught Tracey's attention first. Her heart beat faster at the sight of the woman in the bed. Mom was almost as pale as the bed sheet covering her. "Mom?" Tracey crept to the bedside and touched her mom's cold hand. "Mom?" Tears sprang into her eyes when there was no response.

"Press the call button," Jilly urged.

Pull it together, Tracey! Seeing her mom, the strongest person Tracey knew, lying deathly still sent bolts of fear through Tracey. Her gaze snapped to the head board. There were several buttons. She pressed them all.

Nothing happened. There was no ding or blart of sound. *Did it work?* Her brother, Peter, pushed open the door with his elbow as his hands were occupied with two disposable steaming cups. He froze at the sight of her. "Tracey?"

"Where's Dad?" she asked.

Her brother's stare shifted to Jilly. "He's gone home to grab a shower and change his clothes. What are you—?"

The door snapped open, crashing into Peter's back, sending scalding coffee over his hands. "Ahhh!"

"What's going on in here? Who pressed the call button? Oh!" A red-headed nurse with big hips and a pink uniform immediately jumped into action, taking the cups from Peter's hands, pushing him into the adjoining bathroom to shove his hands under the cold-water tap. He didn't say a word. The nurse poked her head back out to peer at Tracey, her frown turning into a soft smile. "Distracted, were you? I've got this." She returned to the bathroom. "Keep your hands under the water, dear."

Peter's head appeared. "Tracey?"

The nurse bustled out of the bathroom and checked Mom's chart. Her Mage-kind bracelet was covered in plastic. "What do you have there, hun, something for your mom?" She eyed the blanket with interest.

"It's flowers. There's something on the petals," Tracey said. "It's what's making Mom sick."

The nurse's eyes widened. "What? How do you know?"

"I was told."

"You were told there's something she's allergic to on the flowers?"

"No, just that something on them is making her sick. I found the flowers in Mom's room. It's magic, a spell of some kind."

"Has anyone else come into contact with these flowers?"

"I don't know. We put the blanket around them."

"Right, then you've both potentially been exposed. We'll have to test you too. The red-headed nurse pulled latex gloves from a bin on the wall and snapped them over her hands. She took the wrapped bundle from Tracey. "Stay here, girls. The doctor will be in to examine you shortly." Her face softened. "It's all right now, your mom is being well cared for. This is a huge help. You may have just saved her life." She rushed from the room.

Tracey shared a look with Jilly. "We can't wait here."

"Agreed."

"Tracey, what are you talking about? What's going on?" Peter appeared in the bathroom doorway.

"Peter." Tracey inched toward the door. "Jilly and I have to go—" she kept talking, raising her voice over his protest, "—it's about the stones, Peter. I have to go."

"But, the tests?"

"We're running out of time. If Dad's going home, he's going to flip out when he sees—Grandma did a spell and, oh it doesn't matter. We *have* to go." She peered at her mom lying so still on the bed. Her breath caught. "I'm sorry, Mom. I have to go." Her gaze darted to her brother. "Make sure they save Mom."

"What if you're sick?" Peter's hands were dripping water on the floor where he stood. Tracey put as much pleading into her eyes as she could and sent assurance, trust, and promises from her core, hoping her magic would sway him where her words had failed. His concern hit her like a wave, but at last he sighed. It was music to her frayed nerves. Peter's shoulders slumped as if he had no energy left to stand up straight. He didn't glance back, waving to dismiss her.

Tracey grabbed Jilly's hand. "Let's go."

Tales
by
The Lost

Following <u>219</u>, Followed by <u>0</u>
click **<broken link>** to follow <u>The Lost</u>!

Day 1283

[cont …]

Do you know what that does to a person?

It's not good…

<u>0</u> likes, <u>0</u> comments, <u>0</u> reshares
click **<broken link>** to like this post!:D

T.B.T.L.

29

"Where do we go now?" Jilly asked.

Tracey halted just outside the hospital's sliding doors. They closed behind her with a soft sigh. *Mom will be fine. The doctors will figure it out. They'll fix her.* Tracey forced worry that she and Jilly might be sick to the side. Mom had been ill for weeks before she ended up in the hospital. They had to focus on the stones. Doctor Chan poisoned her mom to stop her knowing Tracey was in trouble. Why? It had to be because Tracey knew something, or that Tracey had a way to find the stones. He wanted the Butterfly Stone so badly. It had to be because he thought he could use it to find the other stones. They didn't have Doctor Chan's knowledge, so how would they find... *oh.* The journal Doctor Chan had been waiting for... the one Tony had redirected... the one stolen from her schoolbag.

Ugh, if only I had the journal. She narrowed her gaze at Jilly. "Did you...? I had a book in my bag. It was stolen at school. Meena didn't take it."

Jilly sighed, her face turning pink. "I—"

Tracey grabbed Jilly's shoulders. "I knew it. Where is it?"

"Jonny has it."

"Jonny?" *How could he do that to me?* "Why—"

"Never mind that now. Jonny's unconscious. We can't ask him where he hid it," Jilly said.

"We have to wake him up. We need that book. I think it holds a clue to how we can find the other stones."

As they bolted to the bus stop Tracey's phone rang. The display said Agent Malden. "Hello?"

"Tracey, good, you're there. Listen. There is an emergency at your home—"

"It's not an emergency," she blurted.

There was silence on the other end and then Agent Malden spoke again, his voice a lot calmer. "Explain."

"Did my dad call you?"

"He did."

The bus pulled to a stop in front of them. Tracey jumped on with Jilly right behind her. They sat in the front seat. "Call him back. Grandma cast a spell. It's connected to the stones, not Mom's illness. Tell him not to touch anyone in the living room. He has to go back to the hospital to get tested."

"Tested? What for?"

"Doctor Chan poisoned Mom with flowers he sent to the house. Dad might be affected too."

"Doctor Chan?"

"He is still in town."

Jilly jerked, mouthing, *No.*

"You need to send people to Miltern Falls Motel Seven. Room 407."

"Where are you?"

"Please, Agent Malden." Jilly jerked in her seat at the name. She glared at Tracey, making hand signals telling her to hang up. Tracey shook her head. Jilly pursed her lips. *I know, I know.*

"Where are you?" Agent Malden repeated.

"On my way home."

"Very good. Stay there. Your dad said your family is awake. Tracey, I am on my way and—"

"I'm almost there," Tracey told him. Through the bus window she recognized the street they were on. Slamming her fingers on the bus's stop button, she jumped up. "Gotta go," she said into the phone and disconnected the call. She grabbed Jilly's hand. "They're all awake. I know a short cut. Come on."

Tales
by
The Lost

Following 219, Followed by 0
click **<broken link>** to follow The Lost!

Day 1611

There is a girl at my school.

A strong Mage-kind.

She doesn't like me.

0 likes, 0 comments, 0 reshares
click **<broken link>** to like this post! :D

T.B.T.L.

30

The stitch in Tracey's side dug sharply into her ribs, but she forced herself to keep running. "Just through Mrs. Jenkins's yard," she puffed.

Jilly ran beside her, strides loose and easy, relaxed in a way Tracey would never be when she ran. Jilly panted, her face slightly flushed. Tracey probably looked the same, though nowhere near as radiant. How did Jilly look fabulous after all this exercise? Tracey was nothing more than an exhausted, sweaty mess.

She raced up her driveway less than a minute later. Dad's car was parked haphazardly across the lawn. "Dad!" she shouted, flinging open the front door.

"Tracey! Agent Mald—"

"I know." She stumbled to a halt. Grandma was sitting up but looked awfully pale. She leaned against Tracey's dad. Tony and Sarah sat on the couch. Tony's head was in his hands and Sarah held a bucket to her chin. Laura and Jonny sat in the armchairs on either side of the room sipping slowly from plastic cups.

Jonny moaned. "What hit us?"

Tracey could hear Simon and Charlie in the kitchen chatting. They appeared in the doorway with more cups and handed them around. Sarah took one gratefully. "We woke up and you were gone. Where'd you go?" she asked.

"Hospital," Tracey told her sister. "They—we—they know why Mom is sick now."

"What?" Dad's head snapped up. "M-Force are on their way. Tracey, come sit with me and tell us what, oh—" he spied Jilly and shifted on his knees. "Who are you?"

"Please don't get up," Jilly said. She shuffled a step behind Tracey hiding in her shadow.

"Dad, this is Jilly. A school friend."

"Tracey." Dad's gaze stayed on Jilly. "What's going on?"

"You should go back to Mom. They know what's wrong now. They can fix her."

Dad groaned as he climbed to his feet and helped Grandma to the sofa. Sarah slid over to make room. Dad groaned again as he straightened up. "How do you—"

Tracey threw her arms around him and burrowed her face into his chest. Tears leaked from her eyes. "It's my fault, Dad. It's all my fault."

He held her tightly. She didn't want to move. Jilly's shock and impatience bubbled up against Tracey's shield, but she didn't care. She cried into her dad's woolly vest. All she wanted was for him to tell her everything would be fine. He didn't speak. "Dad?" She peered up at his blurry face and dashed her tears away with shaking fingers.

"What happened to Mom?" Sarah asked. She put the bucket down in her lap.

"Doctor Chan poisoned Mom."

Jonny stood up and wobbled before he fell back into the armchair. "Why would he hurt your mom?"

"To stop me from finding the stones."

"Those damned stones." Dad's frown took up most of his face. "I thought Agent Malden was working on this case."

Jilly pulled on Tracey's arm. "We came—"

"Yes, right." Tracey moved closer to the boy sitting on Mom's favorite armchair. How could her friend have betrayed her by stealing the journal? "Jonny, did you steal the journal from my bag?"

His eyes widened, "Um."

"Jonny? How could you? You took it and didn't tell me?"

He dropped his head into his hands. "I, um. I . . ."

"Where is it? There is important information in that journal! I'm sure of it."

He lifted his head and glanced at Jilly. "I hid it."

"Why?"

"Jilly told me too."

Tracey's fury swelled. She glared at the girl by her side. "I knew it. I knew you were behind it! Give it back."

"I hoped it held a clue to removing the curse on my family."

Tracey's anger simmered. She breathed deeply and spun around to glare at Jonny. "Where did you hide it?"

"Aw, man, don't be mad." He leaned over and pulled a large book from his school bag. He shrugged at Tracey's dark look. "What? I was going to tell you."

Tracey flipped through the book quickly. Jilly pressed into Tracey's side and read over her shoulder. "Oh!" Jilly reached in to turn back a few pages. "Tracey, I saw something."

Flinching away from the girl, Tracey pulled her book out of Jilly's reach. She read out loud, "—I cannot believe it has gone this far. I am distraught watching flames wreak destruction upon my home. It is a nightmare from which I can never wake. Memories of my parents prey upon my mind. Everything is lost. I cannot return. My foolish heart has led me astray as my sister had warned. I have only Matthew now, but I fear it is already too late. I had to see. I had to know the limits of my strength. I am a fool—"

"Tracey?" Laura's voice broke her concentration. "Is that Stephanie? It doesn't sound like she knew what she was doing. It sounds like she made a mistake."

"What?" Lifting her head brought Tracey's attention to the ache between her temples. Even the bridge of her nose hurt. She squeezed the skin between her eyes like it was a particularly nasty pimple. For a second, the pain lessened, and she was able to focus. She glanced at Jilly. "What did you see?"

Jilly snatched the book from Tracey's lax hands and flicked back a few more pages. She continued reading. "I have experienced feelings of familiarity as though I have walked these corridors before and yet I find nothing familiar. I must ask the others if they have undergone a similar experience. Happy accident, or something else? Can we truly use these vessels to communicate over vast distances? Our experiments seem to have traveled in a direction we could scarcely imagine. I feel a connection. At times, I even suspect I can sense my companions' thoughts. Certainly, we share our emotions. I am curious and a little afraid. What else have we created, unknowingly?"

"What does that mean?" Laura asked.

"The stones are connected. Tracey, I think you *can* use your stone to find the others," Jilly gushed.

Tony's eyes widened. "Tracey? I know what spell we can use."

The same thought occurred to Tracey. The communication stones she and Tony had spelled at camp! It was so simple. Why hadn't they thought of it before? *Fruit tingles, we had the right spell all along.* "Dad, we have to go."

His stern expression stopped her cold. "Honey, I want you to stay here."

"I can't, Dad. I have to go. If we find the stones it will all stop. Doctor Chan and Timothy will leave us alone. Mom will be safe."

"You should wait for Agent Malden. He's on his way."

How could Tracey explain the urgency that thrummed in her body. "Dad, I can't." She gestured to her friends. Laura, Jonny, Tony and Sarah all climbed to their feet. "You have to look after Mom and Grandma. This is something I have to do. Please let us go?"

His frown stayed in place but after a tense moment of silence, he nodded.

"I love you, Dad."

"I love you too, honey. Stay safe, please. Look out for Sarah."

"I will, Dad. Promise me, you'll go back to hospital. They have to test everyone who's been in contact with Mom." She glanced at Grandma who looked like she had fallen asleep on the sofa. "Take Grandma. She might need to be checked out too."

His lips tightened.

"I'll wait until Agent Malden's people get here," he said and turned his back on Tracey. He walked over to Grandma, his steps slow. His shoulders slumped as if he carried a heavy weight.

Tracey's stomach hurt watching him go. She wanted to call him back and hug him again. She turned away, swallowing her emotions and glanced at everyone. "Tony, we need to do that camp exercise." There was a gap next to Sarah. "Wait, where's Kylie?"

All of Tracey's friends gaped. Sarah's head whipped around as if she had only just noticed. "She was here before," Sarah said, her voice rising.

Dad shrugged. "There was no one else here when I arrived."

Weird.

"Tracey?" Jilly shifted her weight, rubbing her hands against her thighs. "You must focus."

Maybe Kylie had woken up before the others and gone home to get some help? The young girl's disappearance disturbed Tracey, but Jilly was right. She had to focus on the stones. "Sarah, call Kylie. Check that she's okay?" Tracey grabbed the book and waved it around. "Let's go into the kitchen. We have to do this spell before Agent Malden gets here."

"I'll get the salt. Laura can you help me with the circle?" Tony asked. They both disappeared through the kitchen doorway.

"She's not answering," Sarah said lowering the phone. Her lips trembled. "Do you think she's okay?"

"Sure," Tracey said. Jilly's cold hands clamped like a vice around Tracey's arm. "Agent Malden. Is he an M-Force agent?"

"Ah, yeah."

"You didn't tell me M-Force was involved."

"Well you didn't ask. Don't look at me like that. Agent Malden is a friend of my uncle's and—"

"They cannot be allowed to get their hands on the stones," Jilly said.

Jonny came up beside her. "What?"

"The stones are dangerous, Tracey. You don't seem to realize how easily you use its power. The stones must be kept out of M-Force's reach."

"Why?"

"Why? Oh my God! You truly know nothing."

Tracey pushed Jilly's arm away. "You're right. I don't know anything. I got dragged into this whole thing by accident. It was just a stupid necklace. A case for my uncle and now my mom is in hospital, Dad's angry, or frightened, or both, and I'm just me. I don't know what to do, Jilly.

Okay?" Walls swayed as she gasped. *Breathe you idiot.*

Sarah came up beside Tracey and took her hand. "Let's go get the stones."

"Right," Tracey breathed out. She shot one last glance at her dad and grandma on the sofa and nodded. "Let's go."

Tales
by
The Lost

Following 219, Followed by 0
click **<broken link>** to follow The Lost!

Day 1611

[cont …]

I have made friends with her Norm

friends and they actually believe

my story! They say we need

to tell her the truth.

0 likes, 0 comments, 0 reshares
click **<broken link>** to like this post!:D

T.B.T.L.

31

Laura was drawing a circle on the kitchen floor with the giant bag of salt from the pantry, her hair fell over her shoulder in a dark swathe as her head ducked under the kitchen table. Jonny and Tony pulled the heavy table out of her way as Sarah ran around shifting the chairs.

Laura finished the circle. Jonny pulled plastic bowls, a bottle of water, and a birthday candle from the kitchen pantry at Tony's order.

Tony crouched in the center of the circle and wrote out the symbols from their camp task in his notebook. He was the most familiar with them having done this spell several times before. Tracey and Tony originally stuffed up the spell the first time they had tried it. The camp exercise called for them to spell two river stones to find each other, almost like a find-my-phone app. Instead they had created two stones that vibrated when they tapped them, turning them into communication stones instead. This time they *had* to get the spell right. He tore off each page and placed it in the circle. "Better not stuff it up again," he muttered.

"What does that mean?" Jilly asked.

"Nothing," Tracey said. She looked at Tony. "Will it work with only the one stone?"

"Dunno? I hope so. I mean, the stones of power are already connected, right? So we only need to *find* the others."

"Okay, everyone move out of the circle." Tracey couldn't take off the Butterfly Stone without experiencing excruciating pain, so she wrapped her hand around it instead and stepped into the circle. Pressing her hand against the symbol Tony placed in the center, she let her magic out and closed the circle. Invisible lightning pricked her exposed skin. Her bracelet buzzed against her forearm, the only sound in the thickened air. She could feel the eyes of her friends on her, watching, waiting, praying the spell would work.

Tony chanted the words to their exercise. "Stones once spelled together, stones now lost. Stones of —"

Tracey took over. "— magic, locked in place and time. Protectors forsworn to be guardians forever, stones of power find thy fate and destiny." The words were not part of the spell. They came from deep within Tracey. In her mind, she stretched out beyond the circle, beyond the clearing, beyond the town. She reached into the void and the void answered. Six swirling colors filled her mind's eye. A silver strand, the strongest, wrapped around Tracey's body and absorbed into her skin. The other colors danced. Blue, black, gold, green, and red. Each darted away from Tracey's body in different directions. Two colors were stronger than the others, not as strong as her own silver light, but thicker and brighter than the other three — a golden line and a smoky black line. Both rose out of the void, undulating and tugging her forward, begging her to follow them home.

She opened her eyes and found the gold and black lines manifested as streamers that skated along the ground. "Can you see them?"

"No." Jilly's gaze scoured the ground searching for what Tracey pointed at.

"See what?" Jonny asked. He glanced at Tony and Sarah. They shook their heads.

"What do you see?" Laura asked.

"Two paths. But I don't know which is which? Gold or black?" Tracey released a slow breath and drew her magic back inside her core. She hadn't needed to tap into the Butterfly Stone's power. She pressed her hand over it but it was quiet and cold. Tracey unbound the circle by swiping her hand across the salt. Colors and sound crammed into her brain overwhelming her senses in an instant, filling her ears with noise and her vision with light — bird song and splashing water, wet earth and rain in the crisp air. She shook her head trying to make sense of the chaos. Sarah crept to her side and took her hand. Her sister's magic muffled the madness in Tracey's mind. "Thanks," she whispered. A bright smile appeared on Sarah's face.

Tracey stared at the ground. "Black or gold?" she asked.

None of her friends spoke up. She wished they could see the magic lines. Then she could have sent each of her friends after one of the stones but, only Tracey could see them. Sarah jiggled Tracey's hand. "Which one feels right?"

Tracey released her hold on the Butterfly Stone. "Gold," she announced.

"Then let's go find the gold," Jilly said.

Tales
by
The Lost

Following 219, Followed by 0
click **<broken link>** to follow The Lost!

Day 1611

[cont …]

Oh, but what is the use?

She will forget.

She will always forget.

I've done this before.

0 likes, 0 comments, 0 reshares
click **<broken link>** to like this post!:D

T.B.T.L.

32

They ran toward town, looking like a pack of hyenas following the golden line. "I hate exercise," Tracey panted. Jilly looked magnificent, barely breaking a sweat, puffing lightly while Tracey was a sweaty, disgusting, gasping mess. So gross.

"You're doing really well," Jilly said, catching her grumble.

Gah, and patronizing too. "Please," Tracey gasped, unable to say anything else because she didn't have enough air to form words. She glanced back at her friends. They seemed to have no trouble keeping up, even Laura in her fancy boots.

"How ... are ... you ... so ... fit?" she whined to Jilly. Everything hurt, from her lungs to her throat to her knees. Why did the back of her thighs hurt? *This is torture.*

"Hunter training."

"So ... you ... fight?"

"Yes, though I have never had to in real life," she replied smoothly, and Tracey hated her a little bit more for it.

A tug pulled Tracey to the left.

"I ... think we're getting close," Jonny panted, racing up to Tracey's side.

"How can you tell?" Sarah gasped.

Tracey stumbled to a stop. "That." She pointed ahead, her other hand pressed to her knees as she doubled over. Heat poured off her face, sweat soaking her collar and down the middle of her back.

"Whoa!" Tony jogged up beside Jilly.

Tracey stared into the sky. What had been a clear and bright day had turned murky and the golden line headed straight into it. Flashes of light in the distant storm clouds Tracey mistook for lightning became obvious as they moved closer—*bursts of magic*. Someone was under attack.

Jilly gasped.

A figure stood in the eye of the storm. His shield was under attack from all sides as the swirling maelstrom pressed down upon him, buckling his form and sending him to his knees. The shield contracted around the man's body as his magic faltered.

"It's wearing him down," Tracey shouted.

The figure tilted, swaying before calling on a last breath of strength. To Tracey's inexperienced battle eyes even she could see he was going to lose. The screaming and wailing should have drawn curious bystanders but there was no one nearby, except for a car trapped on the edge of the storm. A dark colored SUV.

Jilly powered up beside Tracey, glowing with yellow gold magic. Her dark hair created a wild, windblown halo around her head, her bracelet burning fiery red in the gloom.

"Tony, you and Sarah take the other side. See if you can get around the edge of the storm. Sarah, I need you to shield Tony like we did in practice with Grandma," Tracey ordered.

"Stay safe," Tony shouted and ran off with Sarah.

Expanding her own shield bubble over Jilly, Tracey flung open her little closet door and filled her hands with power.

"Someone's in the car!" Jonny yelled. "We have to get them out."

The man in the center of the storm let out a scream that raised the hairs all over Tracey's body.

"We have to help him first," Jilly shouted.

"I'll punch a hole through the storm," Tracey told her. "Tony will help from the other side. Jonny, I need you to grab the guy and drag him out. Laura, can you help whoever is in the SUV?"

"On it," Laura yelled, and ran toward the stalled vehicle. Jilly widened her stance, shifting one foot fractionally behind the other. Tracey copied her and found her stance was stronger and more secure. *I could learn a lot from her.* In the distance Tony and Sarah ran around behind the whirling wind. "Ready!" Her sister's shout almost disappeared under the roar of the storm.

"Ready?" Tracey asked Jilly.

"When you are."

Knowing this time she would need all the help she could get, Tracey prayed she was strong enough to keep control and latched onto the Butterfly Stone with one hand. Immediately Stephanie ripped into her mind, slamming Tracey into the back seat. Words to a spell Tracey couldn't hear were shouted through a mouth she no longer controlled. A beam of ice shot into the swirling monstrosity, burning a frozen path all the way to the man huddled at the center.

Let me help, Tracey thought-screamed at Stephanie. The powerful Mage-kind spirit ignored her, pushing Tracey's mind away. *No!* Tracey fought for attention as Stephanie turned her attack on the storm. *No! We get the man out and run!* It was the only reason she had called for Stephanie's help in the first place.

Stephanie laughed, building a wall inside Tracey's head to trap her in place. Tracey pushed through the thick pressure in her mind and managed a sliver of vision. Jilly battled to hold her shield over the hole Stephanie punched through the storm. On the other side, Tony braced the gap, keeping it open. Sarah covered him with her shield. Jonny's slender form raced out of the ice tunnel with the man slung over his shoulder in a fireman's carry.

Tracey's vision turned black as Stephanie pushed her away. Her mind floundered, lost. *Which way is up?* Dizziness hit her, which was crazy because she had no body. It was like being underwater. She was surrounded by blackness. Floating. Unable to determine up or down. Choosing the wrong direction would mean becoming forever lost. Everything spun as her hold on reality disappeared.

No sound.
　No light.
　　No weight.
　　Floating.
　　Falling.
　　　Empty.

Where am I?

　　　　　　Darkness.
　　　　　　Blackness.
　　　　　　A void.
　　　　　　Nothing.

I'm forgetting something.
Who am I?

Spinning.
　Lifeless.
　　Lost.

Lost? This is not real. This is not the end.

Thud thud.
Thud thud.

　　　A beat.
　　　Life.
　　　Her life.

Thud thud.

My heart.

Mine.

Mine.

Which way is up?

"Tracey!"

Sarah?

Focus on the voice.

It will lead you home.

Thud thud.
Thud thud.

A heartbeat.
　Her heart.
　　Beating.
　　　Faster.
　　　　Harder.

"Mine!"

Light exploded around Tracey, blinding her. She blinked.

I blinked.

Cold air hit her throat.

Air.

I'm breathing.

"Mine," she gasped, hearing the word fill her ears, her heart, her soul. She was back. She had come back. She was inside her body again.

Sparks of pain like fireworks erupted from every part of her form. Sharp objects dug into her knees. Cold air stung her lungs. Her nose dripped. She sniffed, sending knives of ice into her brain.

"Tracey?"

She blinked, bringing the blurry image in front of her into focus. Sarah and Jilly knelt at her side. Jilly's wide dark brown eyes had gold in them. Her ruby lips were bitten and bleeding. They twitched and then lifted as she smiled. "Hey. Are you in there?"

"I'm back." Tracey's voice sounded like crunching gravel and the creak of a door.

"You you, or you her?" Sarah asked taking Tracey's hand to help her stand.

"Me me. Ugh! What happened?"

Everything was covered in a film of dirt including her clothes. "Whoa!" Grass had been flattened in a wide circle around them. Trees lay uprooted and flung across the road. In the distance a dark-colored SUV lay on its side. Laura had climbed onto the SUV and was peering into the window. "Tracey?" she yelled and waved her hands around madly to get her attention.

Tracey, Sarah, and Jilly ran toward Laura and the SUV. "Tracey!" Jonny shouted.

She skidded to a halt and peered back to find Jonny and Tony leaning over the prone figure of the man from the storm. "Hang on!" she shouted back. "I'll just be a second."

Jonny waved his hands around. "What about—"

"Just a second." Without checking to see if Jilly followed, Tracey ran to the overturned SUV. The engine still growled, but there was no smell of petrol. Glass sprinkled the road where the windows had been smashed in. "Is the door stuck?"

Laura pulled Tracey up onto the side of the SUV. "Look!"

Tracey peered inside. A swirling, dusty mist filled the vehicle. Two eyes peered up at her and blinked. "What are you?" the monster asked. Its voice was a hiss of wind and sand. The dirty mist swirled in sharp waves like thousands of ribbons clenched tightly together. Little wisps like fog floated out when it spoke.

"What is it?" Laura gasped. Jilly climbed up beside Tracey. She reared back at the sight of the Dust Devil in its current compressed form.

"A watcher!"

"A what?" Tracey didn't take her eyes off the mist, afraid it would pour out of the window and attack them. Her shield thickened to protect her friends.

"What are you?" it hissed.

"Jilly?" Tracey asked, not taking her eyes of the creature.

"A watcher is an agent of the council." Jilly's eyes were wide, spooked, terrified. Tracey had never seen Jilly afraid and it sent an icy river of fear down her spine. "This is not good, Tracey. The council is watching you."

"What are you?" the Dust Devil—the watcher—demanded again.

What a weird question. "I'm a girl."

"You are not just a girl," it rasped, then jerked as if stuck on something. Tracey couldn't imagine what held it in place.

"What do you want?" she demanded.

"I was sent to test you."

"Why?"

"You are a danger to yourself and others. The council is watching." The swirling mist flared bright, making Tracey cover her eyes. When she could see again the SUV was empty.

A number of papers lay scattered over the windows where the car rested on its side. Tracey couldn't reach them, but she did see a name.

Her name.

Tracey Masters.

Fruit tingles. An address was written on one of the papers. United

Kingdom. *The council?* Her heart clenched. *A test?*

"Tracey?"

She glanced back at Jilly. "Yeah."

Jilly's wide eyes and flared nostrils exposed her terror. "This is not good."

"So you said."

Laura shook Tracey's arm. "Jonny's calling you."

They helped each other off the SUV. Jilly held out a hand to stop Tracey. "Can you still see the stones?"

Tracey blinked and lifted her head. "Yup, gold and black. Two lines. The gold line is really strong, leading to … Oh."

Tony and Jonny stood at a distance from the man on the ground. Sarah huddled behind Tony. Tony's shield bubble was raised. "Tony?" Tracey shouted, running toward them. "What is it? What's wrong? Who is he?" The gold line ran straight to the prone man.

"It's Doctor Chan," he shouted back.

Tracey's blood turned to ice. She stopped running. Beside her, Jilly swore. "Laura, stay behind me," Tracey said. They approached cautiously, watching the man for any sudden movement. "Is he alive?" she asked.

"Yes—barely," Jonny said.

Jilly shoved past Tracey. "Finally." Her magic crackled around her like live electricity, sparking and popping.

"Jilly, stop! What are you doing?" Tracey shouted.

Jilly only had eyes for the unconscious man on the ground. "He must be bound, before he can wake and use his magic. He is powerful, Tracey. My family gifted me with the magic to hold him so I can fulfill my destiny and take him home to face justice. It will freeze his magic inside his cold black heart and—"

"Wait, we have to find the stone first. Jilly, you promised we could have the stone he holds, remember?" Tracey could see the emotions swinging back and forth in her new friend's eyes. She pointed to the gold streamer she knew Jilly couldn't see. "It's here. He has it. We have to be careful. We might not be able to get it off him."

"He won't be wearing it. He is using it for ill will. He is no protector.

Only the stone's protector can wear it," she snarled. "Tracey, where does the line go?"

Tracey pointed to Doctor Chan's feet. "There!"

Tony, the one closest to Doctor Chan, snatched off the man's shoes and cheered, shaking the left one about. The largest grin Tracey had ever seen spread across Jilly's face. She took the shoe from Tony's hand. "We found it," she whispered.

Tracey pressed close to the girl's side, trying to catch a peek at the object in her hand. It was a stone the size of a Conker, orange with a thick band of black running through the center. Tracey gasped as the power it contained raised the hairs on her neck and buzzed against her skin.

"The Tiger's Eye. Yes!" Jilly closed her fist around it. Tracey was having none of that. She shoved Jilly hard, pulling at Jilly's wrist with both hands.

"Stop it! Don't!" Jilly shouted, doing her best to pull out of Tracey's grasp.

Tracey winced as the shout became a scream jabbing into her eardrums. "Let me see it," she demanded.

"No, it's mine."

Tony pushed between Tracey and Jilly. "Hey!"

"Whoa, what's going on?" Jonny shouted.

Sarah yanked on Tracey's shirt. "Tracey stop!"

Tracey shoved magic into her hand and pushed. Jilly and Tony flew back, hitting the road with twin thumps and a screech. "Stop it!" Laura shouted. Tracey stared at the stone in her hand feeling the buzz of energy spread out over her body. *So much power.* "Tracey!" Laura grabbed her arm as Jonny pulled the stone out of her hand.

What did I do? Tracey clutched her temples, her head pounding—a drum growing louder and faster. "Jilly?" *What did I just do?*

Jilly moaned.

Tracey fell to her knees. Apologies tumbled from her mouth as she reached for Jilly to help her sit up. "I don't know why I did that."

Jilly shoved Tracey's hand away and lay on the street staring up at the sky. "I do. It's the stone. It's dangerous. I can feel it calling to me, wanting me. Do you feel it?"

"Yeah." Tracey slumped beside Jilly's legs, forcing her stare from Jonny's hand. He shoved the stone inside his pocket, out of sight but not out of mind. The urge to take it was strong. Tracey's fingers trembled. She clenched them into fists. "You're right. It is dangerous." Jilly struggled to sit up. "Don't let it in."

"It wants me too," Jilly admitted.

"I know." Tracey waited, her breath caught in her throat, watching Jilly's battle. Longing and hatred crossed Jilly's face in waves. Behind her Tony and Sarah's expressions were pure longing. Laura stood between them, her hands outstretched as if she could stop them if they tried to move past.

Finally Jilly sat up, her face pale. The shadows beneath her eyes were more pronounced, like she had been awake for days. "Damn."

"Yeah."

"I'm so tired."

Tracey clapped her hands once. "Right, do you know how to break the curse?"

Jilly gaped at her. "I—I've been looking for the stone for so long I didn't think to... Oh no." She stared off into the distance. Her lost expression drove a wedge into Tracey's heart.

Tony smacked his forehead. "We don't know how to break the curse?"

They all stared wide-eyed at each other. *Now what?*

"What about Stephanie?" Jilly asked.

Tracey shook her head. "I'm not sure I can ask her. I can't let her in again. I—she won't—I nearly lost myself. I can't do that again." Her body sagged, exhausted in a way she had never been before. The urge to lie back on the ground and just close her eyes was hard to ignore. But ignore it she did and heaved a giant sigh before struggling to her feet. "Come on."

"What about him?" Jilly snarled, glaring at the unconscious body of Doctor Chan.

"Bind him. We'll leave him here. Agent Malden can hold him until you can organize a way for your family to take him home." Tracey pulled her cell phone from her pocket. Jilly leaned over Doctor Chan, her hands bright with magic. Tracey glanced at her phone. Only twenty percent battery left. She typed a quick message to Agent Malden. *Doctor Chan is unconscious on Stock Street, south side of Jessie Park.*

She hit send and her phone trilled barely a second later. Without looking, she turned it off and shoved it into her pocket. "I can still see the black line. Until we figure out what to do with the Tiger's Eye, let's go find the other stone."

Tales
by
The Lost

Following 219, Followed by 0
click **<broken link>** to follow The Lost!

Day 1611

[cont …]

Tried when I was younger.

I wanted friends so desperately.

0 likes, 0 comments, 0 reshares
click **<broken link>** to like this post!:D

T.B.T.L.

33

Before long even Jilly could tell where they were going.

"There!" Tracey pointed, gasping from their long run. The black line led directly to the school. "Why here?" Night was falling rapidly and making it hard to see the black line at all. Tracey squinted, following it across the front walkway leading to the school's administration office.

Jilly shrugged. "No one would think to look here. It's night time. There are no kids or teachers around." Jonny came up beside her and took her hand. Jilly smiled brightly at him and threw herself into his arms giving him a giant hug. Though Tracey couldn't see Jonny's face, embarrassment dripped from his body even as he held the girl tighter. "Ah..."

"But what about the security guard? How did the stone even get here?"

Laura froze. Her head tilted to the side. "What's that noise?"

Floodlights lit the sports ground. Calls, shouts, and groans — all male — and then Tracey made out the crack of hard plastic. "Football training?"

"Now? It's just gone dark," Laura said.

"Maybe it's a special training session?" Tracey replied with a shrug. "Charlie and Simon have had a lot of sessions lately. Said the coaches have some sort of bet on." The black line traveled toward the bleachers. "It goes over there."

"One of the players must have it," Jilly said pulling away from Jonny. She tugged her hair back behind her ears and tied it up in a ponytail.

"What do we do, Tracey?" Sarah whispered.

"We have to be careful." Tracey stared at each of them to make sure they were listening. Jilly wouldn't look her in the eyes. "Timothy is dangerous. If he's possessed one of the team, he might attack us when we try to get the stone. The other players will be in danger too. We need to figure out who is holding it before we make our move. Maybe we should call Agent Malden?"

"No, we shouldn't call him," Jilly said. Tony's face paled in the light shining from Jilly's cell phone. She shook her head. "We don't even know where it is for sure." Her student bracelet shone vibrantly red.

"Cover it," Tracey hissed. Her own bracelet was still faintly green beneath her sleeve, muffled enough that it couldn't be seen from a distance.

The red glow disappeared. "Your hands are lit too," Tracey warned.

That light disappeared too.

"What do we do?" Jonny asked. Everyone turned to look at Tracey.

"Let's see where it goes. Find who has it then we can call in Agent Malden." Quietly, with only the light from their cell phones to guide them, they moved to the corner of the building and peered across the sports field. "Oh no," Tracey groaned.

The huddled football players broke with a cheer and headed straight toward Tracey and her friends. "Fruit tingles," she whispered recognizing several players.

"Tracey, hey." Damian looked exactly the same as every other football player in uniform. But his voice and stance were unmistakable. He gave her a wave and stopped in front of the bleachers to grab his gear. His team mates spread out around him, some yanking their stuff from the ground, some headed for the change rooms. Many just milled around, watching to see what was going to happen.

Her face heated uncomfortably. "Hi Damian."

Dave One and Dave Two walked in front of her crush. So, the two Daves were friends again? Not a good thing for Tracey, but it had to be good for Dave Two. She searched the darkness for the black line, hoping it would run past the boys. It ran straight to Dave Two's left leg. She squinted. No, right through his legs. She ignored the Daves and dragged Jilly around them. A chorus of *hey man*, *yo*, and *dude* followed as Jonny weaved between the boys. Tony traveled in his wake, face red, eyes glued to the ground.

Laura got one whistle. Everyone fell silent as Laura froze and speared the perpetrator with a long dark look. After a moment he shuffled his feet and looked to his friends for backup. None came. "Sorry," he mumbled. Laura tilted her head in acknowledgement. Jilly snorted. As Dave One and Dave Two passed her, Tracey felt the gentle press of Dave Two's magic. Gratitude. He was happy she hadn't made a big deal out of him talking to Dave One. Sheesh, what had he thought she would do?

"Did you watch us practice?" Damian asked, pulling off his helmet. His sweaty hair stuck to his head in some places, stuck up in others.

What? Oh my God, how embarrassing. If she said yes, he would think she was here to watch *him*. If she said no, then what *was* she doing here? Jilly's presence at her back served as a bucket of icy water, keeping Tracey's attention on task. She blinked. The black line ran straight to Damian's chest. Heart thumping loudly, she shuffled closer. *Not Damian, please no.* It was really hard to see. The dark corner they stood in was filled with the shadows cast from the school gymnasium and the light from Tracey and Jilly's cell phones. Damian didn't seem to need a response. His hand crept up to scratch his neck as his eyes dropped to her chest. "Oh hey, that's pretty."

"What?" Tracey glanced down. The Butterfly Stone was resting on the outside of her shirt. The rainbow of lines springing forth from it would be hidden from his Norm eyes. Still she hadn't meant for him to see the stone at all. "Thanks," she said, tucking it back beneath her shirt.

"It looks like Kylie's necklace. Must be by the same artist, huh?"

Tracey's jaw dropped. "Kylie has a necklace like this?" She heard Sarah's gasp and turned to share her sister's wide gaze. Tony and Laura both looked shocked.

"Damn," Jonny muttered.

Damian shot their reactions a long look. He coughed and returned his gaze to Tracey. "Well, sorta, yeah. Hers has a picture on it too, but it's not a butterfly. It's a snake or something."

Kylie had been missing from Tracey's house.

Sarah tugged sharply on Tracey's sleeve. She nodded at her sister's unasked question. She kept her voice light as she asked, "Hey Damian, do you know where Kylie is? Is she at your place?"

"Dunno, haven't seen her. Wasn't she with your—hey, your sister is here."

As he shifted Tracey followed the black line past his chest toward the main school building. *She's here?* "Where did, ah, Kylie find it? The stone I mean."

Damian's tone sharpened, "I found it. Up Mount Hawthy, near the river. It was pretty so I gave it to her."

Tracey closed her eyes briefly and inhaled slowly. *Fruit tingles.* "Can you call her?"

"Why? Tracey, what's going on?" Damian stepped closer, his voice dropping lower. "Should I be worried?" He pulled his cell phone from inside a towel. "She's not answering," he said a minute later.

"Tracey!" Sarah's tone matched the urgency on her face.

"Okay. I—uh, have to go."

"I'm coming with you," Damian said, his gaze running over Tracey's friends again.

"But—"

"Tracey," Jilly's voice was urgent.

"If my sister is in trouble, I'm coming," Damian insisted.

An invisible tug to Tracey's chest jerked her forward. She stumbled. Damian caught her by the shoulders holding her upright. "Tracey?"

The stone. Someone was using it. "This way," she shouted and took off running toward the school. Her friends, Sarah, and Damian ran close behind her.

Tales
by
The Lost

Following <u>219</u>, Followed by <u>0</u>
click **<u>\<broken link\></u>** to follow <u>The Lost</u>!

Day 1611

[cont …]

I thought I could handle having to

repeat my story day after day,

reminding them of who I was and

that I was their friend. I couldn't

do it for long. It hurt too much.

<u>0</u> *likes,* <u>0</u> *comments,* <u>0</u> *reshares*
click **<u>\<broken link\></u>** to like this post!:D

T.B.T.L.

34

The empty and gloomy school corridors reminded Tracey of a horror movie. The echoes of their pounding footsteps were louder than they should have been and would warn anyone that they were coming. A weird chemical smell floated up from the recently cleaned floors. The black line Tracey followed grew darker, thicker, enough that she could have reached out and grabbed it with her hands. "The library," she gasped when the double doors came into view.

"Kylie's probably doing homework." Damian's voice faded as he realized the school was dark around them. His footsteps slowed. "Tracey, what's going on?"

Tracey skidded to a halt beside him.

Jilly passed them before she realized they had stopped and doubled back. "Let's go," she urged.

Tracey caught a glint of orange against Jilly's chest. "Jilly, no. You didn't." The stone was undeniable. It hung on a silver chain around Jilly's neck.

Jonny slapped a hand over his pocket. He looked aghast at Jilly. "You... you... the hug?"

"I'm sorry. I had to. You know I did."

Tracey sighed. Jilly couldn't possibly know what she had done. "Can you take it off?"

"What is going on?" Damian interrupted, waving a hand around. "What are you just standing around talking for? Why is my sister at school? Wait, isn't she supposed to be with you, anyway?"

Jilly couldn't hold Tracey's furious glare, nor could she look at Jonny. Guilt dripped from every limb as she turned away.

"Hey Tracey, what is going—"

"Damian, just give me a minute, okay?" she snapped. "If we go storming in there, Kylie will freak out. I think I should—"

"Tracey, let me come with you." Sarah stared up at Tracey, her set face expressing her determination to help.

A flicker of memory crossed Tracey's mind. Sarah's terrified scream, her pale and frightened face searching for help as the man in the red mask grabbed the back of her neck. Sarah, brilliant and brave Sarah, helping Tracey and her friends fight the Shadowman. She had attended the same training as Tracey, sat through the same lessons, performed the same tests. Sarah was as experienced as the rest of them. Tracey had to trust that Sarah could look after herself.

"But if it looks—"

"I'll run. I promise."

Tracey checked her cell phone. The red battery symbol was flashing. She glanced over at her friends. "Tony, call Agent Malden. Can you, Laura, and Jonny go around to the emergency exit, in case she—"

Tony's stare darted to Damian. "Sure." The three of them took off running toward the rear of the building.

"Tracey, what is going on? You are really freaking me out—"

"Damian." Tracey made sure to hold his gaze. She took his hand. The heat of his skin soaked into her cold fingers. "Whatever happens in there—it's not Kylie's fault."

His eyes sprang wide. He pulled away from her grip. "What's happening? Is my sister in danger?"

Oh, how Tracey wished he had stayed behind. The sharp glint in his eyes and his clenched fists told her there was no stopping him from joining them now.

If Kylie was under Timothy's thrall, Damian would fight to save her just as hard as Tracey had fought to save Sarah from the Shadowman. Only Damian wasn't Mage-kind. He would get hurt.

"Just stay behind us." She gestured to Jilly and Sarah. "When we get Kylie free, get her out of there. Okay?"

Damian spared her a glance before his attention returned to the closed library door. Tracey bit back a sigh. She shot Jilly a warning glance. "Don't hurt Kylie."

Jilly's mouth became a tight line. *No promises huh? Great.* Tracey glanced at Sarah. Through their connection, Sarah seemed to understand Tracey's concern. "I'll watch her," she whispered.

Tracey nodded. "We really should wait for Agent Malden," she tried one last time.

Damian's jaw was set. "I'm going. You wait for whoever. It's my sister in there. I dunno what's wrong but it's my job to protect her."

Tracey bit back a sigh. This was all about Kylie now. She had to focus. Shooting a look at Damian to ensure he stayed behind her, Tracey pushed open the library's double doors.

They swung shut behind them with a soft swish. All was dark inside the library. Damian's hand found Tracey's. "Can't see," he whispered. Tracey's heart thumped at the touch of his warm hand. She sent a spurt of magic into her vision, knowing Jilly and Sarah would do the same. Using her Sight, Tracey examined the usually familiar room.

Sickly green light infused the comfy reading area, revealing the two-person tables had been pushed out of line. Enough room had been left for a circle in the middle and when Tracey glanced down, she could just make out a chalky outline. It shimmered under her magically-enhanced gaze. A figure hunched inside the circle, frozen still and silent.

"Where is she?" Damian muttered. In the dead silence of the room his voice was a thunder clap, startling the figure upright. Tracey flicked a hand toward the wall where she knew the light switch was located. With a ticking sound and a fluttering flash of light, the overhead fluorescent tubes woke up. Under brilliant white light, Kylie Carter was revealed. She stood, head bowed, her long blond hair covering her face. As she peered up through her hair, Tracey gasped. Kylie's eyes were sunken and dark, like the deep holes of a skull.

"Oh no." Sarah whispered.

"Kylie!" Damian shouted. He jerked forward. Tracey tugged on his hand to keep him behind her. She pushed magic into a barrier to stop him from getting past and in the way. He grunted, trying to force his way through. Using the distraction, Jilly inched away from them heading for the stacks. Sarah followed, staying a step behind Jilly.

"It's not Kylie," Tracey told Damian through gritted teeth.

He fought hard but was no match for Tracey's magic. He pulled back and glared daggers at her. There went their budding friendship. She shook her head and faced the possessed girl. A pained sound erupted from Damian's mouth—half moan, half question. "Kylie?"

Tracey ignored him. "Timothy, I know it's you," she said to the monster possessing the young girl's body.

"Tracey. How good of you to bring me two of my desired prizes. And it's not even my birthday."

"Timothy. Let the girl go," she demanded.

"No, no. I quite like it in here. I should have realized a young mind would be easier to control. And to have magic again." Timothy spun Kylie's body around. The sight turned Tracey's stomach.

Jilly sidestepped further, putting a wider space between them, creating two targets for Timothy. She hissed at Tracey, "What are you doing?"

Driving daggers into Jilly with her eyes, Tracey shouted into Jilly's mind, *Don't get anywhere near Kylie with your stone.*

A tiny nod was Jilly's only acknowledgement that she received Tracey's warning. Sarah stood behind Jilly. Tracey could feel the fear and uncertainty Sarah felt though she was trying very hard to hide it. Tracey's eyes narrowed, her hand fluttered close to the Butterfly Stone. She didn't want to call on the power of the stone. If she did, Stephanie would take over again and this time Tracey would be lost for good. But what else could she do? She wasn't powerful enough to defeat Timothy on her own. Staring wildly around the library she searched for inspiration, anything she could use to fight Timothy. She spied a tousled head on the upper level behind the history section and reminded herself she was not alone. Tony was here, and Laura, and Jonny, and they would have called Agent Malden. All Tracey had to do was stall long enough for help to arrive. Tracey didn't look up again, not wanting to draw attention to Tony and her Norm friends.

The strange standoff continued. No one made a move to call on their magic. The possessed Kylie stood inside the circle, meaning Timothy could enact whatever spell he had prepared in an instant. Jilly and Tracey would be caught outside the circle, unable to stop him. Tracey's heart pounded and her breathing quickened, anticipating the fight to come. She thought about Stephanie's possession of her own body. She had managed to force herself to the surface to see out of her own eyes and hear what was going on around her. How close to the surface was Kylie? Could she hear Tracey? "Kylie?" she called.

There was no flicker of awareness on the girl's face.

"Call to her, Damian," Tracey ordered, stepping further away from Jilly.

"Ky? Kyls, are you there? Kylie?" Damian's voice trembled, clearly upset by the cruel expression on his sister's sweet face. She blinked as her face contorted into a pained grimace.

"Yessss?" her gasp was filled with pain.

"Fight him, Kylie," Tracey urged.

"Enough of this!" Jilly sprinted forward, her hands alight with magic. She sent a spear of magical energy straight at Kylie's chest. Sarah cried out, reaching for the older girl but Jilly slipped her grasp.

"No!" Tracey thrust out her shield bubble, but both her shield and Jilly's spear shattered into sparkling diamonds as they hit the invisible boundary wall of the circle.

"You're the impatient one I see," Timothy laughed. A bitter, horrid sound that sent shivers through Tracey's body.

Jilly — enraged — flew toward the circle, pounding her fists against the magical wall. Inside the circle, Timothy cackled. "Such raw anger. Perhaps I should have chosen you over this child."

"Let her go then," Tracey shouted, racing to Jilly's side to grab her hands and stop her ineffectual rain of destruction.

Sarah pressed her hands to the circle's impenetrable wall. "Kylie, please! I know you're in there, please come back. Break the circle. Let us in."

"Tracey, help my sister," Damian pleaded. His soft voice carried over Timothy's hysterical laughter and Jilly's angry growls.

The broken sound tore at Tracey's heart. What did he think she was trying to do? "Call her again." Tracey dropped her bubble and focused all of her magic into a pinpoint beam to drill into the circle wall.

"Kylie? Please, Kylie," Damian begged.

A full body shiver betrayed the battle going on inside the young girl. "Help me," Kylie hissed.

Jilly's animalistic roaring did not cease.

"Jilly!" Tracey snapped. The pupils of Jilly's eyes were blown wide as she channeled her magic into the wall like a giant fist. Thank goodness she hadn't thought to use the Tiger's Eye — yet. Tracey had to get Jilly back in control. She couldn't risk battling two out-of-control Mages. "Jilly come on. I need you. I need your help." Tracey kept up her pinpoint magical drill etching ever further into the wall. "Damian, keep Kylie's focus on you."

"Jilly. Help us," Sarah begged and ran to Tracey's side. "Use my magic, Trace."

Tracey nodded feeling Sarah's magic swell up and blend with her own. The magical drill grew stronger.

Above them Tracey felt another source of magic. Tony had dropped his shield too. *I'm here.* Tracey's eyes widened. That was Tony's voice in her head.

Me too, Sarah thought at Tracey. Tracey's drill thickened with Tony's added magic.

Jilly! Tracey called. *Help us.*

Laura's at the door ready to let Agent Malden in when he gets here, Tony thought to Tracey. Damian continued to plead with Kylie, shifting around the circle, turning Kylie away from Tracey and Sarah, calling for his sister and begging her to break free. Flinging out a hand, Tracey grabbed Jilly's sleeve and yanked hard.

Jilly's focus shifted and Tracey felt her awareness return with a snap. After a moment Jilly opened her mind and merged her power with the rest of them. Music played in Tracey's mind. Peppermint and strawberries filled the air. Tracey's magical drill became a jack hammer. Timothy growled.

Kylie screamed.

The scream became a howl as the wall wobbled. Tracey pushed harder.

Damian placed his hands against the circle's boundary and pushed with all of his strength. Tears crept down his cheeks. "Kylie." His voice was only a whisper, yet it found purchase.

Kylie wailed and reached for him, the sound piercing Tracey's ears. She heard Sarah, Jilly and Tony cry out in pain. Energy pulsed through Tracey. *Open yourself to me*, Stephanie whispered, her voice caressing Tracey's ear like the warmest honey. Tracey shoved the ghostly woman back, feeling Sarah's magic strengthen her will against her ancestor. Tracey focused on Kylie with everything that she had. Her friends did the same. Timothy let out a pained bellow and fell silent. Kylie dropped to her knees. The circle wall disintegrated. Tracey, Sarah, Jilly, and Damian hit the ground as the invisible line they pushed against disappeared. In the upper stacks Tracey heard a thump that had to be Tony's body falling to his knees. She swiped her hand over the chalk to disrupt the circle.

Damian scrambled to Kylie's side and pulled her into his arms. She blinked up at him. "Damian?"

Tracey rolled onto her back. *Oh, thank goodness.*

Jilly moaned, "Oh my head."

Mine too. It pounded as if she hadn't slept in days. She dragged her head up to check on her sister. "Sarah?"

A few feet away Tracey spied Sarah's hand flop up and down. "I'm here."

Tracey rolled her head. "Kylie?"

"What happened?" Kylie's voice trembled. Comforting sounds came from Damian as he hugged her tightly. Kylie's blond hair fell over his arm as she buried her head in his neck and sobbed.

Tracey let out a tiny "whoop" at the sound of the girl's young voice and dragged herself closer. Damian's eyes were shiny and red. He searched Tracey's face. "Is it over? Is Kylie okay now?"

Jilly crawled to Kylie's other side and stared into her eyes.

"Who are you?" Kylie asked. She inched further into Damian's embrace and away from Jilly.

"I'm a friend of Tracey's. My name is Jilly Cho. Can you follow my finger?" Jilly held up one finger and moved it from side to side. Kylie followed the movement with her eyes. Jilly glanced over her shoulder. "I think she's fine." She touched Kylie's head, checking for something, lumps or wounds probably.

Kylie grabbed Jilly's necklace with one hand and thrust her palm out at Tracey. Before Tracey could cry out a warning, she was flying backward. She hit the wall hard enough to rattle her teeth. With a startled cry Sarah slammed into Tracey's legs.

Moaning at the new aches in her body, Tracey flopped over. "Sarah?"

"What happened?" her sister flicked hair out of her face and squinted at Tracey.

Laughter filled the library. Kylie held the orange stone with the chain still attached to Jilly, dragging the girl up to her knees with it. Kylie's eyes burned with fire.

Fruit tingles. Timothy had tricked them. He was still in control of Kylie's body and now he had Jilly and the Tiger's Eye.

Tales
by
The Lost

Following 219, Followed by 0
click **<broken link>** to follow The Lost!

Day 1611

[cont …]

And they don't even know the hurt

they cause when they ask if I am a

new student, or when they introduce

themselves to me over and over again.

0 likes, 0 comments, 0 reshares
click **<broken link>** to like this post! :D

T.B.T.L.

35

Head spinning like her favorite childhood toy, Tracey pushed up onto her elbows and peered around.

Hard cardboard from the pile of books she landed on dug sharply into her back. Kylie was still possessed. Timothy had pretended the girl broke free of his control, a trick designed to get closer to Jilly. Timothy's laugh reached cartoonish levels. The possessed girl sat in the center of the disturbed circle, his hand clasped around the Tiger's Eye still attached to Jilly's neck by the chain. The jerking movement of Kylie's hand, controlled by Timothy, and her clenched teeth made Tracey realize Timothy couldn't break the chain. Jilly's hands tightened around Kylie's wrist, holding her in place. "Tracey help!" she screamed.

Sarah scrambled to her feet. "What do we do?"

Tracey's hands flew to the Butterfly Stone. She yanked them back before she could touch it. *No.* If she used the stone Stephanie would take over. Tracey might never come back. But how could she fight Timothy without the stone? Something Dave Two shouted at her a few months ago popped into her head. *"Stop pulling at me."* It was how she used her magic—her natural way. "Sarah, raise your shield against me. Run and find Tony."

"What are you...? Oh. *Oh.*" Sarah's shield snapped into place and strengthened against Tracey.

"Tony and Laura are upstairs. Go!" In her head she shouted to Tony. *Shield now!* Checking she hadn't raised her shadow shield from instinct, she threw open the closet door in her chest and drew on her own power. Blinking rapidly, she activated her Sight. The two stones radiated with color, one black, the other gold. For the first time in a long time Tracey opened herself fully to her own magic and called for more.

As she suspected, a thin golden line immediately spiraled toward her from Jilly's core. Swallowing the fear that sat like a peanut in her throat, Tracey checked the Butterfly Stone was completely locked down and drew more magic. A faint black line joined the golden one. *There you are.* Tracey tried something she had never done before. She let go of Jilly and focused wholly on Timothy's magic.

"Wha...what is that? What's going on?" Timothy spun Kylie's head, searching for the source of his power drain.

What are you doing? Jilly's voice boomed inside Tracey's head.

Tracey couldn't spare her the concentration to explain. She pushed an image of Jilly pulling away from Timothy, stone and all, in Jilly's direction. A tug on her chest jerked Tracey forward. *Fruit tingles.* Timothy had figured out her plan. No matter. This was something Tracey could do in her sleep. She drew on more power. Coils of energy thickened and danced before her eyes. Beautiful streamers spun up and down in the air, moving toward her, filling her with extra magic. Her fingers began to tingle. The hairs rose up on her arms as she absorbed Timothy's magic. Tracey could taste the cold bitter blackness of Timothy's mind. *Let her go!* She shouted at him with her mind.

Timothy thrust both hands at Tracey. A wave of energy slammed into her, knocking her back into the wall.

Both hands.

He had pushed Tracey away with *both* hands. Which meant he had let Jilly go.

Jilly fell back and scooted away, out of reach. Tracey had a split second to enjoy her success before she was flung sideways into another wall with a crack that slammed all air from her lungs. Ropes of red shadowy magic wrapped around Tracey's body, tying her up like a tangled skipping rope. Bruises on top of bruises flared over her skin. The shadowy rope writhed and tightened with every movement, leaving a burn line in its wake.

Gaping like a fish, Tracey found she couldn't breathe. Sparks ignited behind her eyes. Dark shadows crept into her vision, triggering all of her nightmares at once. There was a shout and a scream. She couldn't work out where the sounds came from. *Air, breathe, help.*

Her eyes fluttered shut. Everything hurt. She fought for oxygen but there was no way out. No escape. *Breathe.* It became a chant she couldn't make sense of. *Breathe!* Timothy's laughter filled her ears.

"Tracey." Her name whispered across her mind. *Mom?* "Fight. Live." A burst of magic from a place she couldn't comprehend filled her core. The magical rope loosened and suddenly Tracey could breathe again.

A different voice, soft and pleading, surrounded her. Tracey's body swayed as she was pulled into a strong embrace. "Tracey, wake up. Please. You have to save my sister. Please. Wake up."

She followed the voice and opened her eyes. Damian held her, rocking her body against his own like he had done with Kylie only moments ago. He whispered into her ear, "Wake up."

Tracey struggled against her bindings and turned her head.

"Hey man, don't you know girls don't like clingy stalker dudes?" Jonny shouted. He stepped out from behind a leaning bookshelf and pelted Kylie's possessed body with books, breaking Timothy's concentration. Eyes wide, Timothy gaped at the sight of Jonny.

"Where did you come from?"

Laura appeared from behind a different bookshelf. "Let her go." She held a stack of books. Her aim true and the large hardcover slammed into Timothy's leg. Beside Laura another figure stepped into view. Broad shoulders, shaved head and still dressed in his football uniform, Dave Two sneered at Timothy, "Let her go butt-head."

Tony and Sarah popped up from either side of the library and together threw balls of magical energy at Timothy. The ropes around Tracey fell away.

Tracey stared up at Damian. "Thanks," she whispered.

"Your friends are awesome," he said.

"They really are."

With Damian's help Tracey clambered to her feet. Timothy bolted into the stacks. *Run!* Tracey screamed at her friends. Jilly's wild flowing hair in the distance and the clack of her shoes against the library floor snapped Tracey's attention to the true danger. Timothy wasn't running from Tracey. He was chasing Jilly.

Timothy wants the stone!

Tracey threw up a wall of power between the fleeing girl and Kylie's possessed body. Timothy spun and sent a dark wave of power straight back at Tracey. She dove to the floor, barely avoiding the wave. It slammed into the wall beside her. She rolled to dodge the next attack. Damian cried out, diving away in the opposite direction. Tracey reversed course and slid to Damian's side. The floor beneath her feet cracked. Jilly's power spear flew past Tracey's ear. Another flash of light and this time Timothy screamed as Jilly's next throw connected.

Jilly back tracked through the stacks and fired at Timothy again. Tracey pushed Damian behind a column and peered around the other side. Timothy yanked the second spear out of his shoulder. It disintegrated in his hands. Releasing a snarl, he turned on Jilly, sending a powerful blast her way that sent her flying.

It was a demonic game of back and forth. Tracey let loose another attack, returning Timothy's attention to her. Jonny's book throwing skills were spot on, a hardcover slammed against Timothy's shoulder. He spun to face the boy, his tone incredulous. "Where do you keep coming from?"

Tracey's gaze was frantic searching the dark book stacks for help. Where were Agent Malden and his team? They couldn't keep this up for long. They had to get Timothy out of Kylie. Officer Jameson had only held Timothy's stone. When he no longer held it, he had been fine, returning to his normal self with no memory of what had happened, but Kylie was Mage-kind. The stone might fix to her in the same way the Tiger's Eye had locked onto Jilly and the Butterfly Stone had attached to Tracey. To remove it from Kylie they would have to get close, and get Timothy to drop his guard. Tracey remembered her own bias back at their ill-fated training camp with Prince Henry. He had tricked them all by hiding his magical self from their Sight. She hadn't looked for a Norm void during the fight, only the swell of magic. It was why Jonny and Laura kept surprising Timothy now, and why Jilly had underestimated Tracey when she had been shielding her full strength. Tracey's gaze fell on Damian. Why had Doctor Chan failed to get the stone off Tracey?

Because Mage-kind can't remove it.

Maybe a Norm could.

"Damian, I have an idea, but I need your help. Can you get up?"

He rolled over. "What's the plan?"

"I'll give you an opening. When it's clear, you need to tackle Kylie. Knock her out cold. Timothy can't be allowed to get his hands on Jilly or me. You have to get Kylie's necklace off and throw it as far away as you can."

"But Kylie—" He gestured to his hard football uniform. "I'll hurt her."

Tracey grabbed Damian by his jersey collar. "You have to do this. It's the only way to save her." Timothy would not see Damian as a threat. It was how they had beaten him before. Norms were Timothy's weakness. "Stay here and hide. Then tackle her. Got it? For Kylie."

"Yeah." A determined light filled Damian's eyes. He gritted his teeth. "For Kylie."

Using the stolen magic she had pulled from Timothy, Tracey shouted in her mind to her friends scattered throughout the two levels of the library calling to each one separately, opening the mental audio chat between them. Timothy's mind was not invited so he couldn't hear her plan. *Hide!* Tracey raised her shadow shield and suppressed her magic down as far as she could manage, making herself practically invisible to Timothy's senses. She flicked off the lights and plunged the library into darkness. Kicking off her shoes, she spun on silent feet and ran deep into the stacks.

Tales
by
The Lost

Following 219, Followed by 0
click **<broken link>** to follow The Lost!

Day 1611

[cont …]

Tracey thinks I'm mean.

Who wouldn't be, having

to repeat the same story

over and over again, with

the ending never changing?

0 likes, 0 comments, 0 reshares
click **<broken link>** to like this post!:D

T.B.T.L.

36

Surrounded by darkness, Tracey's instinct was to stop running. She fought it with all her might. She knew this library backward and forward. Better than Timothy. Better than Kylie. This was Tracey's campus. This was her home ground and she had the advantage.

There was a gap in the shelves just ahead. Holding out her arms to touch the books on either side she found the gap she wanted when her fingers met air. Turn right, then left and stay straight ahead. *History Section*.

Murky grey light filtered in around her as her eyes adjusted to the darkness. She had to get behind Timothy and drive him toward Damian for this to work. She tilted her head and listened to the echoes of the library, calling on her memory of the floor plan. Ahead was where they kept the abandoned large map storage cabinets, and beyond that another gap. Timothy stalked the stacks behind her. She could hear his footsteps. "Come out, come out, where ever you are." His taunting voice—in Kylie's high pitch—sent a shiver down Tracey's spine. Hopefully, the others were well hidden. The quiet of the dark library compounded her fears. She was afraid she would hit a shelf and alert Timothy to her position, or maybe he would hear her racing heart and hone in on her direction. He was stronger than her, more powerful than her. She was going to fail.

A pop, tiny, nothing more than a spark of pressure ignited in her mind. *Sarah!*

Tracey, we're safe. Whatever you're going to do, do it now.

Thank you. Stay low. She swung into the next gap and headed back to the study area. Her stocking feet made no sound against the aged linoleum.

She was positive she was now in the *Fantasy & Sci-Fi* section. A thump and a shout reminded her she was also hidden from Jilly. Thudding footsteps two aisles over ran toward Jilly. *Fruit tingles.* Keeping her shield up and still masking her magic, Tracey pressed her palms together and prepared to create a ball of energy. She needed Timothy to chase her, not Jilly. She had to get his attention back. Listening carefully, Tracey aimed just ahead of where she thought Timothy would end up and dropped her shield. Timothy roared, sensing Tracey's suddenly restored magic. "Got you!"

Tracey threw her power ball. It hit Timothy square on and the library lit up from the explosion. Kylie dropped to her knees. Timothy roared. Black smoke poured from Kylie's mouth. The familiar screech sent a knife into Tracey's mind. The light in her hands sputtered out. *No! Not him.* The Shadowman — Timothy's smoky henchman. Tracey thought she had seen the last of him when she beat him in Sachorn Forest.

The Shadowman rose up in a cloud of red smoke and shrieked, flying down at her fast, solidifying into the shape of a man. Tracey restored her bubble just in time. He struck Tracey's shield and recoiled. The Butterfly Stone on Tracey's chest burned. She could feel it urging her to use it, and heard Stephanie's voice begging to be let back in. Honey tones and beautiful music. Tracey froze it out, thinking of ice and snow and freezing wind that chilled her to the core. The voice faded. The stone grew cold.

Tracey drew out her own magic, filling her body with true warmth and joy. She knew the difference now. The Butterfly Stone's magic was a false warmth. It didn't resonate with her deep inside like her own magic did. Tracey had been using the Butterfly Stone to search for that illusive warmth and she had never succeeded. The stone made her stronger, yes. It certainly made using her magic easier, but the joy was not the same. It was empty — empty of life, empty of hope, empty of love.

It was time to end this.

Tracey drew on as much magic as she could stand, pulling it from everywhere like a black hole. No magic escaped. No one — not Jilly, not Timothy, not even the Shadowman — were safe from her pull. Tracey thrust the excess energy into the library's lighting system, blasting white hot energy out of every tube, illuminating the library like the flood lights over a stadium and exposed Jilly and Timothy. The Shadowman screamed long and loud and high. It shot up into the ceiling but the light only grew brighter as Tracey poured everything she had into the electrical systems. The Shadowman froze, mouth open in a silent screech and exploded like a firework raining down over the library and vanished. "Damian, now!"

The boy appeared from the stacks behind Kylie and pounced. There was a click, like the snapping of metal. "Tracey!" Damian threw the stone in her direction. Kylie wailed and thrashed against her brother. He pressed her into the floor, holding her still, begging her to come back to him. Tracey raised her hand to catch the stone. To touch it, to hold another stone, would lead to unending power. The magic would all be hers.

No! Tracey shoved the voice with those thoughts out of her mind and created a tiny magical sling to catch the necklace.

That was one.

She ran to Jilly. The girl lay on the floor, exhausted, staring up into the lights blankly. Jonny knelt beside her, holding her hand. "Tracey help."

"Jilly, I need your stone," Tracey said.

Jilly blinked at her. "I can't." Her hands covered the Tiger's Eye, pressing it into her chest. "I can't take it off."

"I'm sorry, Jilly." Tracey looked at Jonny. "Take it off!" Without questioning Tracey's order, Jonny ripped the orange stone from Jilly's neck. The girl quivered and seized, her feet and head tapping a rapid drumbeat into the carpet.

Jonny gasped. He dropped the stone and it clattered to the ground as he grabbed Jilly by the shoulders and turned her onto her side. "Tracey? Help!"

Tracey wrapped a second sling around the Tiger's Eye and pulled it to her. She now possessed all three stones.

Jilly screamed. Her head slammed against the floor and her body fell still. "Tracey!" Jonny shouted.

"I can't, I have to—" Tracey held up both stones in their magical netting and brought them to her chest. She touched the three stones together.

The world screamed.

Tales
by
The Lost

Following <u>219</u>, Followed by <u>0</u>
click **<broken link>** to follow <u>The Lost</u>!

Day 1611

[cont …]

It's easy to be bitter.

It's not fair.

I never asked for this life.

<u>0</u> likes, <u>0</u> comments, <u>0</u> reshares
click **<broken link>** to like this post!:D

T.B.T.L.

37

Tracey stood in the white room. In front of her danced the red and blue shapes she was familiar with. From the corner of her eye something moved. Spinning around, Tracey found a purple circle undulating with a grey octagon. Suspecting what she would find, she turned again and found a line of green swirling with a wave of pink.

"Hi," Tracey said to the heart of the stones.

Her words echoed, a chaos of sound, but inside Tracey's mind she only felt peace. She was also cold. Rubbing her fingers together she puffed out a breath and watched fog ghost out of her mouth. She pictured a beach and flooded it with hot sunshine. Her imagination didn't work. A shiver wracked her frame.

"You refused the power of the stone." The statement came from her blue and red friends.

"Refused," echoed the purple and grey.

"Power," repeated the green and pink.

"Yes," she said, and she was proud of it. She had beaten Timothy and fought Stephanie's temptation. She had fought and won. Closing her eyes brought the constantly moving shapes into the blackness behind her eyes.

"Why?"

"Why?"

"Why?"

The voices were inside her head, not in her ears. She couldn't block them out. The first voice she recognized from her previous visits. The others were unfamiliar. Not Stephanie, not Timothy. They belonged to the stones. "The stone's magic is not my magic," she said.

The shapes stopped moving. Tracey had the strangest feeling they were communicating with each other outside of her hearing.

"*What do you want?*"

"*You.*"

"*Want.*"

"I—" She wanted nothing and everything. She wanted her mom healthy again. She wanted her dad happy and her sister safe. She wanted her friends and Damian to like her.

"*Why have you come here?*"

"*Come.*"

"*Here.*"

"There is a curse on my friend Jilly. A curse that makes Mage-kind forget her. I want to break the curse. I want to help her."

"*Why?*"

"*Why?*"

"*Why?*"

"The curse is wrong. It's not fair. Jilly's whole family has been forgotten. Jilly didn't do anything. Why should she be punished?" Tracey remembered Jilly knocking into her on the walkway outside school. The image played back in her mind like a silent black and white picture. The colors were inverted, wrong. In her memory, Jilly smirked as she stared at Tracey, her face twisted and ugly.

No, no, that's not what really happened. Jilly hadn't looked back at all. Tracey now remembered Jilly's shoulders slumped, her head low as she walked around Tracey, full of sadness. Another memory played—Jilly walking away with Laura, laughing happily. Her eyes were cold, her mouth was contorted with nastiness. Again, Jilly looked at Tracey and smirked. But that wasn't true either, was it? Jilly's head tilted wrong. Something was trying to convince her that her memories were real, but they weren't. She could see that now. Jilly hadn't stolen Laura and Jonny away from her at all. Jilly wasn't nasty or angry or bitter. She was sad and it broke Tracey's heart.

"End the curse," Tracey begged. "It wasn't Jilly's fault. She doesn't deserve this. Let her go." Tracey fell to her knees. "Please."

"*Jilly is a protector.*"

"The power will be hers."

"How can we trust her?"

"Am I not a protector, too?" Tracey asked.

"You will vouch for her? Can you promise the past will not return?"

"Past."

"Return."

How could Tracey make such a promise?" "I don't know. I—"

"Do you lead them?"

"Lead."

"Them."

Wait, what? "Lead them?"

"The other."

"Girl."

"Girl."

They had to be talking about Kylie. "But she's just a kid." Thoughts of Sarah filled Tracey's mind. The same age, they were both too young to face such danger. "Not her. There must be someone else."

"She accepted the stone."

"Stone."

"Accepted."

This was wrong. Kylie was too young, too angry. Tracey's stomach clenched. "Timothy is still in the stone. He took over her mind. Can you stop him? Can you help Kylie keep control?"

"For now."

"Now."

"Now."

Tracey's skin was icy cold. "Is there no other way?" She got no answer. Damian was going to kill her. "I—I will vouch for her." Tracey spun in a circle, glaring at every shape. Her heart filled with sorrow. "Break the curse."

"For now."

"For now."

"For now."

That didn't exactly sound final.

In a flash Tracey was back in the library. Noise returned an instant later. Damian's high-pitched voice urged his sister to wake up, Jilly sobbed softly in Jonny's arms, curled up rocking back and forth. A dusty, dry smell of old books filled Tracey's nose. She slid to Jonny's side. "Is Jilly—"

"Something's wrong. She's in pain, Tracey," Jonny snapped. "Where ever you went, you'd better be back now. We have to help them. You'd better fix this."

"I will," she swore.

"Tracey?" Jilly's voice drew Tracey's gaze down to her sweaty face.

Jilly's beautiful black tresses had fallen out of her ponytail and were knotted in a monstrous snarl. Her dark eyes overflowed with tears. Tracey knelt beside her. "Hey there."

"Tracey, I'm burning up. What did you do?"

Her insides aching, Tracey scrubbed a hand over her face.

"What's happening to me?" Jilly asked.

Tracey held out the Tiger's Eye. Jilly took it with a trembling hand. As she placed it over her head a golden glow spread and traveled over Jilly's body.

The last of Tracey's memories returned with a snap, filling holes she didn't even know she had. Memories of Laura and Jilly explaining the curse to Tracey over and over again... Of Laura, in tears, telling Tracey she had to leave, that the curse was too strong, that they would find a way to help. Tears rolled hot lines of shame down Tracey's cheeks. "I remember everything."

Giant, heaving sobs burst from Jilly's mouth. "It's gone? The curse is really broken?" Her shoulders jerked as tears poured down her face.

Tracey wrapped her arms around Jilly and held her in her grief. "I've got you," she whispered. She let Jilly cling to her, knowing it would take time for her to truly believe her hell was finally over.

Tales
by
The Lost

Following 219, Followed by 0
click **<broken link>** to follow The Lost!

Day 1611

[cont …]

The actions of others did this

to me, and what, I'm just

supposed to accept it?

Be all smiles and charm

and pleasant cheer?

0 likes, 0 comments, 0 reshares
click **<broken link>** to like this post!:D

T.B.T.L.

38

Tracey left Jilly in Jonny's care and crawled to Damian's side. "Is Kylie okay?" Sarah sat on the floor beside them, watching over her friend.

"Tracey, what's happening?" Sarah whispered.

"Where are Laura, Dave, and Tony?" Tracey asked instead.

"Waiting at the door for Agent Malden." Sarah swiped tears from her eyes. "What do we do? Kylie won't wake up."

Tracey clutched Kylie's fingers and reached into the unconscious girl's mind. *Kylie?*

Who's there? Kylie's thoughts were so tiny it was hard for Tracey to understand them.

Tracey Masters, she thought back. She tugged on the tendrils of Kylie's young fractured mind. *Come back with me,* she urged.

He'll hurt me, Kylie said, her voice that of a scared child.

He's gone, Tracey thought back.

Really?

I promise.

Kylie's eyelids twitched. She blinked and let out a moan.

"Kylie!" The emotion in Damian's voice brought a lump to Tracey's throat. She sat back on her heels.

You have to do it, Tracey. You have to give her the stone. Her heart thumped madly. Could she really condemn this girl to a life of danger and temptation? She didn't have a choice, but that didn't make it any easier. Damian clutched his sister to his chest in a giant hug.

"Ugh! What's going on?" Kylie asked, trying to push him away. He wouldn't let her go. "Everything hurts! Tracey, why does it hurt?" Her face scrunched up in terrible pain. Kylie clutched Sarah with one hand

and Damian in the other. Wide blue eyes stared up at Tracey, begging her to make the pain stop. The promise the stones had extracted from Tracey thudded inside her chest. *I have to give Kylie the stone.*

But what about Timothy? The stones had promised to stop him from possessing Kylie again, but could she trust them?

Kylie's fingers clenched around Damian's hand so tightly Tracey heard his bones creak. She didn't want to do it, but it was the only way to stop the girl's pain.

With Damian's breath heating Tracey's shoulder and her own heart spasming from her decision, she knelt over the girl and focused on Kylie's eyes, forcing her to meet Tracey's stare.

Tracey pictured her core as a small ball of white light. Keeping her shield bubble compressed around the Butterfly Stone, Tracey breathed slowly and deeply, watching until Kylie inhaled and they exhaled together. Tracey built a room in her mind, Kylie's bedroom. She imagined bright orange sunlight streaming through the blinds and Kylie's soft bed with its pretty floral cover front and center. There were books galore surrounding them and Tracey made the room smell of peppermint and chocolate. It was a safe and happy place. She called for Kylie in her mind to join her in this safe space.

"Tracey?" Kylie's form was ghostly, Tracey could see right through her and figured she probably looked much the same to Kylie. The blonde, almost transparent girl wobbled and sat down on the bed. Her eyes were enormous as she stared around the imaginary bedroom. "What are we doing in my room?"

Tracey joined her on the bed. "We need to talk."

"What's happening?" Kylie asked. "Everything hurts. Even breathing. Damian's scared. I can feel it all around me."

How could Tracey explain? "Let me tell you about something that happened to me a few weeks ago." As Tracey spoke about the Shadowman, Stephanie, and Timothy she watched Kylie's face. Emotions darted across it like a movie.

"Why did he pick me?" Kylie asked when Tracey fell silent.

"Do you remember the necklace you were wearing?"

"The one Damian found? The black one with the red snake on it? I like it, it's pretty." Kylie's eyes shone with unshed tears. Tracey pretended not to see them. Kylie's lips trembled. "So, it's all my fault?"

"No! No, Kylie. Don't think that. Timothy is..." Tracey wanted to say evil, but that was hardly going to help. "Timothy is troubled, upset, angry—"

"—like me?"

Fruit tingles. "Maybe he recognized the emotions and thought you'd understand."

"Why are you telling me about him?"

"You're in pain now because I took the stone away from you. I tried to take mine off and it didn't go well."

"Am I going to die?"

"No! Of course not. I'm giving the stone back to you."

Kylie pushed Tracey away and leaped from the bed. The sunlight shining through the blinds turned grey, as if storm clouds had eaten the sun. "I don't want it, I don't... please don't give it to me." Her whole body quivered and dissolved. Tracey bit her lips and waited for Kylie to concentrate on returning to the safe space. It took a while. Tracey hated herself for what she was doing to this brave girl. When Kylie returned, she stayed on the opposite side of the little room.

"Kylie. Do you remember the white room I just told you about?"

"Your Vision? Yeah, kinda. The stones were talking to you?"

"Yes. They told me you need to keep it. That you are a protector, like me." The stones had promised to keep Timothy away from Kylie for now. They had better uphold their side of the bargain.

Kylie blinked slowly, considering Tracey's statement. "Can I control it?"

"Yes. And I'm going to help you."

"Promise?"

Tracey nodded as solemnly as she could. "I promise."

"Okay," Kylie sniffed and stretched out her hand. Tracey jumped off the bed and clutched it tightly releasing the breath she was holding. "I want you to picture your magic bubble around your body. You'll probably push me out of this bedroom in your mind so I might disappear, but that's okay. When your bubble is as strong as concrete, I want you to open your eyes. Remember, I'm here and I'm going to help you."

"Okay."

Dizziness washed over Tracey as she was propelled from Kylie's mind. She found Damian cuddling Kylie tight and calling her name. Sarah leaned into Tracey's side. Tracey could feel her sister's magic curling around her, helping to steady her. Power also flowed from Jilly who sat right behind Tracey. Jonny sat with her, holding her hand. Dave's voice popped into her head. *Hey, is everything okay now?*

Dave! You can hear me?

Yeah. You're really loud, you know?

Is Agent Malden here yet? she thought back. She felt his *yes* before she heard it.

Pulling in now. Seven cars and two ambulances. We'll be inside in a second. Laura and Tony are talking to Agent Malden through the car window.

Thanks, Tracey thought back to him. *And thanks for coming to help. How did you know we needed you?*

Laura came to the change rooms. Just marched right in and told me you needed help, he thought to her.

Tracey smirked at the image. She totally believed Laura had done that. *Well, thank you. We really needed you.*

Yeah, you did. I'll have to hang around a bit more, huh? Keep you out of trouble.

Tracey sent him a smile. *You'd better.*

Besides, the guys all think it's cool that Laura just walked in there like that. I couldn't say no.

"Is the kid okay?" Jilly asked, bringing Tracey's attention back to the library. She kept her voice soft, probably so Damian didn't hear them. Tracey doubted anything could penetrate his walls of concern for his sister.

"I hope so." Tracey leaned over and slipped the chain attached to the black stone over Kylie's head.

"Whoa! What are you doing?" Jilly's shield bubble sprang up, prepared to defend them all against attack.

"Helping." *I hope.* Tracey held Kylie's hand and checked on the girl's shield bubble. It didn't waver, remaining strong, unbreakable.

Kylie's face relaxed and her eyes popped open. "Hey."

"Kylie!" Damian's cheer filled the library. His gaze darted to Tracey and in that split-second Tracey knew she had made the right decision. His smile warmed her entire body.

"Hi Kylie, how are you feeling?" Tracey asked.

"Everything hurts, but—I can see it now."

"Push Timothy away if he tries to talk to you. Don't let him in," Tracey told her. "It's your choice now, he can't make you."

Kylie's eyes shimmered but the color had returned to her cheeks. "I won't."

"I don't like this," Damian said. His smile fell away as his expression darkened, his mouth formed a tight line. He touched the black stone and for a moment Tracey was afraid he would tear it away.

No one moved. It was like they were all waiting for something to happen. Damian's hand dropped to his side.

"So now what? I feel weird just sitting here with all of you staring at me," Kylie said.

Tracey started laughing. After a moment, Sarah and Jilly laughed too. The library doors sprang open and two figures ran in. One stumbled to a stop, huffing and puffing, his face red and shiny. "Uncle Donny?" Tracey jumped to her feet.

Agent Malden approached at a slower, steady pace, stepping in front of Tracey's worried uncle. Magic whipped around his body like he was trying very hard to hold it back. "What happened?" he demanded.

Tracey held up both hands. "I can explain."

Tales
by
The Lost

Following 219, Followed by 0
click **<broken link>** to follow The Lost!

Day 1611

[cont …]

Ugh. No.

Besides, it doesn't matter.

She won't remember…

0 likes, 0 comments, 0 reshares
click **<broken link>** to like this post!:D

T.B.T.L.

39

The explanation wasn't easy. Tracey had to stop when the M-Force paramedics came inside insisting they check everyone over. Tracey pointed them straight to Kylie and Jilly. She pulled Agent Malden and Uncle Donny toward the librarian's desk as her friends were escorted outside.

"I'm very proud of you, Tracey," Agent Malden said when she finished speaking.

"Really? I put everyone in danger and poor Kylie, I—"

"Breathe," Uncle Donny said, his hand resting on her shoulder. She took comfort in his presence. He had come despite his anger after the *Saving Time* interviews.

Tracey inhaled until her lungs were full to bursting. It gave her time to think about what she was going to say. "Agent Malden, I am a protector."

"Yes, protector of the Butterfly Stone," he said. Uncle Donny bounced from foot to foot. Several times his mouth opened. He mashed his lips together without uttering a sound.

"Jilly is a protector, too," Tracey said. *Here it comes.* "And so is Kylie."

Agent Malden's eyes widened. "They have a stone? Each?"

"Yes. And you can't take them off," she said. "It hurts. Really, really hurts."

"What about Timothy?" Agent Malden's mouth turned inward. His hand fluttered beside his waist as his shield strengthened reflexively. He shot the library doors a long look like he could see through them to her friends outside. Maybe he could.

"Timothy's gone." *I hope.* The look on Agent Malden's face made Tracey's tummy twitch.

"Are you certain?"

"Well, mostly. We have to teach Kylie a way to fight him off if he returns."

"The M-Force paramedics have a tool that might help that—temporarily. It strengthens one's will against possession."

Tracey jerked as her body reached out. "Can I get one of those?"

Agent Malden smiled. "As I said, it's temporary. Used primarily to transport patients to hospitals safely. I'll speak to the techs. Perhaps we can work on something for the longer term. Besides you're doing pretty well with your stone," he told her.

Ha! Yeah, that was the biggest lie ever told. Tracey suspected Agent Malden knew it too, but he had said it anyway to make her feel better, or himself.

Tracey recalled Tony's warning. Maybe she shouldn't have told Agent Malden about the stones. She peered around the destroyed library. He would have guessed even if she hadn't told him. "Do you know anything about my mom? Is she okay?"

Uncle Donny jumped in. "She's fine. Better than fine, actually. She's cured. No traces of what affected her remain. Your dad told me she is being discharged this evening."

Tracey burst into tears. "I don't know why I'm crying. I'm happy," she insisted, burying her head in her hands. Uncle Donny pulled her into a hug.

"It happens. Adrenaline and worry. It's good news," Uncle Donny said and patted her back until she lifted her head.

"What about Grandma?"

"She's fine. Overexerted herself with that memory spell, but that's all. She just needs to sleep it off."

"My agents confirm that, Tracey. They are all okay," Agent Malden said. He stepped away as the paramedics approached. Tracey tried to avoid her uncle's stare but couldn't hold out for long. His gaze crawled over her skin like a worm. Or maybe a caterpillar. Something with a lot of legs. Each one pricked her skin where it stepped.

"I'm sorry," she said before Uncle Donny could speak.

"What for? You did very well, Tracey. Everyone is safe."

She rubbed hard at her breastbone. "Kylie is Sarah's age."

"Yes, and she's going to need your help." Uncle Donny peered around at the destroyed library. "Come on, let's go outside and check on your friends."

They walked slowly. Tracey focused on the good news about her mom. "Oh, I forgot to ask Agent Malden if they found Doctor Chan where we left him."

"That imposter?" Uncle Donny spat. "Oh yes, they have him locked up. It was a surprise to find him all trussed up like a turkey at Thanksgiving. Did you do that?"

Tracey shook her head but didn't say anything else.

"I understand there has been an extradition request. I don't know what his future is but I'm glad he has finally been caught. For your sake and your Mom's."

Tracey was positive that request had come from Jilly's family. She wondered if Agent Malden would let Doctor Chan be moved or if he would try to keep him here.

As they stepped outside the library Tracey's thoughts returned to Kylie and Jilly, and their new status as protectors.

"What about Kylie and Jilly's parents?"

"I'm sure Malden will talk to them. You're going to have new friends to add to your little gang."

Tracey's gaze fell on Kylie, sitting in the back of the ambulance. She glanced at Jonny standing with Jilly, Tony, Sarah, Dave and Laura. They smiled and waved. Tracey spied Damian standing guard beside the ambulance. She hunched her shoulders. *Fruit tingles!* He had asked Tracey to help his sister with school and look at what had happened since. "Hold on, Uncle Donny, I'll be back in a minute."

With slow steps and the sound of a heavy bell tolling in her head, she walked over to Damian. He leaned against the wall beside the ambulance. "Can we—um—can I talk to you?" she asked.

He huffed out a breath. "Be quick."

Ouch. Her heart sank. "I'm sorry Kylie got hurt."

"She said it was the necklace." Damian scrubbed a hand against the back of his neck. "I gave it to her, Tracey. It's not your fault. It's mine.

Mom and Dad are going to kill me. I'm supposed to look after her. This is all my fault."

They were each blaming themselves. What a pair they made. "I don't think it's anyone's fault," she said. "Bad stuff happened, but everyone is okay now."

"You gave it back to her. That stone took my sister away and you just gave it back."

"I know. But I'm here and so is Jilly. We've got one." Tracey touched the necklace hidden beneath her shirt. "We'll help Kylie stay in control."

"I wish she wasn't Mage-kind," Damian blurted. He stared at the library doors like they were the cause of all his problems.

His words stabbed into Tracey's body like a spear, right under her broken heart. "Yeah, I can see why you'd say that. Damian, Kylie can't help who she is. She needs your support right now and your love." *So do I.*

"She's not strong enough. It should be me. Why did this have to happen to her?"

Tracey released a shallow breath. "I—"

"There are police here, Tracey. Mage-kind ones. This is bad. I just—I can't really deal with it all at the moment."

Could a person actually hear their heart break? The look on Damian's face and the way he couldn't meet her eyes terrified her. He was scared.

Scared of her.

"I-I understand. But if Kylie needs me, I'm here, Damian. Anytime. You can trust me."

He didn't answer her. He wouldn't even look at her. Tracey walked away feeling a hundred years old. *I want Mom.*

"Tracey?" Kylie's voice pierced the darkness of Tracey's thoughts.

She raced to Kylie's side. "Hey, how are you feeling?" The paramedic was packing up his bag. He ignored Tracey entirely, so she ignored him back. She sat down on the edge of the ambulance. There was a strange green device wrapped around Kylie's head. It pressed around her skull like a headband, squashing her hair flat. That must be the anti-possession device Agent Malden mentioned.

"Like my new gear? The M-Force special paramedics said it would keep me safe."

"It's to stop Timothy," Tracey said. She reached out but didn't touch the headband.

"They don't know if it will work for long," Kylie said.

"How are you feeling?"

Kylie held up her bracelet. A flashing red line ran through the center. "Bubble is still up and going strong. It feels weird to be using magic at school though."

"Yeah. You'll be allowed to do that from now on. Any pain?"

"No. The stone is warm. Is that normal?"

Tracey's hand drifted to her own necklace. "It reacts to your emotions. You're probably just stressing about it and it knows you're stressing about it." *Please believe me.*

"I can't hear his voice anymore," Kylie whispered. Her eyes were cast down, staring at her sneakers.

Tracey bumped her shoulder against Kylie's. "Good. If you do, tell me straight away, okay?"

"Okay." Kylie wiped her eyes. "Are my mom and dad going to be angry?"

"Mine were, but they'll calm down eventually. You've got lots of friends here, Kylie. Me and Sarah and well, my whole family too."

"And me," Jilly said appearing at Tracey's shoulder.

Tracey jumped, pressing her hand to her chest. "Give me a heart attack, why don't you?"

"Sorry," Jilly smirked. Jonny stood at her side. Tony, Dave, Sarah, and Laura were right behind them.

"You need like — a bell — or something," Tracey told Jilly.

Jilly nibbled at her bottom lip. "You still remember me?"

"Yup, and guess what, you're still annoying," Tracey said. She smiled, hoping Jilly wouldn't take her too seriously.

Jilly's laugh was loud and bright. Kylie chuckled too.

"How are you doing, Tracey?" Laura asked.

Tracey held out a hand to her sister. Sarah grabbed it and squeezed tight. "I'm okay," she told Laura. Tony gave her a smile.

"Good, because, no offence, but you guys are killing my social life," Dave said, sending them all into peals of laughter.

Agent Malden walked in their direction. "Oh, oh, the cops!" Tracey whispered. That cracked them up again.

"I'm not even going to ask," Agent Malden said. His lips twitched. "Ladies and gentlemen, I'm glad to see you're all feeling better. We need to have a little chat and—" A buzzing sound came from the pocket of his trousers. He yanked out his cell phone. "Oh."

"Sir? Agent Malden?"

Tracey's heartbeat increased and the longer he stayed silent reading whatever it was on the screen, the faster it got. Tony's gaze turned inward, his mouth downturned.

"Well then," Agent Malden said and looked straight at Tracey.

"Who was it?" she asked.

"Prince Henry."

Tracey released the breath she was holding. "What did he say?"

"He found another stone. Looks like you and your friends are going to England."

ABOUT THE AUTHOR

Laurie Bell is a former teacher who has worked with children of all ages in the literary sphere. She is a science fiction aficionado who is regularly featured by publications such as the Antipodean Science Fiction E-Magazine.

Laurie maintains an active blog of science fiction, fantasy, and flash fiction pieces, and serves as a volunteer in her local theatre company.

Discover more about Laurie Bell at:

www.solothefirst.wordpress.com

A Thank You From The Author

I'd like to that the following people who helped *The Tiger's Eye* become what it is — so much fun.

Linh, Margo, Carolyn, and Edmund for your CP & Beta-ery goodness! Every time I receive an email from you my writing becomes better. You are all just fabulous. Keep on keeping on. I can't wait to read your words soon.

Mum and Dad, who keep reading and bugging me to find out what happens next. *Shhhhhhh spoilers*

Helen, for your unending support.

Kate Foster. Your advice as always inspires me and keeps me going.

Brigitte, for believing in me and supporting my writing journey.

For all the kids I taught in the few short years I was a teacher — you will always inspire me.

Hayley and Stefanie (Always! BFFs forever.)

Lauren Lynne, THANK YOU!

D.C. McGannon, Michael McGannon and Holly McGannon — for believing in this series and in Tracey's journey. Thank you for jumping onto the merry-go-round once more with me.

James Gatherum-Goss and the Team at Dymocks Knox City in Victoria, Australia. Thank you for all your support. To see my book on your shelves is a dream come true. Thank you for supporting local authors. Readers... get out there and support your local bookshops and booksellers! They are truly awesome people.

Oh, and to Lisa, Jen, Kathy, Luneah, Stefanie, Hayley, Justine, Blair, Amber, Anthony, Cathy, Brian, Berny, and Helen - Sorry for making you wait so long.

Gerry. I love you.

Thank you!

Another stone is coming...

For this and other exciting titles, visit:

www.WyvernsPeak.com

www.twitter.com/WyvernsPeak
www.facebook.com/WyvernsPeak

Sign up for our newsletter, get free stuff, and be the first to know when new books from your favorite Wyvern's Peak authors are released.

Follow Laurie Bell on Twitter

@LaurienotLori

Like Laurie on Facebook

www.facebook.com/WriterLaurieBell

Visit her website at

www.solothefirst.wordpress.com

CPSIA information can be obtained
at www.ICGtesting.com
Printed in the USA
BVHW080837300720
584991BV00001B/165